Also by Byron Lane

A Star Is Bored: A Novel

Big Gay

Wedding

Big Gay Wedding

A Novel

Byron Lane

HENRY HOLT AND COMPANY   NEW YORK

Henry Holt and Company
Publishers since 1866
120 Broadway
New York, New York 10271
www.henryholt.com

Henry Holt° and 🄗° are registered trademarks of Macmillan
Publishing Group, LLC.

Library of Congress Cataloging-in-Publication Data is available.

ISBN: 9781250267146

Our books may be purchased in bulk for promotional,
educational, or business use. Please contact your local
bookseller or the Macmillan Corporate and Premium Sales
Department at (800) 221-7945, extension 5442, or by e-mail at
MacmillanSpecialMarkets@macmillan.com.

First Edition 2023

Designed by Meryl Sussman Levavi

Epilogue art by Laura Hartman Maestro

Printed in the United States of America

10   9   8   7   6   5   4   3   2   1

This is a work of fiction. All of the characters, organizations, and
events portrayed in this novel either are products of the author's
imagination or are used fictitiously.

For those who paved the way.

Contents

Big
Gay
Wedding

Part 1

Announcement

Sweetheart, announce an engagement with soft tongue, for what is a marriage if not also a funeral? Consider mamas who weep as their virgin sons and daughters perish into adulthood! Enough! To calm their hysteria, simply serve chilled pineapple slices or affix leeches to the discontented abdomen.

> —*Mrs. Jeannie Laffite's Undisputed Guide to Respectable Southern Nuptials,*
> *volume III, page 22*
> *(copyright 1912 by Mrs. Jeannie Laffite)*

Chapter 1

Countdown to Damnation:

13 days / 11 hours / 10 minutes

THE screeching rips peace and quiet from every soul within a mile of Polite Society Ranch. The farmhands outside the barn drop their rakes and bags of feed, step away from the animals in their charge—the blind chicken, the alpaca with alopecia, the pig who's too thin.

All hearts are alarmed, all available eyes looking for the source of the racket, then at each other, then all at once to their leader, their boss: Chrissy Durang.

"Stretch those spines," she shouts from her side porch, her graying hair carefully styled, presenting as easy but respectable, exactly as she requested from her hairdresser. "It's gonna be a Category 4 today."

The thick posts holding up Chrissy's porch mirror her poise, her perfect posture, her five foot six inches of straight line from crown to heel. She breathes coolly and calmly, signaling strength, decreeing the dignity she expects from her staff, no matter the storm.

The next burst of wailing, even louder now, like metal grinding on metal, causes the ground to vibrate and the macaws in the barn to chant their panic, sounding alarm with the only words they know.

"Good morning!" they shout frantically.

"You're so pretty!" they shout in blood-curdling bursts. If only the birds had a wider vocabulary. If only they knew how to say, "Warning." Or, "It's getting closer."

Chrissy's hands smooth her new white blouse. Her fingers delicately check that her gold-chain necklace is clasped perfectly at her nape. Her thumbs trace the waistline of her good jeans. She tugs on her belt, an old, cracking leather strap punched with letters spelling out "Farmer Mom," her preferred title, her prized possession made years ago by her son, Barnett, when they first moved to Mader and he joined the Boy Scouts.

The town is perfect for the typically quiet ranch, located in one of the most rural parts of Louisiana, a heavily wooded part, a part far outside New Orleans, a part no one really wanted in The Purchase. Mader was born as an afterthought of an official hurricane evacuation route, rich with local pride in its recently blacktopped two-lane road that wiggles through forest like a pine snake.

The screech—

"It's here!" the macaws would warn, if only they could.

As if out of thin, humid air, from a tunnel of untamed brush, atop the sweltering blacktop road, emerges a yellow school bus full of children. It lurches into view in front of the ranch, the driver riding the rusty brakes, which continue their blaring protest.

The young lives aboard the bus are bouncing in their seats, the namesake of their oppressor stenciled along the side of their chariot: "Mader Elementary School." The kids, frantic as fire ants, sense their arrival on this long-awaited field trip, built on the backs of underpaid teachers and exhausted parents and tattered permission slips signed at the last minute.

These kids are the summer schoolers, the victims of poor grades or poor manners—neither of which is their fault, in most cases—enduring their August penance filled with spelling tests and word problems and, mercifully, today's outing.

A total of seventeen students make up the third-grade summer school class, median age eight, all of them somehow bound to the soil of Mader. Their parents own farms here, work on farms here, run supply lines for farms here.

But none of these kids have ever seen a farm like this one. Or met a farmer like this one, a Farmer Mom like Chrissy.

Polite Society Ranch is well manicured and beautiful. Animals are treated with love, not as property, never as a future meal. The sign out front has the ranch slogan stenciled clearly and in a stately font, exactly as Chrissy requested of the artist: "A Place of Dignity."

Encircled in white picket fencing, a large clearing with grass as green as a tree frog gives rise to five structures. The barn is painted bright blue, the chicken coop is bright blue, the kennel is bright blue, the stables are bright blue, and Chrissy's home is bright blue. It's a shade presenting as cheery but grounded, exactly as she requested from her handyman. On perfect days, when she's not hunkered down because of rain or blinded by sweat or rushing to feed this animal or that, she notices that the blue of her house perfectly matches the blue of the sky, and Chrissy nods with pride, as if receiving confirmation that she and God are in cahoots.

The yellow bus screams and growls into the driveway of Polite Society Ranch, barely clearing the ditch. Finally, those poor brakes do their job, delivering the day's headache to Chrissy's feet.

"Let's do it," Chrissy says to Pauley, her chief farmhand, who stands at her right side, at least for now. "Remember the rules. Respect. Dignity. And don't hog-tie anyone under nine years old unless it's an emergency."

"Sorry about that," Pauley says through his square jaw. He's somewhere in his midtwenties, though in Mader, value comes not from time lived, but from time lived on a farm, and by that metric Pauley is practically an old man.

"Close your mouth, please," Chrissy says to Pauley, who's as stunned as she is that so many kids are on the bus. Chrissy wasn't even expecting a bus, she was expecting the old Mader Elementary van. *This will strain the schedule*, she thinks.

Except for his look of shock at the day's oversize tour, Pauley is otherwise exact in mandated appearance, as are the other staffers milling about: blue jeans, white T-shirt (tucked in), clean fingernails.

At last, Pauley has stopped wearing his ratty baseball cap. For months, Chrissy issued polite signals to him. "Baseball cap," she'd point out. And the next day, "Baseball cap," and the next, "Baseball cap." Eventually, she asked him to step into the farm's office. "Sweetie, I'm not calling you 'Baseball Cap' as a nickname. I'm telling you a baseball cap is not part of the dress code."

"Oh, shit—I mean—shucks, Miss Chrissy. Sorry about that," Pauley said, grabbing the cap with his whole hand and dragging it from his skull like a shameful toupee.

"This isn't *Casual* Society Ranch, Pauley. It's *Polite* Society Ranch. But you're welcome to wear a cowboy hat if you'd like."

"Yes, ma'am. Thank you. Sorry again—"

Chrissy reached into a desk drawer and lifted two gifts, each neatly wrapped in thick, glossy-white paper and sturdy red-velvet ribbons tied into big blossoming bows. One package was large, one smaller. She handed the large one to Pauley.

"What's this for?"

"A little appreciation gift."

Pauley ripped it open and stared at the Stetson beaver roper cowboy hat, factory dusted, soft, pliable, premium, medium pinch front, Silverton crown, made in the USA, color: acorn. "Holy shucks, Miss Chrissy!"

"You don't have to keep it or wear it. The receipt is in there if you want to exchange it. Or if you need the cash and want to return it, that's okay, too."

"I don't know what to say, except, shucks, again."

"You deserve something nice, Pauley. Thanks for all you've done for me and my critters out here. LSU will be lucky to have you. You're gonna be the best vet this side of the lake."

Pauley blushed, smiled. "You're gonna make it real hard to say goodbye."

"Nonsense. That's what family is for. I have Barnett."

Oh, Barnett, Chrissy thought, awash in her usual delight at the very mention of her son's name, a thrill almost as meaningful as actually seeing him on his rare trips home, or as comforting as hearing his voice on one of his calls. Just by talking to him on the phone, Chrissy can tell if Barnett needs a haircut. He phones often to tell his mother, "Good night," or, "I love you," or, only half-jokingly, "Just making sure you're not dead."

Pauley popped the cowboy hat atop his noggin, a grin upon his face. He eyed the other gift, the smaller one. "Is that for me, too?" he joked.

Chrissy held the package carefully. "This one is for Barnett."

Pauley studied her face, still beaming from thinking of her son. Pauley wished his own mother would glow in that way, effuse any semblance of pride. "How is Barnett? How's his job? How's his . . . roommate . . . thing?"

Chrissy's eyebrows twitched. Not many people ask so directly for details about Barnett these days. She smiled, stood, and said, "Let's get back to work."

Pauley also stood, headed for the door, opening it a little wider than he did when he first entered so his exit would accommodate his new headdress. "Is Barnett coming for a visit anytime soon?"

Chrissy held the small gift in her hands even more tightly, as if much depended on its contents. "Monday," she said.

"Monday!" the macaws would shout.

"It's here!" they would shout, if only they could.

The day came as fast and as loud as the yellow bus now parked out front of the farm. Chrissy adjusts her Farmer Mom belt and double-checks that she put a five-dollar bill in her front pocket—bribe money for when one of the kids visiting the farm has a tantrum. Chrissy has learned that five bucks can stop tears in an emergency, when Hershey's Kisses or Elmo Band-Aids don't do the trick.

Chrissy reaches into her back pocket and pulls out a small orange notepad and half a pencil she accidentally stole from Saint Michael the Archangel Catholic Church. She licks the tip of the pencil and holds it beside one of the items on her to-do list: "9 a.m., tour arrives." Just under that is written: "10 a.m., Barnett comes home."

Chrissy looks at her watch: 9:10 a.m. The tour is large, and late. Barnett's plane, if on time, if all is going according to plan, should have already landed at New Orleans International Airport, a facility built not in New Orleans, but in the neighboring city of Metairie—an airport for a city within another city. *The world makes no sense*, Chrissy thinks. *I'm never leaving the farm again.*

She returns the orange notepad to her back pocket.

The school bus engine ends its roar in the driveway and nature takes its cue, picks up the slack. Birds and breeze and insects resume whispering sweet nothings.

Chrissy looks at her watch again. Barnett will get a ride to the farm. Even though the drive from Polite Society Ranch to the airport is a whole tank of gas away, she would have gone to pick him up. She always offers. She's always relieved not that he declines, but by how he declines. "I can't possibly take you away from the ranch. Those little animals need you more than I do. I'll get an Uber," Barnett said. And then, "I don't have a return flight yet. I'm hoping we can find time *to talk*."

Find time to talk. Those were his exact words, Chrissy recalls.

Chrissy almost laughed as he said it. *Oh, Barnett*. She knows what he wants to talk about. She's been planning it for years, and accepting it of late: her retirement, her passing the farm to its heir, her son, Barnett, her "Farmer Son," just like it says on the brand-new leather belt in the neatly wrapped small white box with the sturdy red-velvet ribbon tied in a big blossoming bow in the office.

No wonder he doesn't have a return flight. He's moving home, Chrissy thinks. She and Barnett talk in circles about it all the time. "This farm will be yours someday," she's said so often that the macaws occasionally repeat it.

"My favorite place on earth," Barnett always says right back to her.

Outside the bus, Chrissy and Pauley can hear the kids' teacher, Miss Iva, giving her usual speech about behaving. "What do we do?" she asks. The students repeat the words with her—"Listen! Learn! Listen harder!"

Chrissy and Pauley compose themselves as if the ranch is Downton Abbey and the lords and ladies are about to step from their carriage. Pauley touches the brim of his acorn-colored cowboy hat and nods to Chrissy like a hero in a Western. And gazing at the blues and greens and white picket fence behind him, Chrissy fills with pride, wondering if she should have named it *Perfect* Society Ranch instead.

The kids on these tours always remind Chrissy of youth, and its absence. She never had a singular moment when she realized she was old. She figures she's old simply because she doesn't feel young. Of course, she's noticed occasional aches and pains through the years. But nowadays, everything hurts even when she's standing still. Caring for other lives all day has led her to consider, more than once, *Who will take care of me?*

Oh, Barnett, she thinks.

Recently, at a whisper past one in the morning, the motion light outside her barn popped on with a click. It turned out to be nothing, but she jolted up in bed. Jolting up in bed isn't what it used to be, not for Chrissy, not for anyone in their sixties. Plus, she was new at it. It used to be her husband who did the jolting up and running out of the bedroom and out the back door.

Oh, John, she thinks.

John Durang once killed a fox. He once killed a coyote. In later years, she scolded him something fierce when he grabbed her good bread knife to chase off a critter. "You think that raccoon is made of corn bread?" she asked. "Why didn't you just take the shotgun? What if it was a person out there?"

He shook his head, looked at the floor. "I don't think I could pull the trigger," he said. "I don't know if I can kill. I don't think I have it in me anymore."

And sometimes, there on the farm, Chrissy feels she doesn't have it in her anymore, either. Not enough of it, anyway. She's ready to pass it along to Barnett. She thinks of her son in colorful snapshots like in the pictures beside her bed. Her favorite photo is from Barnett's graduation from high school over ten years ago. Chrissy took the picture with a disposable camera. She feels she captured Barnett at his best, at what she knows is surely his happiest, him looking directly at her. Photos of him—and John, but mostly Barnett—also line the long hallway in her home. That boy's smile—it's caffeine. All the pictures tell a history of his growth, of her parenting. But the pictures don't chronicle Barnett's path all the way to now. It's hard to find a picture of present-day Barnett Durang, age thirty-four. Chrissy used to update the wall regularly, until Barnett moved away, until the time when she could no longer control him, no longer vouch for his values and whatnot. *Your child is a reflection of you, up to a point*, she figures. *Barnett's adult life is nobody's business*, she thinks.

The school bus doors open with such force, Chrissy steps back slightly.

Miss Iva exits the bus first. "Hey, honey. I miss you."

The two ladies hug in earnest for the first time since Chrissy left her life as a teacher way back when Barnett was a boy. "You should try retirement," Chrissy says. "I promise it's way easier to teach chickens than to teach kids."

"Honey, how's things?" Miss Iva asks.

Things. That's another way of asking about him—*Oh, Barnett.*

Chrissy is still getting used to the fact that her son somehow, sometime, grew up, got smart, moved away, and stayed away from Mader, to live in Loony Tunes, California. "It's Los Angeles, Mom," Barnett said on his last visit, almost a year ago.

"I'll call it whatever I please, thank you very much," Chrissy said. "All that sunshine is unnatural."

Miss Iva ushers the kids off the bus as Farmer Mom watches. She looks at their shoes as they step onto her farm. Shoes don't lie. Sneakers that light up are telling. Flip-flops hide nothing. Boots hide a lot. Name brands stick out. Knockoffs fall apart. The wear of the sole says much of its owner. None of the kids at Mader Elementary ever have new shoes. But the depth of remaining sole, the degree to which the sock is actually buffered from the ground, is often the measure of poverty these kids exist within.

The first half of the bus files out. Chrissy steps forward to collect them. "Come with me," she says.

She looks at her watch. *Almost Barnett o'clock*, she thinks.

She turns to the kids. "This is Polite Society Ranch, not Uncivilized Society Ranch. So, when I say, 'Come with me,' you all say, 'Yes ma'am.' Understand?"

One of the boys, the biggest one, a youngster profoundly covered in freckles, spits in the dirt, not at Chrissy, but not away from her, either.

"I see," Chrissy says to the group. Then she turns to The Freckled Spitter. "You're lucky that saliva went in the dirt and not on my shoe or I'd make you clean it." She holds eye contact with him for a second longer than natural. Then she adds, "I hate to say it, but that was pretty good aim."

The boy, indeed all the kids, stare at her with suspicion.

"Where did you learn to spit like that?"

The Freckled Spitter looks down at his wet spot in the dirt, as if hoping his DNA will rise up and offer an answer for him. "Dunno," he says.

Chrissy stares back, looks at her watch, then smiles. "Look, I won't treat you like babies if you don't treat me like an enemy. I'll walk you around and you can listen or not listen, as long as you pretend to be learning incredible things whenever Miss Iva looks over here. Deal?"

The kids start to show their devious grins and unmaintained teeth. "Cool," The Freckled Spitter says. And the other kids nod their approval.

"And if you see an animal going to the bathroom, you turn your back. This is a place of dignity. Understand?"

"Yes ma'am," The Freckled Spitter says, to looks of surprise from his peers. He's not one to hand out "ma'ams" and "sirs" unless they're earned.

Chrissy's faint smile acknowledges the moment. "For this group, we start at the cemetery." Chrissy leads the kids to the gravestones near the barn. They pass a white picket fence and enter a secluded area with colorful wildflowers offering company to a smattering of graves. The tombstones are simple, made by a guy in New Orleans. Each is a piece of slate engraved with a name.

Here lies Jerry Seinfeld.

Here lies Cosmo Kramer.

Here lies George Costanza.

The animals were all named after characters from John's favorite television shows.

"Good morning, Frasier," Farmer Mom says to the tombstone.

"Good morning, Newhart."

"Good morning, Blossom." (Barnett was allowed to name that one.)

And there's the marker for "Farmer Dog," an old black Lab, brought to Chrissy by a local boy, who had nowhere else to go. The dog was too sick to earn its keep at the boy's parents' farm, so he was instructed to "get rid of it." The boy came to Chrissy, and Farmer Dog lived his final weeks awash in leisure and fried chicken dinners.

And there's a marker that says simply "JD." Chrissy can't manage to greet that one. She has to swallow hard to avoid getting all worked up.

Oh, John.

He didn't want anything fancier. And everyone agreed that putting more than his initials, especially putting his full name, telling the kids there were human remains there, even if just his ashes, would only cause freak-outs and cost more five-dollar bills and Hershey's Kisses. The empty space next to John's plot is unmarked, but not unspoken for; Chrissy plans to go beside him there one day, when the time comes.

"What's a *Seinfeld*?" The Freckled Spitter asks.

I'm definitely getting old, Chrissy thinks. She ushers the students past the stables. Two horses live on the farm—Niles and Roz. They're old and useless, inherited from a neighbor who was going to put them down.

One pig, a few goats, and an alpaca live in the kennel. The alpaca, Alice, is bald and looks like a toddler's attempt to draw a baby giraffe. The pig, Nanny Fine, belonged to a New Orleans newscaster who was raising her as a piglet until she could no longer fit in a Mercedes. Recently, Nanny Fine has lost so much weight, it's not even worth trying to stop the cancer.

One of the goats, Urkel, is so old he may have dementia. He seems to think Nanny Fine is his mother. Chrissy will put him out of his misery when it starts to look like misery. For now, it looks like love.

A handful of old chickens kick up dust. Sam is blind but capable. Diane and Woody prance and preen. Lilith is unfriendly, but her eggs are decent. "Hi, babies," Chrissy says to them, tossing a handful of corn feed. To the students, she says, "You can throw feed *to* them, not *at* them."

All the animals know Barnett. Chrissy thinks of her handsome son so often, her constant monologue leaks like the old water pump in the barn. She talks about him to herself with such repetition, the animals recognize his name like it's a signal: "Git back," "Come eat," and "Oh, Barnett." When they hear it—*Oh, Barnett*—they know Chrissy's in a good mood.

"He's coming home to take care of us," Chrissy whispers to the chickens, sprinkling feed beneath their feet—three of their toes pointing to the front and one to the back, making each of their footsteps a peace sign in the dirt. She looks at the kids. She looks at her watch. She tosses a bit of feed, then a bit more.

The purchase of this farm decades ago was a challenge. It was a dumpy, regular farm back then. John raised and sheared and bred and sold sheep and horses, and grew and sold a few vegetables. He did it alone for a while, until Chrissy quit teaching and joined him. It was mostly a real farm until he died three years ago. He went limp in the living room. The two of them were laughing at a rerun of *Cheers*. John got a real kick out of Cliff, the mailman. Chrissy thought John fell asleep. She looked at him flopped over and blue from, she thought, the glow of the television. She stared at the lines of his face and smiled with affection like a fool. She considered leaving him there for the night. *Oh, John*, she thought.

Staring at him, counting him among her life's blessings, smiling as giddily as the day his chipper eyes had first met hers, she didn't think it was all over until she smelled him. He had soiled himself. He wouldn't wake up. He absolutely ruined that dang recliner that cost a fortune. A very thin doctor said it was quick, that John's "heart was rotten." *Those were his exact words*, Chrissy recalls. She tried every kind of cleaner on that recliner, but the memory of the scent was something the Dawn and vinegar and toothbrush couldn't scrape away. After the service, after Barnett had gone back to Loony Tunes, Chrissy, sobbing, dragged John's pitifully empty chair outside and onto the porch and across the yard. The chair's legs, sides, and back tore up the lawn. It looked like a plane had crashed. It took two and a quarter hours, but that chair made it to the burn pile. Chrissy calmly watched the smoke go up—all the way to John in Heaven. She figured all the physical labor involved in dragging furniture while wailing must have helped her grief. But all this time later, even after the remodel, she hasn't replaced the chair. The space where it used to sit is still empty. The divots in the hardwood floor remind her of the before-time, a ghost chair for her ghost husband.

Thank God for life insurance, Chrissy thinks, often. The remodel started shortly after John died. She stopped the farm's slaughters and procurement of new animals to breed and sell. For years prior, she had been casually collecting misfit animals. John had reservations but gave his blessing. But after his death she began to rescue with real gusto. Chrissy built fences, she carried feed, she woke at all hours to feed a blind newborn goat who thought she was his mother.

She has Pauley, until he quits for school. Soon.

Then, she'll have Barnett, when he finally comes home. Any second.

"You got kids?" The Freckled Spitter asks Chrissy.

She stuffs a handful of hay in Roz's mouth, wishing the horse could answer the question on her behalf. "Why do you want to know that?" she asks.

"I dunno," he says. "Just being nice."

"Well, thank you for being nice. Yes. I have a son. He's all grown up."

"You a grandma?"

Chrissy looks at the boy, tries to look through him, to judge intent or innocence, whether he's curious or cruel. "It's complicated," she says. "Now, be quiet and appreciate nature."

Barnett was always sensitive, even as a child. It was especially obvious in the way he cared for the animals, befriending the lame ones, like Elaine, the charity case, the last of the Seinfelds, the last of the Durang family's heritage sheep, the kind native to Louisiana, the only kind acclimated to Louisiana parasites. Louisiana heritage sheep can't survive anywhere else, a lot like most of the people in the state; most people born in Louisiana never leave.

Elaine has only three legs. She's a pampered senior now—seventeen years old—but was the runt of the litter. She was rejected by her mother, kicked away from the nipples, breaking her leg in the process so it needed to be amputated. Mother sheep sometimes reject the weaklings so the others have a better chance of survival. Chrissy tells Elaine almost every day, "Sometimes mamas have to do terrible things."

As Chrissy leads the group of kids from the barn, she slows and watches Elaine, her saddest ward. *Depression*, Chrissy thinks. It started in earnest a year ago, right after Kramer died. The two were best buds. Elaine never bonded with any of the other sheep, or with John or Chrissy or Barnett. Kramer was her whole world. Once, Elaine ran away, escaped her pen. John felt like a clown as he chased her through the pasture and woods out back, but eventually he gave up, and she was gone. That night, she came home on her own, snuggling up with Kramer. She'd rather be with him than be free. Sheep are like that. Loyal, foolish.

Once Kramer died, and with John gone, too, and Barnett off in Loony Tunes, Elaine had no choice but to bond with the only one left: Chrissy. It was a bond of circumstance, a bond of shared history. But Chrissy has whispered to Elaine, "I'm lonely, too."

Elaine is the kind of sheep they put in children's books, the kind you're supposed to count in your head at night. Chrissy falls asleep each night counting Elaine, and only Elaine. Counting the same sheep over and over again, Chrissy counts: "One, one, one, one."

The second-worst thing Barnett ever did was wash Elaine's wool using Woolite. The chemicals turned her coat blue for a whole year, and they had to use special chemicals on the wool before they could sell it. It was innocent and amusing to everyone except Elaine. Perhaps she's forgotten. Perhaps the Woolite incident is another thing that's scarred over around here, just like The Big Thing, which is the number-one worst thing Barnett Durang ever did.

Chrissy and the kids finish the tour at bright-blue picnic tables, enjoying sack lunches and homemade animal cookies and "Polite Society Punch," Pauley's stab at rebranding little cups of Kool-Aid.

Soon enough, the farm endures the renewed screeching of the bus's exit.

"Good riddance!" the macaws would shout, if only.

But in the resulting, refreshing quiet after the kids' departure,

Elaine, Niles, the chickens, and the other animals all pause at the sign of a threat, a new one. And Chrissy finds herself doing the same, copying them or mirroring them or maybe even having become one with them over the years. She soon hears what the chickens hear, the horses hear, Elaine hears. A car pulls into her farm's private entrance, her home's driveway, a symphony of crunching gravel. Chrissy is in such oneness with her property, she could almost recognize the sound of every rock and pebble supporting those tires, that car, this homecoming.

"Another Category 4?" Pauley asks.

Chrissy is lost in thought—*Oh, Barnett*. She steps away from Pauley and toward the house, as if in a trance, toward the private driveway, toward the heralded heir to Polite Society Ranch. "He's finally home," she says.

Chapter 2

Countdown to Damnation:

13 days / 10 hours / 5 minutes

BARNETT Durang lays eyes on his childhood home and begins picking at a hangnail on his thumb. Where the protruding dead skin meets the living, it's bright pink. Almost bloody. Almost time to see his mother. Almost time for *the talk*.

"This your destination, man?" the Uber driver asks.

My destination? Barnett considers. *My fate? My end?* His stomach contracts.

To Barnett, the driver's modest sedan feels like a child's toy parked in the driveway behind his mother's big Chevy—what used to be his father's big Chevy. Parked in the Uber in the farm's private driveway, Barnett wonders how long before she finds him.

Barnett can see almost the whole farm from the back seat window and at once feels like a kid. It's not that the bright-blue house and bright-blue barn and bright-blue chicken coop and bright-blue kennel and bright-blue stables remind him of his youth. In fact, when he was growing up, everything was colorless—gray and moldy—from years of being unpainted, exposed to nature. It wasn't until his father died that his mother applied her relentlessly blue touch.

Barnett feels like a kid here because that's how Chrissy makes him feel—young, small. It's an aftertaste he can't swallow away. His mother is the adult and he's the child; those are their poles. They're two magnets always pushing an exact distance apart, two magnets that will always have space and time between them, unequals forever, eternally misaligned.

"Hey, man. This your destination?" the driver asks again, tapping on his phone at maps and alerts and other bits of a digital record of this analog arrival at a farm for misfits. The driver looks at Barnett in the rearview mirror. "Helloooo?"

"Yeah, yeah, sorry," Barnett mumbles. "Memories."

Chrissy never cared that the property was a bit run-down when her husband was alive. She never cared that the wood was rotting here or there. But with John's life insurance money, Chrissy remade her world, said goodbye to the painful reminders that John was dead. She covered the house and the barn and her whole life with a coat of oil-based cheer.

Chrissy had little time or energy to worry about the farm back when John was alive. He and Chrissy (and young Barnett, after he did his homework) were happily exhausted together at the end of every day. Their hard work raising and selling everything—animals, chickens, eggs, plants—left them too depleted of energy to care about the little grievances plaguing many other families. John handled their lives with otherworldly grace. He paid bills. Managed business. He even cleaned the bathrooms occasionally. Chrissy cooked whatever she wanted, or didn't cook at all, and John was fine. He once ate three apples for dinner because neither he nor Chrissy felt like cooking. And when she protested about the sugar high, John said it would simply make him "more crazy in love" with her. She and Barnett never wanted for anything, in part because of John's careful parenting. If Barnett wanted a new He-Man action figure, John would say, "We can get you a He-Man, or we can buy more feed for the sheep." Barnett always chose the sheep. *Oh, Barnett*. And John would get him one of those He-Man things for Christmas. *Oh, John*. Chrissy's one true love had a superpower. John emoted contagious completeness.

Chrissy loved her small life. Until it got smaller. Until Barnett moved away. Until John died.

"Thanks for the ride," Barnett says to the driver, picking at his hangnail again as he exits the Uber. He closes the door gently and inhales the notes of the pine trees cluttering the old homestead. The smell carries a million memories of animals and air and genealogy. To all of it, Barnett is fully allergic. He's taken his allergy shots. He's inhaled his Flonase. He's set his boundaries.

Barnett closes his eyes and tries to quiet his nerves. The smell of pine reminds him of the big drought that struck the area in '96. He was collecting sticks for his father's burn barrel. He spotted a dead branch still holding onto a tree trunk. He pulled and pulled and when it finally snapped off, the vibrations were so intense they were visible up the tree, as if he was in his own episode of a He-Man cartoon. He could soon see the havoc he unleashed as the snap of the branch loosened every single bright-green pollen spore up that tree's long trunk, even reverberating to some of its neighbors, all of nature in cahoots. And then, release. All that loose pollen, like a dry deluge, fell from the cloud of his own making. Barnett was the center of a green dust storm, covered in pollen, choking on the taste of it, filthy like a tiny coal miner after a hard day. Farms can be dangerous.

"Popping the trunk," the driver says from his open car window. "Need help with your bags?"

"No, thanks," Barnett says. He walks to the popped trunk and hauls out a large suitcase and a carry-on bag—both bright red, so he can easily find them in baggage claim, avoiding fights with other passengers, setting himself apart from all the ordinary.

"Thank you," he yells, slamming the trunk closed, stepping away as the driver backs the car out of the driveway and onto the blacktop escape.

Barnett hears the birds more clearly now. He hears the chickens. He hears the hum of whatever collusion of insects gives Louisiana its soundtrack. He turns from the road that leads away, and looks at his childhood home, wipes the sweat increasing on his brow, scans the landscape for her.

As a kid, little Barnett used to throw himself around his mother, hugging her with arms thin as Christmas wrapping-paper tubes. He'd wear tattered old He-Man T-shirts while helping her around the farm. Now, he wears fancy khakis and polo shirts that hardly fit over his grapefruit-size biceps.

He's been in Loony Tunes, away from the farm, away at school, and away from his mother's watchful, adoring eye for sixteen years now. Barnett tells people he's a nurse, though he scoffs at the term. But it's easier than explaining radiology, that he operates an MRI machine all day. It's easier than saying that for a living, Barnett looks inside people.

Barnett's eyes water every time they fall upon his mother, always in the first seconds of his visits.

It's the heat and humidity, he'll tell her.

It's the love, he'll tell her.

But really, it's the increasing surge of gray in her hair. It's the way gravity is pulling her skin, her very life, closer and closer to the dirt, to the land she tends with her whole heart. It's the parchment-paper skin of her hands. It's the age spots and the easy bruises, which have scant time to heal, not when all these animals need love. But it's the redness around her smile that moves him most, the freshness of her delight, her face not used to smiling much these days, and he knows of all the chores he'll do for her, making her smile is his sweetest gift.

Barnett's smile, however, will be a little forced. It'll be hard to see his mother growing frail, especially this trip. Especially when under his generous greeting will be his nerves, the race of his heart, his fear that this might be the trip that breaks hers.

We need to find time to talk. Those were his exact words, he thinks. *I've prepared her for what I have to tell her*, he thinks.

Standing in the driveway, the same old gravel under his feet, the same old nerves kicking at his guts, he steadies himself. He doesn't even need to move. He knows she will come to him, she will find him. Nothing happens on an inch of Polite Society Ranch that doesn't have the imprint of Chrissy's finger—or thumb.

"EH!" he hears in the far distance and spins around. He's wont to holler back but his old country boy ways kick in, and he plays it safe and stealthy—*Never give up your location; you never know when you're the one being hunted.* He listens carefully—hears nature and the usual rumblings of Pauley and the others near the barn. This disruption came from farther away, almost a ghostly outburst.

Barnett squints in the direction of the sound—is his mother calling him? And he catches a flash of a man far out in their pasture. The man is wearing a red-and-black checkered lumberjack shirt and dirty old orange cap with jeans. The figure moves into view, and out, in a blink.

Barnett doesn't take his eyes off the spot, hoping for another glimpse. He drops both of his suitcases in the dirt and steps toward the man—an act of futile curiosity; the man is simply too far away, hardly within earshot not to mention clear sight, not at all within walking distance, and almost impossibly far away for Barnett to have seen him in the first place.

Still, Barnett stares, tracking.

Was it real? Was it a trick of the mind? Was there really a shout? A person? Someone wearing . . . that *outfit?* Barnett wonders. Chrissy would never allow an employee to wear such attire—her white T-shirt and blue jeans rules are strict. Chrissy would never allow a guest to wander out to that part of the farm. And of course, it can't be the other option. It can't be a ghost. It can't be his dead father, even though that lumberjack shirt, that orange cap, that style of jeans—that's what John Durang wore every day of his life.

Barnett stares and stares. Then, another apparition pulls his focus.

When he turns from the pasture, she appears. Farmer Mom rounds the corner of her home, past the old Chevy in the carport, and lays eyes on her son.

"Hi, Mom!" Barnett sucks in a deep breath and his eyes fill as he effortlessly smiles.

Once more he glances behind him—to the trespasser—and seeing nothing, turns his full attention to Farmer Mom.

Barnett and his mother come together in a hug so tight, it's as if their blood cells know each other, old friends snapping together like grooves of a Ziploc bag, those magnets somehow finding a way to touch, at least for a moment.

"You stopped parting your hair on the right?" Chrissy asks into her son's chest.

"Good to see you, Mom." Barnett laughs, tightening his arms around his mother. Her body always feels shockingly small, incongruous with her personality, with the towering and tough version of her that lives in Barnett's head. She feels skeletal. *Where does she keep all the might and muster?* he wonders.

Barnett's favorite MRI scan is of the spinal cord. Brains are interesting, sure. Eyes and feet are cool. But the spine of a person says so much. Hugging his mother, Barnett figures she must have perhaps the stiffest spine ever known. And he worries that his spine is more like a plastic Slinky.

"I liked your hair parted on the right," Chrissy says.

"I've missed ya, Mom," Barnett says, rocking his mother back and forth in his arms, her C1 anterior arch flexing perfectly, her prevertebral soft tissue expanding exactly, her old boots holding steady as she rocks from one transverse tarsal joint to the other in the gravel.

She smells like the old ladies used to at church. As a child, Barnett imagined all those ladies wore the same perfume, as if they were in a club. Barnett misses the scent of his mom from times past, after a long day, the lingering smell of the animals, of fresh-cut hay, of his father's aftershave hugging her neck.

"Let me see your face," Chrissy says. She pushes Barnett an arm's length away. She studies the skin that God himself must have draped upon Barnett's baroque bones. At that thought, Chrissy's rare smile changes. She touches Barnett's face. "You look more and more like your father." Feeling his skin, she longs for her own memories, her own sense-flashback of what John's face used to feel like: the roughness, the sun-beaten dark spots, the dirt so deep it seemed as if John was earthen. But Barnett's face doesn't deliver. His skin is shaved tight. Not a pore in sight. Not a mark from sun or scandal. The lines from his smile come and go with ease. Chrissy pulls her hand away. She once again grinds her boots into the gravel, then looks at Barnett standing in her driveway.

He stares back at her, hoping that in his face she can see his longing, that she can see how badly he wants her to ask about him, really ask about his life, really ask how he's doing instead of talking about the weather or his hair or the dreaded—

"How's things?" Chrissy asks.

Things. The question makes his Slinky firm up. His MRI would show swelling in his adrenal glands.

How's things? Barnett has a chance to tell her right here and right now. All he has to do is answer her question honestly, buck the unofficial policy of willful ignorance, show his mother the true picture, share the real intent of this visit, spill his guts—

"Fine," Barnett says, pick, pick, picking at that hangnail. He consciously tries to emote with his eyes, to signal his desire to tell her his news, but Barnett's face is one of blanket kindness. It doesn't emote longing of any type. Despite all the easy privilege his handsomeness provides, to be vulnerable with his mother, to win her approval or even her direct interest in the details of his life, he will have to work.

"How many tanks of gas did it take to get here?" Chrissy asks.

"I have no idea."

"Your suitcases are *very* red," Chrissy observes. "Why are they in the dirt?"

"They fell," Barnett says, glancing quickly again to the pasture. "I thought I saw someone out there."

"Were people staring at you the whole trip?" Chrissy asks.

"What? Why?"

"For twirling around the airport with those loud red suitcases."

"I don't think so," Barnett says.

"At least no one will steal 'em, right?"

"I guess," Barnett says. "Good thinking, Mom."

"Is this all you brought?" Chrissy asks, again surveying his two pieces of luggage as he gathers them from the ground.

"This is all I need right here."

"You sure do move light," Chrissy says. "Good boy. Come on."

Barnett steps inside the bright-blue farmhouse and tries to find the remnants of his happy childhood, anything original, unvarnished.

"Let's hide these in your room," Chrissy says, pulling Barnett's suitcases away from him as he tries anew to take in all the changes his mother has made over the years.

Chrissy's boots tap, tap, tap on the warm hardwood floor as she walks away from him. She chose to paint the floor black against all advice, but Chrissy saw it in a picture in a magazine at Rhett's Corner Grocery. And she liked it. She had grieved for a respectable year after

John died. Then, one day, she decided if she couldn't build a life with John, she'd build a life for Barnett, build something nice to leave to him someday. And she'd start with black wood floors just like in that glossy picture. She bought the magazine, she was so inspired. Rhett Johnson couldn't believe it, clanking the keys of the register as he rang up her usuals: "One head of lettuce. One potato. One tomato. One box of oatmeal. One bag of coffee. One bag of Hershey's Kisses, and one *Southern Living* magazine." He looked at her over his dirty glasses. "I thought all my magazines were 'devil's literature'?"

Chrissy leaned toward him. "All but one. Anyway, mind your business, Rhett. And I'll mind mine." She winked at him. He winked back.

Barnett survived the usual rites of passage in that home—ruining his church suit trying to wash it, losing his He-Man action figures in random spots all over the farm, the unfortunate time he stained Elaine with Woolite. Barnett smiles seeing all the little scenes of the little crimes. But his face grows sober with one memory, the one that isn't funny, the one that's The Big Thing.

Barnett killed his father. Or, at least, that's what Chrissy sometimes thinks. She believes Barnett shredded John's heart, tore it into a dozen strips. It was years ago, but a dam takes years to build, one tiny rock at a time. And The Big Thing, Chrissy believes, started the heart problems that would spell John's demise in the middle of *Cheers*. When that very thin doctor said John's heart was rotten, Chrissy believes the rot started with The Big Thing.

Barnett was a junior in high school when it happened. He always knew he was different. His friends would talk about the thrill of being with a girl—the feel of her warmth, the smell of her skin. Barnett dated girls, but it was never a thrill. Every sexual interaction Barnett had with a girl was a chore, and most could hardly be called sexual, especially if Barnett had any say in it. He always steered dates to conversations about family or algebra. Mostly, there was kissing, a battlefield of sticky lip glosses and lipstick colors that stained his shirts, his lips, and his sense of taste—these girls with their cheap tubes of moist colored waxes. He dated girls with the flippancy people use to select avocados: low stakes, no passion, hard to tell if it'll be brown inside. Then, he realized it wasn't fruit he wanted; it was Brätwurst.

His name was Duncan, an exchange student from Germany, with curly black hair and deep brown eyes and dark, perfect skin and that accent and that confidence and how did he know how to roll his pant legs like that? Duncan, and thoughts of Duncan, for Barnett, those were a thrill. Those lips were unvarnished.

Barnett stalked Duncan until one day, after their American literature class, Barnett mustered the courage to say hello, to investigate this gravitational pull, to see if it was God somehow calling Barnett to enmesh himself in Duncan's life in some way.

"How about this damn class?" Barnett asked, out of breath from chasing Duncan down the hall.

"Huh?" Duncan asked, fidgeting with the necktie he was wearing as a belt. (Wow! Style! How did he know how to do that?)

"I said, 'How about this damn class,'" Barnett repeated. "I'm in your American literature class."

"Right, yeah," Duncan said, his accent doing the heavy lifting, his sensuality a bully to Barnett's fragile parts. Barnett had never been that close to Duncan—nerves kept him away until now. But there, up close to him, Barnett could see each follicle where facial hair was sprouting on Duncan's beautiful skin. "If it wasn't for my girlfriend I'd be flunking," Duncan said.

Girlfriend. Barnett had the courage to talk to Duncan, but not to dig deeper. And when Duncan kept on about his girlfriend and kept on about his lust, Barnett knew what Duncan was not. And Barnett knew what he was.

Could it be Barnett's nerves? Barnett's untamed hunger? Barnett's pent-up lust? Something burst from him, broke inside him. It wasn't sadness—*girlfriend*. It wasn't rage. It was clarity. Later that night, it was a mess in a dirty sock. It was the endless topic of every guilty confession with every priest, so much so that his local pastor eventually seemed gleeful to welcome the sordid details of Barnett's sexual awakening. On one occasion, Barnett chose only benign things to confess, but Father Perfect (their local pastor's nickname) lowered his head, leaned close to Barnett, and whispered, "What about the sexual stuff?" At the time, Barnett thought the Lord or the Holy Spirit or Jesus himself made Father Perfect a mind reader. Nowadays, long after Barnett has left the church, he realizes Father Perfect was a worse sinner, probably.

It wasn't just the church telling Barnett that homosexuality was a sin. It was his small town, his world, every path in every direction from that blinking yellow light at the intersection by Rhett's Corner Grocery. It was condemnation via disassociation. Barnett didn't know any other homosexuals. His home had no Internet. His home had only one television and his father was in charge of the remote. Whom did he have to talk to? Whom did he have to look up to? Who would teach him about butt stuff? Certainly not his sex ed teacher, Mrs. Badeaux, who had ill-fitting dentures and mysteriously referred to genitals as "ropes and pulleys." So, Barnett did what always worked for him, the trick that helped him get all those As in all those classes—study, research.

Barnett ordered a book from Amazon. He paid with a prepaid credit card from Rhett's. Sweating through his T-shirt at his school library's computer, with seconds left in the thirty-minute time limit, he clicked the yellow "submit" button and placed the order. And the day before its scheduled delivery, a surprise. It came early. He arrived home from school and found the box. It was open. His mother was in tears. His father was looking at him—for the first time in Barnett's life—with disappointment. Barnett's book, all $14.99 of it, was splayed across the family dinner table: *Being Gay for Dummies.*

"Is this a prank?" Farmer Dad asked.

Barnett's spirit sank and, unable to manage a modicum of poise, he looked down at the floor. He shook his head, *no.*

"Are you confused about nature?" Farmer Dad asked.

Confused? Barnett wondered. He shook his head again, *no.*

"It's unnatural!" John yelled.

Barnett replied to his father, quietly, bravely, "It feels natural to me."

SLAP—John smacked his hand atop the book, wrapping his fingers around the edge and carrying it toward Barnett.

"John!" Chrissy cautioned.

Barnett took a step back, but Farmer Dad turned, returning to the table to also grab the box the book came in, the address label affixed to it like an act of betrayal with its black-and-white finger pointing, which said, "To:" then clearly, shamefully, "Barnett Durang."

"Come with me," John said, pushing past Barnett and out the kitchen's back door. Barnett followed his father past Jerry Seinfeld, past Kramer and Elaine, past Niles and Roz, and to the old burn barrel. John tossed in the book. John tossed in the box. Old ashes rose up in a gray cloud and for a second, Barnett thought he saw the cruel outline of a heart. "Go get what you need to burn this," John said.

Barnett walked slowly to the barn and fetched lighter fluid and matches. He returned to a father who wouldn't look at him. No words were spoken as the lighter fluid streamed like piss onto the book and the box.

"Do it," John said.

It took Barnett a couple of attempts to light a match, but then the fire went up fast and grand and would have been beautiful, if not for the truth behind all that heat.

Sin rose from the pages in black bilious vapor, every glossy page fighting for life in smolder and smite. John and Barnett's hair and skin stunk for two and a half days. The smoke gave the pigs diarrhea. Sometimes, Chrissy swears she still smells it.

"Anything else like this in my house, boy?"

"No, sir," Barnett said.

"There's a natural order."

"Animals do it—"

"Wrong!" John shouted. "It's wrong. Animals get confused, too. They come back. They change back. Or there wouldn't be any animals. It's a phase."

"Dad, it's not a big thing—"

But John kicked over the burning barrel, the fire and embers and remains of *Being Gay for Dummies* aflame, sliding out like lava, hissing and charring the green grass. Barnett backed away and John approached slowly, emotion in his eyes, heaving of his body. "It's a big damn thing." THE Big Thing, it would turn out, and the only thing the little trio of a family would ever lose sleep over, would ever ignore, until this very homecoming.

"Your room," Chrissy says to Barnett, snapping him out of his worst memory. "If you still recognize it."

"Thanks, Mom."

Barnett's room was also remodeled during Chrissy's storm of change. She wanted something vaguely masculine but neutral and settled on wallpaper with bicycles in blocky patterns. Barnett's Boy Scout patches are still framed on the wall, a constellation created when he got too old for scouting, too big for his uniform, and too attached to his many accomplishments. His trophies from running track still line his windowsill, each statuette also draped with ribbons from those winningest years on the team. The bed where he cried himself to sleep believing the devil was inside him still sits in the corner, still too small. He suffered many sleepless nights in that bed until the good Lord helped Barnett forget Duncan and all of it, helped Barnett shut it down in time to bring girls to junior and senior prom and ignore the fetid taste of their lips, at least until college.

"How's the farm?" Barnett asks.

"It's great," Chrissy says, "now that you're home."

Barnett doesn't tell Chrissy his big news right away, nor as he and his mother mend the old fence around the pasture later that afternoon. He doesn't tell her as they laugh at the determined chicken who thinks an old tennis ball is an egg. He doesn't tell her as she looks at his hands, at the raw hangnail he's been anxiously picking around his thumb.

"Your father's hands," she tells him as they walk home under a classic Louisiana sunset. She knows something's wrong, making him nervous, something's unsaid, and that awareness covers her arms in a fresh crop of goose pimples.

Chrissy wants a spectacular life for her son. "He's only *gay* because of that damn Internet," she's told Frasier and Niles, and Sam and Diane. "It's a phase," she's told Newhart and Nanny Fine.

It's nobody's business, she thinks, though she discusses it regularly with Father Perfect at Saint Michael the Archangel Catholic Church. Father Perfect keeps a candle lit in church for Barnett. It costs Chrissy ten dollars per month to keep it going but it also comes with a bottle of La Gracè Vino, the official church wine. Father Perfect tried to sell Chrissy a second candle and wine subscription after John died. It would have been another ten dollars. Chrissy scoffed, "John doesn't need a candle. He's already in Heaven."

Chrissy is Catholic the way some people are smokers: it's a habit. Her beliefs have never been challenged. Or discussed. Even all these years later, even after Barnett's move to Loony Tunes and his graduation from college and John's death, religion remains an easy container for The Big Thing, the big secret.

When mother and son are back inside from the day's toll of tours and travel and manual labor, washed and pajamaed, and full of fried chicken dinners from Rhett's Corner Grocery—with mashed potatoes, buttery biscuits, and green beans with bacon—Barnett starts his fidgeting. It's a meek, adorable dance he's always done—starting as a kid—to signal it's time for bed, as if he's ashamed to be tired. Before he says good night, Chrissy pipes up.

"So, this is it, right?" she asks.

"This is what?"

"What you want to talk to me about?"

"That I'm going to bed?"

"No. That you're home."

"Um, it's complicated, Mom—"

"Not that complicated," Chrissy interrupts. "For goodness' sake, you're home, it's not a secret. You're standing in front of me. I'm not hallucinating, right?"

Barnett—his skin shiny from his mother's soap, his green sweatpants cut perfectly into short shorts that show the outline of his thigh muscles, his T-shirt still clinging to the scent of his luxe laundry detergent from Loony Toons—momentarily longs to flee. "I have news, but—"

Chrissy kicks her feet out, leans back, sinks deep into the sofa, throws her arms up, and says, "Go ahead. Make it official."

"Tomorrow?" Barnett asks, begs. He and his mother have plans to visit Paw-Paw Durang at his retirement home. He's Barnett's grandfather, John's father, but he may as well have raised Chrissy, too. Her father died when she was a teenager and her mother was often real busy. In Louisiana, *real busy* is another way to say drunk.

Once Chrissy started dating John, Paw-Paw was the one who taught her how to drive, how to grill, how to clean a gun. He taught her how to protect herself, how to fight.

"Good idea," Chrissy says to Barnett, her smile appearing slowly, those face muscles getting their workout. "Paw-Paw will love it. And my heart might crack from the happiness. It'll be good to make the announcement around family."

Barnett smiles and turns his back to his mother, turns for his bed that's too small, his plans that are too secret.

He looks out his bedroom window and for a split second thinks he sees someone in the front yard—almost comically the silhouette of a man in a red-and-black checkered lumberjack shirt and a dirty old orange cap. But in a breath, the figure disappears.

Barnett spins to look behind him, as if it was just a reflection in the glass. But his room is empty.

Barnett dashes to his bedroom door, turns off the light, and jumps back to the window—nothing. He stares into the darkness, barely able to see the empty expanse of the farm outside, barely able to see his own reflection. An MRI would show his neocortex and thalamus acting up. Travel and exhaustion can do that. So can stress, about tomorrow, about *the talk*, about what he has to tell his mother and Paw-Paw.

It'll be good to be around family, she said.

Still staring into the dark abyss, Barnett mumbles to himself, "It'll be good to be around witnesses."

Chapter 3

CAMILLE Manor Retirement Gardens has a golden rule, which is also the silver rule and the platinum rule: don't molest the squirrels.

The nurses—a word that loosely and almost certainly illegally describes the overworked and underpaid attendants—are free to forget to serve the vanilla pudding before bed or to switch the television to Bob Ross during lunch. Hell, they can even accidentally kill some of the residents—most of whom actually wish there were occasional manslaughters to liven things up.

But, by God, whether nurse or neighbor, leave the squirrels to their sovereignty.

"Come here, April," Paw-Paw Durang chants in baby talk to a fat and neurotic Eastern Gray who showed up in the month of her namesake. "You, too, Red," Paw-Paw says to the critter with a crimson wisp who's peeking around a planter proudly housing a dead Japanese boxwood. "My daughter-in-law is on her way to visit. And my grandson. Hide your nuts."

Nine squirrels provide daily, unquantifiable amusement to the residents of Camille Manor. The number is almost worthy of being called an infestation, were it not for the ancillary benefits. As one gets older and human beings become harder to tolerate and to engage (visitors are few), squirrels are a good replacement, the one thing slightly more entertaining than *Judge Judy*.

"You like these?" Paw-Paw asks the squirrels, offering in his palm an assortment of roasted and salted mixed nuts, which the residents of Camille Manor Retirement Gardens buy in bulk at the Walmart.

"If you love nuts, you'll love my family," Paw-Paw tells the critters.

Camille Manor Retirement Gardens is less a nursing home and more a marketing marvel. Glossy brochures hail the caring staff, but the workers in the pictures are all actors and models from Hollywood. The brochure isn't even printed locally. It's a bulk order from a company in Dayton. Television commercials tout the lush property, but the video was shot on a beautiful sunny day on an estate in Virginia. When Chrissy and John and Paw-Paw first visited the place, Chrissy said it should be called "Camille Manor Retirement Pavements." There's no garden, not to mention "Gardens." There's no landscaping. There's only concrete: a "courtyard" with concrete benches atop concrete paving, a concrete parking lot, a concrete sidewalk around the cemented half acre of property. The managers say every blade of grass is a liability when every resident is a fall risk. Monthly, the suggestion box is packed with a zillion versions of the same request: more grass, more shrubbery. Not for aesthetics, but for fear. Residents worry the squirrels will burn their little feet as they scurry from the adjacent green spaces onto the veritable prison yard of Camille Manor Retirement Gardens.

Ironically not mentioned in the facility's glossy brochures: squirrels.

The squirrels take nuts from elderly hands, making those hands feel needed. The squirrels have daily routines. They expect and feel entitled to their roasted and salted peanuts and almonds and cashews, as if nature herself is stretching down a breast to provide for them.

"You'll appreciate this," Paw-Paw tells April and Red. "In cereal terms, my daughter-in-law is a Frosted Flake. And my grandson is a

Froot Loop." He pauses for laughter from his audience, which never comes, an almost alarming reminder for Paw-Paw that the bulk of his most meaningful socializing is with rodents.

"Hon?" a woman's voice calls from inside Paw-Paw's apartment.

He rolls his eyes and whispers to the squirrels, "Ignore her." He's surprisingly self-conscious of what they'll think of the scenario: an old man tossing salted and roasted mixed nuts as the untoward voice of an eighty-two-year-old seductress beckons. Inside, the room's thin curtain is billowing in the weak air-conditioning. Paw-Paw wishes it was from a breeze.

"Hon?" she calls out again. "I'm in the bed."

"One second! I'm with Red and—whatever-her-name-is."

"July?"

Paw-Paw doesn't answer.

"Do you care more about those squirrels than me?" she asks.

"Yes!" he shouts.

The woman is Frances from room 214. Paw-Paw's dead wife was also named Frances. This coincidence is very helpful at Camille Manor Retirement Gardens, though among the sexually industrious residents, it's no insult when anyone calls anyone else another name—whether in bed or on insufferable bingo night. Calling someone the wrong name is as common among the elderly as a little throw-up during sex. (Passing gas is also common but absolutely ignored—in part because no one can hear it and no one is confident it wasn't them. "Hell," Paw-Paw often points out, "we all eat the same food!")

"Come make love on me before *Wheel* starts!" Frances from 214 yells.

"I can't smell like I made love," Paw-Paw says. "My daughter-in-law and grandson are coming."

"Take a bath!"

"Baths are Wednesdays!"

"I have needs! Unless you want me to go down to 202!"

"GODDAMMIT!" Paw-Paw's greatest competition is McCoy in 202, a man who has lost most of his muscle mass but still has a grotesquely thick head of hair. *ANYONE CAN GROW HAIR! CORPSES GROW HAIR!* Paw-Paw has protested, and still lost lovers.

Frances from 214 tosses back the comforter and steps her tiny feet onto the floor. "It took me thirty minutes to get my stockings off!"

Paw-Paw throws his hands up. If his timing is right, she'll have her house dress on, her walker in hand, and her dappled ass out of his room in three, two, one . . .

SLAM!

Red and April scurry off at the sound of the door mocking Paw-Paw's exploits.

"GODDAMMIT AGAIN!" Paw-Paw yells. He throws his remaining handful of nuts into the concrete yard as his room's phone rings with the passion of a foghorn. The blast of noise stuns him. Disoriented, he has to grab hold of his old white lawn chairs to settle.

Before he can groan or wince or even think *LOUD*, he first thinks *DEAD*. It's not the worst place for his brain to land. In his eighty-eight years of life, his mind has had many home bases. As a youth, his imagination was fueled by serials. During meals and school and church he was always somewhere else—imagining superheroes and magic superimposed over daily life. In his teens, his brain's home was sexuality—even the hint of a hardened nipple on a woman would send him into such a fit that he'd sometimes have to change underwear. In his twenties, thirties, forties, fifties, sixties, seventies—each era seems to have been programmed with similar catch basins, the spot to which all thoughts would flow: family, career, wealth, health, pain management, and life expectancy, respectively. And now, in his eighties, his go-to mental resting place is death. Every ache—DEATH. Every unruly gas bubble—DEATH. Paw-Paw's latest years have been home to honest questions about his death: *When will I go? What will be my last thought? Will my last thought be of the phone's nonadjustable goddamn ring volume?*

The phone rings again.

"GODDAMMIT THRICE!" Paw-Paw yells as the phone quiets from its latest outburst. He knows another blast is coming. He wages war with the curtains and goes inside and shuffles toward the wicked device as it howls yet again. "HELLO?" he asks, ungently.

That phone. It's one way they try to kill him, one way they try to kill all of them. Every death is a victory at Camille Manor. Death is profit. Shareholders cheer, reading funeral notices like NASDAQ. Paw-Paw is certain there's a chart in the back office. He's certain whichever nurse scores the most deaths gets employee of the month. Every time someone dies, the decedent's room is re-rented with a big price hike. The new tenant, already full of bash and bile because of being forced to live there, is viciously mistreated by the other residents as if the new tenant killed the previous tenant themself. Eventually, after a time, the dead resident is forgotten. The new resident finds their clique. And glorious equilibrium is reached. Until the next death.

"You have guests up front," a voice says over the phone. "Okay to send them back?"

"Okay to send them back?" Paw-Paw mocks. "Let me tell you something. It's bleak in here, you understand? You never have to ask me that. If an outsider asks for me, just send them back. Send anyone and anything back! I don't care if it's a gator! I'm lucky if it's a hungry goddamn alligator! You understand? Hello? Hello?"

Paw-Paw hangs up the dead line and takes a deep breath to gather strength for what's about to happen: the farcical hugging, the examining of bodies, and the "you look great" comments, which are always utterly offensive in their reach. He opens his room door and braces for it. The touching, the lies.

"You look great!" Chrissy says to her father-in-law, attempting to beam genuine cheerful affection from the doorway.

Paw-Paw says hello to Chrissy, and HELLO to his damn fine grandkid. "Mr. B!" Paw-Paw says as Barnett reaches in for a hug.

"Come on in," Paw-Paw says. He leads them inside as if there's much to show in the square box of the so-called apartment. Instead of rooms there are the four walls—the wall with the kitchenette, the wall with the water closet, the wall with the bed, the wall with the sofa. It's hardly a personal space, save for a single photo above a dresser, an eight-by-ten picture of his wife, Frances, in a frame with cracked glass. She looks like the model for every classic antique cameo pendant. Her eyes follow them around the space, follow Paw-Paw in judgment of all his exploits. "We can fight about it in Heaven," Paw-Paw often says to the picture.

The three Durangs sit at a tiny table and chairs. "Damn, you look just like your dad," Paw-Paw says, seeing in Barnett the beautiful face his son, John, once gifted the world, a face Paw-Paw has in pictures—*somewhere around here*. But that's a loss, unlike that of his wife, that he can't display, a loss he can't bear to face every day.

"Barnett has some news," Chrissy says.

"What's the news, Mr. B?"

"Uh," Barnett says, twitching in his chair. "We just got here. We don't have to—"

"I can't wait," Chrissy says.

"Yeah. I could die at any second!" Paw-Paw laughs. "Spit it out."

"I'm engaged," Barnett blurts. His head spins from the inertia of the statement, the confession, the words from his mouth, sweat dripping from his armpits, and again his picking, picking, picking at his angry, red hangnail. By now, the blood is poised to emerge from his thumb, so he squeezes the wound. The MRI would show a fissure ancillary to the distal phalange, it would show a bright spot. The pain is real, and a relief—a welcome distraction. "I'm engaged," he repeats, savoring the words aloud.

"Engaged in what?" Chrissy asks.

"Engaged to be married," Barnett says. Adding meekly, "To a great guy."

Whether it's his bad hearing or senility or modern brainwashing, Paw-Paw misses not a single beat. "Congratulations, Mr. B!" But Chrissy misses every beat, her mind racing, trying to reconcile how this *gay* thing, this monster, this plague on her joyful paradise, this parasitic flaw, this glitch in her life, this isolated imperfection infecting her son, has emerged, again. The Big Thing is exposed, free, undead after all, even bigger, and with a new sting. The mention of it makes more painful the years of Barnett not having a single serious girlfriend, years of vague descriptions of his weekend plans, the phone calls where she and Barnett spent an hour talking in passionate circles about the weather, and his most recent passive-aggressive updates about his *roommate*.

"Not this again," Chrissy says.

"Mom." Barnett feels his thumb throbbing in sync with his heart rate, his tenor willing his plastic Slinky into steel. "Just because we never talk about me being gay doesn't mean I'm not."

"You know how I feel about all that," Chrissy says.

"I really want you to be a part of my life, Mom."

"I am part of your life," she says. "Nothing can change that, believe me."

"What's his name?" Paw-Paw asks. "Is he a bum?"

"No," Barnett laughs. "He's great. His name is Ezra." Barnett beams at the very mention of his sweetheart's name.

"Ezra," Chrissy says, introducing it to her lips with barely veiled distaste. She recognizes the name, of course. Barnett has worked on the soft pitch for quite a while now, making increased mention of "Ezra doing this" and "Ezra doing that." Chrissy never asked a follow-up question. She never said the name aloud, until now. "Okay. So now I know."

"And I'd like you to meet him."

"I'm leaving!" Chrissy says, standing up so fast her knees force her chair to topple behind her.

Barnett stands, more a polite reflex than a challenge. "Mom—"

"This is not *the talk* I imagined us having."

"It's the talk I've been dreading for years. You ignore this part of my life. It feels like you have a don't ask, don't tell policy."

"Nope. You can ask me anything you want."

"Could Ezra come down and meet you?"

"Oh, Barnett," Chrissy says, her hands in fists at her sides. "Do you really want to do this in front of your paw-paw?"

The old man laughs. "Don't mind me. This is way better than *Jeopardy.*"

Chrissy groans. She locks eyes with her son. His eyes have already been locked on her.

"Ezra and I have been together for three years," Barnett says. "This is a really exciting step for us. I'm in love."

"Oh, Barnett!" Chrissy repeats. She feels the collapse of her central nervous system, the pain of thinking, of processing, of doing the math, the reconfiguring of vague and dismissive mentions of Barnett's life in Loony Toons, the reality of the untold unmentionables she hoped would never find voice. The future she had planned for herself and Barnett is now decimated.

Still, Barnett smiles. Barnett smiles with compassion, with regret— maybe this would've been easier on his mother if he'd had the courage to bring it up sooner. Or if there had been other boyfriends before now, but none were serious enough or worthy enough to make him stir up The Big Thing. Maybe as a kid he should have dreamed of being married, shared his hope that such a day would come, but back then it was unheard of. It wasn't even legal. He's considered: *Why wake the dragon?* Because while Barnett loves his mother, for the first time, he now loves someone else more.

Barnett looks at his mother, the two of them standing there like fools at Paw-Paw's little table. "One of us should probably storm out," he says.

Chrissy looks at Paw-Paw, then reaches behind and picks up her toppled chair. She sits at the table, folding one hand on top of the other, politely.

"Okay, I'll go," Barnett says. He steps behind Paw-Paw and holds his elder's shoulders. He leans down. "Talk again soon. Love ya, Paw-Paw."

"Love ya back, Mr. B," Paw-Paw says. Then, "Hey!" Paw-Paw extends his hand. "Secret handshake?"

The two Durang men do the "secret handshake." It's the one Paw-Paw taught Barnett as a kid. The secret handshake is actually a regular handshake, but young Barnett didn't know any better, and neither man has had the heart to ever bring it up, ever let their little joke get old or fade away, even these decades later, because each time they do it, for a moment, they both feel young.

Barnett calmly and quietly leaves the room, gently closing the door behind him.

Chrissy turns her head slowly to look at Paw-Paw.

"Go after him," he says. "Being gay is on him. Losing him will be on you."

"How can you be so flip? I don't accept the gay thing."

"Reality doesn't care if you accept it or not."

"And I definitely don't believe in gay marriage. John must be rolling in his grave."

"John!" Paw-Paw laughs. "If that's true, my son is a big hypocrite. I remember when you two were dating—not to mention all the *dating* he did before he met you—when he committed all kinds of sins."

Chrissy blushes at the memory of her first time with John. He loved sex, and Chrissy loved it with him. She lost her virginity to him. And he lost his wilds with her. And to Chrissy, what happened between them felt like the opposite of sin.

"You and John met when you were both a little too young for all that, as I recall," Paw-Paw says. He and his late wife opposed John's relationship—not to mention marriage—with Chrissy. They saw her as too immature, though they never said that part out loud. But their son loved her. It was the kind of love Paw-Paw scarcely understood; his love for his wife was always full, but it was never the dangerously rewarding kind of fireworks he saw between John and Chrissy. John had the kind of focus on Chrissy that superseded all the other reasonable benchmarks of the mind. That kind of love settled every decade of John's life not on his triumphs or pains but on his union with a little hick girl named Chrissy Boudreaux. "Remember what happened when I forbade John from seeing you?"

"Your memory is especially sharp today."

"I'm only conveniently senile," Paw-Paw says with a thin grin. "If John were alive, I think he would grow and adjust. And my advice is that you should, too." Paw-Paw leans closer to Chrissy, as if the nurses are listening outside the door. "Gay grandsons are all the rage here at the home," he explains. "I didn't always feel this way." He leans even closer, speaking even more quietly: "They made us watch every season of *Glee*."

Chrissy's right leg is bouncing, her bootheel tapping the floor so hard, Paw-Paw worries the vibrations will spread and she'll start rumors. He doesn't have time to interject before she lays it on him.

"If John came to you and said he was engaged to get gay married, you would have killed him. I'd be visiting you on death row."

Paw-Paw motions around him. "Welcome!"

"You know what I'm saying," Chrissy says. "What would you do? If John did this?"

Paw-Paw looks at his hands, withered and perpetually salty from the mixed nuts. He brushes his palms on his pants. "These hands hit John more than I would have liked, for far less than Barnett is doing now. But this is a different time, Chrissy."

"A different time for who? Because it's not a different time for me. It's the same time. I'm living in the same time. I didn't switch dimensions."

"The boy is engaged. He wants you to meet his friend and be happy for him. That's all."

"I can't." Chrissy is surprised by a touch of shame. "I just can't. I hate it. It's not what I want for him. The world is so crazy." She feels the familiar warnings of emotion, her ribs threatening to cave in, her sinuses swelling, her eyes awaiting their cue. But her tears dried up years ago; there were so many back then, back when she lost John. "I thought Barnett's big news was that he was moving home to take care of the farm. And me."

"Maybe he will, still," Paw-Paw says. "Maybe you'll love his little gay friend."

"God," Chrissy says, dropping her head into her palms. The thoughts that pop in her mind at the phrase "gay friend" include, but are not limited to, a slideshow of saggy, speckled, stubble-faced pedophiles she's seen on *Dateline*.

Paw-Paw puts his hands on the table and starts to push himself up. It nearly flips the table over and Chrissy quickly brings her own palms down to stop the tumble. "Come with me," he says.

Paw-Paw makes the slow trek of a few feet to the sliding glass door.

He swats at the curtain like it's a cobweb and steps out. His silhouette in the day's light makes it look like he's walking into Heaven and gives Chrissy the briefest pause as she wonders whether she's allowed to follow him, allowed there, doubting for a moment whether there's a place for her in the golden light.

"Come on, dang it, I don't have all day," Paw-Paw scolds.

Chrissy follows and sits in the stained plastic chair beside him. He points to the vast landscape of concrete before them. "Squirrels are just rats," he says. "I'd give my life for one of them. I would." He starts to get choked up, sharing the deepest of confessions, fit for voice only from a senior, from someone to whom truth is as essential as hope is elusive. "And they're just rats."

Chrissy struggles to see any squirrels in the gray landscape, but then a shadow shifts and betrays a lone creature staring at them with maybe fear, maybe favor.

"They're the same in important ways—attitude, brain, body— except for the tail, really," Paw-Paw says. "But rats are shunned. Squirrels are celebrated. The only difference is that someone said rats are bad. And someone said squirrels are good. And everyone collectively agreed to go along with it. To pretend it's different is just to be at war all the damn time."

Paw-Paw reaches down and pops the lid off a container of nuts. He grabs a handful of the good stuff and tosses it onto the pavement, the treats landing in a shape reminiscent of a spread of moles on the back of Winnifred from 243.

April, Red, and a few others emerge from wherever such cherubs go when they're not needed. Chrissy watches them, regretfully understanding what it is that captures Paw-Paw's aged affections. "Rats are misfits," she muses aloud, looking out at the gaggle of nature's troublemakers, filling their soft cheeks, judging her, daring her to be tough, daring her to somehow save her son's soul.

"I have a secret, too," Paw-Paw says. "Barnett called me and asked my advice. About how to tell you about the engagement. I told him to come visit me and tell us together. That I'd help soften the blow. So, that part is my fault. Now, the part about him being gay is probably your fault, you know. Your side of the family and all that."

Paw-Paw can't keep a straight face.

Chrissy smiles against her will, but only for a moment.

Paw-Paw twists, aims to make eye contact with Chrissy, but settles for her profile instead, since her eyes are still focused on the expanse of rats before her.

"Barnett isn't asking you to put an ad in the paper for gay rights. Or host a big gay wedding. He's just asking you to love him and be interested in his life and the person he loves. Do it—or at least pretend to—or you will lose him," Paw-Paw says.

BARNETT sits in the lobby of Camille Manor Retirement Gardens. He did two laps in the halls until he felt the walls close in. Four hallways support the square building, making a loop. That way, the residents are never lost; they just keep running into the lobby. That's where Barnett found a seat, waiting for his mother.

Beside Barnett sits an elderly woman in a wheelchair. He guesses at her radiology report: pulmonary lesions, shadowy corners of the brain common after a stroke, likely herniated disc in the L3 region.

Working an MRI machine is like looking into a crystal ball. Patient after patient will get their scan, then ask Barnett, "How does it look?" He always knows the answer. He can see the scan. It's not rocket science. He can see large masses in breasts or displaced vertebrae stabbing spinal cords. He can see when a brain tumor will be inoperable.

"Above my pay grade," he has to lie to the new mother worried about cysts or the kid wondering what's up there causing his head-aches.

The old woman's MRI wouldn't look good.

As he stares at her, she looks back at him. This old woman has seen things. Her eyes are frosty and her lips pink from a tube of lip-stick that she's owned since 1981. She used to collect lipsticks as a girl, woman, mother, grandmother, great-grandmother. But now there are only a few tubes left in her life. She's vowed she will use all of them up, then she expects her time will come. Lipstick, one of her favorite things in the world, will count down her death.

Barnett's heart is fragile as he awaits his mother's fury, or not; he doesn't know what to brace for. But he affixes a smile and his best puppy dog eyebrows. He gently nods at the old woman, cocks his head, his kindness tick going full force. "Hi there."

"Up yours!" she shouts. She grabs one wheel of her chair and tries to spin herself in his direction, so she can face him head-on and give him a good wallop. But her chair's brakes are on, and she's reminded yet again that her life is frozen, stuck in what feels like a fever dream, assaults apparently hurled at her nonstop, even if only in her mind. The worst part of being forced to live in the present is when the present sucks, when the present doesn't seem to want you.

"Calm down, Miss Dottie," a nurse says kindly, stepping behind the old woman and offering some sort of comfort, perhaps if only to assure Miss Dottie that she's still alive, not in Hell, not yet.

Barnett turns from the fracas he caused to see his mother standing in the hall, watching her son's tenderness, the cause of so much of her suffering. She nods to the front door and Barnett follows his mother to the Chevy, walking quickly ahead of her and opening her driver's door for her. "Sorry, Mom."

"Please don't ever get advice from Paw-Paw again."

Barnett wants to argue, but he nods his agreement. Chrissy gets in and Barnett closes her door. The engine is purring and the truck is barely in drive before Barnett is seated beside her and back on the subject.

"I hope you'll meet him, Mom. I think you'll love Ezra."

Ezra. Chrissy tightens her grip on the steering wheel.

"He's all the things you wanted for me. Except the penis part."

Chrissy resists driving her truck off the road and into a pine.

"Wanna know how he proposed?" Barnett asks.

Chrissy doesn't answer. She accelerates.

"It was a Sunday morning. He made pancakes—"

"I really don't think this is the right time for this—" Chrissy starts.

But Barnett continues. "Making pancakes is ordinary for Ezra on Sundays. We ate, then went back to bed. Later, we went to the farmers' market and had a tiff over which soap to buy—vanilla or lavender. He bought us both. We made dinner and watched a couple episodes of an old season of *Survivor*. Again, it was all very ordinary. And then, before we went to bed, he held my hand and asked, 'Can we be ordinary together forever?'" Barnett pauses, gets emotional, brushes it off. "Later, he said the whole thing was his second idea. His first . . . He wished he could have had you there to be happy for me. He gave me the plane ticket I used to come here. He said to tell you in person, to trust that mothers love their sons." Barnett pauses. "Ezra is kind, beautiful, funny, smart. He's my age, he's a teacher just like you used to be. He's my life, Mom."

Barnett, always polite, found the sweetest way to say: *He's my future, not you.*

"Please buckle your seat belt," Chrissy says, politely.

THAT evening, Chrissy works the stables for an hour longer than usual.

She gives the chickens extra attention.

She takes extra care with the goats and the pig and the alpaca in the kennel.

When Chrissy enters the barn, she finds Barnett there.

Mother and son don't speak to each other immediately, don't even acknowledge one another. Barnett begins by greeting Elaine. "What's wrong, girl?"

"She's depressed," Farmer Mom says. "She misses Kramer."

"She has you, doesn't she?"

"What we have is less a bond and more a concession," Chrissy says, tidying up the horse saddles, restacking the buckets for chicken feed.

"Do you think it's real?" Barnett asks, gently petting Elaine, trying to look into her cloudy eyes. "A bond? A connection like that?"

Chrissy doesn't answer. Not out loud. It's not lost on her that the way Elaine's life is ending—unceremoniously, separated forever from her family, seemingly dying from loneliness—could be her own fate eventually. "I thought your big news was going to be that you're moving home to take care of me. And the farm."

"I'm sorry, Mom," Barnett says softly.

Chrissy doesn't ask her next questions, though Barnett is prepared with answers: *I'm not ready yet.* And, *I don't know when or . . . if.*

"If you aren't coming home to take over the farm, why don't you have a return flight?"

"I was hoping Ezra could come out and we could have a nice time and I could maybe stay longer than usual."

Chrissy turns to Barnett. "How much longer?"

"I don't know."

She refills water bottles for the macaws. "And if not?" she asks.

"I guess there are flights every day back to Loony Tunes."

Chrissy grabs the hose and drags it toward Elaine. Ezra on her mind, she aims the spray at a pile of Elaine's poop, the water blasting it from existence.

"Ezra can't wait to see this place," Barnett says. "I've told him so much about it. And about you."

"If you love it so much, why don't you visit more often?"

"It doesn't always feel very friendly here, Mom. Know what I mean?"

Chrissy doesn't answer. She twists and pulls the hose around her arm, looping it again and again, perfectly.

Elaine pokes her nose at Barnett's hand. She wants his touch, and he smiles and pats her head again, then rubs her belly. "I love you, too," he says to her.

"Ezra," Chrissy mumbles to herself, not with fondness or humor. "I find myself thinking that I just wish his name was, like, 'Mike' or something."

Barnett smiles. "He's got a great sense of humor. You could call him whatever you want."

"Be careful what you wish for," Chrissy says.

Then, speaking either to Elaine or his mother or both, Barnett says, "You'll love him. I just know it."

Chrissy is silent.

"Good night, Mom. I love you."

He starts to walk back to the house. "Fine," Chrissy says to the ground.

Barnett stops and turns around, caffeinated smile blazing. "Wait. Is that a yes?"

Chrissy looks at her boy, wonders what power he has over her that he can warm her so. "And if I do this, you can stay longer?"

"Be careful what you wish for," Barnett says coyly.

Chrissy hangs the hose back on its hook, her shoulder aching, her knees enflamed, her mind reeling. *How much longer can I endure all this?*

As Barnett walks away, an unmistakable new buoyancy in his step, Chrissy gives Elaine a good-night handful of hay, again reminding her woolly friend, "Sometimes mamas have to do terrible things."

Part 2

Interlopers

Sweetheart, joining families in marriage requires one part patience and two parts manipulation. Apply fake countenance! Loosen lace-cuffed fists! To keep the peace with future in-laws, I recommend a meal of Campbell's delicious soups or stews, finely canned with the latest scientific technology. Nothing says love more than a fashionable meal of exquisitely canned product!

> —*Mrs. Jeannie Laffite's Undisputed Guide to Respectable Southern Nuptials,*
> *volume III, page 37*
> *(copyright 1912 by Mrs. Jeannie Laffite)*

Chapter 4

Countdown to Damnation:

11 days / 8 hours / 17 minutes

THE moment Ezra Tanner arrives at Polite Society Ranch, Chrissy's eyes lock on him like a hawk about to snatch a Chihuahua from a backyard.

Just in time, Chrissy thinks. By the barn, Pauley has nearly finished with today's tour. The group, from an elementary school a couple towns over, should be leaving soon. *At least none of the kids will be traumatized if they see him*, she thinks.

Ezra is still sitting in Chrissy's Chevy, parked in her carport, in the passenger seat, beside her only beloved son. *Look at this gay stranger, this gay . . . boy*, she thinks of Ezra, a thirty-three-year-old man.

Chrissy can't believe Barnett took the truck to pick him up, all that gas, all that wear and tear. She wouldn't have been too upset if it broke down, died, if this meeting of Ezra was delayed by days or hours or minutes. Or forever, if she's honest.

She's standing in the doorway to the carport, her truck, son, and foe a few feet away. One step forward and she's outside approaching them, or one step back and she can stay in her home and avoid the whole thing a little while longer.

She watches Ezra look at Barnett. The two exchange some quip and Ezra laughs so loudly, you'd think the truck windows were down. So loudly, a nearby goat named Cousin Balki is stunned and falls over.

Chrissy reaches into her back pocket and pulls out her orange notepad and little pencil. She flips to a new page and writes, "EZRA." Below that she creates two columns: "Pros" and "Cons." Under "Cons" she writes, "Laughs too loud."

Chrissy looks up from her budding list of grievances and back to the boy, Ezra. Beside him, Barnett is beaming. Both boys look over and see her staring at them. She looks sad, out of sorts, right there in her own doorway.

Ezra looks nothing like the gays Chrissy has seen on TV, not like the ones with AIDS, not like the nearly naked ones in those parades, not like the obscene one from that show *Will & Grace*.

Ezra's black hair hangs just past his steely jawbone. His mouth closes in a permanent, gleeful simper. His eyes hover open in a way that makes girls swoon and straight men suspicious. Gay men either try to bed him or take his photo to their plastic surgeons begging, "Make me look like this!"

Chrissy licks the tip of her pencil and adds to her list: "Unkempt hair."

To Chrissy's eyes, there's a way young men should look. She mostly recognizes it when driving behind them. They preen a certain way as they look around traffic. Their short-haired silhouettes are as clear through a truck's back window as a Winchester. But not Ezra. Chrissy wonders if the drivers behind Barnett and Ezra thought they were man and woman.

The doors of the Chevy open and there's a SLAM-SLAM sound, two parties in devious harmony, and the one with the contestable hair is now standing on Chrissy's farm, firmly planting himself in Chrissy's life.

He's dressed in all black, in an artist-type getup of baggy jeans and what appears to be a sensible woman's capelet. He looks stylish by Loony Tunes standards, probably. But in Mader, he looks more like one of the lovebugs mutilated on the Chevy's grill. *The black pants are too black*, Chrissy thinks. She writes in her notepad, "Offensive dress."

Ezra meets Chrissy's gaze and maneuvers around the truck like one of those demon shadows from the movie *Ghost*, approaching, approaching, approaching.

"Mom," Barnett says. "This is my Ezra."

My Ezra. Chrissy could cry, scream, die right there in the dusty carport as the strange boy gets closer and closer. She always imagined Barnett with a pretty redheaded girl, like his old classmate Renée Bilson. Or a pretty brunette girl like Annie Simmons from church. Renée is agoraphobic, but Annie is due for parole any day now.

As Ezra approaches her, Chrissy struggles to come up with a perfect, warm welcome. Looking at this boy who's interloping with her son, she says, "Nice to meet you, sweetie."

"Nice to finally meet you, Miss Durang," Ezra says, his hand extending for a shake. He bends slightly, almost as if he's about to bow.

She shakes the boy's hand. "Oh, it's Chrissy, please."

"Chrissy," Ezra corrects with a gentleman's nod.

"*Miss* Chrissy, technically—" she corrects.

"Mom—"

Chrissy looks at her son. "I think I'm doing really well so far."

"Great to meet you, Miss Chrissy," Ezra says. "What a beautiful farm you have here."

Chrissy continues to observe him, his kindness that's still and calm, effusive but steadied, like soda with no ice, like they have in Europe, where Chrissy recalls all the communists live.

Ezra looks at Barnett then Chrissy, but both of them are looking at him as if he's in charge. "Have you two been having a nice visit?" he asks.

"Really nice," Chrissy answers, thinking, *It was. I wish it was continuing, uninterrupted.*

Chrissy notices her son's shoulders relax with Ezra beside him, as if a great weight has fallen off Barnett and onto Chrissy, for she tenses as Barnett's fingers find comfort in Ezra's, as the boys briefly touch foreheads then lips, as Barnett beams—*all that caffeine.* Chrissy looks at Barnett's hands—John's hands. Barnett has stopped picking at his hangnail, stopped hurting himself, drawing his own blood, as if Ezra is a salve, a comfort, one of those SSRIs they advertise on television that could cause blurred vision or stroke. How could Chrissy possibly compete?

She writes new "Cons" on her notepad: "Controlling. Manipulative."

"What are you writing?" Barnett asks.

Chrissy brushes it off. "Grocery list."

"Hey, are you responsible for Barnett parting his hair on the right?" Ezra asks, thumbing toward Barnett's head.

Chrissy pauses, suspicious. "No. I like him to part his hair on the left."

"Me, too!" Ezra says, turning to Barnett. "See! Your mom and I agree."

Chrissy cringes.

"Let my hair have its own life," Barnett jokes. "Now, come see the house."

Barnett pulls his *friend* by the hand, through the carport, away from the Chevy, past Chrissy, and into the farmhouse. Ezra looks at Chrissy as he passes her, like he's taunting her, and with that black hair in his face, rolls his eyes playfully and shrugs as if to say, "Golly! Look what your son is making me do!"

Chrissy writes on her pad, "Con artist."

Ezra steps through the doorway and into the Durang living room slowly and deliberately. He breathes deeply, willing the smells and sights and sounds into his mind, fueling the universe of his thoughts. He puts his hands over his heart. "Babe," he says to Barnett. "This is where you grew up."

Ezra looks around, studying the floor, the furniture, the walls—and allowing his mind's eye to remove the coats of color from everything, so he can try to see it as it was when Barnett was a boy, as it looked when it held so much promise, before all the death, disappointment, and remodeling. He imagines what the wood paneling looked like when it was raw. He imagines the hardwood floors as bare tree planks smelling of nature and life, expanding like an ocean in all directions beneath occupants in their prime: a young father pouring his morning coffee, a young mother lacing her boots, a young boy surrounded by imagination and He-Man and love. "Wow," Ezra says. "It's so nice."

Barnett tries to nudge Ezra along. "This is the living room. Kitchen is behind us; my room is this way down the hall—"

"I put out some coffee and chocolate," Chrissy interrupts, slamming the door to the carport behind her, shutting off the outside world, sinking the boys lower into her den, her home advantage. "Please, sit."

She points to the coffee table, which holds a tray with a bowl of Hershey's Kisses and a steaming pot of coffee. She steps to the sofa and sits down, motioning for Ezra to take a seat in the side chair across from her, the one remaining chair in the room, the one upon which her husband did not die. "I'm excited to get to know you," she says flatly. "I have so many questions."

Ezra's eyebrows raise and he steps forward and sits opposite Chrissy, his hands folded one atop the other at his crotch. As if prepared to meet any fate, he says, "Shoot."

"No!" Barnett says playfully, stepping behind Ezra with a big smile.

"Mom, don't shoot." Barnett laughs at the image his mind has conjured, his mother holding one of his dad's old shotguns like a bumbling Annie Oakley, the butt askew on her shoulder, her finger misplaced on the trigger, her eye looking through the sight improperly, ready to launch steel and lead at Ezra as wildly as she sprays the hose on the horses in the summer. "Never tell a Farmer Mom to 'shoot.' She might be looking for a target. Right, Mom?"

Chrissy's mind involuntarily produces her own fantasy with a shotgun, and unlike Barnett's vision, hers is not comical.

"Miss Chrissy," Ezra says. "Ask me anything. I've been under Barnett's spell for the last few years." Ezra looks up at Barnett—the same way Chrissy looks at her son's pictures beside her bed—as if it's an addiction. "I'm in love," Ezra says. "I'm smitten. I'm gobsmacked." Ezra's toes wiggle nervously in his weird black ninja-style shoes. "One time, Barnett was dropping his car off at the mechanic and I was going to drive him home, so I was following him in my car. And the whole time, all I could think was how I wished I was in the car with him. Just *with* him. Just talking about nothing and everything, together. I'm so desperate to be near him I forget what happiness is when we're apart, and I miss it. I miss us when we're not together. I love us."

Barnett leans down and touches foreheads with Ezra. They kiss briefly, just as they did in the carport, their little couple's move. Both men then look at Chrissy.

She's holding the bowl of Kisses at them like a weapon. "CHOC-OLATE?" she asks Ezra, loudly. "Barnett said it's your favorite."

"Possible to take you up on that later?" Ezra asks.

Barnett pulls Ezra's attention. "Come on. You've experienced enough of the living room."

"What's the rush? I'm chatting with your mom. Are you afraid I'll spill a secret?" Ezra asks.

"What secret?" Chrissy asks quickly, slamming down the bowl of Kisses.

Barnett playfully tugs at his lover's arm. "Come on."

As Ezra stands, he looks at Chrissy. "Sorry. Chat later?"

Chrissy nods cautious approval as she pulls out her notepad and writes, "Sneaky. Saccharine."

Barnett leads Ezra down a long hallway, pulling him into the first door to the left.

"My room," Barnett says, hugging Ezra tightly. The guys are hardly alone for a moment before Chrissy appears in the doorway.

"How did you meet Barnett?" she asks.

The two men separate and Ezra sits on Barnett's bed, the springs so noisy he wonders if it's a message, or a warning.

"A dating website," Ezra says, smoothing the bed's lumpy comforter. "They match you based on how you answer a bunch of crazy questions. And of course, you can post pictures."

Chrissy jots on her notepad. "Pornographer."

"It's not pornography, Mom," Barnett says, reading his mother's mind. Then, to Ezra, "Mom thinks every website is porn."

Ezra laughs, softly this time—something between polite and amused. "The website asks questions like, 'What's your idea of a perfect Saturday?' Or 'What do you hate about your body?'"

Chrissy jots on her notepad, "Indiscreet."

Then she turns to her son. "And?"

"And what?" Barnett asks.

"What were your answers?"

As Barnett opens his mouth to respond, Ezra pipes up, "This was three years ago, but I still remember those answers. Barnett's perfect Saturday is a summertime afternoon working at his mom's farm."

Chrissy swallows hard. "And?"

"And he hates his calves," Ezra says.

All eyes turn to Barnett's legs.

Barnett shrugs, "Yeah, I hate my calves."

"I see he got those thin little calves from you," Ezra says to Chrissy, pointing at her legs. "Right?"

Chrissy looks down at her limbs. She hasn't considered her form in years. She even pauses at the mention of the word: "calves." Is that still what they call those?

Her jeans are snug enough that the meat from the back of the knee to the Achilles is svelte. "I guess he does get those from me," Chrissy admits. She thinks, *My son gets something from me—something he hates.*

"For the record, you both have beautiful calves," Ezra says.

Barnett flexes one leg and the next, but his muscles seem maxed out. "I still wish mine were bigger."

"Beautiful man," Ezra says. "Can't we all be friends with our bodies?"

Chrissy looks at Barnett's bedroom wallpaper. All those bicycles atop and around each other in the print make it feel like the three of them in that little room are in jeopardy, in some stage of danger. It's more violent than she remembers.

Ezra looks once more at Barnett's room, stands and studies some of Barnett's Boy Scout patches framed on the wall, then reads the engraved brass plates on the track and field trophies on Barnett's windowsill—"First Place Covington Regional, MVP Mader High Track." Dangling from the trophies are ribbons—mostly blues, mostly firsts.

Barnett steps back into the hall. "Let's continue the tour. Bathroom, guest room, and Mom's room are down this way," he points.

Ezra examines the hallway around him, the one covered with pictures of a familiar, perfect smile. "Lots of pics of your teeth, babe," he says, squaring step-by-step with the photos of Barnett lining their tour.

"The guest room is on the left," Barnett says. "And that's my mom's room on the right."

"Come back this way," Chrissy orders.

She leads them back through the living room and down another short hall. "My sewing room—which is really just a laundry room—is back here. And an office."

"No office in the barn?" Ezra asks.

"We have a granny flat instead," Barnett says.

"Don't be impolite!" Chrissy scolds. "It's an apartment. We chose to put *an apartment* in the barn. In case I have to live there one day. When Barnett gets married and has kids." Chrissy pauses, expecting the show of modest sympathy she always gets while lamenting with Father Perfect. But such moans about her lost fantasies do not arise. "It's where we store the chicken feed these days."

"Nice," Ezra says.

"Wanna see the farm?" Chrissy asks with a tone of obligation. "It might be a mess because we had a tour just before you got here."

"Sure," Ezra says. "Oh, first, should I put my suitcase in Barnett's room?"

"No, you'll take the guest room," Chrissy says.

"Mom!" Barnett protests. "We live together—"

"Please, Barnett. You're not *married* yet."

Barnett's chest swells and he takes a deep breath to facilitate a full-throttled response, one he's been expecting to have to deliver, one he's been practicing, but—

"Absolutely, Miss Chrissy," Ezra interjects. "Your house, your rules. I understand."

Barnett points to Ezra. "Butt kisser!"

"Barnett! Be polite!" Chrissy scolds.

She walks the boys past the sewing room and through her modest office. "Butt kisser," she writes in her notepad, discreetly.

"Love your office," Ezra says.

Chrissy waves away the compliment. "Don't call it my office. Please call it *the* office. I never wanted to grow up to be a person with an office." She breezes past a futon and a desk, straight to the back door. "The farm is this way," Chrissy says.

As the door swings open, the sound outside is penetrating. They're all struck by the size of the tantrum, the day's latest Category 4: a kid wailing and inconsolable.

"I guess the tour hasn't left yet," Chrissy says. "Stiffen your spines."

Near the barn, Pauley is tending to the screaming child. He's tried all the usual techniques, including an Elmo Band-Aid and offer of chocolate. But the screaming. It's the kind Chrissy worries can rupture an eye vessel.

She steps away from Barnett and Ezra.

Pauley looks up at her. "He doesn't want to leave. His classmates are already in the van."

"Did you try a fiver?" she asks, quietly.

"No luck," he says. "Kids these days. Not capitalists."

Chrissy turns to the crying boy. "SHHH! What's wrong?"

The boy ignores her.

"Now look, young man!" Chrissy says. "I don't see a drop of blood or a single protruding bone. What are you going on about?"

As the boy sucks in air during a sob, Chrissy continues, "No one else is crying. Why aren't you acting like the other kids? What are they gonna think of you, huh?"

As the screaming resumes, now with even more shriek, Ezra approaches. "May I try?" he asks.

Chrissy laughs, then realizes he's not joking. "Be my guest."

She steps away and swings her arm out, offering the problem, the boy, to Ezra. She steps back toward Barnett. Pauley steps back with her, as if what's about to go down could be contagious.

Ezra kneels in the dirt, the mess and muck attaching instantly to his too-black pants. "Hi," he says to the crying boy.

The country boy stops sobbing long enough to look at Ezra with a type of curious horror. "What are you tryin' to be?" the boy asks.

"I'm an Ezra." His eyes are warm and glowing, his smile approachable and disarming.

"Oh," the boy says, calmly.

"Hey," Ezra says. "What color are your body's vibes right now?"

"What's vibes?"

"Like feelings, but 'vibes' is cooler to say," Ezra says. "Are your vibes red and angry? Blue and sad? Yellow and nervous? Green and chill?"

The boy wipes his eyes, shrugs his shoulders.

"All those vibes are okay. Sometimes we can't help it. But if we can figure out which one your body is feeling right now, we can maybe help you feel better. Like changing the channel on a radio station. If you want."

At her safe distance from Ezra and the boy, Chrissy whispers to Barnett, "This is ridiculous."

Barnett grins. "Watch this."

Ezra looks with care, eyes locked with the kid. "It looks like your body is feeling red vibes?"

The boy nods, *yes*.

"I'm sorry. I know that's hard. Red is my least favorite. Wanna go to a calm-down spot in your mind?"

"Okay," the boy says.

"Okay," Ezra says. "Close your eyes. Think of a nice place, a really cool spot." He pauses for a moment, opens one eye to make sure the kid is following instructions. "Okay. How cool is it?"

"Reeeeeally cool."

"Perfect! And no one knows what you're seeing in your mind. It's all yours. Notice how nice it feels, how safe. And everything is friendly, because it all comes from you, and you're friendly. You imagined something really awesome, and that means you must be really awesome."

The boy's features soften, the air of smile returning.

"Aaaaaand, open your eyes," Ezra says. "Feel better?"

The boy nods, *yes.*

"Pfft!" Chrissy says from several feet away.

Ezra hears her but smiles and keeps his focus on the boy. "I can see your body seems more relaxed. Were you able to help your body feel calm?"

The boy nods, and smiles.

"Woo-hoo!" Ezra shouts. He puts up his hand and the boy high-fives it.

Barnett whispers to his mother, "The 'woo-hoo' is an essential part of it."

But Chrissy is busy with her notepad, and reads aloud to Barnett what she just wrote, "Witchcraft." Beside that she writes, "Woke." Beside that she writes, "Bad teacher."

Ezra gives the boy an aw-shucks look. "Hey, what happened right before you felt the red vibes?"

"They showed us a sheep in there," the boy says. "Her name's Elaine. And they say she's old and sick and I don't want her to die."

Before the boy can start to cry again—

"You know what?" Ezra says. "I don't want her to die, either. But instead of feeling red vibes about that, I'm going to think about how happy that sheep is today. She got to see you. She gets to live here on this cool farm. And that gives me green vibes. You?"

The boy considers, then nods agreement.

Pauley steps away from Chrissy and Barnett and toward the boy.

"Shall we?" He takes the boy by the hand and leads him to his awaiting school van.

"What the hell was that?" Chrissy asks Ezra.

"The Vibes Method. It's a modality rooted in the cognitive-behavioral approach to psychosomatic stimulus and related verticals. It helps validate feelings and create a path to unmolested emotional regulation. It gives kids a language when they don't have one. That's why dismissing them or ordering them to behave doesn't work. Can you believe some caretakers even bribe their children to behave? They actually use cash sometimes!"

Chrissy blinks twice. "I'm gonna go get started on dinner," she says. "Hope you like Lean Cuisines."

CHRISSY spends two hours and seventeen minutes pacing the hallway of her own home, glaring into the eyes of each of the portraits of Barnett on the wall. His bedroom door is closed. It's quiet inside. The guest room door is closed. It's quiet inside. *No one pulls one over on me,* Chrissy thinks.

Certainly, she thinks, the boys are fornicating in one of the rooms, closing both doors to fool her. She tries to consciously will all of her senses awake. She stands with her face inches from Barnett's bedroom door. She closes her eyes. She inhales deeply. *Does sin have a scent?* she wonders.

She holds her breath to improve her hearing. She leans even closer to the door. She recalls people on television putting their ear to a door to hear inside. *Does that work?*

Her ear moves closer and closer until—

"MOM?" Barnett calls, swinging the door open. Both son and mother are startled and jump away from each other. "What are you doing?"

"What are YOU doing?" she asks.

"Napping."

"Oh, really?" She calls into the room, "You can come out, Ezra."

"Miss Chrissy?" Ezra says, poking his head out of the guest bedroom behind her. "Everything okay?"

"Great. Yes," Chrissy says. "I've just been . . . worried . . . about . . . when to start the microwave for your dinners."

"Can we eat in a few minutes? We were just about to FaceTime with Ezra's parents."

"Parents?" Chrissy says, disoriented for a moment by the news that Ezra was procreated. The thought that he's a son to someone hadn't occurred to her, in the way kids don't always comprehend their teachers are real humans who carry purses or have spouses. "Where are your parents?"

"They live in New York."

"They're nice," Barnett says.

"You've met them?" Chrissy asks with suspicion, wondering what she's being excluded from, what's being hidden from her.

"Yeah, well, Ezra's mom is . . . pushy," Barnett says. "I didn't so much meet her as experience her."

"Wanna join our FaceTime, Miss Chrissy? My parents would love to see you."

"Absolutely not, thank you. I'm not dressed for FaceTime."

"Mom, please. You don't even know what FaceTime is."

"I do so," Chrissy says, turning to Ezra. "Please tell them hi and I look forward to meeting them, maybe, one day. And don't tell them about the Lean Cuisines. That's only because you arrived on short notice. I'm not great with surprises."

The guys follow Chrissy down the hall until she goes into the kitchen. They continue onward, nearly crashing on top of each other on the living room sofa.

Chrissy listens carefully from beside the fridge, resenting the dreaded ringtone she can hear forced through the tiny speakers of Ezra's phone. FaceTime's ring sounds sadder than that of a regular call. She knows the sound well. Rejection. Barnett has for years tried to get her to FaceTime with him. He'd initiate it and she'd be terrorized by the ringtone and which buttons to push and so she flatly refused the stress of it all and insisted on the regular old telephone. Barnett didn't concede immediately. The standoff gave them both what they wanted—a way to communicate less, a way to keep their walls up.

At last, "HELLO DON'T HANG UP!" a woman shouts from the speakerphone.

"Hi Mother," Ezra says.

"I'm in the bath," she responds. "Am I using the correct camera? Do you see my face or my—?"

"Your face, Mother. I see your face. I'm calling with Barnett."

Ezra's mother squints into her phone to see him. "Ah. Hello, wonderful Barnett. How are your breasts?"

Barnett laughs, pounds his big chest like Tarzan. "Still big, Victoria. Thanks for asking."

"Mother, we have news. We're engaged."

"AHHHH!" Victoria shrieks into the phone, dropping it in the process. As if in slow motion, the phone flips backward, a possible pornographic disaster in the making. There are shimmies and shines and suds and Victoria's scream muffled under the bubbly water.

It's unclear to either man what might be visible in the depths.

Eventually, the phone is rebirthed, shaken, and again at the mercy of Victoria Tanner's floppy fingers. "WHEN? WHEN? HOW? HOW?"

"Calm down," Ezra pleads.

In the kitchen, Chrissy continues to spy, quietly opening the freezer, quietly taking out three Lean Cuisines, oblivious to their coldness, quietly closing the freezer door.

"I'm so damn excited," Victoria yells. "YES! Your father is gonna freak out when I tell him!"

"Doesn't he hear you screaming?" Ezra asks.

"My screaming is pretty normal at bath time."

"Is that what time it is?" Ezra asks, accusingly. "It sounds like maybe it's drinky time."

"They overlap," Victoria says, dryly.

Chrissy puts one of the frozen Lean Cuisines to her forehead.

"What's your address, boys? I'm sending you a valuable gift," Victoria says.

"Please, do not, Mother."

"Barnett, what's the name of the farm again?" Victoria asks. "Peabody Society Ranch?"

"Polite Society Ranch," Barnett corrects, with a grin.

"Don't give her any intel!" Ezra says. "Last time she sent me a 'valuable gift' it was HER! She sent herself first-class to visit me and wouldn't leave."

On the list of "Ezra Cons" Chrissy writes: "Insane Mother."

"Ezra, you should appreciate me!" Victoria yells. "All children should respect their mothers!"

Chrissy pauses, nods slowly, scratches out "Insane Mother."

"You're drunk, Mother!" Ezra yells.

"And beautiful Barnett, what about your mom? Is she happy for you?" Victoria asks.

"Um," Barnett hedges. "Of course, of course."

"Deep down," Ezra adds.

"What?" Victoria says. "She should be jumping for joy and guzzling champagne."

Chrissy's eyes widen and she writes quickly back in the "Cons" column: "Insane mother."

"My mom says hi and she can't wait to meet you," Barnett says.

"Well, put her on."

"Oh, no, no," Barnett and Ezra say together in various overlapping objections.

Chrissy panics beside the fridge. She turns to the counter and reaches for a knife, then reconsiders. She grabs a frozen Lean Cuisine as if a shield.

"Is she there?" Victoria asks.

"She's in the kitchen, but—"

"MOM? BARNETT'S MOTHER?" Victoria calls out through the phone. To Barnett she asks, "What's her name?"

"Chrissy," Barnett says.

"SHH!" Ezra says.

"CHRISSY!" Victoria calls out.

And from the kitchen, Chrissy asks, "Barnett? Could you please come here a moment?"

"Is that her?" Victoria asks as Barnett dashes around the corner to find his mother squeezing a frozen Lean Cuisine with such force, by now she's cut two minutes off the defrost time.

"What's happening?" Chrissy asks.

"She wants to talk to you—"

"Chrissy!" Victoria calls over speakerphone.

"Please don't do this to me, Barnett."

"I won't. Don't worry."

"Take me to her this instant!" Victoria demands of Ezra.

Chrissy looks to Barnett with fright.

"Don't worry," Barnett says. "He won't."

Ezra enters with the phone. "I'm so sorry!" he whispers.

"Chrissy?" Victoria asks as Ezra points the camera at her.

"Hiiiiii," Chrissy says into the phone, hiding the Lean Cuisine behind her back.

"Hey!" Barnett scolds, quietly.

"I'm a victim!" Ezra replies. "My mother is a master manipulator!"

Victoria squints into the camera, as if trying to see Chrissy more clearly. "Cheers! Can't wait to meet you and celebrate our boys. We should throw them an engagement party posthaste."

Chrissy hedges. "Oh. Really?"

"Everyone loves a party," Victoria says.

"Yeah. More or less."

"We could even do it there on your farm," Victoria suggests.

"Um. Yeah. Maybe—"

"Great. I can be there in twenty-four hours," Victoria says.

"What? Wow—" Chrissy says.

"Wait! Wait!" Ezra interjects. "No, no, Mother. Absolutely not." Ezra turns the camera back onto himself.

"Why not?" Victoria asks. "Chrissy just agreed to it.'"

"She's not used to New Yorkers," Ezra says. "She's . . . polite."

Chrissy firmly nods approval of his defense and fights a surprising feeling of warmth. It's been a while since another human being has seen her so clearly, defined her so perfectly.

"I can bring my gayest dress," Victoria says. "Chrissy, we can do a photo shoot with our gay sons! I'll call the *Post*!"

"Oh my God!" Chrissy turns to Barnett. "She won't stop. Like a termite."

"No. Mother. Stop," Ezra pleads.

"Your engagement should be celebrated! Your father and I love New Orleans," Victoria says.

"No, no, Mother. We are . . . the farm is . . . way outside New Orleans," Ezra says.

"We'll see you soon!" Victoria yells.

"No! Mother! Please don't come! Mother!" Ezra pleads, until his phone's screen goes black, his head drops, and he lets his arms fall limp to his sides.

"Ezra will undo it," Barnett says to his mother. "Or I'll meet them at the airport myself, if I have to, and turn them around."

Ezra turns to Barnett and Chrissy. "I'm so sorry. I'm so embarrassed. I'll keep calling and texting and try to stop her."

"What are the actual chances she'll come?" Chrissy asks.

"I don't know for sure," Ezra says. "But I would say one hundred percent. Chances are one hundred percent. Yeah. They'll be here tomorrow."

"OH, BARNETT!" Chrissy cries out.

"We'll simply send her away," Barnett says.

"No. I can't uninvite her," Chrissy says.

Barnett shrugs. "Why? You never invited her in the first place."

"For what it's worth, you'd get a kick out of my mother," Ezra says. "She's a real character, a socialite, charmingly difficult," he says with pride.

"And your mother approves of—" Chrissy asks, waving the frozen Lean Cuisine wildly at Ezra, from his head to his toes, "—all this?"

"You'll have to be more specific," Ezra says.

"And your father?" Chrissy asks.

"He's a . . . quiet type," Ezra says.

Barnett jumps in. "Ezra's mom is just as caring as you are. She's careful and concerned. She's a good, protective mother."

"Protective?" Chrissy asks with curiosity.

"She has awards," Ezra says. "Motherhood awards. Not kidding."

"Motherhood awards?" Chrissy asks, her face brightening slightly.

"That's why she wants to meet you. She's protective," Ezra says. "And she loves a party."

Chrissy stares at Barnett and Ezra together, as again their fingers intertwine like a fresh bucket of worms from Rhett's, as again their heads touch and they kiss briefly. The two of them, they look happy. They look perfect, except for Chrissy's belief that they're not.

"May I talk to Barnett alone for a second?" Chrissy asks of Ezra, her eyes locked on her son in such a way it's as if Ezra has already left.

"I'm so sorry, Mom. Honestly," Barnett says. Then, "But, maybe it would be nice? Maybe it would be fun? Or you can say no."

Chrissy turns red and struggles to find replacements for the expletive she wants to hurl. "GOSH! DARN! IT! I cannot say no and you know it. And that's why this is all unfair."

"Why can't you say no?"

She leans close to him. "It's 'Polite Society Ranch'! Not 'Asshole Old Maid Ranch'!" Chrissy turns her back to Barnett, trying to steady the lightning cloud inside her. "Not yet. No thanks to you."

Barnett takes a deep breath. "I really am sorry, Mom. But it's okay to decline. Ezra's mom is a hurricane. Legitimately. You joke about the kids on the tours. Victoria Tanner is Category 5."

"Maybe you should have called and gotten Paw-Paw's advice," Chrissy snaps. She rips open one of the Lean Cuisine boxes and pulls out the frozen plate of food.

Barnett steps forward. "His advice was to not tell anyone about the engagement at all and just elope. His advice was to quit working so hard to try to keep people in my life if they don't want to be there."

A chill shakes Chrissy and she drops the Lean Cuisine. The cold mixes with the warm air, making the dinner appear to smoke as it falls to the floor, where it cracks into uneven chunks, bits of frosty glazed chicken with roasted potatoes and assorted vegetables scattering across her otherwise perfect hardwood floor.

Barnett kneels down to clean it up.

Chrissy joins him. "She supports all this? Your *engagement*? With all her motherhood awards?"

"I think so. We only just told her. I guess there's room for you to turn her against us if that's on your mind."

"Don't be impolite," Chrissy scolds. She picks up a frozen pea, a frozen piece of diced carrot. "I'm not cooking."

Barnett smiles like he just won a 5K. "Of course not. Ezra and I will take care of everything—"

"Where will they sleep? Here? The barn apartment is a mess. Ezra already took the guest room."

"Mom, we have plenty of options."

"I'm not moving my—"

"—sewing room. I know, I know. I'll figure it out. Don't worry."

Barnett reaches for a piece of frozen broccoli, and Chrissy reaches as well, in her mind, for help, for a coconspirator, one with awards, one as protective as her. "Leave it for me," Chrissy says. "I'll take care of all this mess."

Chapter 5

Countdown to Damnation:

10 days / 16 hours / 32 minutes

VICTORIA Tanner doesn't exit the limousine; she emerges. She tugs on her black business jacket and smooths the front of her matching black skirt. The air-conditioning from the white stretch is so cold, it billows out and around her like fog in a horror movie. She tilts her head back and shimmies her hair into place, her bob so razor-sharp, so severe, that every movement carries risk of decapitation. She looks at the rural Louisiana sky, deeply inhales the breezy fresh air, the cleanest air she's sucked into her body in years. "Ew," she says, and coughs.

Inside the Durang farmhouse, Chrissy is shifting left to right in her boots. She fumbles with the gold chain around her neck. "Oh, no," she says, standing in the living room, staring out the window at the strange new houseguest in her driveway. Chrissy tries to steady herself on John's chair, the one he died in, the one she dragged onto the burn pile three years ago. She nearly falls and has to look down to remember, to snap back to reality, to again acknowledge John's chair is gone, to notice her losses anew—first John and now Barnett, the latter being sucked away by this gay business, which Victoria Tanner could be dissuaded from supporting. Chrissy has done the impossible before; she once taught a rooster to play fetch.

Chrissy rushes to the kitchen and flings open the back door.

"BOYS! BOYS, SHE'S HERE! SHE'S EARLY!" Her eyes strain in the afternoon light, struggling to find Barnett and Ezra through the trees and piles of hay and orbs of sunshine hugging every speck of dust. "BOYS?"

Elaine lets out a little "baa" and the chickens flop about. But Barnett and Ezra are unheard, unseen. Chrissy steps outside and closes the door behind her. She yells once more, "BOYS?"

Crickets.

Chrissy's face reddens. She told the boys to stay close. She warned them, "What if she gets here early?"

Alone, Chrissy makes her way toward the driveway. She brushes wisps of hair out of her face and runs her fingers ungently around her lips. It's an effort to remove any bits of food, and maybe add color, if one should care about such things. Chrissy looks down at her body—breasts: fine; hips: fine; calves: *ugh*.

And as she's always done, she marches on, steadied—or at least trying to fake it—to greet her potential teammate in hopefully trying to talk sense into these boys, to have them call it off. Surely she will. *Protective. Motherhood awards.* Those were his exact words.

Victoria Tanner suddenly stands taller beside her limousine, her senses firing like a Xenomorph's, her attention activated by an instinct accustomed to predators. She turns to the little bright-blue farmhouse, looks up the driveway, and locks gaze with what seems to be a little peasant man.

Chrissy waves, cautiously. "Hi."

Victoria says not a word, doesn't even open her mouth lest she crease her dark, glassy, brown slivers of lipstick. She jets her finger high in the air as if to say, "WAIT!"

Chrissy stops, a primal and submissive—and surprising—reaction for her. She figured she'd be used to any beast by now, especially the city type. But she nods her agreement, accepting a yield but giving her alternative one last try; Chrissy turns quickly and shouts to the ether, "BOYS!!!"

As she turns back, Victoria, in all that makeup and wool and humidity, is making a slow and stealthy approach, her black high heels playing Russian roulette with the gravel driveway. Her toes are flexed in her shoes, her back level and determined. Victoria puts her hands on her bony hips and stops in front of Chrissy. "Not a hotel in sight but no shortage of cows defecating."

"Pardon?" Chrissy asks.

Victoria Tanner steps back. "You're a woman!"

Chrissy blinks, then blinks again. "Yes."

"From over there I thought you were . . . not."

Chrissy seals her eyes shut, takes a deep breath, makes a wish, reopens her eyes. *Nope.* Victoria is still there, formally announcing herself.

"Victoria Tanner," she says, pointedly not offering to shake hands with Farmer Mom.

"I'm . . . Chrissy." It comes out sweeter than she intends. The tenor of her voice, the deference therein, reminds Chrissy of kowtowing to bullies when she was a girl.

"Indeed! Chrissy, yes! We did the FaceTime and you invited us here!"

"Oh, more or less," Chrissy says.

"You know, the drive from the airport cost us one thousand dollars," Victoria says. "And there were no olives!"

"Olives? In the car?"

"In the limousine. Yes. For the vodka. There were none," Victoria says, accusingly.

"I don't believe I've ever seen a limousine in these parts," Chrissy says.

"Never?" Victoria flashes a look of worry, then shimmies her head until her bob reconstitutes perfection.

"Are you here alone?" Chrissy asks.

Victoria motions to the limousine as a man cartoonishly exits. "Winston Tanner," she says, as her husband lifts his short personage out of the vehicle, restuffs his undersized shirt into various folds of his body, tugs his slacks up to his imperceptible waist, tips the driver (generously), and approaches the ladies.

"Oozing sexuality as ever, Winston," Victoria says. Winston opens his mouth to respond but Victoria cuts him off. "Winston's father invented the flip-top lid for dish soap."

Winston opens his mouth to respond, but—

"Are you going to get the bags?" Victoria asks.

Winston opens his mouth to respond, but—

"Posthaste!" Victoria shouts.

Winston turns away, relieved to part ways with his wife, if only for a moment, and to have a task that's objectively accomplishable.

Victoria turns to Chrissy. "Years ago, Winston asked me, 'Want an apple or a blackberry?' And I said 'apple' because I thought he was talking about pie and I didn't want to stain my brand-new veneers. But it turned out he was talking about stocks and Blackberry bombed. So, I like to say that he inherited our wealth, but I preserved it."

Chrissy nods like a student who doesn't understand the assignment, then starts walking toward the house. "Come on inside. Did the trip take a lot out of you?"

"It didn't put enough IN me," Victoria says, flipping her hand like she's knocking back a martini. "Know what I mean?"

"So, what can I get you to make you comfortable?" Chrissy asks. "Food? A nap?" She then whispers, politely, "The toilet?"

"Only if that's where you keep the vodka," Victoria whispers back.

Chrissy laughs.

Victoria scowls.

"Oh, I don't think I have vodka. I have wine," Chrissy says.

"Is it in a bottle? With a cork? I'll take it. Meanwhile, might you summon your butler? I'd like to send him out for some provisions."

"The butler?" Chrissy asks. "Oh, yeah. He's . . . in the back." She looks out to the woods, now desperately. "BOYS!!!"

BARNETT and Ezra are naked, back by the pond, or what's left of it. Every summer the water dries up nearly completely. The heat sucks the moisture from the ground, creating a cracked clay landscape that looks like another planet. It would smell, it would attract bugs, but a Louisiana summer spares nothing, and the heat turns the clay to a sort of ocean of fragile gray terra-cotta.

Barnett and Ezra are both lying with their bare backs on the hot, dried mud, smelling of each other and sweating, still breathing heavy in the way young couples often do. They're looking up at the blue Louisiana sky, a color so calming they can't believe it can exist alongside the crushing humidity.

"The color of your farm matches the sky," Ezra says.

"It's my mom's farm."

"Actually, it *almost* matches the sky," Ezra says. "Your farm is more like the color of a Porta Potty."

"God, don't ever say that to my mom."

"Should we head back soon? My mother will expect me to greet her. Not that I don't love it out here." Ezra looks around. "Is this mud going to give me leprosy?"

The boys laugh. They touch foreheads and kiss.

Barnett looks at his love, then back at the sky, back where God used to live, back when God was alive in him. "I used to come out here all the time as a kid. I never thought in a million years that I'd feel 'in love' or have a boyfriend. Even further from my mind was that I'd be able to have a boyfriend out here at the farm. That I'd be able to really share my life with someone. Young Barnett—inside me—he can't believe his life right now."

Ezra swallows hard and resists the urge to say some hocus-pocus about how it's impossible for two people to ever meet, to ever really know each other, to ever really know what's inside another person. He resists the urge to acknowledge the cosmos, to let it join them, to let it make their moment anything other than a nice, deeply human, mortal connection. "I never really wanted to get married until I met you," Ezra says. "Young Ezra is also freaking out. I have a feeling young Ezra and young Barnett are very proud of us right now."

Barnett feels alongside him for Ezra's hand, and when the two men's fingers find each other, the digits move with lust. They intertwine their fingers tightly, squeezing as if on a roller coaster, squeezing as if they could get thrown from this ride if they don't take all the precautions, as if they could be ripped apart, woken from a dream, as if everything has led to right now.

Barnett and Ezra are not exactly alone. They share the clay with crawfish, who are living in holes bored into the ground. The crawfish dig and dig, rolling mud into asymmetrical balls which they pile around the opening to their hole, creating a small tower with a hollow center, almost like a roll of toilet paper. Some towers are four inches tall, some six, some squat and some lean. They rise around the boys like little chimneys, scattered about, gray and unassuming, no judgment from the underground.

"Wanna know something gross I used to do as a kid?" Barnett asks Ezra.

"Absolutely yes. I'm not even kidding."

"I used to use the crawfish towers in an . . . unchaste way," Barnett says.

Ezra sits up, startled. "You fucked crawfish holes in the ground?"

"No!" Barnett says. "Just the clay tower things. And I would pull them off the ground first. When they're a little wet they're kinda, you know?"

"Ew! No, I certainly do not know! The engagement is off!" Ezra says. Then, "Just kidding. Keep going. Tell me everything."

Barnett laughs. "Can you believe you're gonna marry a swamp creature like me?"

"HA!" Ezra laughs. "What to do about our swamp creature babies?" Ezra reaches, smearing the white goo on Barnett's chest and flicking a handful out to the empty pond floor.

The two men laugh and Ezra forces himself up. He flings a leg over Barnett and straddles him.

"Remember what your dating profile said was the part of your body you hated the most?" Barnett asks.

"Do you?" Ezra challenges.

Barnett pinches a small bit of belly fat near Ezra's belly button and wiggles it. "I still love this," Barnett says.

Ezra dips his head down. Barnett's world closes in as Ezra's long hair falls over the boys' faces. Barnett takes in the scents: Ezra, the pond, the farm, home, happiness. He closes his eyes and sees only dancing blasts of light, a pink, blood-fueled glow through his eyelids. His hands reach and cup Ezra's buttocks, his touch gentle, so as to tickle the faint hair Ezra has on his cheeks. Ezra giggles, delighted. So does Barnett.

Ezra pins Barnett's arms out to his sides like a crucifixion. Barnett's fingers wrap around his lovers'. "You need to clean your fingernails, babe," Ezra says.

"How did I find someone so romantic?"

"Algorithms—" Ezra starts, but Barnett turns away.

"Did you hear something?" Barnett rises to his elbows, the curtains of his lover's hair gone and the world revealed to him once more. "Oh shit. Are they early?"

And over the crickets and gentle breeze, Barnett hears a faint whisper, as if God is naming this picture-perfect moment: "BOYS!!!"

VICTORIA opens the pantry door as if an audience were inside, expecting her. It's organized but sparse—canned food and an open bag of Hershey's Kisses. But Victoria's attention is on the dozens of treasures on the floor and first two shelves of the pantry: red wine. She grabs a bottle and squints to read the label: "'La Gracè Vino.' Is this Italian or French?"

"It's free," Chrissy says. "It's a gift from church. Apparently, wine is cheaper than candles, so when parishioners donate to light candles we get a free bottle of wine."

Chrissy hands over a corkscrew. Victoria stabs it into the bottle, violently extracting the cork as if the wine is choking and she just let it gasp. She looks at Chrissy's huge supply. "You must light a lot of candles."

"I need a lot of help."

"Like, servants?" Victoria asks, opening cabinets until she finds any vessel to hold liquid, settling on a coffee mug.

"Like with *the boys*?"

Victoria dumps several glugs of wine into the mug, takes a big sip. "I KNOW! If you would've told me that when I turned seventy, my husband's testicles—"

"No, no," Chrissy interrupts. "I'm talking about our sons!"

"Our sons? What about them?"

"They're engaged. You invited yourself here to celebrate them."

"Did I invite myself? Well, New York is disgusting this time of year and the renovations on our place in the Hamptons aren't finished," Victoria says, taking another taste of wine.

"How do you feel about the engagement?"

"Mixed. On one shoulder is an angel saying have fun and on the other shoulder is the devil saying get sober."

"Ezra says you've won several mother-of-the-year awards. That's nice," Chrissy says. "Must put a lot of pressure on you to make the right choices."

"It's a burden, really. But I win every year. Of course, it's an award from my own foundation. Honestly, how would it look if my foundation named someone else mother of the year? And my attorneys said the foundation has to do *something* to keep taxes low—feed the homeless, provide drinking water to turtles, or something. Recognizing the excellence in my motherhood was the least amount of work."

"Congratulations."

"Thanks. I've won thirty-six years in a row, starting two years before I even had children."

"Yeah, how do you feel about it? The engagement thing?"

Victoria shrugs. "Ezra has been in love before. What do I care? I always say: 'Do whatever you want, just don't TOUCH the CarMax stock.'" She raises her glass as if to toast a ghost.

"Do you ever think, as a mother, you know, about whether we should support it? Should we unite to talk to the boys about the true meaning of marriage?"

"I married for money and look at this suit!" Victoria spins.

"But, *gay* marriage. I know it's *allowed* but is it *right*?"

The kitchen door opens like a small explosion and Ezra Tanner stands in the doorway, backlit by the brewing Louisiana sunset. "Mother!"

"Who? Me?" Victoria Tanner asks.

Ezra walks toward her for a hug.

"Don't spill my wine," Victoria says, then notices his dirty clothes. She holds up her hand as if to scream STOP! "Were you recently buried alive?" She looks at the mud and mess covering Barnett. "You two look terrible. Of course, it could be my low blood alcohol levels."

Ezra motions to his fiancé. "Barnett and I were just doing, uh, yard work."

"Like in a penitentiary?" Victoria asks.

"Barnett," Chrissy interrupts. "Victoria was just asking for the butler."

Barnett looks at Victoria. "Hi. I'm the butler."

"Hmm," Victoria says. "I'm starting to have concerns."

"Barnett, why don't you go pick up some chicken dinners at Rhett's," Chrissy says. "There's cash in my purse."

"What the hell is a 'Rhett'?" Victoria asks, as Winston enters, loaded down with luggage. "And where should he put all our stuff? Is there a tent set up for us somewhere?"

"The guest room," Barnett says. "Ezra just moved out."

Victoria turns to her son. "Are you not sleeping in Barnett's room? Trouble in paradise?"

"No, no, Mother."

"My mom has traditional rules," Barnett says, nodding to Chrissy. "But don't worry, Mom. We're cool. Ezra can move in with me, take my bed, and I'll sleep on the floor."

"The floor? Dear God," Victoria Tanner says.

Chrissy blushes, flush with heat, feels for her gold chain, wonders whether the air-conditioning is working properly. "Yeah, so, how long are you staying?"

"Generally, if I stay in any one place longer than forty-eight hours my hair will wilt."

"Then we should do the so-called engagement dinner immediately?" Chrissy asks. "So you can get the heck out of . . . this humidity? It'll be short notice. I'm not sure how fancy it can be or whether many people will come—"

"If there's wine, it works for me." Victoria shrugs, taking another gulp.

"Like, tomorrow, then?" Chrissy asks.

"Mom?" Barnett tries to interject, but Victoria interrupts.

"Fine," she says. "Tomorrow. Now, where's the spa?"

Chrissy turns her ire to Barnett.

"She means the bathroom," he says.

Chapter 6

Countdown to Damnation:

9 days / 10 hours / 33 minutes

FOR Chrissy, peace and quiet doesn't sound like ocean waves or jungle sounds or even absolute silence. For Chrissy, peace and quiet sounds like her barn at the crack of dawn, when her chores start.

It sounds like the macaws fighting with each other in their favorite words, "Good morning!" And, "You're so pretty!"

It's the echo of Elaine's "baa" as it fills the first floor of the barn and bounces off the rafters above. Unlike the exterior, everything in the barn is painted white, except for the dirt floor. Cool air flows in from the apartment, which is more like an enclosed loft with a bedroom, bathroom, kitchenette, air-conditioning, and bags and bags of chicken feed.

After her rounds of feeding the other animals, the sunshine hard at work fulfilling its daily duty, Chrissy returns to the barn.

This is perfect, Chrissy thinks, just herself and the macaws and Elaine.

Chrissy sits in Elaine's special corner, on the far side of the barn, under the apartment, the most sacred spot, the warmest spot in the winter and the coolest spot in the summer, the spot with the best views outside, the spot with the softest hay, the warmest blankets.

"Baa," Elaine says.

"My, how things change," Chrissy says. She looks around.

Newhart, the unmilkable cow, used to live where the tractor is now parked.

Blossom, the turkey spared on Thanksgiving Day after her owners burned their house down in an oven fire, used to live where the hay baler is stored.

"I have to go inside," Chrissy tells Elaine.

"Baa!"

"I know, I know. But—" Chrissy looks at her watch. "The boys left to collect provisions for the dinner tonight, then they're picking up Paw-Paw so he can enjoy the festivities. So this is the perfect time to go snooping through Ezra's things."

"Baa!"

"But, counterpoint, if I go now, maybe I can also avoid Victoria and Winston. I bet they're still sleeping."

"Baa!"

"Thank you for understanding."

CHRISSY sneaks quietly back to the house, past the carport—empty of the Chevy the boys took into town. She sneaks quietly into her own home, up her own hallway.

She approaches Barnett's room. The door is slightly ajar, and she gives it a push. She's filled with dread at the meaning of the sheets ripped from the bed, the sleeping bag on the floor barely ruffled.

The room smells of the boy, the long-haired one. His scent covers—overwhelms—her son's. She can tell which suitcase belongs to Ezra—it's not a suitcase at all but a tote, like a huge black purse. Her body moves to it, unzips it. There are delicate clothes, scarves, a book of poetry, and pieces of silver—wait, no, silver foil. She picks up one of the silver squares, slightly larger than a cube of sugar. She picks at the foil. She sniffs. CHOCOLATE! She pulls out her orange notepad, and under "Ezra Cons," she writes: "Diabetes."

Chrissy moves on to examine his toiletries, oils for his hair, herbal toothpaste, silicone-based lube—

She pulls out her notepad: "Disgusting," she writes.

She looks for any hard evidence of wickedness, but their life together looks innocent, except for Chrissy's belief that it's not.

She makes her way quickly to the kitchen, hoping to get in and out before encountering the Tanners. She opens the pantry to grab one of her Hershey's Kisses, though Chrissy always thinks of them as John's Kisses. She tells herself that she still buys them for him, a habit that started years earlier when John started waking up before her, and eventually going to bed before her. She bought the Hershey's Kisses and told him, "Now you get a kiss from me first thing, and last thing. And don't blame me for the cavities." (John never had a cavity. He had perfect teeth, never had braces. John gave Barnett the same perfect teeth, to match what could have been the perfect life. Sometimes, Chrissy would tell John she wished she was as pretty as he and Barnett. "My girl," John would say with fiery affection, healing pity, sending shivers down to her toes, touching her face, often with filthy fingernails.)

And now, when Chrissy needs them most, after enduring Ezra's arrival and that of his parents, not only are her Hershey's Kisses GONE, but the bag is still there, EMPTY! It's a sin worse than putting a dry milk jug back in the fridge. She picks up the brittle shell of a bag and smells the dark spirits of the chocolate that used to be inside. She closes her eyes and inhales again. Smells like rage. It's when she opens her eyes that she sees the note scribbled on a torn paper towel: "I'll buy you more okay see you later thanks love Ezra."

No punctuation, Chrissy notes. It pales beside her other grievance:

the boy ate all HER Hershey's Kisses when he has all those chocolate squares in his big purse.

She writes: "Greedy!"

She goes back to Barnett's room, back to Ezra's black tote bag. She pulls the zipper open, grabs a silver square and unwraps it, eats it, and another, and another—

This one is for eating my chocolate—

This one is for stealing my boy—

This one is for ruining my—

Tears and sobbing start their procession but Chrissy won't have it. She wills herself stoic, demands calm and comfort via this act of personal chocolate revolution.

And another, and another. She stuffs the empty foil wrappers in her sock until it—and she—are full, calmer, and strangely satiated.

She sits on Barnett's bed. She stares at the bicycle wallpaper, perhaps for too long. The bikes seem to be moving. She's lost in wonder, timelessness, and one small note: *This room needs a clock*, she thinks.

Back in the hallway, the foil digging into the skin of her ankle, another abrasion emerges.

"I hate it here," Victoria Tanner says coldly. "I can't sleep without city noise, apparently. And I'm a little nauseous but that's on brand. Winston thinks I'm drinking too much wine but I think I'm not drinking enough."

"You look so pretty," Chrissy says, her eyes wide and bright. "You look so different. You have a strange glow."

"Well, my parents were socialists," Victoria says. She resets her hair. "Look, what do I wear tonight? What says 'engagement dinner'? I wanted to wear a gay dress but, upon reflection, are all dresses gay? The world is changing so fast. I try to keep up if I can. Then,

I wondered if there's a certain color I should wear tonight that will repel the bugs?"

"Have you done something with your skin?" Chrissy asks.

Victoria touches her face. "I use a cream made of little fetuses. You don't see any tiny fingers do you?"

And instantly, that's all Chrissy can see—a million little fingers waving to her from inside the pores of Victoria Tanner's tight face. "I need a minute to catch my breath," Chrissy says. Her body is heating up, her blood pressure rising, her hallway walls barely static. "Something really weird is happening. Do you feel that?"

"Are you high?" Victoria asks. "You look like Ezra when he's cracked out."

Chrissy lets her head fall back and roll around her shoulders. "Weee."

"Good Lord!" Victoria says. "You didn't touch any of Ezra's possessions did you? You could get a transfer high. It's why I refuse to take the subway."

Chrissy floats to her bedroom. She hears something that for the briefest fraction of a second concerns her, then delights her. It's nothing. It's just the sound of the quiet, empty room. She almost laughs, but she can't remember how. And then there's something wrong with her body—or something right. She feels—nothing. The usual tension on the right side of her neck is gone, replaced with a sensation that is almost orgasmic.

She goes into her bathroom and is shocked to see her face. "Nice to meet you," she says to herself. Then, "Are you high? Are you?"

She kneels down to pull the foil wrappers from her sock and puts them in the trash. "Bye, friends," she says. Then, "Were you crack?"

She stands, her body feeling like it's making snow angels in a silo of clouds. She looks at her bathroom countertops with wonder. The granite swirls. It's alive. It's speaking to her. "Hi, right back at ya," Chrissy replies.

When her body involuntarily moves itself outside the bathroom, she enters Oz. The colors in her bedroom are singing to her—reds and blues and greens in symphony, not just of sound but of feeling, something dazzling in her eyes, and she's almost brought to tears. "Vibes," she says to herself. She gasps.

"Are you insane? Do you need help?" Victoria Tanner asks, standing at the bedroom door with her hands on her hips, her pores still waving the tiny fingers of the little child laborers who keep her looking so young and fresh. Winston, behind her, cocks his head in a familiar judgment. He opens his mouth to speak but—"Let her answer!" Victoria interrupts. "Posthaste."

But Chrissy doesn't answer. She wanders. She walks past Victoria and Winston, glides past them, almost desperate to get outside into the open air.

"This is my whole life," Chrissy says.

The grass just off the step of the back door captures her attention. Each blade is a singular miracle. Chrissy worries she will never be able to exit her home again for fear she'll step on these living beings and harm them. They're waving. To her. Or waving her away. Or pointing. Each blade sways to the left, to the left, to the left, and Chrissy looks over to the barn, to old, feeble Elaine, who is standing like a human being—shockingly—on her one hind leg and waving with her woolly right trotter. "Get the heck over here!" Elaine shouts.

"My sheep can talk," Chrissy says, eyes wide with wonder.

Victoria says from the doorway behind Chrissy, "Wow. All right. I'm going back to bed IMMEDIATELY." Then, once inside the house, as she's closing the door on Chrissy, "Winston, get me some La Gracè Vino, posthaste."

"Come," Elaine yells again, motions again for Chrissy.

Chrissy follows the order, moving weightlessly to the barn and Elaine's enclosure.

"Shithole, I know," Elaine says. "But the rent is cheap."

"Sheep go 'baa,'" Chrissy says.

Elaine rolls her eyes. "Open your mind."

Elaine lies on her hay and blankets in her special corner of the barn and Chrissy snuggles beside her, the hair of Chrissy's head dancing up and out and mingling with Elaine's wool, so bright and white it looks like she's been bleached.

"I'm gonna miss this place," Elaine says.

Chrissy laughs. *Elaine*, Chrissy thinks, *you're all talk.*

"Planning to escape again?" Chrissy muses.

Chrissy wants to sit up, wants to look Elaine in the eyes, but she just can't muster the strength. Anyway, she can see Elaine without looking at her. Chrissy has every curve of Elaine memorized, the tuck of her nub of a tail, the sharp points of her hooves, the slight downward tug of her lip.

"I'm dying," Elaine says.

Chrissy knows the signs, she's seen them, she's been denying them. She touches Elaine's shimmering, soft wool. "Please don't. Please don't you leave me, too."

"You're not as alone as you think," Elaine says.

Chrissy's tie-dyed universe spins into darker colors. She looks out into the field, seeing the wavy image of a man, as if through heat waves off hot pavement. The man's lumberjack shirt and orange cap are familiar—too familiar. "JOHN?" Chrissy cries out.

She stands, screams for him, her late husband, who is, it appears to Chrissy, walking around outside the barn door, showered in heavenly light and tending to his farm, his other true love, after herself and Barnett, of course.

"JOHN! JOHN!" Chrissy cries.

He doesn't acknowledge her. "You see him, right?" she asks of Elaine, stepping closer and closer to the barn door, but holding back, or somehow being held back.

"Sometimes they return," Elaine says. "To collect someone else."

Chapter 7

THE nurse behind the front desk at Camille Manor Retirement Gardens is sweating and gesturing wildly. She has a phone receiver to one ear and with the other ear is trying to understand whoever's at the front of the long line.

Barnett cranes his head to try to figure out what's going on. "Hope Paw-Paw is okay. This is weird."

"Our crab legs are going to spoil," Ezra says.

In the front parking lot, in the back of the Chevy, ice chests are full of their engagement dinner. The best of a New Orleans eatery called Mama Creole is wrapped into tinfoil balls the size of pumpkins. Some of the goodies will need to be thawed and cooked (pork for the red beans and rice), other items simply reheated (corn bread, beignets), but most will be easily ready when the guys get home with Paw-Paw in tow. If the nurses can get it together.

"Please be patient. We'll be right with you," one of the nurses says to the line.

Barnett turns to Ezra. "This is why we should have eloped."

"We can do it right now. Elope now. Abandon Paw-Paw. Go to the farm and pack our bags. Or just leave our bags there, screw it. Go to New Orleans. Or Vegas. Or anywhere. Be done. Be official. I'll have an eternal soulmate," Ezra says.

"I'll have better health insurance," Barnett says. Adding, "Just kidding, my eternal soulmate."

Ezra beams. "Thank you, my eternal soulmate." Then, coldly, "By the way, we can never tell anyone that we talk to each other like this, understand?"

"Absolutely correct," Barnett laughs.

Ezra thinks about the Carrollton Corned Beef and Braised Cabbage in the Chevy. And the Bayou Beef Brisket with rice and gravy. And the Cajun Jambalaya with Alligator—*does it really taste like chicken?* And the Eggplant Tchoupitoulas, battered and fried, with crawfish cream sauce over angel hair pasta. He can't wait to have the Trout Napoleon, with lemon-lime cayenne almond sauce. Or the Saint Charles Shrimp with white wine, garlic, and ham. And there are two thirteen-foot-long po-boys—fried oyster and fried catfish—intended to be cut up so everyone can try a bite or two.

The line expands and contracts as those coming to visit loved ones at Camille Manor Retirement Gardens—mostly elderly people visiting spouses or friends—start to inhale and exhale their fear. In a nursing home, there's only one: that time has finally come, that death has kept its word.

The frail woman in front of Barnett and Ezra turns to the boys, her eyes searching for someone to save her, comfort her. "The last time it was crazy like this in here was because there had been a death," she says. "I hope it's not my Tante."

"NEXT!" the front desk nurse cries out, toweling her sweaty brow.

The woman ahead of Barnett and Ezra steps forward, braces herself on the desk, ready for the worst news. Barnett and Ezra lean forward, eager to hear her fate.

"Hello? NEXT!" Another nurse says, waving at Barnett and Ezra. And the men step forward.

"Hello there," the nurse says to Barnett. "Who are you here to see?"

"Durang. Room 102. Please tell me he's not dead."

The nurse taps and clicks on her keyboard. Ezra looks over at the frail woman beside them. She looks back. She smiles. "Not my Tante! Someone else croaked, thank God."

Ezra turns back to Barnett in time to hear the nurse tell him, "Mister Durang isn't dead. I'd tell him you're here but he makes a fuss every time we call so just go on back. NEXT!"

PAW-PAW stands in his kitchen holding a black-handled steak knife from his limited supply. He took an extra Lipitor today, just after he heard the news that Elmer in 131 moved out (died). The men saw each other yesterday for their standard lunch appointment: egg salad sandwiches and conversation about whether Richard Nixon is in hell.

Elmer had a mole on his forearm the shape of Alaska, but rarely were his forearms exposed. An impeccable dresser, even in a nursing home, he wore brightly colored suits with matching cummerbund and shoes. Paw-Paw called him a weirdo. Elmer called Paw-Paw a caveman. And both men called each other friend, even though friendship is different at their age; it's rare, it's fleeting.

Paw-Paw's steak knife is average, but sharp, gets any job done. And as he squeezes the handle, taunting his arthritis, he's startled by a knock. "Who is it?" he grumbles.

"It's me, Barnett. And someone I really want you to meet."

"Damn near cut my arm off." Paw-Paw walks across the room, the knife still in his grip, waving in the air as he opens the door. "You're early."

"Whoa!" Barnett shouts and puts his hands up. He steps protectively in front of Ezra.

"What?" Paw-Paw asks. "I'm not gonna stab y'all."

"What are you doing with that knife?" Barnett asks.

"I'm going to do a burglary."

"A what?" Barnett asks.

Paw-Paw looks at Ezra. "You the bum?"

"Nice to meet you, sir," Ezra says, stepping around Barnett.

Paw-Paw shoves past Barnett and Ezra and walks quickly down the empty hallway. "We don't have much time," he says. "How's things? With your mother?" He asks as he rushes past rooms 106, 109, 115.

"Not great," Barnett says, chasing after his grandfather, Ezra trying to keep up. "Where are we going? We have to get you to the engagement dinner."

Paw-Paw again looks at his watch. "I'm going to break into Elmer's room and steal his clothes."

"No. No, you're not, Paw-Paw. Please don't."

"Not all the clothes," Paw-Paw says. "Just the suits and shoes, mostly."

"Absolutely not. You're not going to steal. And who is Elmer?"

"My friend," Paw-Paw says, racing past rooms 116, 117, 118.

He leans against the wall at room 119. He's out of breath, profoundly tired, and as he allows his head to droop down—relief for his neck—Barnett notices the prominence of the occipital bone, the protrusions of the atlas C1 and axis C2 vertebrae.

"Feeling okay? Have you been losing weight?" Barnett asks.

"I've been thinking," Paw-Paw says. "I have some more advice about your mom, Mr. B."

"No. No more advice from you. It's not been good advice."

"My first advice was not to tell anyone and elope!"

"Yeah, actually. We do wish we had done that," Barnett admits.

"Let's go," Paw-Paw says with a look at his watch, an almost other-worldly burst of energy driving him onward, now past rooms 122, 123, 124. "This is not stealing. Elmer gave the clothes to me."

"Oh, really? You have that in writing?"

"Narc!" Paw-Paw shouts. He stops at the door to room 131. Paw-Paw shoves the knife into the space between the door and the frame, right where the door handle meets the stop.

"We don't want to be late for the engagement dinner," Barnett says.

"They can start without us," Paw-Paw says, carefully adjusting the knife just so.

"We're the grooms," Barnett says.

Ezra holds up his finger to emphasize the point: "And, more importantly, we have all the food."

Paw-Paw gives the steak knife a little twist, the door swings open, and Paw-Paw slips inside with the comfort and confidence of a man who's done this before, maybe done this a lot. "Don't put anything in your mouth!"

Barnett looks left then right down the quiet hallway, shrugs at Ezra.

"Get in here!" Paw-Paw yells.

Ezra steps around Barnett and enters. "I think this is exciting."

"Don't encourage him," Barnett says, throwing his hands up and following the guys into Elmer's room. The door closes itself behind him. "Where are the nurses? Where is security?"

"You've seen too many movies," Paw-Paw says.

"Wow, look at this stuff." Ezra turns his attention to what's left of Elmer's life, the ghosts of a man he'll never meet beyond looking at his face in old photos, his spirit in little treasures—a memoriam portrait of a French bulldog, a marble-and-jade chess set in starting position, crystal bowls of various candies and mints, bowls that will never be refilled.

"Paw-Paw, come on," Barnett says.

"You come on," Paw-Paw says. "You're the one ruining my afternoon plans."

"My engagement dinner is your afternoon plan."

"That's my evening plan. And you're early."

Barnett studies the maps of Paris framed on the wall, then looks over to Ezra, who's smelling one of a dozen red carnations in a vase atop a dresser.

"Hmm, fake," Ezra says.

Barnett looks back to Paw-Paw. "I can't believe your afternoon plan includes petty larceny."

"You're petty! Mind your own business, Karen."

"God, where do you seniors learn to talk like that?" Barnett asks.

"TikTok," Paw-Paw says from the closet, two mirrored sliding doors the only barrier between him and an improved wardrobe. He puts his hand on the mirror, flat, palm down, and shoves it open, leaving a greasy handprint, geriatric graffiti.

The closet slides open easily, the colors inside dazzling. Ezra gasps, stepping toward the wardrobe like it's a portal to a new dimension: Planet Elmer.

"Elmer was gay," Paw-Paw announces. "Always, you know. But he was married back in the day. Then the wife dies and the kids become assholes and hey, screw 'em, right? Can you believe I finally made a gay friend at my age and now he's dead?"

That fact is one of many that keeps Paw-Paw alive. For the young, the game of life is more like Jenga, made of heavy blocks that stack and sustain. At a certain age, a life is more like a house of cards: the easiest breeze, the slightest stir, and the whole thing comes tumbling down. And at eighty-eight, all those thin cuts of glossy cardboard can feel like jokers. But a friend can be a king. A new outfit can be an ace, a reason to keep going a little longer, make the deck a little stronger.

Paw-Paw grabs two armfuls of colorful clothes and pulls them free from the closet. They smell of Elmer. "Take these, ya bum!" he orders Ezra. Then Paw-Paw grabs another armful. "For you," he says to Barnett.

One sweater didn't make the grab, and Paw-Paw stares at it, a wild number, knit with loops of orange, black, blue, and yellow, in big clumps of yarn that twist together and around. He tugs it from the wooden hanger. He grabs several pairs of shoes, each of them in a cloth bag, the sequins and gems inside making it look like the bags are filled with fine jewels.

Paw-Paw gently closes the closet door, catching his reflection in the mirror, distorted by the earlier smudge of his hand. He's still stunned and saddened anew every time he sees himself. *Where did it all go?* he wonders. Then, "Run for it!" he yells.

The three men slip through the door, enter the empty hallway, make their way past rooms 130, 123, 110, and finally into Paw-Paw's apartment, before the door to ole Elmer in 131 even clicks closed.

Paw-Paw throws his new sweater and new shoes down on his bed, and his body beside them, catching his breath while barking out orders. "Put that shit wherever," he says to Barnett and Ezra. The two lay their piles on top of the lonely sweater, never to be lonely again.

Paw-Paw adjusts his weight on the bed. He motions to Barnett, who follows the instruction to sit beside him. "For what it's worth," Paw-Paw says slowly, his breathing labored, "Elmer pointed out to me that gay and trans people have been around since the beginning of history. In some cultures, they were considered gods because they were seen as the most complete humans—male and female in one. And Jesus never said a dang thing about being gay or trans. People should be able to do whatever they want with their bodies. I support gay rights and trans rights fully!"

"You're the best, Paw-Paw."

The old man swats at the compliment. "You boys, come watch," he says, and with Barnett's help, he stands and walks to his patio, Ezra following.

When it comes to death, the custodians are almost as numb as the patients at Camille Manor. Their custodial hands gloved in ill-fitting blue latex, they stoically roll a huge laundry cart into Elmer's room, to be filled with Elmer's prized possessions. Moments later, they emerge in the first of their trips, the cart full and covered ceremoniously with a deep purple satin cloth, as if it's a religious moment and not a real estate one. They file out, rolling the cart full of Elmer's life, or what's left of it, down the hall. The administrative staff has already gone through his things—that happened while his body was still cooling in bed. Elmer's family would have had the chance to come and take anything valuable, but they're estranged, not that it mattered. Family members rarely bring anything valuable when checking their loved ones into Camille Manor. The facility discourages it for liability reasons, and greedy relatives are all too eager to "hold it for safe keeping." None of the women at Camille Manor have their heirloom earrings or engagement rings from husbands long grieved. None of the men have the watches they were given at retirement or the military medals for bravery they barely remember. The kids already have them, trading them like game pieces, their prior owners almost forgotten.

"All the things you imagine you can bring with you to a nursing home, you can't," Paw-Paw says. The three men are sitting in plastic lawn chairs, staring out, not at the squirrels, but at the dumpsters. "They're not allowed to bring the good stuff. No silver spoons. No valuables. No alcohol. For whiskey you have to see Bernice in 213. She arrived here kicking and screaming and now she's like a prison capitalist. She trades in contraband—drugs and cigarettes and hard candies."

"Drugs? What kind?" Barnett asks.

"Tylenols are on fire here." Paw-Paw never turns his attention from the dumpsters. "After every death, we stare at the trash to watch their life go away. That's our mourning ritual, that's how we say good-bye, watching our last friends' clothes and possessions pour out like a waterfall into the trash."

Two blue-handed custodians emerge from the building's back door with their cart rolling noisily to the dumpsters. They don't try to talk to each other over their loud journey. They move like characters in a play they've performed repeatedly, eight shows a week for years. At the dumpster, they stop. One of them looks around, as if he can feel the eyes of the residents watching him. He removes the purple cloth and hangs it from his neck like a shawl. Each man then takes a side of the cart, and they lift it up. They tilt one side so the contents—Elmer's remaining clothing, the picture of the French bulldog—topple over bags of cafeteria trash.

Paw-Paw watches helplessly, not enough fight left in him to scold the system or write another letter to the manager or even call out to God. Prayers take too long at Camille Manor. Paw-Paw feels he might as well just share his complaints with his creator face-to-face, when the time comes.

The custodians shake the empty cart over the dumpster—just to be sure there's not a scrap of Elmer left.

"Farewell, friend," Paw-Paw mutters to himself, his eyes focused like he's about to salute, but he does not. The cart comes back down to earth with a loud crash. The custodians start their loud journey back, to do it all over again, another haul of Elmer, another haul of someone else, eventually.

"Elmer says he asked for his ashes to be returned here and put in that dumpster so he could be with all his shit, even if it's scattered at a landfill. They won't. His family doesn't care. They'll put a nice picture on Ancestry.com and then edit all the fun stuff out of his bio. Sometimes, I think about whoever empties out my closet when I'm dead. I want them to think I lived a life like Elmer in 131, a life that has nurses and residents and janitors fighting over my shit."

"Paw-Paw?" Barnett asks. "What should we pack for you? To bring with us?"

Paw-Paw stands and makes a slow path to his kitchenette, opens the cabinet under the sink, and pulls out a white trash bag. He shakes it open. "Here's a bag to pack."

Barnett watches his grandfather meander to his closet and slide the mirrored doors open just as he'd done in Elmer's room. "Help me throw out all my gray shit. When I go down, I want it to be in technicolor."

Barnett turns to Ezra, who shrugs, and mouths, "Why not?"

The two lovers help Paw-Paw with a touch of quick, impromptu summer tidying—throwing out practically everything and replacing it with Elmer's wardrobe.

"What if Elmer's stuff doesn't fit you?" Barnett asks.

"That's the good thing about being around people this old, Mr. B. We're all basically the same size now." Paw-Paw grabs handfuls of his wardrobe. "Nothing in my closet sparks joy. I learned that on Netflix."

The trio fill two bags full of old bland suits and sweaters and slacks.

"Leave 'em outside the door and they'll collect 'em," Paw-Paw says, his voice breaking. "That way a little of Elmer and a little of me can hang out together at the dump."

Ezra and Barnett share another look, and after a few quiet moments, Barnett asks, "Paw-Paw, do you have a bag packed?"

"Right there." He points to a small bag on a dining chair. "Add some of Elmer's clothes and shoes in there, will ya? And there's a bag of meds and stuff in the bathroom."

"I'll grab it," Ezra says.

Paw-Paw's bathroom feels like a sacred place, with dim lighting and blue vibes. Ezra smiles at the evidence of Paw-Paw's recent hard years. Bottles of alcohol and peroxide and a tube of Neosporin sit on the floor, a pack of Band-Aids is stuffed atop a bath towel, medicines are overflowing in drawers—all signs of past or ongoing suffering. An old plastic grocery bag sits in the sink, with toiletries and bottles of meds, one of which catches Ezra's eye. He pokes at it to make sure he's reading it correctly: "Bosulif."

Ezra looks up and into the bathroom's small mirror. He watches his own smile fade.

Ezra steps out of the bathroom to see grandfather and grandson sitting side by side on the bed, their silhouettes matching only in the tilt of their necks, the synced swinging of their right legs.

"Next stop, engagement dinner," Paw-Paw says. "Get me a wheelchair. I don't leave the home without it. And let's go celebrate your homosexual love which is totally normal!"

Chapter 8

Countdown to Damnation:

9 days / 1 hour / 32 minutes

CHRISSY is frozen as if the sight of John—not just alive but walking around outside the barn—has turned her to ice. It's when a breeze puffs the trees and a dusting of sunshine touches her that she awakens from her trance.

"*Are—you—high?*" Chrissy hears in her head, each of Victoria Tanner's words tapping over and over again to the beat of a rude metronome. But Chrissy blinks, and in that instant the vision of John vanishes. Now, it appears, John has stepped away.

"No, no, wait!" Chrissy pulls herself up from the dirt and hay. "Oh, John!" She starts toward the barn door but then quickly turns to a wall and begins to primp her hair and clothes in a mirror. "Oh, I can't let him see me like this."

"Like what?" Elaine asks.

Chrissy pauses for a moment to take in what she's actually seeing. "I look . . . young."

"That's a wall, not a mirror," Elaine says.

But Chrissy is focused on her reflection—*this must be a mirror*—her better self appearing as a hologram, as if brought to life by the wood and grain of the wall of this old barn.

And as if in a Disney movie, John steps behind her in the magical mirror. Chrissy jumps but stares at him with a steady gaze, not frightened of him being there but scared of turning around and him being gone.

"John?" she whispers.

In the reflection, John nods. He's young, too. It feels so comfortable, so casual, like time is a lie that just came unraveled without pomp.

"I miss you," Chrissy says. She reaches out her hand and touches the wall, touches the image of John. "I'm scared to turn around. I'm scared to see that you're not really there."

She watches John look over at Elaine and walk to her. He pats her head and she nuzzles against him.

"Come join us," Elaine says to Chrissy.

Chrissy, so afraid that her vision is only that, closes her eyes and turns, blindly following Elaine's voice.

"This way," Elaine says. "This way."

Chrissy feels for the dirt, then the hay, which gets thicker as she finds the spot where she was lying earlier. She feels Elaine's blanket and sits. Chrissy sweeps her legs out, hoping they bump him, hoping they prove he's real. *Oh, John.*

"MOM?" Barnett shouts, rushing into the barn and kneeling beside Chrissy.

She opens her eyes to see her son—*Oh, Barnett*—and no one else.

"What are you doing?" he asks.

"I was about to have a talk with your father."

"What?"

"Elaine is dying," Chrissy says. "And your father was here. I swear. Elaine, tell them!" She sits up and turns to look at Elaine, but the old gal is across the barn chewing a wad of hay, looking suspiciously at her human visitors, then releasing a stream of pee, which forms a neat, noisy puddle in the dirt. "She can talk!" Chrissy says. "She was just talking to me!"

"Mom, are you okay?" Barnett asks.

"Your whole gay thing. It's terrible timing. Elaine's dying!"

Firmer now, Barnett says, "MOM! What's going on?"

Ezra steps forward. "Shhhh," he whispers to Barnett, gently putting his hand on Chrissy's shoulder.

"Your hands are disgustingly gorgeous," Chrissy says to him.

"Why do you think Elaine is dying?" Ezra asks.

"She told me," Chrissy repeats. "She can talk!"

Ezra smiles, leans close to her. "Nice dilated pupils you got there, Miss Chrissy."

Her face is awash with guilt. "You stole my chocolate Kisses," Chrissy says.

"I'm sorry. I have a chocolate addiction and found your stash." Ezra holds up a plastic bag from Rhett's Corner Grocery. "I got you replacements."

Chrissy cringes. "That was very nice of you."

"I see you found *my* chocolate," Ezra says.

"It was so good," Chrissy confesses. "I saw fingers in your mom's face."

"Ah, the fetuses," Ezra says. "Yeah, I know those guys. You ate my magic mushroom chocolate."

"I knew you were a drug addict! Someone hand me my notepad! Write 'drug addict'!" Chrissy yells. "Why do you have drugs?"

"They're organic mushrooms, Miss Chrissy. They help with my migraines. I take a little as needed. It's called microdosing," Ezra says. "Micro is the key word there. But that's not what you did, right?"

"Nooooo," Chrissy says. "Nooooo. Nothing micro about what I did."

"Oh, my God," Barnett says.

"It's okay," Ezra says. "Will you get us a cool washcloth?"

"Yeah, great," Barnett says, dashing out of the barn.

Ezra sits and scoots his body closer to Chrissy and cradles her head.

"What's happening?" Chrissy asks.

"You're one with everything," Ezra says.

"With ROACHES?"

"You're getting confused with words. Let's try to enjoy this time without using words."

Chrissy's face twists with confusion.

"Words are first-generation thinking. The first lie is the belief, 'I am.'"

"But *I am*," Chrissy says.

"You think you are, but you're not. You think you're the one doing your thinking, but you're not. You're being thought, just like your lungs are being breathed, and your heart is being beat, and your eyes are being blinked."

"Who told you that?" Chrissy asks.

"Who told you 'tree'? Who told you 'sky'? And you believe them and you believe you're separate."

"But I *am* separate," Chrissy says. "I am not a tree."

"No, no," Ezra says. "You think you're separate but we're all connected."

"My son is connected to you?"

"Yes," Ezra says.

"But you're so wild," Chrissy says.

"I'm an animal," Ezra says, "and your wonderful son is a farmer."

"A farmer. Just like I always wanted." Chrissy is enchanted—either she is warming up to this young man, or it's the mushrooms. "My mind is messed up."

"Mind is a lie. There is no separate mind. There is only one mind."

"Oh," Chrissy says. Her eyelids draw closer as she strains to see, to understand this alien who captured her only son's heart.

"I want to hate you but also eat you," Chrissy says.

"I know," Ezra says. "I get that all the time." He rocks Chrissy back and forth like she's a lamb.

Chrissy studies the disconnection from her body. Her arm moves—*Who moved that?* she wonders. She wiggles a toe—*Who did that?* she wonders. *Do I really control my heartbeat, my breathing, my sickness, my health, my thinking? I am not my body.*

The body of Chrissy Durang closes its eyes. It tries to hum, but no sound emerges. It tries to make the sound in its mind. *Isn't that where it exists anyhow?* And in the darkness of its consciousness, the line forms, bursting forth as if cigarette smoke is forced through a syringe. In its mind, it sees a smoky line that stretches to the imagined sound: *HMM*, as if before now, it knew anything about music or tones or meditation.

In that moment, Chrissy forgets about her body. Her body has no pilot. And her body moves without her. Then it has thoughts without her, laughs without her. Then it hears sounds and turns its head without her, turns to the window without her.

"Ew, you live in a barn?" comes a fried young voice from behind Ezra. The new creature is confusing to Chrissy. She looks back and forth from the new one to Ezra, the new one to Ezra. The two of them, they look remarkably alike.

"Are you multiplying?" Chrissy asks.

"This is my twin sister. My mother invited her as a surprise," Ezra says. "Surprise!" Then, he whispers, "I'm so sorry."

Chrissy turns to the young woman. Staring at this new entity, Chrissy asks, "What's its name?"

The twin steps forward. "I'm Nichole, spelled n-i, like the element. And c-h-o-l-e, as in the Punjabi word for chickpeas, but pronounced traditionally 'Nicole' like Scherzinger."

"Where is she going to sleep?" Chrissy asks.

"Mom," Barnett says, returning with a dripping washcloth and a glass of cold water. "She'll sleep in the apartment. She doesn't mind the chicken feed in there."

Chrissy writhes. "I'm overwhelmed."

"I know, I know," Barnett says, placing the cool cloth on her forehead. "But everything is okay. Paw-Paw is here. The food is almost ready."

"Ready for what?" she asks.

"The engagement dinner."

Chrissy turns to Ezra. "I'm gonna need a lot more of your special chocolate."

Chapter 9

Countdown to Damnation:

9 days / 0 hours / 8 minutes

CHRISSY stares out at the scene before her, into the night, dim save for the fairy lights above her, above all of them. But she's focused on him—*Oh, Barnett*—sitting at the old picnic table in the backyard. Like Chrissy, the table is rotting but no doubt has a few good years left. Like Chrissy, the table politely accommodates anything weighing down the evening.

It's the sight of Barnett and Paw-Paw—in an unusually flashy suit—sitting together, and the others around them, that brings Chrissy fully back into her body, the smoky stretch of *HMM* in her mind evaporating into the shapes of her family.

Paw-Paw looks like an ancient version of John. Barnett looks like a young version of John. It's moving in its sweetness and its cruelty—seeing John in bits, little teases, while the John Chrissy knew and loved best—the middle-aged John, the real flesh-and-body John—is still immaterial. She can't remember the feel of his face. She can't see in Barnett the age and wisdom of her late husband. She can't see in Paw-Paw the vigor John carried so fully in his faulty heart.

Chrissy smiles. She touches her face to confirm—*yes, yes, happiness*. Or, at least, *calm*.

She scans the table before her—steaming piles of rice ready for their spicy red beans, a few crab legs left of the two dozen Barnett ordered and collected, the still-warm corn bread and corned beef. The plates around the table are full—Ezra loves the trout; Winston loves the brisket and the shrimp.

Victoria is partial to the jambalaya and Nichole to the eggplant.

Chrissy helps herself to one slice of fried oyster po-boy and two slices of fried catfish po-boy. She puts both on her plate and looks up at Barnett, noticing his plate matches hers exactly. "I wish I could have helped more with all this," she says. "Sorry. I don't know what got into me."

"I do," Ezra says.

Chrissy fumbles with a stray piece of fried oyster. "Nice to officially meet you all and welcome you, Nichole. Please tell me we aren't doing engagement dinner speeches."

"I have a song prepared but we can wait till later," Nichole says.

"And what a pretty name: Nichole," Chrissy says.

"I had an assistant named Nichole," Victoria says. "I fell in love with the name so I took it and paid my assistant to change hers to Cheryl."

Barnett plays with a disintegrating piece of greasy fried catfish. "Mom, you're in a great mood. Those mushrooms still working?"

"I hope not. Sorry about that. Sorry again, Ezra. I hope you're all enjoying your stay."

"As long as you keep the wine stocked," Victoria says, one open bottle of La Gracè Vino in front of her and an unopened, backup bottle behind it.

"When are the nuptials, Mr. B?" Paw-Paw asks.

"Can we get through the engagement dinner first?" Chrissy laughs. "No one's in a rush."

"I am! I'm eighty-eight!" Paw-Paw says. He looks to Barnett. "What's the plan?"

"I don't know," Barnett says coyly. "What do you guys think we should do?"

"You need a big gay wedding," Nichole says, licking hot butter and garlic dipping sauce from a crab leg.

"We talked about eloping," Barnett says.

Paw-Paw holds up half a biscuit as if it's a judge's gavel. "Told you! Eloping is easy and cheap and no one will get on your nerves but the one you're marryin.'"

"No child of mine will elope!" Victoria shouts. She looks to Nichole and says quietly, "It's fine if *you* do it."

"Ezra and I have been together three years," Barnett says, grabbing Ezra's hand, displaying their unity for all to see. "It feels like we've already been married this whole time, anyway."

"And we should say we think marriage is stupid," Ezra adds. "All marriage. It's a tool of control by religion, a construct imposed on families by society, and a governmental infraction on personal freedom. That being said—"

"It does mean something to us, though," Barnett says. "Marriage is a contract between two people, an agreement for all to see that we are building something together. Also, it's important for assets and health care decisions."

"It's way more than that," Chrissy says.

"Good!" Barnett interrupts. "Good. I want it to mean the most it can possibly mean. I want it to be serious, forever. I want it to scar me. I want it to change me. I want Ezra tattooed on my heart forever." He looks at Ezra. "I don't want a tomorrow without you."

Ezra beams back at Barnett and addresses the table. "We're ready. Marriage feels like a no-brainer, like no big deal."

"It should be a big deal!" Victoria says. "My God, it's your wedding! Each of mine were so magical, so memorable that it's taken decades of self-medicating to suppress them all."

"We were thinking maybe we could just dash to New Orleans and get it done," Barnett says.

"When?" Chrissy asks in a panic.

"I can't tell you that or it wouldn't be eloping," Barnett says.

"Do it next weekend," Nichole says. "It's good astrologically. The sun is in Leo until the twenty-third, when it enters Virgo. Your stars are aligned!"

Barnett looks at Ezra. "That's kinda sweet, right?"

Ezra nods his agreement. "The universe is conspiring to help us."

"Um, Nichole," Chrissy interjects. "Have you had a piece of corn bread?"

"Yeah. I loved it—"

"Eat another one!" Chrissy shouts.

"Why elope when you could just marry here on the farm?" Victoria asks.

Chrissy laughs. She thinks it a farce, she thinks it a joke that her son and his gay lover would get gay married on her farm. She looks at Barnett's face and her smile drops. "You're serious?"

Barnett squirms, starts to pick at his thumb. Ezra gently puts his hand over Barnett's, and Barnett exhales, looks at his lover, his comfort. "We actually did talk about having a little farm wedding."

Ezra chimes in. "Our time here so far has been magical. Barnett and I are ready, all the family is here. And, I guess, it's not eloping if you already know the location and the date."

"And I can't think of a better place for saying my vows than my childhood home, where I saw my parents in love for so many years. And Paw-Paw is getting older, you know?"

"Up yours!" Paw-Paw says. "Age jokes are only funny when I do 'em!"

"So, what if we do it here? What if we have a little wedding here at the farm next week?" Barnett asks. He turns to Chrissy. "Mom?"

"The pictures will look great in the *Post*," Victoria says.

"Can I plan it?" Nichole asks. "We could turn this farm into a real partyscape! Live music! Entertainment! You guys like fire jugglers?"

"That sounds fun!" Ezra says.

"Let's take it slow," Barnett cautions, trying to catch Ezra's eye. "We said *little* wedding."

"UMM," Chrissy interrupts. "It's an interesting idea. But it would traumatize the animals to do something like that here, I'm afraid."

"True," Barnett says. "We would have to be respectful of the ranch."

"The animals won't care if they're all invited," Nichole says. "Plus, they already put up with those tours with kids and that's worse than a wedding. The only ones who may be the slightest bit inconvenienced are the neighbors because of the party noise, but I have a twofold plan to handle that. One: bribe them. Two: burn down their farms."

"Or we could just invite them," Barnett says.

"Barnett," Chrissy says, giving her son *the look*.

"I hear ya, Mom. We can be on the same team, slow and steady, small and easy."

"Also, a wedding takes so much planning," Chrissy says.

"Hello!" Nichole says. "I've been full of ideas since I got here. Like, traditional lighting can be replaced with thousands of fireflies, which we can order in bulk as larvae and hatch just before the service. We can hire models to make the ceremony look well attended by beautiful people, and we can have clever bathrooms: a big, circular trough for the gays, stalls by the pond for the straights, and each lesbian can get a shovel and map of the woods."

"Nichole, we were thinking just Ezra and me and the people at this table," Barnett says.

"But it's fun to dream, right?" Ezra says. "Why not make it extra awesome if we can?"

"Yeah!" Nichole says. "Invite all your friends from Los Angeles. And New York. And here. People can make it work. Or they can tune in on FaceTime or something. We can really turn this farm into a modern gay wonderland, with glitter and lasers and parrots."

"Ha! Love it!" Ezra says.

Barnett cocks his head. "Parrots?"

"We can have them trained to say 'Welcome' as people arrive," Nichole says.

Chrissy shakes her head. "Won't they fly away?"

"Not if they're in chains."

"Um—" Chrissy begins.

"I know what you're thinking," Nichole interrupts. "But we can find parrots on short notice. They ship overnight from Cuba with a guarantee that at least forty percent will still be moving on arrival."

"No," Chrissy says. "We have plenty of birds already with the macaws."

"Okay, sure. We'll train your macaws."

"That's not what I'm saying. I'm saying 'no animals,'" Chrissy says.

"But what about snakes?" Nichole asks. "They can be trained to spell out the word 'congratulations.'"

"Over my dead body," Chrissy says.

Nichole pounds her fist on the table. "Event planning is my calling!"

Victoria nearly spits out her gulp of wine but sucks it back in so as to not waste. "Excuse me, I thought your calling was fashion design, and then it was baking cupcakes, and then it seemed you had settled on a master's in spending my money." Victoria looks at Winston, "*Our* money."

Nichole turns to Ezra. "You're my dear brother. No one knows better than I do the kinds of things you would love." Nichole shrugs. "I'm single and probably will be forever because men are pigs, so why not have the wedding of my dreams, but for my brother?"

"Love you, Nic," Ezra says.

"Love you, Ez," she says back. "Now, here's a brainstorm—"

Nichole ungracefully extracts her legs from the picnic table and stands. She circles the group while looking around the farm. "We can repaint the buildings from this bright blue to a crisp white, except the barn, which will be painted a new shade of red that was only invented earlier this year. We'll have knee-high tables for the goats, ankle-high tables for the chickens. We'll have a menu for each animal. The horses will have hay with apple puree dressing."

"What about menus for people?" Victoria asks. "I need organic foods. This southern stuff is making my skin itch. Is anyone else sweating?"

"Honestly, I'd try the hay with apple puree dressing," Paw-Paw says.

Nichole, unbothered by the interruptions, continues. "New Orleans's own Bourbon Street Jazz Players could perform on a stage that could be set up there," she says, pointing to the pasture. "This area could be for pictures, but we will have to paint the grass because it's a bit dull. And we'll have to paint the rocks something more realistic."

"More realistic than what?" Chrissy asks. "They're rocks. They're not painted at all."

"Exactly," Nichole says with derision. She points toward the stables. "This would be the route of the roller-coaster tracks."

"Absurd," Chrissy says. "People are not riding a roller coaster at a wedding."

"Not people. Just Paw-Paw. The tracks will be designed for his wheelchair. That way, we can just put him on it and leave him be."

"If there's a chance it'll kill me," Paw-Paw says, "I'll do it!"

"And with him and his wheelchair out of the way, we don't have any needless mucking up of the runway."

"Runway?" Chrissy asks.

"Yeah. Instead of an aisle to walk down."

"Who's gonna be the flower girl?" Ezra asks with excitement.

"Pick a horse!" Nichole says. She turns to the backyard. "We can have a massage area here, happy ending massage area there." She turns to the table and throws her fist into the air. "Gay rights!"

"GAY RIGHTS!" Ezra shouts.

"We can put a dunking booth with Celine Dion here," Nichole says. "We'll have ten to fifteen swans in the lake."

"Wait, what? Celine Dion? And what lake?" Chrissy asks.

"Bulldozers could be here in an hour. I have an app."

"Celine is a good woman, but she's a real terror when wet," Victoria says.

"Lightning round, Nic!" Ezra shouts. "Wardrobe?"

"Nudity."

"Flowers?"

"Trees!"

"Finale?"

"Fireworks."

"They're illegal," Chrissy says.

"These ones are organic."

"For kids?" Ezra asks.

"Nothing," Nichole says. "No kids."

"I like that," Victoria muses, refilling her glass.

Nichole looks into the distance, wistfully. "Socializing will be in the barn, with designated areas for otters and twinks, and a common room next to the glory hole. We'll need four bars to survive this thing, with custom drinks depending on the strain of marijuana contained therein. Expect fog machines. Expect snap fans. And expect a drag bar."

"A what?" Chrissy asks.

"An area with wigs and dresses and heels so everyone can take some fun, fabulous pictures."

"Hey," Paw-Paw says, "I can bring trash bags full of my dead friends' wigs and clothes from the dumpster at the home. It'll be a real gas."

"Wow. You really think you could do all that in a week?" Ezra asks.

"No," Chrissy and Barnett say in sync.

"Yep," Nichole says. "Less, probably. I only need two days to get the firefly larvae."

"I'm still a 'no,'" Chrissy says.

"Barnett, what about you?" Nichole asks.

Barnett looks at the table and at Ezra. The men squeeze each other's hands. "Um, we don't need a new lake. But, uh, Mom—" He looks at Chrissy. "Doesn't some version of this—some smaller version—sound better than us eloping? Don't you want to be with us? And when will we all be together again? The timing is nice."

Chrissy feels all eyes on her.

"The end of summer can be the beginning for us," Ezra says. "All of us."

"Maybe after this, all of you can come spend summers with us in Los Angeles," Barnett says.

The end of summer, the end, the end, Chrissy thinks. *This will kill me*, she thinks. *Maybe Elaine and I will go out together*, she thinks. "I feel depressed," Chrissy says.

"That's the mushrooms talking," Ezra says.

"Sure it's not the sudden big gay wedding?" Chrissy asks.

Barnett pushes his plate away from him, his appetite unable to compete with such a huge serving of wedding planning. "It doesn't have to be big."

"But it doesn't have to be too little, right?" Ezra asks.

"And what about the expense?" Chrissy blurts.

"Anything for my only child!" Victoria says.

"Hey!" Nichole protests, pointing her finger at her mother.

Victoria waves as if swatting a gnat. "I meant 'my only son.'"

"You're drunk!" Nichole says.

"It's not happening," Chrissy says. "This isn't a circus. These are lives. These are people's lives. My life. Animals' lives."

"It'll be your son's big day," Victoria says. "It's supposed to be his happiest day."

"Believe me, I'm happy," Barnett says.

"What about my happiness?" Chrissy asks. It's the kind of question that should shut down a family event, the kind of question oft on a parent's mind and seldom, if ever, voiced. The silence is quickly broken.

"It's just one day," Nichole says.

"Barnett, can I talk to you?" Chrissy asks.

As they walk away, Paw-Paw shouts, "Before you schlep me back to that damn home, I expect dessert!"

CLOSE to the bright-blue house where he grew up, Barnett tries to calm his mother in a hushed tone. "It doesn't have to be crazy. Nichole is just excited. I'll rein her in. And Ezra."

Chrissy stops near the back door, then leans forward and whisper-yells: "We can't have a wedding . . . like that . . . here. What will people say?"

"They'll say I'm gay and I got married."

"No," Chrissy says. She turns away from him. "What will people say about me?"

"Ahhh," Barnett laughs, though it's not condescending. It's not patronizing. It's affection. It's a release, almost a comfort. Because he knew this could happen. He has over three decades of intel on his mother, three decades of watching her survive losing a husband, say goodbye to so many of her misfit four-legged tenants, and even agree, finally, to get a mammogram from one of the most respected physicians in the parish, whom she called "a witch doctor."

Chrissy takes a quick breath. "What will Father Perfect say?"

"Again, he'll say I'm gay and I got married. It's not complicated."

"I've said yes to everything so far, Barnett. But this is too much."

Barnett nods, understandingly but unwaveringly. "I know this is a lot. But maybe it's only that way because we've ignored it for so long. And I have to wonder, if I got engaged to a woman, would you be acting like this? Or would you be on the phone hiring chefs and marching bands?"

"Maybe you should just do whatever you want, as long as it's not here."

Barnett laughs again; it's innocent because he knows that for all the talk of the farm and Elaine and his dad's old Chevy, *he* is his mother's true prized possession. The smile his mother greets every morning in the pictures of him on her nightstand, it's a smile that's kind, loving, and before Chrissy in real life right now.

"You don't understand," she says.

"I understand," Barnett says. "It's Polite Society Ranch. Not *Real Life* Ranch."

Chrissy, for the first time since holding Barnett in her arms thirty-four years ago, doesn't recognize her son. She storms inside her empty home, shutting herself off from this stranger, from the celebration she wishes was for someone else's baby boy.

Part 3

Pick a Side

Sweetheart, many wedding traditions shall never change. The bride must always have an aromatic bouquet to obfuscate her body odor. The service must always begin on the half hour to mirror the clock's small hand rising to praise Him. And the bride and her family must always be on the left so the groom's right hand remains free for sword fighting.

> —*Mrs. Jeannie Laffite's Undisputed Guide to Respectable Southern Nuptials, volume III, page 81 (copyright 1912 by Mrs. Jeannie Laffite)*

Chapter 10

Countdown to Damnation:

8 days / 20 hours / 16 minutes

CHRISSY gasps for air and grabs her chest. She's wet—*Am I sweating?* she wonders. She's confused and fumbling in the dark—*Is this a nightmare?*

Her left arm flies up. Her hand finds a light switch.

Clarity comes to her in a shocking, sobering instant. The light from her bedside lamp fills every void and answers every question.

The clock tells her it's just past midnight.

She's been asleep for a few hours.

With her awareness come whiffs of remembrance—storming from the engagement dinner, hard words with Barnett, a wild trip on strange psychedelics.

She gets out of bed, turns on the shower, thinking, *Rinse it all away—the snakes who will spell out 'congratulations,' the drag bar!*

She reaches and feels the water—warm.

She can't remember the last time she was awake at this hour, showering at this hour, but she's compelled to get ready; she has somewhere to be.

Chrissy slowly undresses, remnants of Ezra's mushrooms still present in her, as if she's absorbed them. She feels like one does after a massage, or as she used to after making love, like John's touch is still lingering. Her body has been on an unwanted adventure. So has her mind. And now, as the water rinses through her hair and over her shoulders, and the heat warms her back, she feels—paradoxically— even more rigid in her horror. *Why is Barnett doing this to me? How did I let it get this far?*

Her damp towel tossed aside is the only evidence of her haste. She carefully affixes the gold chain around her neck. She pulls on the first pair of jeans within reach. She grabs a sweatshirt and a much-loved but respectable knit cap. She puts her ear to her bedroom door. *A fugitive in my own house!* she thinks.

Silence.

She opens the door onto a darkened hallway.

Silence.

Chrissy's bare feet lead her past Victoria and Winston's guest room—door closed. Then Barnett's room—door open, but vacant. Chrissy steps inside and tries to smell her boy, the old scent of school clothes and farm work. She scans the room as if she were in mourning, as if Barnett, *Oh, Barnett,* were dead and this is how he will always be remembered, his red suitcases in order, his life looking tidy, contained, if not for the evidence of intrusion—the other bag of clothes, the other person in Barnett's life, the one who's easily blamed for this whole dang thing.

Chrissy pitter-patters to the kitchen, which is mostly cleared of the dishes that covered every surface, making it only half the gluttonous crime scene it was earlier. The dishwasher is pounding away at the debauchery, ridding the world of the stain of the homosexual engagement dinner—the meal, the waste, the sin.

One beignet is uneaten on the table, laid out on a plate as if just for her, carefully sprinkled with powdered sugar. One fork rests beside it, the shiny silver summoning her. And there's one coffee mug out, hers. Enough for one piping cup of chicory brew that waits, as still as glass, in the percolator. It's all laid out, as if she left the party promising to be back in a second. As if when she stormed away earlier, it was a prank. As if when they cleared the picnic table, they set up this spot for her in the kitchen, an offering of peace. For all of it, Chrissy has no appetite.

She steps to the living room—voices, flashes. The television lights up her life's greatest achievement: Barnett. He's awash in whites and blues, that late-night infomercial glow, rendering him almost alive, almost hers again, if not for the blemish, Ezra Tanner, snuggled beside him.

Ezra's head is cocked back, his neck exposed, the most unnatural position for animals in the wild. And this animal, this Ezra, invading Chrissy's ranch and life, sleeps effortlessly, confident that he's safe, that his intentions will never be slain, never executed before him. Ezra, this stranger, just interlopes and gets away with it.

Chrissy is—she hates that it comes to her this way—feeling red vibes. It's enraging thinking about her own life in Ezra's infrastructure. It's rage on top of rage. Her summer with her son: ruined. Her hopes for her boy: gone. Her night of trying to be open-minded: ridiculous. Her conditional love: exposed.

Barnett and Ezra are holding hands as they sleep. Here's her son choosing Ezra over her again. Here's her son choosing Ezra over poor Elaine, over all the animals, over the entire goddamn farm she planned to run with him and leave to him when she eventually has to make her own tragic journey to the granny flat and then Camille Manor Retirement Gardens and then the graveyard out back.

Chrissy stares at her Barnett. He must have fallen asleep waiting for her to return from her sojourn to her bedroom several hours ago. She wants to touch his hair, grab him, shake him. She wants to talk to him about why she's struggling with this whole thing, this glacier ripping apart her plains. She wants to hold him, tell him she loves him. But she does not.

Chrissy slips on her shoes in the carport and fires up the Chevy. It practically drives itself, like it knows the route it's taken a million times.

The ride to Saint Michael the Archangel Catholic Church kicks up as much dust as it does memories. This was the route to John's induction into the Knights of Columbus to get medical insurance. This was the route to Barnett's successes in Sunday school and confirmation and youth group. Father Perfect once thought Barnett could be a priest. *A priest!*

Chrissy was in the choir for one day, long ago, giving it an honest try, but she preferred to spend her time at the farm, singing praises of Elaine or Roz or Cousin Balki.

The old trusty Chevy takes her as if by the hand to the edges of the church property, and Chrissy feels relief fall over her as if she's entered a magical wardrobe and is safe and sound in the squeeze of a childhood fairy tale.

The turn onto the church grounds is transformative, if for no other reason than it's lit. The church has about a dozen New Orleans–style streetlamps that mark the property entrance and guide guests to the parking area. The streetlamps line the wooded, two-way driveway, casting a warm glow on the pine needles and oak leaves. It renders the green ombré; only the foliage close to the light is illuminated, the shade of green darkening to black as the light fails to twist and bend and clear a path through the whole night. But, oh, Chrissy wishes that the light would go everywhere, into every heart. And everyone could see clearly how she's suffering, how they're causing her pain, disruption, disrepute. If they understood, wouldn't they stop?

The lights drape the occasional statue, which at one time had

Chrissy slamming on the brakes for fear someone was rushing from the woods, but she's used to them now—

Hello, Saint Francis.

Hello, Saint Anthony.

Hello, Saint Jude.

The lights usher her to the parking lot, which is a clearing with no stripes, no guidelines, only trust that all the elderly congregants can figure out parking for themselves on busy Sundays. Father Perfect gave a sermon about it one day. Tired of all the complaints about parking, he challenged his loyal followers: "Do you love Jesus? Loving Jesus in these sacred walls is not enough. You have to love Jesus when you get cancer. You have to love Jesus when your kid gets cancer. You have to love Jesus when you get a speeding ticket or get fired from your job or get stuck in traffic. Do you love Jesus then?" And with a little spittle flying, he asked, "Do you love Jesus when you're fighting each other in the dang parking lot outside?"

By that point, Father Perfect was kinda more of a Father Redface. He was so furious about the pettiness of fights over parking spaces. He brought up the high cost of painting stripes. The youth group offered to paint the stripes for free, but he stuck to the idea that the lot should remain unstriped as a penance, a reminder that, "You don't love Jesus if you take up two parking spots!"

The Chevy finds Chrissy's usual Sunday space, far away from any parking controversy, even though she could have pulled up right out front.

When the Chevy's engine silences, Chrissy hears voices and reaches up to turn off her radio—but it's already off. She listens— men's voices. She grabs the handle for the driver's window and rolls it down a crack so she can listen.

The church is dark, all the better, so no one sees how close she is to crying. *Oh, Barnett.*

She turns and looks out the back window. She can make out a few figures sitting on the church's front steps.

The rectory has one outdoor light on. Maybe Father Perfect is still awake. She should have called first. *Whatever.* She rolls her eyes like one of the six-year-olds who tour her ranch. She tithes, she's given plenty of money over the years for those saint statues, those streetlamps, this pavement, the sacred candles inside. Father Perfect can handle her emergency.

As Chrissy exits the Chevy and walks closer to the sacred space, she notices kids outside. No, teenagers. They're those youth group kids. *Good eggs*, she's always thought.

"Good evening," she says, her voice low and professional, adult, a register that makes it easier to establish courage and authority, to hide the cracks of her sorrow.

"Hi, hi," the kids say, in their meek teenage way.

"What's going on tonight?" Chrissy asks.

"Youth group," one of the boys says.

"In the middle of the night?"

"What's your excuse?" a young man asks, accusingly.

Chrissy sucks in a breath to respond, but at the risk of it becoming an actual sob, she declines.

"Ignore him," another boy says. He nods to the rectory and Father Perfect's car parked out front. "He just went to bed. Want me to see if I can still catch him? If you need to talk?"

The kind act is like a slaughter. Chrissy's defenses fall. She nearly crumples into tears right there in front of these holy hooligans. She doesn't answer the boy, can't without wailing.

"I'll go get him," the boy says, and all Chrissy can do is nod, and walk past them, and enter the dark sanctuary, lit only by the altar candles.

The little country church is all tribute to its namesake. Saint

Michael the Archangel effigies abound. The lorded, winged, sword-wielding soldier slices through his enemies, protects the innocent children, defends the church atop pools of blood.

Inside, the church stinks. The original structure was a barn built in 1910. A rogue priest from a seminary many towns over wanted his own church to rule, his own game to play, so he set up shop in a barn in Mader, promising the barn owners fast entry into Heaven if they let him spread the good news. His first parishioners were simple farmhands and construction workers who were initially hired to turn the barn into a church. The big con was that the workers—once paid by the church to build the church—were convinced to join, thereby paying the church to be part of the church, tithing to the rogue local priest who saw his parish grow so fast, the archdiocese of New Orleans made Saint Michael's official. Then the real money arrived. They took the barn apart—saving all the boards—and built a new church in 1951. They used the salvaged barn planks to cover the new interior walls. The church felt fresh and solemn in its tribute to history, incorporating its past into the present, except that the aged, abused barn planks stank to high Heaven from years of humidity and stray cat piss and every imaginable excretion from every beast to ever find solace within those old walls.

The congregation, back before Dawn or OxyClean or unleaded paint, tried pressure washing and sanding and incense and ventilation. Nothing ever really worked, until that old rogue priest died, and Father Perfect arrived and found a solution fit for his namesake.

Instead of removing the planks or deep cleaning all the sacred out of the sanctuary, Father Perfect bought candles. Not the white, waxy, unscented candles from the wholesale church supply store—he goes to the Walmart and buys scented candles in all colors, shapes, and sizes. Now the nave smells of "evergreen mist," or "orange exuberance," or "ocean tide."

A few of the old timers find the colored, scented candles an out-
rage, but where else are they to go? Saint Michael the Archangel Catholic Church is the only house of worship for miles and miles.

Chrissy sits at her unofficially assigned pew and waits.

She breathes in the smell, tries to steady her emotions. Tonight's
scent is "white apple oakwood." Father Perfect lists the scents on a
wall plaque that was intended to display the day's scripture quote and
hymnal pages. But Father Perfect got tired of people asking about the
candle scents. His solution: perfect.

The scented candles aren't cheap, but parishioners pay. Sometimes they pay big. Candles in church are the new voodoo dolls and
witch's brews. *That* flame is for Miss Tennyson's sick husband. *That*
flame is for Mr. and Mrs. McGee so their daughter doesn't go to college and become a Democrat.

Father Perfect enters the church with light steps, both respectful
and cunning. Not much happens on these grounds, or in this town,
without him knowing. To say he keeps secrets is incomplete. He
deals in secrets. They're his currency. Every person's deepest, darkest
secret, he knows. He catalogs the good stuff, the abortions, the lust,
the innermost desires of everyone from the cleaning lady (she hates
having sex with her husband) to the mayor (he lies to his wife about
having sex with the cleaning lady).

Father Perfect, even after midnight, is still wearing his black priestly
garb with white collar, his outfit looking like it just came from the
cleaners. He's always in proper dress. His outfit: perfect.

"Did the kids outside try to charge you admission?" he asks as he
sits beside Chrissy.

Chrissy shakes her head, *no*. She'd tell him they were mostly kind,
that she's grateful for the boy who fetched help, but she's still on the
verge of an unflattering crumbling.

"They're youth group kids. They use the group as a social club more than a Bible study. I don't mind it. It's better than letting them run in the streets. Their parents are happier having them here than somewhere else. One of them once stole a bottle of La Gracè Vino. I found the bottle in the woods. But the boy confessed to everything. He was trying to get drunk. He wanted to see what it was like. It wasn't worth the hell he heard during confession, I'll tell you that, and it wasn't worth the summer afternoon of work he had to do on the church as part of his penance." He looks at Chrissy. "That's why the church has freshly painted railings out front."

"The kids were fine," Chrissy says. "Maybe they were scared of me weeping all over them."

"Oh, Chrissy," Father Perfect says, scooting closer to her, putting his arm around her. Through her sniffles, she can smell his deodorant.

"Barnett came home."

"I heard. That's nice."

"I thought he was moving home to take over the farm. I'm losing Pauley to vet school and no one else on the staff is capable, you know? And I can't do it forever. And I thought he was gonna come home but . . . he's not."

"It's hard when children take their own path," Father Perfect says. "It's painful when we realize our path to happiness was dependent on theirs. It's painful when we hold others hostage to our happiness."

"He's getting married," she says. "He's trying to get married. He wants to get married. To a man. He wants to do it on the farm."

Father Perfect looks from Chrissy to the altar, to Jesus staring down at them from the bloody cross.

"I kinda set myself up," Chrissy says. "There were warning signs, I guess. I mean, we knew about the gay thing. But it hasn't come up in years. Then Barnett asked if I would meet his *roommate*. Then if I would meet the boy's parents. Then, here's the boy's twin sister. Then, they want to have a wedding at the farm." She looks at Father Perfect.

"Am I using all the right words? Is 'wedding' a religious word? Is it even possible to have a 'gay wedding'?"

A drop of sweat makes its way down Father Perfect's back, but he is unflinching. He offers Chrissy the wisdom he dispenses for almost any misbehavior: "There's right and there's wrong," he says.

Chrissy nods her agreement, the same nod she gave him when he told her and John—years ago—not to let Barnett's "gay thing" get out of control.

"Kids are a reflection of their parents. At any age. It doesn't matter," he says.

Chrissy bursts into sobs, puts her hands to her face. The heat of her palms and the spread of her tears creates its own humidity, her face pained and steamy. Slowly, she manages, "What does it say about me? Everyone is going to find out about me. That I'm a bad parent. That I allowed all that to happen under my roof. That I'm part of the whole problem with society, acting like 'gay marriage' is normal."

"We just have to do our best," Father Perfect says. "We're all sinners."

Chrissy reaches to her neck and inside her collar. She pulls on her gold chain until it reveals what's she's looking for: John's wedding band. It's gold but worn, scratched and dinged from a hard life. Chrissy holds it just so, until it catches in the candlelight and illuminates the inscription: *Chrissy & John*. It makes Chrissy smile. John insisted her name be first in the inscription, "Because you're prettier," he said. But when he picked up the ring, his name was misspelled. They forgot the *n*. John laughed it off. "Now it'll be harder for you to pawn it," he joked. Still, they got it fixed. After all, they paid for that dang letter. And if that gold band was going to outlast them all, Chrissy at least wanted it to be an honest record.

Father Perfect watches as Chrissy's attention leaves the moment, her mind elsewhere. "What would John say?" he asks.

Chrissy tucks the ring back in her collar and then says, "Father, I need an ally."

Father Perfect nods. "I'm your ally." He waves his hand around him, to his left and then to his right, to the pews usually full of her neighbors, the walls saturated with prayers and hopes and smells, the Archangel Michael armed in the windows and crannies, the altar and the body of Christ within. "This church is full of your allies."

His answer, Chrissy thinks: *perfect*.

Chapter 11

Countdown to Damnation:

8 days / 10 hours / 8 minutes

EZRA wakes mindfully, that is, trying to ignore his mind altogether. When his mind exits dreamscape and enters awareness, he works hard to throttle emerging thoughts. He keeps his eyes closed, says, *Okay, okay*, to himself—his mantra—as the thoughts and duties of the day start to rush toward him like a colony of ants.

Of course, awareness insists, persists, drips and soaks and floods every cranny in a self-gratifying process. That's why it's so difficult to train dogs not to dig a hole in a yard. The moment they break ground is the reward. By the time a correction is ordered, it's too late. Humans are like that with obsessive thoughts. The thoughts are an addiction. They justify themselves all day long.

A few of those thoughts slip into Ezra's consciousness: The position of his body—he's upright with his head back, *Ah, right, I slept on the sofa with Barnett*. His body is cold—*Barnett must be gone*. The body hungers, thirsts—*I must have slept too long*.

And awareness wins, as Ezra opens his eyes, thinking he's uncomfortable, alone, and starving.

Ezra adjusts himself and walks quietly out of the living room to the kitchen. "Hello?" he says softly. The table is a reminder of the night before—Chrissy abandoning her guests, her son. The setting he and Barnett made for her is untouched.

Ezra walks to Barnett's room and hears the shower running, smells the steamy, soapy scent of his lover.

The hot water gives a little spit from the showerhead, the signal it may run low, a tick that's haunted these pipes even back when Barnett was growing up here. But the water still hits his back with great force as Barnett rubs shampoo in his hair, working up the lather, considering again prodding his mother to get a new hot water heater, but in the fresh light of this new day, that's low on his list of serious things he needs to talk to her about.

"Hey," Ezra says.

The sound of his voice rushes a smile to Barnett's face. "Hey. I can't see anything. Lemme wash out this shampoo."

"No," Ezra says. "Don't move."

"What?" Barnett asks playfully. "Why not?" He hears rustling of clothes, the slapping of bare feet. It fills him with restlessness, a primal desperation to see Ezra's nudity. "What are you doing?"

"Don't look or you'll get shampoo in your eyes."

"I'm gonna wash it out!" Barnett laughs. He reaches up to gently guide his head back into the flow, but Ezra grabs his hands. Ezra lowers Barnett's heavy arms to his sides. He pulls Barnett's wet, warm body out of the stream of water and against his cold, dry one. Ezra kisses Barnett's chest, neck, jawline.

Barnett moves to meet his lips with Ezra. "No, no," Ezra says quietly. "I'll find you."

Barnett squeezes his eyes closed even tighter.

Ezra kisses Barnett's chin, his left jawline, his cheek, the skin under his eye, the skin beside his nose, the tip of his nose, beside his nose on the right side, under his eyes, his cheek, and then, the men's lips connect.

The water spits again and Barnett giggles.

"What's so funny?" Ezra asks.

"The shower always farts every time I get sexy in here."

"Every time? How many times have you been sexy in this shower? I'm outta here," Ezra jokes.

"No, no," Barnett says, reaching to his eyes and wiping them. "Sexy with myself."

"What do you mean?" Ezra asks coyly. "I think I'm gonna need to observe it to understand."

They touch foreheads and kiss again.

They hold each other.

"Things are heating up," Ezra says.

"I know." Barnett rocks Ezra back and forth a few moments. "Can I tell you a secret? I don't wanna force my mom to do anything if she's not ready."

"I meant things are heating up in here between us," Ezra says.

"Oh, right. Sorry. In fairness, I do have shampoo in my eyes."

"Are you saying you want to ditch the wedding idea?"

"No way," Barnett says. He grabs Ezra's shoulders. "If Mom doesn't want it here we'll find someplace else."

Ezra nods.

"Should we go talk to my mom? See if she's cooled down?"

Ezra, hot-blooded, wrapped in steam and suds and the arms of his love, grabs a handful of Barnett and says seductively, "Maybe in a few minutes?"

CHRISSY Durang is out on the farm trying to balance a deep prayer—*Please, God, show me the way*—and a rowdy kids' birthday party. "No running!" she shouts.

This Saturday morning private tour is a party for a spoiled young lady from affluent Mandeville, and her spoiled friends.

"Be careful," Chrissy charges to a seven-year-old girl running away from chickens and into the pigpen. "CAREFUL!" Chrissy shouts again as the inevitable occurs, and the devil's usual chaos begins: screaming, crying, the fury of a child who shan't rest until the mud on her arms and the pig poop near her mouth are obliterated from her consciousness.

"Some spare clothes are in the Goodwill bin if you need 'em!" Pauley yells to Chrissy as she rushes to render aid to the girl.

"Look, kid," she says over the girl's cries, lifting her and dusting her off. "HEY!" Chrissy yells. "Listen to me for one second." The child seems to relent, the silence feeling tenuous at best, so Chrissy rushes. "I had the worst night last night. The whole day yesterday was pretty bad, too. I really don't know what to tell you. And I refuse to do the vibes method, dear God." She looks over her shoulder. Her focus lands on her home, and her son, and a spike in her blood pressure.

Barnett and Ezra are walking toward Chrissy, hand in hand, defiant looks on their faces, like they know exactly what they're doing, making a spectacle in front of the partygoers. It strikes Chrissy as inconsiderate in so many ways. Chrissy has a wicked flash of what the young minds around her must be thinking, the confusion of their retinas at the sight of the handsome young future farmer and the demonic Lolita!

Chrissy turns to the girl and whispers, "I'll give you chocolate and an Elmo Band-Aid to quit crying."

The girl stares.

"And five dollars cash."

The girl nods her agreement.

"All right, then. Very well. Get lost."

"But I have questions about the chickens," the girl says.

"Yes, chickens have ears, their eyes see in full color, a hen lays three hundred eggs per year, they eat meat, they have dreams, they live five to ten years, they can swim, they can fly about nine miles per hour. Does that do it?"

Stunned, the young girl nods. "Yes, ma'am."

Chrissy pulls a five-dollar bill from her pocket and gives it to the girl, and then turns to the other birthday partygoers. "This way." Chrissy points and the kids follow, making their trek to the barn. "Let's meet the macaws." She turns to Barnett and Ezra as they get closer. They all look at each other. And then Chrissy turns away.

Barnett stops, pulling back on Ezra's hand. "No. That means don't bother her, she's working."

They watch her for a moment more, as she guides the children, offering such great, attentive care to other people's kids.

"Let's go," Barnett says, chin up, as he and Ezra turn and head back to the house. "We could take another shower together."

Ezra laughs. "Maybe we should leave the farm for a little while? Go into town? We're here in Mader. I wanna see your life. Is there someplace special you can show me?"

"Ah," Barnett says. "Like a museum or theater or charming haberdashery?"

Ezra's eyes widen, then his look falls, and Barnett confesses, "Kidding. This town has Rhett's Corner Grocery—basically a gas station—or there's my old high school, but—"

"But nothing. Sounds like we're late for class," Ezra says.

Even with so much space between them, Chrissy hears her son's voice behind her. She watches the kids gather around the barn door waiting for her. It's irresistible, her urge to turn around. And she does. She looks back at the two men, one she's known his entire life, walking away from her, his hand still interlaced with the fingers of the other one, the one she's known only briefly. Chrissy felt that way about a man once. And Barnett is half of him. She hopes he'll turn around. If Barnett or Ezra looks back, she decides, she will meet them, talk to them.

They do not look back.

BARNETT puts the old Chevy in park and picks at the skin around his thumbnail.

"Hey," Ezra says, taking hold of Barnett's hand. "Why are you picking? What's wrong?"

"Nothing," Barnett says.

Before them is the Mader school campus. Three gray, modest buildings lick the land, all three in a row like stripes on a general's jacket.

"This is it?" Ezra asks over the sound of the Chevy's engine still running. Barnett's hands are wringing, his eyes scanning as if for predators.

"Doesn't school make you nervous?" Barnett asks.

"I'm a teacher. So, yes, definitely!"

Barnett tries to laugh it off. "But as a kid, were you nervous? I was always so nervous. About everything."

"Wonder where you got that," Ezra says, opening the truck door.

"Where are you going?" Barnett asks.

"Let's go walk around."

"I'm not trespassing. Are you crazy?"

"A little. No one's here. This "campus" is, like, three sheds. And I'm a teacher and you're a high school sports icon. What's the worst that could happen? Come on." Ezra slams the truck door and starts a trek.

"Ugh," Barnett says, killing the truck's engine and chasing after.

"Hey, you can show me your trophies!"

"Keep your voice down," Barnett says, nodding toward some teens playing basketball on a crumbling concrete court.

"Still scared of teenagers?" Ezra asks. "Are *they* trespassing?"

Barnett shrugs. "This way." His feet drag in the dirt and gravel of the parking lot. As he takes each step, he's reminded of the old days. Feeling the fake smile on his face. A puck in his stomach twists. He picks at his thumb. The MRI would show irritation.

"What's this building?" Ezra asks, stepping onto the sidewalk.

"Junior high and front office." Barnett points to the building to the right. "That one is the elementary." He points to the left. "And that one is the high school. And the gym. The gym is also the cafeteria. The gym coach was also the principal."

"Hmm. Interesting and efficient, I guess," Ezra says. "And which building houses the trophies?"

"This way," Barnett says, taking Ezra to the high school/gym/cafeteria. Barnett points down. "This is the sidewalk where I first saw Duncan."

"Aw. Your first love," Ezra says.

"My first lust. My first heartbreak, I guess."

The two big doors to the high school/gym/cafeteria are old and worn. The handles, once chrome plated, now show the wear of hundreds of hands using them every day, thousands over the years, including one young Barnett Durang.

Ezra grabs the door handle and pulls.

"Wait, wait—" Barnett cautions.

But the door is locked. "Dammit," Ezra says. "My baby's trophies are in there."

"You can't just walk in. Jesus. What if we get shot?"

Ezra rolls his eyes. "By whom?"

"HEY!" The voice is booming and cruel. Barnett and Ezra spin around to see a large man silhouetted in the sunshine, a man who seems at once threatening and familiar.

Ezra puts his hands up. "I'm a teacher! In Los Angeles! I have awards!"

"Oh my God," Barnett says to himself.

"Barnett?" the man asks, in a country drawl thick as mud.

"Clay?" Barnett asks, his voice deeper, his Slinky spine straighter. He steps forward, away from Ezra.

"Hey! Holy shit! Nice to see you," Clay says, approaching. "You look exactly the same. More muscles maybe," he laughs. He and Barnett meet, shake hands firmly, warmly.

"That's Ezra," Barnett says, flicking his thumb behind him. Ezra acknowledges the introduction with furrowed brows.

"Hi Ezra. Y'all checking out the old stomping ground, eh?"

"Yeah," Barnett says. "I was just showing my, uh, teammate around."

"Teammate?" Ezra asks, putting his hands on his hips and a twist on his face.

"What team?" Clay asks.

"The Faggots," Ezra says. "We're really great. We win lots of tournaments."

"Jesus, Ezra!" Barnett says.

Ezra leans to Clay. "I'm joking. I'm his fiancé, not *teammate*. We're getting married. Supposedly in a week."

"Gay marriage. Right on," Clay says.

"Just *marriage* is fine," Ezra says.

"We're excited," Barnett says, trying to steer the ship. "My mom is struggling with it, actually."

"Yeah," Clay says. "It's a crazy town. A little backward. I have a nephew who is, you know." Clay leans forward toward Barnett and Ezra. "He's blond."

Barnett and Ezra both nod their heads as if to placate, *Sure, sure.*

"My kid loves coming to school here," Clay says.

"Holy shit," Barnett brightens. "You have a kid?"

"I think so," Clay jokes. "A son. I always have to double-check my pictures on Facebook to make sure it's true. It's a lot of damn work. He made me quartermaster for Scouts. I'm always here dropping shit off."

"Quartermaster? Do you have a key?" Ezra asks. "I'd love a tour."

Inside, the gym area is obvious, with basketball hoops, a track loop on the floor, deep shadows in its corners like dark circles under weary eyes. A locker near the entrance is still dented from Barnett's fight with Ronny Campion over a science project.

"The court lights used to take forever to warm up and we thought they were haunted," Clay says. "Remember that?"

"Yeah," Barnett says. He turns to Ezra. "In the bathroom, the middle shower stall used to leak and we'd put a bar of soap under it and watch the water bore a hole. Sometimes it took a day, sometimes a week."

"That orange Dial soap would sometimes last *months*," Clay adds.

Along the walls, the bleachers are folded up and replaced with dining tables and chairs. Over there is where Barnett first learned about menstruation. Over there are ghosts of the crusty cafeteria ladies. Over there is the last school day's lunch menu, still written on the dry erase board: cheese pizza or salad bar.

And over there, beside two unplugged vending machines, sits the Mader High School trophy case. It's an old hutch—probably donated. It's meant to display fine, fragile china but is overflowing with dusty plaques and old trophies—some broken, some losing their fake golden hue, some standing tall and untouched for decades.

"Which one of these did you win?" Ezra asks.

"I didn't win any," Barnett says. "These are all team efforts."

"He was a damn king. The awards from our years are back there." Clay points to the rear right of the hutch, where the largest trophies are clumped together.

"The winningest corner," Ezra says. "This is really incredible. Must have been a great feeling."

"Yeah. Really great," Barnett says flatly. He steals a glance at Clay, wondering if Clay ever knew how much unhappiness the so-called king carried.

In the trophy case, Barnett doesn't see the dust or dead bugs, just a snapshot of his life, his sweat and injuries that made their track team unmatched, unbeatable. And made him untouchable: as long as he kept his secrets, he was a star to the athletes and administrators alike.

Mostly, in that trophy case, Barnett sees scars. The largest trophy, three tiers with peeling metallic columns and a gold man running in place forever, reminds Barnett of The Big Thing. The team won this trophy the week it happened. It was on Barnett's mind while he raced. Every thump of his foot on the ground was a stomp, a desire to crush his head-aching thoughts—he's a disappointment, he's unnatural. He stomped to his winningest time and put his team over the edge.

A few trophies are topped with gold cups, vases, chalices— whatever they're supposed to represent, they'll never hold much. They're the size of shot glasses, hardly thirst quenching. Some of these are Barnett's oldest scars. This one was around his crush on Duncan. That one was around the first time he confessed impure thoughts to Father Perfect. That one was around the time he asked Marianne Mouledoux to prom, showering her with compliments, kisses, lies.

Victories.

The trophy with the winged shoe on top was won in Mandeville. Barnett was warming up when another team's runner—pinned with the number 1045 on his chest and back—called him a fag. Barnett was stunned. He wondered: *How did this kid know?* And who else back at Mader High suspected such a thing, but wasn't saying any-thing because Barnett was Coach Murray's favorite? When Barnett won the race, he was flushed with shame at the trophy—a winged shoe? Barnett had the thought, *Light in the loafers*, just as he looked up to see number 1045 sneering.

"I like the one with the flying shoe," Ezra says. "And the one with the jaunty man running."

Of course, the jaunty golden runner is neither golden nor running. He's hollow resin, painted in a shiny gold color, frozen in place forever at midstride, with one knee at a ninety-degree angle, the other leg long and glued down, immobile. He's also aging. His gold facade is fading in some parts, peeling away in others—the bits of gold paint will eventually break off and fall, more movement than the golden runner may ever himself see, hunks of his peeling flesh betraying his lie.

"Do any of these bring back memories?" Ezra asks.

Barnett adjusts his focus from the trophies to the glass containing them, and his own reflection. "Nah," he says.

Silence falls over the gang, so Ezra pipes up, turns to Clay, "When I saw you outside I thought for sure you were gonna beat me up."

"Not you. Maybe Barnett a little." Clay laughs and elbows Barnett. "I still owe you a beatdown from when you put Bengay in my jock."

"Babe!" Ezra scolds.

"Yeah!" Clay says. "I had to go to the hospital. The whole track team showed up in their jocks and jerseys to show support. The head nurse called the police."

"For a guy closeted in high school, this is the gayest story," Ezra says pointedly to Barnett.

"Hey, I'd love to come to your wedding," Clay says. "My wife and kid, too. Would love to see it. Aw, shit. Wait. I don't mean to be rude."

"Not rude at all," Barnett says. "We'd love to have you. If it happens. Supposed to be next Sunday, but—"

"But we're trying to decide exactly how big and exactly how gay the wedding should be."

"Ezra, please—"

"Hey," Clay says. "Remember Hammond?"

"Oh, God."

"What was Hammond?" Ezra asks.

"We had a track meet there, up north." Clay turns to Barnett. "Remember Paul Stolton?" Barnett doesn't answer. "Paul and Barnett were like a dynamic duo. They tied at a meet in Hammond. It was a big deal back in the day. Paul is a cop now, believe it or not."

Barnett snaps from his trance. "A cop!"

"Can you believe they gave that guy a gun?" Clay laughs.

Barnett returns his focus to the trophy case. Clay follows his gaze.

"These sure do represent an interesting time, don't they?" Clay says. "Back then you were really a man."

Ezra heard it. And Barnett felt it. *Were.*

The truck door slams harder than necessary as Barnett fumbles to get the keys in the ignition. "Why are you so pushy about the gay thing?" he asks.

"The gay . . . *thing*?" Ezra asks.

"You know what I mean."

"I didn't think I was being pushy," Ezra says. "I was being honest."

"Then I wish you'd be a little less honest with my friends."

"Really?" Ezra asks. "You want your 'teammate' to be less honest?"

"And while we're at it, don't be so hard on my mom."

"Your mom thinks I'm a demonic, life-wrecking asshole."

Barnett starts the truck, puts it in reverse. "She would never say it like that." The truck starts to move backward. "She's doing her best."

"Sorry. Are you defending her homophobia?"

"You're forcing me to. She doesn't hate *me*."

"Of course not. But she's sure—" Ezra pauses.

"Go on," Barnett says. "Let's hear it. I can take it."

"I'm sorry if your mom is unenlightened and lonely," Ezra says. "It just seems a little selfish and delusional of her to expect you to give up your life and move back to a town with nothing to offer."

Right there in the middle of the parking lot, Barnett stops the truck and puts it back in park with a slow and deliberate, if not exaggerated, push. "Wow," he says. "Well, she's *my* unenlightened and lonely and selfish and delusional mom."

"That's not—" Ezra starts. "Come on, that's not what I was saying."

"And I don't talk about your mother like that, okay?"

"Oh, reeeeally?" Ezra asks, a devilish, affected drawl on the end. "That's because you don't need to. I already know everything about my mother, the alcoholic's alcoholic, the silver-tongued complainer who only flies first-class and has allegedly never, in her whole life, worn something that's one hundred percent cotton. She's not here to support me but to get out of the city. She invited herself here and is now shepherding everyone, it seems, face-first into a huge fight. Look, I know how ridiculous she is. I know how ridiculous my family can be. I just didn't know you thought it, too."

The men are quiet for a moment, Barnett's gears spinning with visions of Nichole's plan to turn a farm into a destination, a love story into a rave, and two grooms into local lightning rods.

Ezra is thinking of him and Barnett, how they were so hopeful as they planned this trip, open to whatever adventure awaited them, whatever obstacles life could throw. They could encounter anything, could overcome anything, as long as they were together. "I feel blue vibes," Ezra says.

"You know, it bothers me when you talk like that."

"No, it doesn't," Ezra says. "It's not what someone does or says that causes your suffering, it's what you're thinking and believing about what someone does or says that's the cause of all suffering."

"Honestly," Barnett says. "I can't handle your hocus-pocus right now."

"Right now? Babe, this is me all the time."

"It's annoying."

"You find my core beliefs annoying?" Ezra asks. "Interesting. Because I accept all of you unconditionally."

"Really?" Barnett asks. "What about when you said my childhood home was the color of a Porta Potty?"

"Just the shade of blue! Not that you live in a toilet."

"What about wanting to hire models to wander around our wedding because my family isn't photogenic enough? Painting rocks because our place isn't classy enough for you?"

"That's Nichole, not me."

"She's your twin! And it's not *all* Nichole. She didn't tell me to clean my fingernails."

Barnett flips the gear into drive, and the men go onward in silence.

Ezra shakes his head and wonders, *Wait . . . what the hell are we fighting about?* He considers the color codes of his feelings, he breathes deeply, his anger turns soft, he taps into empathy, regretting things he said only seconds earlier, and just as he feels the coveted green vibes, timber.

Barnett says, "Maybe my mom is right and this is all a big mistake."

Ezra loses control of his eyebrows, which rise. He loses control of his mouth, which hangs open. "I can't believe you'd say that."

Barnett drives away from the Mader High School campus, full of the familiar spirits that haunted his young adulthood all those many years until he came out: uneasiness and war.

CHRISSY is not in her bedroom, though it's the first place Barnett looks when he gets home. Sometimes, men need their mothers.

Chrissy is not in the living room or the kitchen.

Chrissy is not beside Elaine in the barn. "Where's Mama?" Barnett asks the sheep.

Barnett finds Chrissy in her least favorite place on the farm: *the office.*

I never wanted to grow up to be a person with an office.

But there she sits, in a life she didn't exactly imagine, all grown up, her life's opportunities spent, mostly.

The gentle knock on the door doesn't startle her. She continues looking out the window at her whole world, her plot of land on earth. It's the sound of his voice that alarms her.

"You must be really down if this is where you're hiding," Barnett says.

Chrissy affixes a smile as easy as one on a Mrs. Potato Head doll. She turns just in time to hear her son's voice crack, and his eyes redden and burst. "Mom—" he cries.

She stands quickly, the office chair sliding back and into the wall behind her. He's in her arms in an instant, clamped like a sawfly on oak.

"What's wrong?"

"Ezra and I had a fight," Barnett says, rolling the offenses against her around in his mind—*unenlightened and lonely, selfish and delusional.*

Chrissy ushers him to the futon. They sit atop the thin blanket she keeps spread about so no one stains it during staff meetings. "There,

there," she says, knowing she could do better, if only she knew exactly what to say, if only the situation wasn't so complicated.

"He said things about you. And about me. I don't know if I should be with someone who sees me that way."

She hugs her boy tightly. "Maybe it's for the best. Maybe it's time to let all this go."

And Barnett sobs anew. And then harder.

"What, what?" Chrissy asks. "What is it now?"

Barnett cries even harder still, his perfect face swelling, no evidence his brilliant smile ever existed upon it. He pulls himself slightly out of her embrace. "Mom, that really isn't what I was hoping you would say."

Chapter 12

Countdown to Damnation:

7 days / 17 hours / 54 minutes

BARNETT's broad chest, then neck, then jaw, and then cheekbones are suddenly shaded in darkness, blotting him out like a fast-moving eclipse. As the shadow floats over his eyes, his attention snaps from dream to reality, from peace to panic.

He pulls off the thin blanket his mother draped over him hours ago and wonders where he is. He leans up and spins into a seated position on Chrissy's office futon, his bare feet on the hardwood floor, his senses now accounted for. He reaches gently to move a curtain and peek outside at the barn, to get a look at—*What? An intruder? A familiar ghost?* he wonders.

Outside the window, the moonlight offers nothing but a bright blur. It's white as snow out there. In Louisiana, the clouds aren't always in the sky. The heavens come down. They smother. They smolder. Outsiders might think it a wildfire. Outsiders might think it fog. But Barnett clings to his childhood hypothesis: on humid mornings, when the night temperatures play their cruel, cool game, the clouds come down to hug swamps and sinners alike.

Like any child of farm wilds, Barnett has been boy and man, owner and owned, loved and killed, predator and prey. Every farm is a tactical field in that way, a war zone with a billion little life-or-death battles playing out, sometimes visible and sometimes not, sometimes overt and sometimes in spirit.

Barnett moves into the night, the clouds, the hunt.

He listens, gently swatting at the mist and creating swirls to rival the twisty breezes of *The Starry Night*. Still barefoot, forcing his feet to remember paths forged in youth, he steps forward.

The pine needles, the rough grass, it all feels different now. Maybe he's simply older, maybe his feet are softer, or maybe the grounds are more dangerous than they used to be.

Barnett can almost hear the cloud cover, wisps of Earth's breath tickling the tiny hairs on the curves of his ears. He's moving, but he's listening for the shadow, for a dark fate or an even worse reality—that he's seeing things, that he's a freak and flake and fool—*I should be in bed beside Ezra! Maybe my mother is selfish and delusional?*

Each of Barnett's deep breaths brings more of the cool clouds into his body. He's one with the mystery, if only for a moment. Soon, his temperature is dropping, his pulse slowing, his mind questioning: *Was the shadow a dream? Or is this the dream?*

He hopes it's his dead father out there, haunting the old acres, available for a hug and maybe some advice. But it's been many years since he's believed in such things as ghosts.

Barnett's father used to think his son left the path of righteousness around the time of The Big Thing. But Barnett lost faith in anything supernatural many years earlier, right there in Mader, right at Saint Michael the Archangel Catholic Church, in third grade of Sunday school, when he asked a question of Miss Donna.

"What kind of apple was it?" young Barnett asked, to awed silence from his classmates. "The apple Eve ate. What kind was it?"

Miss Donna, barely out of her teens, with a heart as ripe as her father's winningest tomato at the Washington Parish Fair, smiled at Barnett, then shrugged.

Young Barnett looked to his classmates, left then right, then back at Miss Donna, who continued with the lesson on how to pronounce the word "Eucharist." *She doesn't know*, Barnett thought. *She doesn't know what kind of apple. How can she know everything else about the big stuff—Eucharist, sin, Heaven—and not know the kind of apple?*

Barnett became a dog with a bone, jaws tight, locked onto it, raising the question at every opportunity. "What kind of apple was it?" he'd ask his mother; she didn't know. He'd ask his father; he didn't know. He even asked Father Perfect; he didn't know and even said it was a silly question. Chrissy had to eventually order Barnett to stop "pestering" people with it. That was the first unraveling of the fabric of his faith in phantoms.

Barnett walks to the barn, doesn't hear anything. The motion lights are off. It's just the glow of the moon, a quiet taunt of a nightmare. He walks another short lap, eyes peeled for a flash of his father, or anyone awake at this hour.

The animals sleepily stalk him as he makes the trek—past the gravestones—*Hello, Seinfeld*. Past the burn barrel—*Hello*, Being Gay for Dummies.

Perhaps this is all silly. Perhaps this is all stress. He pees near the barn. He drinks a sip of water from the hose by the pigs. He throws a little feed to the chickens and checks that Elaine is comfy under a warm blanket. She looks old and frail, but comfortable.

Outside at the stables, he grabs a handful of hay for the horses, Roz and Niles. "Sorry for waking you guys up."

But out of the corner of his eye he clocks movement. A reaction takes over, something that feels ancient in his athletic bones. Barnett ducks and swerves behind a haystack, then to the tractor, then to the side of the barn, looking for a predator.

It's not unusual to be spooked by motion on a farm. Flies are in the trough. Maggots are in the fruit. Skunks are in the woods.

But something about this plume of motion that caught Barnett's eye is different. This little spark, this little ping, it sings sinister.

He doesn't see it again. The rolling clouds tumble in drill formations back and forth like traffic between him and it, whatever it was. *Was it a man? Is there an intruder about? Surely, I'm not crazy. I'm not being hunted.*

Nothing.

He sits.

He waits.

Restless, all nerves, he starts doing chores. The clouds are slowly lifting by the time the horses get a fill of hay and Elaine finally eschews her blanket and turns to her morning needs. Barnett, with a nagging feeling, keeps turning to the field, the forest, the shotgun above the barn door, should it come to that.

Elaine nuzzles against him. Animals sense stress. They smell it. "It's okay, baby—"

And Barnett dashes off! He's midsentence one second and midflight the next, sprinting to the barn door, grabbing the shotgun above it and reflexively pumping it full, then flexing and forging forward with those calves, those thighs that won him all those ribbons, the big feet that made him a king on the Mader High School track team.

A blur. And then another. But this time Barnett is moving with it, parallel across the field, the silhouette of a man sticking close to the forest line, moving fast. Barnett considers yelling, his first thought being to shout "Hey" or "Stop." But his next thought warns against giving himself away, making himself a target.

The ghost is fast and sizable, in a red checkered lumberjack coat and ugly old orange hat.

Go, go, jump, jump, next, next, next—Barnett thinks, his familiar dialogue from track and field. *Keep going, keep going. There, there*, he orders his bare feet, now bleeding in opposition to pursuit. *Go, go!*

Barnett has killed before. He once put down a pig.

Barnett has been in fights before, in school and once at church.

The intruder exits the forest and Barnett makes out with certainty, indeed, the shape and colors of his father, framed in swirling, heavenly puffs. Barnett stops and stares, watches the ghost—*The man? Dad?*—as he glides along the edge of the field, maneuvering intently, like he's been there before.

Barnett smells pine in the breeze, but the winds that bring the scent also drown the ghost, stirring the cloud cover that seems to carry it away.

"Hello?" Barnett asks the empty field, a betrayal of his sanity.

He tries to slow his breathing as he walks into the clearing and closer to the spot where someone—or something—is haunting. He looks for clues, tracks. But nothing.

The walk back, under a mile from home, leaves Barnett lost in thought about himself and Ezra, the shotgun and violence, his mother and her safety, his mental health.

As the farm comes into focus, so does clarity. Barnett needs rest, he needs to shake off stress. It's the lack of sleep, it's the stress of his mother and the wedding. It now has him seeing things and running barefoot and charging into the fog with a loaded shotgun. The MRI would show insanity.

He puts the shotgun back in the barn and turns to the house.

And vandalism.

Spray paint drips down the side of his mother's home, each run of color falling from letters carefully emblazoned in sharp bursts: "FAG." The color is a deep shade of green, cruel in the way it matches the beautiful trees and shrubs around them, almost artful in its ugliness. Barnett wonders if it's real, or another apparition, another torment from his subconscious file of fears and oddities. He touches the lowest part of the "F" and looks at his fingers, now covered in winter green paint, fresh and acrid.

Barnett twists around, scanning the property for aberrations, for more blips or blurs. He listens. He walks another lap. He wonders anew about enemies, about possible wars he never knew he was fighting.

SLOWLY, the sun breaks free of night and burns the scraps of fog away, clearing the sky of its sorrow and charging birds like they're solar activated. The horses snap their tails awake. The chickens poke at mysteries in the ground.

And nearby, Barnett, as if a misfit farm animal himself, sits in the dirt, defeated, staring at his childhood home and the scar laid bare on it, now dry and deep: "FAG."

By the time Barnett's feet have warmed enough for him to feel that they're bleeding, Ezra steps from behind the house. "Hey. I was just looking for you."

Barnett looks down, doesn't respond.

Ezra walks over. He steps to the side of the house and leans upon it casually, perfectly, like a model at a photo shoot. It's not pretentious or posing, it's more Gap than Gucci, more Louisiana than Los Angeles. Maybe Ezra is finally feeling more at home.

They make eye contact. Both open their mouths at the same time, but Ezra's breath is faster. "I'm still fighting with you. I'm just coming to tell you to get inside because we're all having breakfast and I could use some backup because my mother is claiming she's never in her life eaten cereal."

Barnett points to the side of the house.

Ezra rounds the corner and stops as soon as it's clear. "FAG."

"Truce," Ezra says.

"Truce," Barnett says.

"Who did this?"

"It's fresh. I just chased him off."

"Chased him off? Like in a movie?" Ezra asks, turning to face Barnett, to see if he catches jest in his gently estranged lover.

"Yeah," Barnett says. "It was a little like a movie. I thought he was a ghost at first. I thought he was my dead dad."

Ezra turns back to the graffiti. "Your dead dad has great penmanship."

IT doesn't take long for everyone to gather around, forgoing their cereal and bagels and the mass of scrambled eggs Chrissy cooked with salt, pepper, and a dash of whole milk.

"Who would do this?" Barnett asks.

Barnett, Ezra, Nichole, Winston, and Victoria—they all look at Chrissy. "I didn't do it!"

Her audience is unmoved.

"I didn't!" she repeats.

"Maybe it was an accident," Nichole offers, with not much enthusiasm. "Or a joke?"

"It *is* such a fun word to say," Victoria says.

"So is 'cunt,'" Ezra says, looking pointedly at his mother.

"I don't disagree there," Victoria says, amused. Turning to Winston, she says, "He sure is my son, isn't he?" She beams with pride. Winston is speechless anew.

"I would never," Chrissy says.

"I know, I know, Mom," Barnett says. "Who do we really think did it?"

"Barnett thought it was a ghost," Ezra says.

"A ghost?" Chrissy asks.

"Wearing his dad's clothes," Ezra adds.

"Oh," Chrissy says, wheels turning.

"Mom? Do you know something?"

Chrissy sighs. "It's not a ghost."

Chapter 13

Countdown to Damnation:

7 days / 11 hours / 8 minutes

CHRISSY wonders which knife is best for killing her neighbor, if it comes to that. Linda—her last name long forgotten—lives to the north. Not that Chrissy hopes to or even anticipates becoming a murderer at her age, but it could be self-defense, it could be son-defense.

Chrissy's knife collection numbers four: four gifts from her father on her last four birthdays before he died. Before knives, he gave her real presents. The knives he gave her were the least valuable, the unloved ones of his collection. They were gifts he could give that didn't cost him anything. She'd inherit all of them, eventually. And when she did, she gave them all away, keeping only the four he gave her, the ones he cared least about, but the ones that, for a time in her young life, she guarded like treasure, the only reminder of her old man.

The knife with the single diamond in the handle is sharp, but Linda is not worthy of fine jewels.

The knife with the short, petite blade is convenient, but Linda is large and thick.

The knife with the serrated edges will work, but while Chrissy considers herself fair, she is not cruel.

The pocketknife with the locking blade. It will do. It will have to do.

Chrissy isn't one to shy away from a fight. Farmwork means something new every day. Today, maybe a knife in Linda's arm, or chest. Chrissy considers Linda's breast and shudders.

The approach to Linda's home is overgrown and hidden. The sight of her home—any home at all in these thick woods—is a surprise. Linda's house is all porch. It wraps around the entire home and is recklessly cluttered. There are a couple of dishwashers, several stacks of phone books; no sign—yet—of paint cans.

The closer Chrissy gets, the colder the knife in her back pocket feels against her butt. All her energy seems to be flowing to the knife, its steely reminder: *I'm here, I'm here.* Her other senses follow, her eyes softening their focus to include the periphery, her eardrums vibrating to the beat of the woods, the bugs, the house.

Chrissy hears chaos, yelping and thunderous barking in the home. Maybe they know she's coming.

"SHUT THE HELL UUUUP!" The yelling comes from inside the house. The animals are instantly silent. "Jesus Christ," Linda says.

To herself? To someone else? Chrissy wonders. She stops. She listens. Nothing. The only stir in the quiet is the faintest brush as she slips her fingers into the back pocket of her jeans, takes out the knife, and holds it—still folded—in her palm.

"Hello?" Chrissy yells from the yard. There's a moment of silence. That moment, that quiet, it passes through Chrissy, Linda, and the beasts she houses. After the moment, the uproar.

"GODDAMMIT SHUT UP!" Linda screams over the raging of the dogs barking around her.

Dogs don't speak English. They don't count. They try to make connections the best they can. When they're howling and their owner starts howling nonsense, the dogs think they're following the pack leader. They hear her yelling as barking, as her joining their quest, whether it's fun or fight.

"SHUT THE HELL UUUUP!" Linda shouts again.

A broken refrigerator and boxes and boxes of—anything, everything—wobble on the porch. And from the wall of junk, as if from a secret passageway, emerges Linda. "Hey, neighbor! Everything okay?" She's wearing a black-and-red checkered shirt and an old orange cap.

"Nice outfit," Chrissy says.

"My uniform," Linda says.

"Wondering if we could chat?" A gaggle of dogs—four or five— rush Chrissy. They yap and yelp and bark and growl. None of them look the same. None of them look friendly. Chrissy's grip on her knife tightens, her grip on this situation easing.

"Get back in here!" Linda screams at the dogs, scooping her arm as if to say, *This way, this way*. The dogs obey instantly, all but one.

The animal, a puppy, all limbs and floppy bits, is country big. Gray like a storm cloud except for white fur on his face—as if he's been frosted—and dark fur circles under his caramel-colored eyes, like an evil raccoon. His fur is wiry, like a terrier, a hunter of rats. But he weighs about forty pounds and stands nearly three feet tall, like an Irish wolfhound, a hunter of wolves.

"Shithead! I said, 'come'!" Linda yells to the straggler. "He goddamn never listens."

The dog approaches Chrissy carefully, disarmingly, and she wonders if the magic she's believed she's had all these years—caring for animals, somehow signaling to them she's a good person—is about to prove itself again.

The dog steps, steps, steps. He looks up at Chrissy, raises his leg, and pees on her shoe.

"No! No!" Chrissy yells and steps back, shakes her foot before drops of urine have too much time to soak in.

"DAMMIT! SHITHEAD, GET IN HERE!"

The dog flops his oversize paws on the ground and takes a few jaunty leaps in what seems to be a celebratory circle, then dashes off into the woods. Linda shakes her head. "Hate that guy. Come on up."

Chrissy catches her breath, wipes perspiration from her lip, and takes her time approaching Linda's home, carefully maneuvering around the junk and up the dark and moldy porch steps. "Watch your foot for dog shit in the house," Linda says. "HEY! GIT!" she shouts at the lingering pack.

Chrissy looks back, out into the woods, out to the spot where the gray killer, Shithead, vanished. He has now reappeared, on the edges, his frosted face and two caramel eyes staring back at her, intently, maniacally.

"Shithead is seven months old. Jesus, don't ever get a puppy. Not that I adopted him. Not that I adopted any of these monsters. I run my own sort of rescue farm—kinda like yours but we're poor." Linda points to the dogs around her. "This one was homeless. This one was shot with a BB gun and then kicked and had a broken rib. This one ate his owner after he died and he was left alone for two weeks. Right, Murphy?"

The flesh-eating dog, Murphy, a big white bulldog, wheezes.

"Is all that true?" Chrissy asks.

"Most of it," Linda shrugs. "Want a Pepsi or a fish stick?"

"No, thanks," Chrissy says, only half imagining the horrors that could emerge from the kitchen.

"Wanna sit?" Linda asks.

Chrissy looks around.

"Yeah, you'll have to make a spot for yourself."

"Look," Chrissy says. "I'm here to tell you, I don't know how you found out about the wedding, and I don't like it, either, but you're making me look bad."

"Come again?" Linda says.

"You're making me look like I'm in cahoots, or on the same team, with a gay hater."

"You're a gay hater?" Linda asks.

"No," Chrissy says. "I don't hate gay people. It's not *hate*. You know?"

"No, I don't know. I'm not a gay hater."

Chrissy almost laughs aloud. "Linda, my son saw you. He saw you on the property this morning. You were wearing that very outfit. That's John's old jacket and hat."

"I know. You gave 'em to me."

"I know! That's why I'm here. You're busted."

"What the hell are you talking about? Busted for what?"

"For being a gay hater!"

"I told you! I don't hate gays!" Linda yells.

"I know! Me, either," Chrissy says, winking. "I'm a Catholic. Hate the sin, not the sinner, you know, all that."

"I love the sin," Linda says. "I'm one of them lesbians."

Chrissy is too stunned to speak. Her chest grows heavy, as if all the rubble around her is falling in at once. She flexes her feet, ruffling a layer of old *Gambit* magazines that line the floor. She slips her knife back in her pocket.

"Yeah, every now and then I sleep with this goddess named Anna who has only nine toes."

"What happened to the tenth toe?" Chrissy asks, regretfully.

"Guess!" Linda says, cheerfully.

Chrissy imagines one of Anna's thickest toes being inserted into Linda's mouth and never again emerging.

"You okay? You look sick," Linda says.

"Maybe I should sit down." Chrissy makes her way to the nearest garbage heap, a stack of newspapers topped with years of flattened cereal boxes.

"It wasn't that bad, losing her toe," Linda explains, shuffling trash and helping Chrissy get more comfortable. "Poor Anna. She got bit by a spider when she was a kid. Right on the little toe. Did you think she lost her toe from a train track? Like, she put her toe on some train tracks? I always think about things like that. Dark things. Like a kid's hand on a train track. Thoughts like that just pop into my head. The mind is so stupid. It's shocking we trust it at all."

"Wait, wait. You're a lesbian and you still painted 'fag' on my house?"

"Fag?"

"Barnett saw you in the field."

"Yeah, my dog got loose. Shithead. You know the one. He loves your property."

"And right after Barnett saw you, he found someone had painted the word 'fag' on our house."

"On your house!"

"Yes. Jesus Christ! Aren't you listening?" Chrissy says, not lost on her the number of times poor Jesus has been called upon during this rendezvous. *Poor Jesus*, woken from his naps, pulled from his fifteen-minute smoke breaks.

"Someone painted the word 'fag' on your house? I'm so sorry to hear this, Chrissy. Why?"

"I don't know. I thought it was you. Sorry."

"It's okay. So, who's the fag, then? Are you—"

"No, no," Chrissy says. "Barnett is gay. He's engaged. To a man. They want to get married on the farm."

"Good for him!" Linda says.

"Is it?" Chrissy asks.

"Every human being deserves the pursuit of happiness. And someone around here is a homophobe! And a vandal! This is war!" Linda stands and paces best she can in the mess. "This goddamn town! You tell me who it was and I'll feed them to Murphy on his birthday!"

"Oh, Linda. I don't support hate but I don't know if I support gay marriage, either. What would John think of me?" Chrissy asks. "Am I letting John down if I accept this? What if this ends up in the church bulletin? This isn't the life I wanted for Barnett. It's scary—is there still AIDS? The images I've seen of the gays include leather and bondage. What if Barnett gets hurt in a—what's it called?—a sling? Oh, my God!"

"Chrissy, darlin', John is dead. Slings are fun. AIDS is treatable. Get over yourself."

"What about Father Perfect? He says gay marriage is 'wicked.'"

"He said that?" Linda asks. "Father Perfect is an ass. Always has been. He's tried to convert me for years. I think he just wants my land. And I don't think he hates gay people. You know Mae Robinson? Her girl is a lesbian and Father Perfect don't care one bit. Course, Mae Robinson doesn't have any money. Lemme ask you this: How many candles does Father So-Called Perfect sell ya every month? How many candles are ya buying to beg God to fix your boy?"

Chrissy's heels rise, and her thin calves start bouncing.

"And how many candles would he be sellin' ya if you loved and accepted your boy? And whoever that vandal is probably got all fired up because of Father So-Called Perfect," Linda says. "Week after week of being told there's danger—*those dangerous gays*—will make a person do something crazy. Imagine if his sermons every week were about doing acts of love. He's no better than a terrorist, if you ask me. And he gives away all that cheap church wine like it's a great prize, like he doesn't get all that shit from the diocese for free. Phooey! He ain't as pure as people think." Linda taps her temple twice, quickly, like she just solved the world's largest puzzle on *The Price Is Right*. "Feel better?"

"No," Chrissy says. "Now I have more problems. A vandal still on the loose. A conniving priest. A son who might hate me. A son I might lose forever. A wedding I maybe ruined. And a new crisis of faith."

"That's not all," Linda says. "You forgot one other big problem. You realize it's Sunday, right?"

Chrissy's face falls in her palms. "Oh, shit—I mean, shoot."

"You missed Mass today, sinner."

"I've had a lot going on this morning."

"The good news is you can go have a chat with Father Perfect right now. And you'll have him all to yourself."

Chrissy's attention suddenly shifts back to the knife in her pocket.

Chapter 14

Countdown to Damnation:

7 days / 9 hours / 10 minutes

SAINT Michael the Archangel Catholic Church smells like the candle clearance rack at the Walmart. The air is thick with guava coconut fusion and evergreen sapwood. Sometimes, the scents are at war. But in the end, anything burns if there's enough heat.

Barnett is sitting far from the scented altar, tucked in a back corner. That way he's surrounded on two sides—left and back—by pieces of the original church barn attached to the wall. He likes to smell the old days, the old church. He's warmed by the thought that even a stinky barn—just like at his farm—could be a house of God.

He's sweaty and wearing an old T-shirt and running shorts, but he figures he can atone for it later. He didn't intend to run to church, but his feet found their way here, a familiar place to think, though most of the thinking was done on the run, as Barnett slipped into his track star hypnosis. Every step was charged with anger at the graffiti, anger he carried here to church, to confront Father Perfect. He must know something.

The old prayers still loll around Barnett's mind, marbles on the loose, so comfortable in there, so permanent they're free to dally, to drop and pop into Barnett's mind at any time, in any place, in any order. There's the Our Father, the Hail Mary, the Prayer to My Guardian Angel.

Angel of God, my guardian dear, to whom his love commits me here . . .

Barnett was an altar boy. He traversed the aisles of this church many times. He loved the cassock. And forget being the smartest in school, he cared about being the best at altar service, standing behind Father Perfect during Mass, closer than almost anyone else to the Eucharist, closer than almost anyone else to God. He rang the bell just right when Father Perfect held up the body of Christ. He practiced ringing that bell on Sundays after church let out. Really, he loved being in the church when it was empty. He had special access to God.

Until—*What kind of apple was it?*

Once Barnett started peeling the layers, religion seemed arrogant and puerile, and at the same time dangerous—creating followers who were aggressive in their ignorance. Barnett came to see religion not so much as brainwashing, but as brainless. It all falls apart if you dig too deep. A Big Mac is delicious until you find out how it's made.

Our Father, who art in Heaven, hallowed be thy name . . .

Another word for culture is branding. Those gold crosses around everyone's necks, the wine, the bread, the priest's colorful costumes, the hymnals—it's big business.

The flames in the scented candles, each a flickering, burning hope for some poor soul—they're paying for the church's new carpet, the thick marble altar, a ticket to Heaven.

It's a shame, Barnett thinks, because it brings him so much comfort. Under all that science in his head, under all those walls around his heart, he's still the kid in love with order, rules, containment. Maybe he's still a bird who loves a cage.

Religion lowered his blood pressure. Gave him access to the metaphysical. Had him believing in conscious unity. Until it didn't.

Hail Mary full of grace, the Lord is with thee . . .

Barnett recites prayers like poetry in his mind until a booming voice interrupts. It echoes off the walls and the pillars, as if the voice of God is calling: "HEY!"

"GAHHH!" Barnett jumps from the pew. His shriek—like the sharp gasp of a dying balloon—also bounces off every surface, the kind of sound that makes a grown man blush.

The blur of the room settles into focus and Barnett sees, lit by the dim chandeliers and flickering candlelight, Chrissy. "Mom?"

Barnett grabs his chest to feel his heart. "Don't tell anyone about that sound I just made." He cocks his head and gives a coy smile, one he keeps in rotation for moments of generosity. He sits again and motions for his mom to join him.

"Why are you sitting all the way back here?" she asks.

Barnett shrugs. "Too risky up front. In case God is a Catholic. I want to avoid bolts of lightning."

Chrissy sits and a loud CLANK echoes through the church—the knife in her pocket awaiting its birthright.

"What was that noise?" Barnett asks.

"Murder weapon," Chrissy says.

"Uh oh. Who did you kill?"

She looks at Barnett and smiles. Sometimes looking at him feels like meeting him all over again. Her focus falls on his clothes. "What in the heck are you wearing?"

"I was out for a run," he says. "How did you know I'd be here?"

"I know my son," Chrissy says.

The remark seems to echo in the church—even louder than a grown man's shriek or the thud of a pocketknife. *I know my son.*

The phrase rattles in Barnett's head—*I know my son.* "How well did you really know me?" he asks.

Barnett's prayers emerge from memory, but Chrissy's prayers rise from her heart. *The Lord is my shepherd, I shall not want.* It's the

Twenty-Third Psalm. It's the prayer Chrissy chose for the back of the prayer card at John's funeral. The front of the card featured Jesus in a white robe, light shining from his exposed heart, his long wavy hair flowing. "Do you have any pictures of Jesus with short hair?" she asked the funeral home director. She had to drive three towns over to make the arrangements. The funeral director didn't laugh or ask questions.

"No, ma'am," he said, politely.

Chrissy was prepared to explain herself. She was prepared to say John was a clean-cut type, respectable type. He didn't like long hair on men. Even on God.

I know my son.

In the silence, Barnett keeps his eyes focused on the altar. "Did you ever think I was gay?"

He maketh me lie down in green pastures.

Chrissy liked Psalm 23. She had an overwhelming number of options but thought John would appreciate the farming references.

Chrissy also had to pick out an inscription to be printed in bold across the top of the back of the card, above the prayer. It was free. "This one is the most popular," the funeral director said, pointing in a big binder to a card with the quote *In Loving Memory*.

Chrissy winced. *Who would say such a thing? How can it be loving, when someone is reduced to memory?*

"This one," she said, pointing to *Gone but Not Forgotten*.

"We don't have to talk about it, if you don't want to," Barnett says.

The problem, now clear to Chrissy, all these years later, is that *Gone but Not Forgotten* is a lie. For John was not, and is not, "gone," not completely. He's with Chrissy; her decisions are still *their* decisions. She still braces to answer to him for things she's done since his death, things that he might frown upon—painting the farm blue, upgrading to the better chicken feed, opening these gay wounds.

Forgive me, John.

Chrissy looks at Barnett briefly and looks away. "Do you remember your friend Alec Arceneaux?" Chrissy asks.

"With the mole on his forehead?"

"No," Chrissy laughs. "That was Timmy Collins. Alec Arceneaux had the deaf dog."

"Macaroni," Barnett says, his smile warm. "That poor dog."

"Ah, yes. Macaroni." Chrissy squeezes her thigh. She leans harder on the pocketknife in her back pocket. She prays God will find a way to stop her, if he doesn't want her to tell the story. "Alec was . . . very . . . different. And you were so drawn to him. You were in second grade. We lived in Metairie. I was still a teacher at your school—"

"Different how?"

"Ohhh," Chrissy says, exhaling deeply, buying time to find the right words. "I didn't know any gay people back then. We didn't—your father and I. But there were always stories, on the news, you know? Gay people were, it seemed, everywhere. Except Louisiana. Except . . ." Chrissy pauses.

"Except for Alec Arceneaux," Barnett guesses.

"I don't know. I still don't know. When I would see you two playing together, I would go up to you and try to get you to play with someone else. I know that was wrong, but," Chrissy stops. "Then we moved to Mader and you changed schools and it was no problem. Alec isn't the main reason we moved away, of course."

Chrissy wonders about Kelly Arceneaux, Alec's mother. She was a kind woman, the type of person for whom no other description is as apt or whole as the word "kind." Kelly worked all the fundraisers, bake sales, whatever was needed. And she had that crazy dog. Barnett loved the dog. Kelly, a mother of a misfit. Chrissy wonders about Alec. *Forgive me, Alec.*

"So, you knew?" Barnett asks.

Chrissy wipes tears at her eyes. "I didn't think the little things were clues. I thought it all normal. Then, your dad helped you run more like a boy. He taught you a firm handshake, you know? You dated some girls."

Barnett laughs.

"No mother ever wants to think her child is ugly. And no mother wants to think her child flawed. But I did have this feeling—I've always had this feeling—"

She can't finish.

"It's okay," Barnett says.

She takes his hand. "Your whole life I've had this feeling that I would always be the only woman in your life."

Barnett Durang, he is at last seen.

"How did you know I'd be here?" he asks.

"I got lucky. I came here to commit felony assault on Father Perfect. You?"

"I came to feel some happy memories. Well, not happy. Simple? To feel a more simple time. And maybe ask Father Perfect some questions. He offered me a cup of coffee and I figured why not. He'll be back any second."

Chrissy nods and lets her head drop slowly, something too heavy on her mind. "Did you know Linda next door is a lesbian?"

"Every red state woman is kind of a lesbian, Mom."

"I'm not!" Chrissy protests.

"You don't have to be so defensive. It's not a disease."

"Is it crazy that we can live with the mystery of God?" she asks. "Or the mystery of Wi-Fi or something? But the first time we don't understand another human being, the mystery of another human being, it's just too much to overcome?" Chrissy turns to Barnett. "I'm sorry. And I'm sorry about your troubles with Ezra. I'm sure you two can work it out. I hope you work it out. I don't know anything. And maybe life is such that you can't do it wrong. If I'm really honest, I like Ezra. More or less."

"He's worried you're lonely."

The church reclaims its silence, its two occupants yielding to the quiet whisperings of a sacred Sunday afternoon. And Chrissy yielding to a realization.

"I'm a little lonely, Barnett." She looks at her achy hands. "I'm a little scared for my future."

Barnett doesn't tell her the rest of what Ezra said. He holds back, as always, though this time he's not being a coward; this time he's being kind, maybe kind as old Miss Kelly Arceneaux.

"I've made a dumb mess of everything," Chrissy says. "Dang it!"

"It's not just about you, Mom. Ezra and I also fought about the wedding and how much to change the farm. The farm is me. I don't want them to erase that," he says. "I don't want them to erase you."

It's the sweetest thing Barnett could have said to her in that moment. She squeezes his hand; maybe she's his SSRI after all. They look at the beautiful altar and the rows of flickering candles. "One of those is lit for you," Chrissy says. "Father Perfect says it's to heal you."

Chrissy and Barnett sit side by side in the pew, in the stinky church, quietly looking dead ahead. Barnett stares at the altar and wonders about the meaning of life, the universe, how he still wants to believe the world is magic. It's as if a magical world is his default, and when rational thought emerges he has to euthanize it all over again. Heartbreak anew. Like his heartbreak over Ezra.

As Chrissy stares at the altar, she considers the nightmare of some poor soul having to dust the nooks and crannies of all those stone-cold, hollow statuettes.

Chrissy sighs. "I do like the idea of fireflies."

Barnett slides closer to his mother. "This is how they sit at cafés in

Paris," he says. "They sit side by side. Unlike here in the US where we sit across from each other. The idea is that being side by side immediately makes us friends. But face-to-face, it's perceived as a threat in our primal brains."

Chrissy leans and lets her shoulder bump with Barnett's. "I think if we were the same age, and we were in Paris, and I wasn't your mom, I'd sit beside you at a café, shoulder to shoulder, and I think we'd be great friends."

Mother and son grin at each other until the moment is broken by doors opening and Father Perfect emerging from outside, letting in sunlight, bringing in judgment. "Hello there."

"Go wait in the car, please," Chrissy says quietly to Barnett.

"I'd rather stay and—"

"Please," she says, her eyes rippling with a mission, her hand touching his leg, and sending more than enough of a signal.

Barnett stands and slips out—passing Father Perfect in the church doorway like he's not even there. "But I have your coffee," Father Perfect says, holding up one of two Styrofoam cups he's carrying. He turns to Chrissy. "Everything okay?"

Chrissy stands and walks slowly down a side aisle, away from Father Perfect, toward the altar.

"Things with Barnett took a turn?" Father Perfect asks.

"You could say that," Chrissy says, her fingers sliding over one pew, and then the next, closer and closer to the front row, to the flaming prayers sending their black smoke up to Jesus.

"A firm position on this is essential. We are in this world, but not of this world. The Bible is clear on Hell, damnation, sodomy. Think of your dead husband—"

Chrissy stops and turns her ear toward him, daring him to finish. He doesn't. She continues onward to the rack of candles, the orange glow warming her heart, the heat warming her skin.

"Which candle is lit for Barnett's soul?" Chrissy asks.

Father Perfect puts the two cups of coffee down on the empty pew closest to him. He walks to the front of the church, to Chrissy. His footsteps echo in the space. Soon, he's beside her. He points to one of the flames dancing, really twirling up a storm.

Chrissy bends over and blows it out. "He doesn't need it," she says. She stands up, stiffening her spine, and looks at Father Perfect; he doesn't look at her. She starts to walk away, up the center aisle, making a beeline for the open door.

"There's something I have to say," Father Perfect begins.

"Do you?" Chrissy asks, stopping halfway to her freedom. "Do you really have to say whatever it is? Why do you have to? Is it a moral obligation to *say* what you *need* to say? Will you face eternal fires? The kind that you say my son will face?" She tightens her Farmer Mom belt, she folds one hand atop the other in front of her, politely. "There's this thing called breaking up with friends. Some people do it and some don't. Most friendships end with ghosting. Have you heard of that?"

"Yeah, Chrissy," Father Perfect says.

"It's Mrs. Durang," she replies sharply.

"Yes, I've heard of it, *Mrs. Durang*," Father Perfect says.

"I wonder what happens when we end our relationship with religion? Or churches? Do we break up with them? Or ghost them?"

"You don't break up or ghost. You stay in it, you trust the institution, you trust the Holy Spirit."

"No, *Richard*," Chrissy says, defrocking the man who for so long has lorded over what her heart is allowed to feel. "Those are all big words that only mean I should be trusting *you*. And it's clear to me now. You and I don't have the same values. No one is *perfect*."

The nearby candle flames flicker in unison for a moment, like a hushed pattering of applause from beyond. It briefly catches Father Perfect's attention. Then he turns back to Chrissy. "This church is full of your allies. You need allies."

"Oh, look around! Your goddamn church is empty!" Chrissy yells, her words echoing off the old wood planks on the walls and the ornate carvings on the altar, causing the holy water to ripple in the bowl by the door. She pauses, expecting some retort from the heavens. "Hmm, interesting," she muses. "No bolt of lightning."

Father Perfect stares, calculating, listening for a cue from God, some inner prompt for what to say next, what to say to not lose another congregant, especially not one so wealthy, at least by Mader standards. But Father Perfect's God must be busy.

"Did you vandalize our home?"

"No," Father Perfect says. "Absolutely not. I don't know anything about it and I'm very sorry to hear about it—"

"Do you know who did?"

Father Perfect shakes his head, looks at the floor. He shrugs. "I don't know. It could be anyone and—"

"Yeah, anyone, right?" Chrissy interrupts. "Interesting. That it could be anyone in your congregation. Anyone! What does that say about you? About what you preach every week?"

Father Perfect's scowl adjusts not a bit, a man with such a loud voice is now speechless.

And so Chrissy fills the silence. "Excuse me," she says, her head high, summoning all the dignity of a superhero. She walks back up to him so they're face-to-face. "In Paris, they don't socialize like this because it's threatening." Her eye contact with him is palpable. "But I don't feel threatened at all."

She turns and walks away, sunshine from the open door guiding her. "Goodbye. I have a wedding to plan. And a homophobe to find."

She pauses, turns, stares him up and down, and standing in the doorway, backlit by God, she says, "*Another* one."

"DID he know anything?" Barnett asks, standing outside his Mom's truck.

"No."

"Did you kill him?"

"Let's just get home," she says.

Barnett rushes around the Chevy to the passenger side and hops in.

"You saw Linda last night," Chrissy says. "She was getting her dog who ran away. I gave her your dad's old clothes—and a bunch of other junk—after he died. But she didn't paint the house. Someone else is the vandal."

"Are you sure?"

"Linda likes you. She invited herself to your wedding, her and four or five dogs and maybe a ferret. Sorry the ghost wasn't your dad. He would be real proud of you. And so am I."

"Ezra says this wedding thing is, like, *your* coming out. As having a gay son. As being proud of a gay son. And he says that's why it's been hard on you."

"Maybe. I guess it is."

"What about the wedding?" Barnett asks.

"Let's figure it out," Chrissy says, backing the truck from the parking lot.

Barnett flashes that smile. "What about the graffiti?"

"You know what?" Chrissy says, letting exhaustion have its way with her bones, letting her shoulders rest, her jaw unclench. "Let them also paint my truck, my barn, my forehead! I love you. And I don't care who knows it." She pulls the gear into drive, taking her boy away from Saint Michael the Archangel Catholic Church, taking her boy home.

Chapter 15

Countdown to Damnation:

7 days / 8 hours / 22 minutes

EZRA Tanner's preference is to lounge in an oversize European bean-bag chair by a swimming pool somewhere in southern Italy. Instead, he has carried two old bags of horse feed—now filled with hay to make big outdoor pillows—to the end of the private driveway of Polite Society Ranch. He's taken up a sort of country residency, all to issue a massive apology.

He made a sign and everything. All he needs is to see his sweetheart as he comes home from wherever he needed to dash. Chrissy is also gone. Ezra hopes she doesn't come home and discover him before Barnett.

Ezra's look today includes an oversize sweatshirt with plaid patterning, worn over a long dress shirt, which has camel-colored tassels and is tucked with bedraggled style into his blue jean overalls. It looks like something off the runway in Milan. But in Mader, the tassels look like hay.

He's good at showmanship; he excels at communication; he's getting better at dramatic gestures of apology. But Ezra Tanner is not good at waiting. Still, he tries. The first hour goes by, then the next. He scrolls his phone to its near death, having read what feels like the entirety of Twitter. The straw hat on his head breaks the lion's share of the heat.

He allows it. Exhaustion, sweat, and exertion will only make him seem more sincere in his sorrow.

He eventually allows his head to dangle slightly.

When he wakes, it's to the sound of tires screeching to a halt and the pounding of threatening steps toward him.

Ezra blinks to force sleepiness from his vision, just as his brain registers an oafish man rushing toward him, reaching for Ezra's arm when—

"HEY!" Ezra shouts, standing up and causing The Oaf to stop abruptly and step back, and then step back once more. A large piece of cardboard, the size of a poster board, wobbles from Ezra's lap onto the ground.

Stunned, The Oaf eventually cobbles himself together. "I thought you were bags of trash."

"And you just stop in the street and go through people's trash?" Ezra asks.

"Yeah," The Oaf says. "I was about to get me a free scarecrow."

"I'm not a scarecrow," Ezra says. "This is fashion!" He motions to his look and then bends over and picks up the piece of cardboard that fell from his lap. It reads in big bold letters: "SORRY."

"What are you sorry about?" The Oaf asks.

"Elitism. Arrogance. Insensitivity. Lacking mindfulness. Impatience with the universe. Distrust of the universe. Not that the universe is real by any certain stretch of the imagination. Everything exists only in our minds. But I get ego-identified. As if a self is even real. As if it's even something that needs defense. Ever. Believing words. Words are just sounds. And our brains say this or that like they have substance but they don't. They don't globally. They might locally. Locally, they can feel real. Very real."

The Oaf kicks at the ground with one of his heavy boots, puts his hands on his hips, his belt hugging his belly like a ring on a beer barrel. His right thumb rests on the handle of a hunting knife.

Ezra looks out at his rusty truck, stopped half on the highway and half in the ditch, still running, pouring out thick exhaust, readied for a quick escape. "Sir, you're committing a traffic violation, I'm sure of it. Leave me alone to stand out here awash in my sorrow."

"Hey, are you one of them weirdos getting married at this farm?"

"No! Not anymore, at least. That's why I have the sign, you see? I have to apologize to my fiancé or it's all over. I've wanted this since I was a kid. I've dreamed of being in love with a guy like Barnett."

The Oaf blinks quite a few times, as if Ezra's words are a sandstorm.

Ezra continues, "Nichole has so many great plans and ideas. And, you know what, she can pull back. She can honor the farm and, you know, our elitism. I didn't mean to insult his mom. No way. Who do I think I am? The decider of all appropriate human behavior?"

"You seem like . . . You seem like . . . you could be a decider," The Oaf says.

"Thank you for saying that," Ezra says. "That's very sweet. But still. I have a lot to learn. I want to learn it all with Barnett, together."

"Yeah," The Oaf says, gears turning faster now. "Yeah, I think you're one of them weirdos."

"Hey, how do you even know about the wedding?"

The Oaf steps forward.

Ezra steps back. "You live around here?"

"What's it to you?" The Oaf asks.

"What were you doing last night?" Ezra asks.

"Nothing that concerns you," he says, stepping forward again.

HONK!

The two men hear the Chevy's horn before they know what else is in store for them—Chrissy piloting her truck directly at them. She honks again and shouts from her open window, "Leave that boy alone."

She slams on the brakes just feet from The Oaf. Barnett is already out of the truck. He's running to Ezra, and Ezra is rushing to him. "I've been out here for hours! I want credit for that!" Ezra yells as they embrace.

The Oaf, again, blinks in awe, or fury.

"Are you okay?" Barnett asks. "Are you in danger?"

Ezra shrugs.

Behind them, Chrissy jingles the Chevy's keys as she makes her way toward The Oaf.

"Hi there, Miss Chrissy," he says.

She approaches cautiously. "What are you doing out here, Lionel?"

But Ezra answers. "We just had a misunderstanding is all." He turns to Barnett. "It's been going around. I treated you like trash. I'm sorry."

"No, *I'm* sorry," Barnett says.

"No!" Ezra says. "I made you this sign." He holds it up and Barnett traces the letters of the word "SORRY" with his finger.

"I was wrong to say that about your mother," Barnett says. "You weren't totally wrong about the farm. Or my mom."

"Um, he was a little wrong," Chrissy says.

Lionel watches the volleying back and forth.

"I was a lot wrong about your mom," Ezra says. "You weren't wrong about my mother."

"Yes, I was. I'm sorry."

"Where were you?" Ezra asks. "That was the longest run in history."

"Church," Barnett says.

"Dammit!" Ezra throws his sign to the ground. "I could have made a dramatic apology by busting open cathedral doors, the dust and sunshine backlighting me, your head spinning to see the chaos, your eyes used to the dark and candles, struggling to see in the light, the blasting light, light like the very sun, those very candles but burning to infinity."

"That's actually kinda beautiful," Chrissy says.

"Mom has turned a corner," Barnett says to Ezra.

Chrissy turns back to Lionel. "What are you doing out here?"

"Sorry. I thought the little weird one was a pile of trash."

"That little pile of trash is my future son-in-law!" Chrissy says. "Now, go on before I call the police."

Lionel laughs. "Looks kinda like the police are already here, ma'am."

Chrissy turns to see a uniformed officer walking up the drive with Nichole.

"I've been giving him the lay of the land," Nichole shouts.

"Afternoon everyone," the officer says. Then, pointedly, "Hi, *Barnett.*"

"Hi, Paul," Barnett says.

"It's Officer Stolton, now."

"You two know each other?" Nichole asks.

"We went to Mader High together," Officer Stolton says.

"We ran track together. He always came in second place if I recall. Right, Paul?"

"You can call me Officer Stolton, understand?"

The tension escalates, a balloon filling too much, too fast, until Ezra pops the quiet as if with a needle. "Geez," he says. "In that case, I'd like to be called Moonshadow Stardust." Ezra throws his hands up. "What is it with everyone's attitudes?"

Officer Stolton asks, "Y'all trying to bring trouble? Like those ones suing bakeries for not making you a gay cake?"

"Fuck off, Paul," Barnett says.

"Watch it," Officer Stolton says, stepping forward.

"You think we asked for this? That we painted 'fag' on our own home?" Chrissy asks.

Lionel giggles at the word "fag."

"'Sup, Lionel," Officer Stolton says, his tone suddenly friendly and charming.

"Just drivin' through," Lionel says.

"I think you need to question this man," Chrissy starts, pointing at Lionel.

"Nah, nah, nah," Officer Stolton says. "I've known Lionel a long time. He's a good, Christian man."

"Aren't they all," Chrissy says.

Officer Stolton turns to Nichole. "Thanks for all the info, ma'am. I'll do my best to find out who did this."

Chrissy glares at Lionel. "Should be a short list of suspects."

"Short?" Officer Stolton laughs. "Your business is all over Facebook."

"Facebook?" Barnett asks. He looks at Ezra. "Are you back on Facebook?"

"No," Ezra says, and turns to the officer. "We don't even have accounts anymore."

Officer Stolton looks at Lionel. "*We* do," he says.

"Everyone knows?" Chrissy says to herself, a reckoning underway in her mind, heavy gears clicking into place.

"It's a small, quiet, family town out here," Officer Stolton says. "I'd strongly recommend you reconsider your life choices."

"To accommodate your bigotry?" Barnett asks.

"To accommodate your safety," Officer Stolton says.

"Everyone knows?" Chrissy asks, again. Then, "Everyone knows," she declares, almost relieved. She looks at Officer Stolton. "We will not go back in the closet!"

"Wait, so, that's a 'yes' on a little gay wedding next week?" Ezra asks.

"No," Chrissy says.

Barnett scratches his head.

"Not a *little* gay wedding," Chrissy says, marching to her truck, turning her back on Officer Stolton, Lionel, and also the past, the regrets, the fears. As she climbs in, she looks back. "We have a week! Let's get this place ready for a big gay wedding! Nichole! You're unleashed! Let's do it all!"

Nichole bounces in place. "Step one: get paint. Let's cover up that graffiti!"

"Wait," Chrissy says. "What if we don't cover it up?"

Chapter 16

Countdown to Damnation:

6 days / 9 hours / 19 minutes

NICHOLE's app reads: 6 days / 9 hours / 19 minutes.

The app is a wedding countdown clock that delivers alerts to Nichole's smartwatch with a small vibration, which Nichole likens to an electrocution.

"I hate you," she says, watching the clock's decorative tick, tick, tick. It's the most efficient tool for staying on track, but it's also the most stressful $1.99 Nichole has ever spent (except for a dining table she bought last summer that turned out to be for a dollhouse).

Nichole looks up from her watch. She stands tall in the living room of the bright-blue farmhouse, a big navy-blue sheet hanging behind her like a theater curtain. "Morning!" she says.

"Morning, Nic," Ezra says groggily. "Did we have to get up so early?"

"There's a lot to be done. My watch is driving me crazy. Everyone here?"

"Yes, for God's sake," Victoria says, shifting on the sofa, a glass of La Gracè Vino in hand. "The tension is making my skin crawl."

"No. My mom isn't here yet," Barnett says, as his mother enters the room.

Chrissy surveys the scene in her living room and zeroes in on the sheet hanging from the ceiling. "Jesus! Did you put screw holes up there?"

"Behold, the Big Gay Wedding," Nichole says, grabbing the sheet with one hand.

"That's my good sheet," Chrissy says, as Nichole tugs it, ripping it from the screws.

"It *was* your good sheet," Victoria Tanner says.

Sheet tatters fall to the ground, along with a dusting of the ceiling, revealing a tripod holding a brown corkboard featuring a map of the farm that would rival something in *Lord of the Rings*. It displays the property cartoonishly, including a very large outline of the land with colorful labels tacked about and bits of red yarn strung from one pin to another, to another. The display is less wedding and more serial killer.

Nichole points. "Let's start here, at the main entrance. Holograms and cool lights are on the way. It's gonna be so cool when people drive up. I hope no one has a stroke." She shrugs. "Then, the valet—"

"Valet? Where did you find valet drivers in this town?" Chrissy asks.

"Leave that up to me."

"And where are they going to park all the cars?" Chrissy asks.

"It's a surprise," Nichole says, getting frustrated.

"Oh, God," Chrissy says to herself. "What have I gotten us into?"

"Then," Nichole continues, "guests will be led to the barn. Mother, how is it going, training the macaws to say 'Welcome' as people arrive?"

"What's a macaw?" Victoria asks.

"We'll chat after and recap your duties," Nichole says, shaking her head disapprovingly.

Barnett stands. "Transformation has begun on the barn, stables, chicken coop, and kennel."

"What kind of transformation?" Chrissy asks.

"You'll see. Don't worry, Mom. We won't touch the house."

"Thank youuu," Chrissy says.

Nichole gives a thumbs-up. "Have all invitations been texted, emailed, Facebooked, tweeted, Instagrammed, Snapchatted, telegrammed, and snail mailed? Let's start with you, Durang family?"

"Yup and yup," Barnett says for himself and Ezra.

"I invited everyone on my Christmas card spreadsheet," Chrissy says. "I'm getting a lot of quick yesses, which I assume is because of lookie-loos."

"As long as they're cute," Nichole says. "And what about the Tanner family?"

"I invited everyone who owes me money," Victoria says. "That ought to cover it."

"Now, on to things that are NOT moving according to plan," Nichole says. "We had to kill the organic fireworks because the kind I wanted were banned after maiming several careless children. We also can't have a chef for animals because that guy turned out to be a fictional character from a *New Yorker* article I misread."

"What about media coverage?" Chrissy asks.

"I have friends at the *Post*," Victoria says before finishing the glass of wine in her left hand.

"Fear not," Nichole says. "We're about to launch a blitz the likes of which this town has never seen! We'll all be famous soon!"

"I think we're aiming for empathy, not fame," Chrissy says.

Victoria feigns offense. "Speak for yourself."

Quietly, Barnett asks Ezra, "What color vibes are 'worry'?"

NICHOLE's app reads: 5 days / 12 hours / 2 minutes.

Nichole climbs atop a picnic table, clipboard in hand, towering over an assemblage of workers she hired from the parking lot of Larry

Massa Lumber Yard. "Artisans!" she starts. "You are heroes! Your names shall be remembered for generations! You're part of something larger than yourselves! You are part of love, history, rebellion—"

"Hey, you pay twenty-eight bucks an hour, right?" someone calls out.

"Yes. Yes, sir, thank you. Thank you for asking."

"When's lunch?" another shouts.

"Listen up! Your lunch schedule, a handwritten thank-you note, and a list of your daily tasks are in a little waxed-canvas gift bag with your name on it on an entry table in the barn. You'll also find a Polite Society Ranch bandanna and free tube of SPF lip balm. And if you have any questions—" she pauses and looks into the crowd. "Pauley? Where's Pauley?"

In the mass, a familiar, blushing face emerges.

"Hi, Pauley," Nichole says. "Isn't he wonderful? He can answer any of your farm questions. Right, Pauley?"

Pauley tips his cowboy hat to the crew surrounding him. "Uhh—"

"Now, if you'll excuse me, I'm expecting some major news outlets to return my calls any second. Have a great day everyone!"

NICHOLE's app reads: 4 days / 3 hours / 18 minutes.

Nichole checks on the lake being dug for the swans; they'll arrive from Florida any time now.

She checks on the construction of the stage and gazebo.

She checks on Victoria's efforts to teach the macaws to say, "Welcome."

"Look at these twats!" Victoria rages, motioning to the birds. "I think I'm allergic. And they keep making fun of me!"

Nichole grabs her mother's shoulders. "Remember, *you* are the apex predator!"

Above them, in the barn rafters, construction workers install chandeliers.

Outside, fairy lights dangle. Tables are built around trees, turning them into centerpieces.

Workers adjust holograms that project downward on the entry drive, alternatively turning the pavement and ground into white marble, a red carpet, a yellow brick road.

NICHOLE's app reads: 3 days / 4 hours / 5 minutes.

The Baker—a willowy man out of France who could just as easily be out of *The Muppet Show*—is hard at work, making a mess of the kitchen, to Chrissy's dismay.

"What's going on with this guy?" she asks.

"I flew him in from Paris," Nichole says. "They hate deodorant there."

"Yeah, but what the heck is he making?"

The Baker hums the children's lullaby "La Petite Poule Grise" as he constructs his masterpiece. He appears to be making a cake of four male feet. Well, not four feet, four ankles. Four naked ankles. The bare feet of two people. Nearby are molds for calves and thighs and—other parts.

"I'm getting nervous," Chrissy says.

"Oh, Chrissy. A big gay cake is mandatory and this stinky Frenchman is the best. Don't worry. I commissioned something special. A cake, a sculptural work of art, depicting two men, one delicately resting his tongue upon his partner's long, thick—"

"Absolutely not."

"Why do you hate art?"

"It's pornography!"

"It's marzipan!"

"*Mes chiennes!*" The Baker interrupts. "You desire taste?" he asks in his thick accent. "*Vous allez l'adorer!*"

"I'm so sorry," Nichole says. "I can't understand you."

Chrissy closes her eyes and tries to ignore their French guest. "What's going on with the media, Nichole? It's important to have some support."

"I'm working on it," Nichole says. "I have a huge lead but I can't talk about it this second because I have to go pee in the yard. I'm creating a urine boundary around the whole farm to keep predatory animals away. The guys who tend the horses told me it works every time. I could use some help." She looks to Chrissy. "Wanna join and—"

Chrissy slowly turns and walks away.

Nichole looks to The Baker. "Do you have to pee?"

The Baker fears he couldn't possibly have correctly translated Nichole's question, but to play it safe, he also slowly turns and walks away.

NICHOLE's app reads: 2 days / 1 hour / 19 minutes.

At the entrance to Polite Society Ranch, a white Lexus with dark tinted windows turns into the drive. One of the artisans installing lights at the front gate flags it down. "Can I help you?"

The dark driver's-side window comes down, revealing a woman who's not quite nouveau riche, but trying desperately to manifest it. "Are you security?"

The artisan laughs. "Nope. I'm doing the electrical tech stuff. There's no security. These people are spending at least three K on digital sequins for the driveway and not a dime on protecting it."

"I'm Jessica—"

"We all know who you are," he says. "The news reporter will be here any minute, they told us. Be nice to her, they told us. So she'll write something nice about us, they told us."

"Aw. Well, it doesn't work like that."

"You're not nice?"

"I prefer to say I'm honest."

The man points. "There's a reserved parking spot for you over there."

The man turns away and Jessica lets her foot lift slightly off the brake, then reconsiders. "Hey, what do you think of gay weddings?"

The man turns back. "This is gonna be a gay wedding? Interesting."

"Do you think it's immoral?"

"What if I did?" he asks.

"I guess you could quit. Not support it. Or protest—"

The man shrugs. "Protest? This wedding pays my bills. Gay money is still money. Real immoral is me not being able to pay my bills. That's even more immoral. Corporate greed. Who's protesting that? You know, people are out there buying all these home security systems, but burglaries are not as big a threat as wage theft. You should do a story on that!"

"Right," Jessica says. "Okay. Thanks."

He shouts as she rolls up her window, "Maybe you should do a story on how real welfare is that corporations don't pay any tax and yet they use our roads and bridges and pollute our air and water, and don't pay their employees a living wage so they need food stamps."

Inside the blue farmhouse, Chrissy sits nervously at her kitchen table, looking up as Nichole enters.

"The media is here," she announces to the gathered, which is only Chrissy. The kitchen has been cleared of workers just for this interview, The Baker using this chance to go to town for more tools of frosted indecency.

Nichole steps aside to reveal Jessica behind her. "Chrissy, this is Jessica Thoreaux of the *Picayune Tribune*. She asked specifically to chat with you, first. So, I'll leave you two to it while I go check on

Celine Dion's dunking booth." Nichole raises her eyebrows at Jessica. "A little nugget you might want to include in your feature."

"Colorful, thanks."

"You're welcome." Nichole raises her eyebrows again before leaving.

Jessica sits near Chrissy, crossing her legs, letting her floating foot bob up and down as if in sync with the ticking kitchen clock, as if she's anxious, or hungry. She pulls a small tape recorder from her purse, pushes record, and puts it on the table between them. Her smile has hardly a false note, but behind her eyes she's plotting. *This could be a sensational exposé*, she thinks. *I could call it "The Sodomite Grooms of the Greater New Orleans Area,"* she thinks. *I could win awards*, she thinks.

Chrissy offers coffee, donuts from Rhett's, Hershey's Kisses. Jessica declines: there's work to do.

"Are you nervous about the wedding?"

Chrissy exhales. "Yes."

"What makes you nervous?"

"Ohhh. My son. He's . . . all I have. I don't want—" She stops. She restarts. "I want him to be happy, all the time and forever."

"So are you going along with this wedding just to make him happy, just because you have to?"

"That's the interesting thing," she says. "I don't feel like I have to. I want to support him. I can't say I want him to be gay, but I do want to support him."

"Hmm. You *want* to. Does that mean you don't really support him?"

Chrissy laughs. "Don't try to confuse me."

"Did you always support the gay wedding?"

"You know, I realized it's important to support my family, my son, one hundred percent."

"But the gay wedding. Do you support that one hundred percent?"

"What is this?" Chrissy asks. "Are you digging for dirt?"

"It's not dirt. It's truth. It sounds like the mother of the gay groom had—maybe still has—cold feet."

"If you're going to put all this in bold print, you make sure you include this: I love my son. I'm proud of him."

"Gay pride?"

"Mother's pride! Muddy the water all you want by putting the word gay in front of words like wedding, pride, and son. Pride doesn't have to be something wild. Pride is the opposite of shame. And I may not understand every sexual variation in every living soul in this world, but one thing I'm not is ashamed of my son." Chrissy stands, the opposite of an invitation. But she says, "Follow me."

Chrissy escorts Jessica to the side of the house, to the "FAG" graffiti. It's untouched. It's not painted over or hidden in any way. There's a bucket nearby full of an assortment of permanent markers, small paintbrushes, and sample-size cans of paint. There's a sign for guests that reads, "What's *your* message?"

"Interesting, right?" Chrissy asks. "A way to reclaim and reframe."

"Mind if I take a pic?"

"Go right ahead. And then I have to let you go. You understand? There's so much to be done."

Later, back in her white Lexus with dark tinted windows, Jessica relaxes. She again pulls out her little tape recorder. She pushes record and dictates, "Are they asking for trouble? Are they inviting it? This family has been attacked once. Will they be attacked again? We'll find out. I'll be at the wedding to get all the dirt. This is Jessica Thoreaux reporting."

Part 4

Time's Up

Sweetheart, nary a wedding passes without at least some sour air. Never fear, relief awaits! Summon a toothful smile! Brighten your eyes! No matter the folly, your worry is for naught. Find solace in this, every wedding is a gay affair.

—*Mrs. Jeannie Laffite's Undisputed Guide to*
Respectable Southern Nuptials,
volume III, page 107
(copyright 1912 by Mrs. Jeannie Laffite)

Chapter 17

Countdown to Damnation:

1 day / 11 hours / 5 minutes

CHRISSY looks at herself in a mirror in the corner of her bedroom. She's wearing an outfit presenting as fun but responsible, exactly as she requested of the saleswoman. It's an off-white dress with a skirt made of lace, intended for blue jeans to be worn underneath, a little country, a little chic. She's wearing her gold chain, her late husband's ring dangling near her heart: *Chrissy & John*.

In the mirror, Chrissy can see the reflection of her big picture window. She can almost see the reflection of her old life.

She sits on the side of her bed. *A weight is lifted*, she thinks. But something heavy remains. She thinks of Barnett, single and celibate and caring for the farm and his mother. And that dream—the dream that felt so real—is so much closer to being dead forever.

Farmer Mom feels as if she's part of a play. The curtain is going up, and she hasn't learned her lines, hasn't even read the script, hasn't approved her wardrobe, isn't sure she's totally on board with the plot. And yet, out there are the lights.

Am I one hundred percent in on this? she wonders.

Am I being carried away?

Am I going to drown?

She looks out the window at her transformed farm. Chrissy's bedroom window is huge, about the size of the big-screen TV she used to have in the nineties, before TV became untoward, impolite, and theirs ended up on the curb with a piece of junk mail taped to the screen upon which she wrote in big black marker, "TRASH." Young Barnett scribbled under it, "works fine," and it was gone before Chrissy could even bring out the remote.

Nothing on that big-screen TV was ever as interesting as what Chrissy has seen out of her bedroom window over the decades. She's never seen a comedy as good as Barnett, in his clumsy youth, chasing chickens. She's never seen a drama as touching as her late husband helping a sheep give birth. Or a show as gripping as the one she's a part of right now—alone in her big bedroom, celebration lurking on the edges of her life, casting light upon something that she once believed should be in darkness.

Chrissy stares out her window. So much is transformed, so much stripped away, so much changed, like an invasion of termites who want unconditional love while they feast.

She watches Barnett change a few light bulbs in the string that crisscrosses the backyard. Ezra is there, too, assisting, holding the ladder. Chrissy imagines they're talking about her—how she's been acting strange, how she tried to ruin the wedding once and might try again.

But outside—"Hold it steady!" Barnett is saying to Ezra.

"Babe, it is not moving."

"My body is wiggling."

"It's a cute look on you."

"We're not even married yet and I'm already fantasizing about divorce."

The two guys laugh.

In her room, Chrissy imagines they're laughing at her.

Chrissy looks to the stables, watching as Pauley and Nichole chat. Nichole is gesturing, animated. The two of them seem lovely together. Mismatched, but lovely. Chrissy considers their youthfulness, imagining their zeal. She wonders if they, too, are talking about her—how they connived, how they pulled a fast one, how they changed her mind about this whole thing.

In reality, Pauley is saying to Nichole, "I used to breed horses full-time."

"Wait! *You* would breed—"

"No, no. Not my . . . not with my . . . you know—not personally."

"Oh!" Nichole says.

"We use horse semen."

"And they have that at, like, Target, or—"

"I . . . extract it," Pauley says, as seductively as possible. "Wanna see how?"

Nichole recoils. "You're a pervert and I'm repulsed!" Then, "Which way to the equine masturbatorium?"

The two walk out of Chrissy's sight, snapping Farmer Mom from her trance.

She reaches to her nightstand and picks up a gift. It's *that* gift, still wrapped in thick, crisp, glossy-white paper with a sturdy red-velvet ribbon tied into a blossoming bow. She's been reluctant to handle it too much. How much touch can one thing take before it stains, scars, revolts, breaks apart?

She flips it over, roughly, jamming her fingernail into the paper covering one of the box's folds. She tears a hole and rips the paper off, the scraps and the bow—once a proud burst, now a spent waste. She stares at the white box that for weeks was hidden within the wrapping.

Chrissy pulls—rips—the box open. She lets the cardboard and the tissue paper inside fall to the floor as she stands and frees the gift inside. It's a belt. She holds the buckle in her fingers and lets it dangle like a dead cottonmouth. When the craftsman handed her the belt—*Farmer Son* stamped upon it just like her Farmer Mom belt—the smell of the leather was intoxicating.

She walks to her closet, steps inside, and turns on the light. Three nails are driven into a shelf. The first nail is for her Farmer Mom belt. From the second nail hangs another, equally abused old belt, "Farmer Dad." Chrissy touches it with fondness. *Oh, John.* On the third nail she hangs the gift, the new belt once destined for Barnett, "Farmer Son," a dream that remains just that, and will forever, probably. She looks at the latter two belts together—Farmer Dad and Farmer Son—and thinks, *two belts, two deaths.*

There's a gentle knocking on her bedroom door, and a familiar voice. "Miss Chrissy?"

"Yes, Ezra?"

"Almost time for dinner."

"Thank you," she says.

"Oh, and the wine delivery is here."

"Thank you," Chrissy says again, then pauses. "Wait. What wine delivery?"

"Back it up," Victoria yells. "Into my mouth," she adds, under her breath.

The pickup truck, filled with cases and cases of red wine, slowly backs into Chrissy's carport. "What's up?" Chrissy asks.

"You're almost out of wine," Victoria says.

"I could have gone to the market."

"No, no," Victoria says. "They only sell La Gracè Vino in bulk to churches."

"Yeah. So how did you—"

"I'm officially a reverend!" Victoria shouts. "My business manager is friends with the business manager for the Pope."

The truck stops and the driver hops out, tips his cap at Chrissy, opens the tailgate, and starts to stack boxes on a dolly.

"This is a lot of wine."

"My treat," Victoria says.

"I wasn't planning to serve wine."

"This isn't for the rehearsal dinner. This is for me. I just told you: *my* treat. I couldn't have been more clear." Victoria puts her hands on her hips.

"Hard to argue with that."

Victoria relaxes, shakes her hair into place. "If you need me, I'll be in my room not speaking with Winston."

As she walks away, Ezra approaches Chrissy. "What's all this?"

"I'm formally worried about your mother's drinking."

"What about it? Has something changed?"

Chrissy motions to the truck, the bottles of red wine, the cases being unloaded into the carport. "It's escalating."

"Is it?" Ezra asks. He grabs a bottle, spins it around, points to the label, and hands it to Chrissy.

"Dinner in five," he says.

Chrissy reads the label aloud, "La Gracè Vino, Vin Cabernet Sauvignon, Supérieur Désalcoolisé." She shakes her head. "I can't read Italian, or whatever. What does it mean?"

Ezra shouts back as he walks away, "It means you have the sweetest heart. It means you really care about the people around you. Maybe too much. Maybe, even when you don't have to worry at all."

Chrissy looks back at the bottle. "This says all that?"

But Ezra is already gone, carefree, maybe careless, but seemingly determined to be happy on the eve of his happiest day.

EZRA is drawn to the lights of the private ambulance parked in the private driveway. The back doors are open. A gurney is out and set up with crisp, fresh, white sheets, patiently waiting for tragedy. Backlit by the strobe lights, beside the gurney-in-waiting, is Paw-Paw, in a wheelchair.

"You're back!" Ezra says, approaching slowly. "And in a fancy ride."

"When y'all don't come pick me up, the home shuffles me around in this thing."

"And I recall you were promised a roller coaster."

"I feel cheated," Paw-Paw says. "But, the ambulance comes with a nurse. And I like the attention."

As Ezra gets closer, his eyes widen. The sequins and glitter and cubed bits of mirror glued to Paw-Paw's outfit—jacket, vest, pants, and shoes—hit Ezra like an acid trip. "Whoa! Is that Elmer's suit?"

"Nice, huh?" Paw-Paw says, raising his arms like he's a preacher, causing a waterfall of mixed nuts to fall out of the sequined pockets. "GODDAMMIT! You can take a man out of Camille Manor Retirement Pavements, but you can't take Camille Manor Retirement Pavements out of the man."

Ezra hands Paw-Paw a little white paper cup—the kind used for ketchup at a greasy fast-food joint—filled with Paw-Paw's meds.

"Harassing my nurse, eh?" Paw-Paw asks.

"She's grabbing a bite and asked me to pass these along to ya. Looks like there's a little something for everything in here." Ezra pauses, leans forward. "Everything," he stresses. He waits a moment. "I'm sorry."

"Vitamins, really," Paw-Paw says. Then, "Don't tell anyone." Then, "How'd you know?"

"I had a student with leukemia. Different regime, but she was also on Bosulif."

"No one else knows?"

Ezra shakes his head, *no*.

Paw-Paw laughs. "And I thought you were a bum."

"I don't like secrets."

Paw-Paw looks down at the pills. "You know something? My life has been mostly black and white. It was bland and awful for some long stretches. I only have a little time left to add color and make it stick. All the pictures of me are so serious, sad. I want to make—and leave—some happy memories." He looks up at Ezra. "Don't ruin my last act."

"You have some water to take those?"

"You know what? I think I'll wash these down with a little champagne. For a special occasion, okay? Who knows how many more I'll get?"

"Fine with me," Ezra says.

"Will you fetch me a glass?"

"Be right back," Ezra says.

As the boy walks away, Paw-Paw looks to the transformed land. The barn is covered in white, billowing fabric or vinyl that hangs—no, flows, in ripples and waves—from the roof to the ground and from the nearby trees to the roof. It's an adult version of a child's fort. It's as if the barn, once blue and nice but functional, is now a white ghost barn, its eyes looking out, its mouth waiting to consume the guests. The other structures are similarly transformed—the kennel and stable and chicken coop. The chickens look like happy floating clouds—thanks to a black light idea cooked up by Pauley and Nichole.

The house remains bright blue, Chrissy's steadfast grasp of grounding. Beyond the back porch, Paw-Paw looks as his odd family, his family-all-of-a-sudden, gathers around the same picnic table where a few generations of Durangs to date have shared so many occasions and announcements. Seats are filling, seats that for a time have been empty—Paw-Paw's wife, Frances, is gone, his son, John, is gone, his own youth and vibrancy are gone, along with thousands of moments he wishes he could take back, live differently, live with more humor and color.

Paw-Paw pours the pills from the little cup into his palm. He examines them, lets them roll around, considers what the bead- and bean-shaped medical marvels would feel like if they stuck in his throat, the tumult they would cause in his stomach. He tightens his fist around them. His hand shakes with force, his knuckles turning red and then white as he feels at least a couple of the orbs pop. He opens his hand and then smashes his palms together. He grinds and grinds, then opens his hands and looks at the mess of powder and chips and thinks, *What beautiful colors.* Together, they remind him of a small terrazzo flowerpot his mother treasured in the house outside of New Orleans where he grew up, a home long ago destroyed in some hurricane, a life long ago washed away by a flick of nature's finger.

He tosses the remnants of the crushed pills in the grass and claps his hands together, dusting them off as if he's done it a million times, as if getting rid of salt from a handful of nuts.

WINSTON sits at the picnic table beside Victoria, the lights from Paw-Paw's nearby ambulance turning the rehearsal dinner into a Michael Bay movie. Though, to Winston, the lights may be crazy, the vibes are more Nora Ephron, lovey-dovey and strangely brimming with rom-com energy. Something joyful seems afoot, a feeling Winston doesn't have very often.

He looks with awe at the wrinkles on Victoria's face—*My, how pretty she is, even after all we've been through.* He looks at the shape of her mouth, the thinning of her lips, and the sharpening reemergence of her cheekbones.

Winston notices her shaking slightly, even more than in the last few days. He notices her dabbing a spot of perspiration, and another. He's not certain, but he thinks there's been a reduction in redness and inflammation in her nose and cheeks. And of all of it, he thinks, *Very curious*.

Winston wants to reach out and touch his wife's hand, to marvel aloud at their experience together, the memory of their own rehearsal dinner all those years ago, the one where Victoria's mother bawled the whole time, not from sentimentality, but because she had been in charge of the cake and had dropped it. Guests laughed at her; a few kids ran up and started eating the unsullied parts off the ground with their hands. But Winston and Victoria didn't care: they didn't give a damn about anything outside of each other's arms, at least on that day.

But now, Winston stays still, stoic, observant. He won't reach out for his wife's hand—he can't—because it's already occupied, holding tightly to a full glass of red wine.

Ezra rolls Paw-Paw up to the picnic table, to one side of Barnett. Ezra sits on the other.

Chrissy takes her place, politely.

Nichole stands. "As the wedding planner and twin sister of the groom and officiant of said wedding, I'd like to welcome you to the rehearsal dinner. Let the festivities begin!"

Waiters in tuxedos emerge from the white fabric–enshrined barn with trays and trays of food. They circle the table and lean forward to present their first offerings—three-cheese chicken penne, a deconstructed quesadilla burger, brewpub pretzels with beer cheese dip.

"The rehearsal dinner is sponsored by Applebees," Nichole says, sitting quickly. She looks at Ezra. "I know it's trash but I had a craving. Have you had their Fiesta Lime Chicken? They use real fiesta!"

Plates are quickly filled, meals quickly consumed. Everyone is stuffing themselves—everyone but Chrissy. She stands. "Excuse me, Miss Officiant, wedding planner, Nichole, twin sister of the groom. May I say a little something?"

"Speeches are after dessert," Nichole says, her mouth full of a crispy, boneless hot wing.

"It's just, I'm too nervous to eat. And I'd rather do my speech while your mouths are stuffed so you can't yell at me or laugh at me."

Nichole rolls her eyes. "It's impossible to make traditions with you people! Fine! Do whatever you want. Maybe we need a little anarchy."

"Are you sure?"

"Yes, yes," Nichole says. "Let's hear it for the mother of the other groom."

To a round of applause, Chrissy smiles demurely and adjusts her lace skirt with blue jeans underneath, though it needed no adjusting. She looks at Ezra, who's smiling. She reaches into her back pocket and pulls out her little orange notepad.

"I can't believe it was almost one week ago that I stood here," Chrissy says, "and aggressively refused every single thing that has brought me so much joy or aliveness in the last six days. But, still, some serious things need to be said." She's poised and confident. She looks at Barnett. His glowing smile downshifts to polite.

Chrissy looks back at her notepad and flips the pages—past the notes about the last Mader Elementary tour, about Pauley's schooling and departure, about Barnett's arriving flight. She stops at the list of Ezra's cons, her list of offenses and grievances.

She scans the list. She winces and looks at Ezra. "Do you mind if I read some of my first impressions of you?"

"I'm begging you," he says.

"They're highly offensive," she warns.

"Even better," he says. "Go deep. I love it. I'm not even kidding."

Chrissy examines her list. "First thing I wrote down is that Ezra laughs too loud."

Faint giggles spread like a contagion around the table. Victoria holds up her glass of wine. "He gets it from my mother. May she rest."

"In peace?" Nichole asks.

"Doesn't matter to me," Victoria says, immediately refilling her mouth with La Gracè Vino.

Ezra looks at Chrissy. "Sorry for being so loud."

"No, no," Chrissy says. "Don't be sorry. My first impression of you was your laughter. Laughter! Joy! That's what laughter is, that's what you brought with you. You brought laughter to this little farm. And shouldn't we be so lucky that all our laughter is loud."

"What else?" Nichole shouts. "He's a butt kisser sometimes. That on your list?"

"Hey!" Ezra shouts at Nichole. "Don't help her, jeez."

"That's on here," Chrissy says.

"OHHH," the table cries out, more like a sporting event than a wedding rehearsal dinner.

"Being an empath is a heavy burden, okay?" Ezra says playfully. "And butt kissing can be fun. You should all try it!"

"Gay propaganda!" Victoria says.

Ezra adjusts his hair and Chrissy points. "Unkempt hair," she says. "That's on my list."

"Guilty," Ezra says.

"Guilty of being beautiful," Chrissy says. "Your hair is incredible, kid." She shakes her head and sets her hair free. She blushes, looks at Ezra, and fluffs up her bangs.

"I like it wild," Ezra says, with others around the table shouting and jeering their opinions.

"Baby steps," Chrissy says, as she gently returns her hair to it's original state. "Baby steps."

When the ruckus settles, she continues.

"All right. I also wrote 'offensive dress' and 'disgusting' and 'drug addict.' Some of these, I guess, I can skip if they're obvious," she jokes.

"It's called microdosing!" Ezra says.

"Excuse me, Mom?" Barnett raises his hand. "Is this just a roast of Ezra?"

Ezra calms him. "Shh, I think this is good, really. This is how you develop intimacy."

"You really want intimacy? With my mother? You should read *your* list of grievances against her."

"Maybe during my vows," Ezra says.

There's laughter, but not from Chrissy.

"I don't really care for your hair," Paw-Paw says to Ezra. "Are we still on that one?"

"You're just jealous, Paw-Paw," Barnett says.

Chrissy continues reading from her orange notebook. "I wrote 'woke.' But I've learned that's just another word for being a good neighbor, for caring about other people." She looks down at her list, almost ashamed. "I wrote 'bad teacher.'" She looks at him. "I'm sorry."

"It's okay," he says. "I'm not for everyone."

"It's just, at first I thought you were not present with the kids," Chrissy says. "Truthfully, you are so very present with them, you vanish among them, you become one of them. You understand them. That's a hallmark of a great teacher in every sense of the word."

"Thank you," he says.

"Don't thank me yet." She turns back to her list. "I wrote that you're 'indiscreet.' But I've learned that you're just an efficient communicator. You're honest. That the truly offensive choice is to ignore things or be vague." Chrissy takes a deep breath. "And, Ezra, I wrote that you're 'greedy.' And that was before I was the one who ate all of your chocolate."

"Not *all* of it," Ezra says.

"If that's true, it's not for a lack of trying. Thank you for sharing with me. Thank you for sharing your life with me, with Barnett. I love you both. To the grooms," Chrissy says, raising her glass.

"To mothers," Barnett says.

"To life," Ezra says.

"Meh," Paw-Paw says. "But I'll toast to youth."

"To love," Nichole says.

"To wine," Victoria says. She turns to Winston. He raises his glass, seems about to make a proclamation, but nods instead. Everyone nods back.

"Cheers," Chrissy says, her voice cracking.

Chapter 18

Countdown to Damnation:

0 days / 21 hours / 40 minutes

DARKNESS falls on Barnett and Ezra, a curtain coming down on their exhaustive youth, this night being the finale of their status as single men. They mark it not with fear or seclusion. They don't mark the close of something. Instead, they celebrate the beginning, with verve, a blanket, and an open sky.

"I'm nervous," Ezra says, scooting closer to Barnett as the two guys lie on the ground beside the new gazebo, camping out at the very site of their destination wedding, considering the future they will begin in earnest, with vows, in several hours.

"Nervous about building a life with me?" Barnett asks. "Or about the vandal?"

Ezra snuggles into Barnett's thick arms. They smell each other, their bodies, their hair. Both feel comfort in the scents of love, of what feels like home, even right there in Mader, right there near the wall where someone painted the word "FAG."

"We're going to look so tired in our wedding pictures tomorrow," Barnett says.

"You'll look tired. I'll look pensive, which is kinda my brand," Ezra jokes.

The men kiss sweetly and silently under the night sky, Louisiana heat broken by the late hour, the ground still radiating the last bits of the day's warmth.

"I probably wasn't going to sleep much anyhow," Barnett confesses.

The vandal. The graffiti. The wall. It's taken so much bandwidth from everyone in the family, but especially from Barnett, who's had to fight an enemy at home, maybe more than one. It's been affecting his sleep since he first saw the ghost. And now he knows ghosts aren't real. But hate is.

He's been considering: *Where would a vandal strike next?* Multiple areas would seem to be ideal—the stage, the reception tables, the gazebo. *Ah, yes. If you only have one shot, that's where to take it—the gazebo, where the vows will be said.*

And that's where Ezra and Barnett are hunkered down, waiting, prepared to defend themselves, to defend their new family.

"I love you," Ezra says.

"I love you, too," Barnett says.

In the country, procuring a bucket of shit is easy. The sloshing contents of a Porta Potty would be sufficient. There are piles of animal excrement all over the landscape of Mader. The town is built on shit. Sheep shit, horse shit, dog shit, human shit. The smell, awful, but one kinda gets used to it.

The vandal's feet step carefully, heavily on the Louisiana ground. He's weighed down by a mission—one he views as holy, a calling from God—in addition to his thoughtfully collected, and very full, five-gallon bucket of excrement and related fluids, some animal and some not.

It started as a joke, a plan hatched over beer and giggles, a bunch of tough construction guys laboring their pedantic talk about the penis and the rectum. Their fits of glee eventually took dark turns, one extreme to the other.

The man, the vandal, knows the route. He and Barnett forged these paths as kids. They'd drawn maps. *There's the oak. There's the gap in the fence. There's the house*, he remembers. "We're spies," he would say to his pal, young Barnett.

And young Barnett would say, "Yeah! And best friends!"

The vandal retraces those long-ago steps under the Louisiana sky, the atmosphere in repose, considering what hell to unleash later today, or not.

And the vandal walks past their old fort, past the old slab of concrete within which he and Barnett's initials are still carved, to the pinch of land between the properties of Chrissy Durang and Linda the Hoarder.

The vandal steps over the rusty barbed wire, still collapsed under the rotting tree trunk the two boys tossed onto it decades earlier—the tree trunk was fresh and alive back then.

The vandal could retrace all their steps, except the ones Barnett took without him, when Barnett grew up and left town, left it all behind, left all of them there, the class of misfits, his so-called best friend, abandoned just as he abandoned all the animals at Polite Society Ranch.

Barnett thinks he's better than me, the vandal thinks.

They all think they're better than me, the vandal thinks.

They all think they're so proper and polite and fancy because they save animals, he thinks. That the Durangs save, means the vandal destroys.

He walks around the stables and the dog kennel and the chicken coop, moving this way and that, knowing the exact steps to take to avoid triggering the motion lights, the same exact steps he took to spray-paint "FAG" on the house, a move that only seemed to empower the sin, not dissuade it.

And finally, this time, he'll give them pause.

And finally, the target is in view.

And finally, the vandal is at the gazebo.

BARNETT and Ezra are asleep, both of them dreaming. The gentle steps toward them don't alarm them; they don't hear anything coming. A hunter knows how to move slowly, how to make his steps sound like the rustling of a breeze.

The vandal is surprised to see them, the two faggots out there by the gazebo, snuggled together, cuddling sin. They're supposed to be defending their love, guarding their wedding, and yet here they are asleep, displaying their weakness, such inferiority.

The vandal slowly, gently puts the bucket of shit down. He slowly, carefully peels the lid off. The odor doesn't affect him, doesn't cause him to flinch, doesn't make him take his eyes off his targets.

The vandal picks up the bucket in his two thick hands. He takes one soft step forward, and then shudders at—

"Clay Parker, you put that down this instant!" Chrissy shouts from pitch darkness.

The vandal is shaken slightly, the bucket of shit sloshing about. He worries some may have spilled on him. A flashlight flicks on. The vandal turns toward the light behind him. All he can see is the illuminated barrel of a shotgun.

"I smelled you a mile away," Chrissy says from the shadows.

Another light flicks on as Barnett and Ezra jolt up, flinging off their blanket and standing. Now two beams shine on the vandal, on Clay.

His face twists, all nerves and fury. He turns back to Chrissy.

"Bucket of shit for your faggot son," Clay says, now turning to Barnett and Ezra. "And his faggot *friend*." Clay storms forward.

CLICK-CLICK. He stops. He knows the sound. A shotgun is being cocked.

"I don't want to," Chrissy says, her eye in the sight. "But I will." The flashlight wobbles slightly in her shaky hand.

But Clay has farmer ears, and hunter ears. He knows the sound of a Winchester, a Colt, an M1 Garand. He knows the tones of bullets and shot and shells. And Chrissy's pump of the barrel was flat, hollow, recognizable: empty.

Clay crosses the imaginary line, rushes toward the gazebo and the boys.

Barnett and Ezra scream, "No!"

Clay flings the contents of the bucket like he does every season to spread grass seeds in his dad's pasture.

The shit sprays with an undeniable THWOP-THWOP across the gazebo, and an undeniable smell.

Barnett is off his feet instantly, flying in the air, forward, jumping to the former friend basked in the unsteady glow of Chrissy's flashlight.

The puddle of shit spreads and follows the beam of the flashlight in Ezra's hand. The mess almost touches the tips of Ezra's shoes.

Barnett's shoulder pounds into Clay's chest, both men flying up and landing hard—Clay on his back and out of breath. Both men claw the earth, wet and stink all over them. Clay fights and flails. But the two men, they know each other's moves.

CHA-CHUNK.

The sound is clear this time, honest as a rattlesnake's tail. And Clay stands and takes a step back, away from Barnett.

"It's loaded now," Chrissy says. "Get outta here before we decide to press charges."

"Decide to?" Barnett says. "We're definitely pressing charges, Mom."

"There's worse things," Chrissy says. "I'm calling his mother."

"You need to call the police," Barnett says.

"I want this over right now," Chrissy says. "And anyway, he's friends with the law. Everything is country complicated out here. Right, Clay?"

"Fuck you," Clay says to Chrissy. "And all y'all."

"What the hell, man?" Barnett asks. "I thought we were friends."

"You're right. We *were*. Then you cut me loose the first chance you got. California. And then all these rumors about you. And I had to defend you. And for what? An email every now and then? And then, it's true. You're a fag and you're not even trying to hide it!"

Clay turns to Chrissy. He spits in the dirt, not at her, but not away from her, either.

Chrissy's grip on the shotgun softens. Her eye leaves the weapon's sight. "You're lucky that spit landed in the dirt or I'd make you clean it up," Chrissy says, the words feeling familiar in her mouth. Then, "Clay, you got a boy? Red hair? Freckles?"

Clay looks at her suspiciously.

"Well, he's welcome here anytime. So are you and the missus."

"Mom!" Barnett protests. "He's a vandal, criminal, bigot, asshole!"

"Don't use that kinda language on my farm! This is *Polite* Society Ranch. Not *Grudge* Society Ranch."

Clay leans from one foot to the next. "You sure are confusing me, being so nice while still aiming that shotgun at my head."

"I'm polite," Chrissy says. "Not stupid. Now, Barnett, you apologize to Clay."

"ME! For what? I'm not—"

She lets the shotgun's aim lower to the dirt. "Listen to me! You're not just of my cloth you're of my world, my land. You're standing on my soil, every inch a part of me, my tears, my blood, the blood of every animal we've hustled in order to own this place and send you to California. This land killed my love. This land is taking my health. This land is burying me and I welcome it. But until that day, this land is a sovereign nation called Chrissy Durang and when your feet are planted on it you listen to ME! Now, Barnett Durang, you apologize this instant. Clay was your friend and you abandoned him. I know how that feels."

Barnett glares at his mother. He looks at Clay, awash in confusion. He looks at Ezra, shocked but also comforted by his lover's smile and nod of encouragement, even after all these red vibes. He looks back to Clay. "Sorry," he says, eventually.

"Now, Clay, you apologize for painting 'fag' on my house and throwing poop all over my new gazebo."

"Sorry," Clay says, eventually.

"Now, git," Chrissy says.

Clay hesitates a moment, then turns and walks into the darkness.

Ezra asks Barnett, loud enough for Clay to hear. "Is it worse when the hate is from someone you know?"

In the shadows, Clay stops to hear the answer.

"I guess Clay was not someone I ever knew. Not really."

At that, Clay vanishes into the void, back onto the path whence he came, toward the overgrown landmarks of his youth, past the rusty barbed wire, past the initials in concrete, past the old fort, and maybe, hopefully, forging a trail to a new way of thinking.

Motion lights click on as Victoria arrives. "AHHH!" she screams.

"Mother!" Ezra scolds. "You're too late. The scream should have come like seven minutes ago. And you're gonna wake Dad and Paw-Paw."

"What happened?" Victoria asks. "What stinks? Ezra, are you making perfume again?"

"We caught the vandal," Ezra says.

Barnett wipes filth from his arms. "Well, Mom caught him."

"Your eye!" Victoria says, approaching Barnett. Ezra holds the flashlight up to see a stretch of blood dripping down Barnett's cheek, a gash above his eye.

"Oh, no!" Ezra says.

Chrissy approaches and puts her hands on Barnett's face, forcing the small wound open, then closed, inspecting whether he needs stitches.

"Ahh!" he winces.

Chrissy's hackles lower. *His face*, she thinks. *It's ruined*, she thinks. But the shotgun at her side helps dull her motherly instincts. Plus, she's seen enough from injured kids to know there's not much to do at this point, when a hospital is not in order, and the only truth is really to embrace it, to simply, immediately, start healing.

"It'll be fine," Chrissy says. "Maybe that face could use a scar or two. Let's get inside."

The future family walks back to their farmhouse, all the worse for wear, some dripping more than others. "Hope you fought back," Victoria says.

Barnett pushes down on his injury to slow the blood. "Nah. Mom did all the hard work."

Victoria turns to her son. "Ezra, what was your contribution to defending your family?"

"Disassociating," he says.

Chrissy stops. "Actually," she says, "y'all go ahead. I'm gonna go check on Elaine."

In the barn, in her special corner, Elaine could hear all of it, the shouting, the rumble on the ground. She recognized Barnett's voice when he cried out.

At all the ruckus, Elaine worries. She wishes she could stand and protect herself and her family, see what's going on, but she can hardly lift her head. She's not sure whether she's lost her sight or the barn is dark, until a sliver of light spreads across the ground, illuminating the darkened decorations, the gently swaying chandeliers.

Chrissy enters quietly. "Hey, sweetie," she says. This causes not a single macaw to stir. They all know who Chrissy is here to see.

"Baa," Elaine cries softly, managing the slightest shimmy of her frail body.

Chrissy reads the movement as restful, a simple stretch.

But really, what Elaine wants to do is leap up, lick Chrissy's face, awkwardly wrap her trotters around Chrissy's neck in an animal's attempt at the kind of hug she's seen Chrissy share with John and Barnett over the years. "The years, the years, the years; at a certain point they start to take back the joys they've given," Elaine would say, if only she could.

"See you in the morning," Chrissy says softly.

Again, Elaine lets out a weak "baa," which is the best scream she can muster, her best attempt at a cry to be held, to be comforted, to beg not to be left alone. But such comfort is not to be, not tonight.

Chrissy turns to leave and is startled to see the silhouette of a man in the barn's doorway. Her shotgun isn't pointed at him, but it can be in a flash.

"Thought I'd escort you home," Barnett says.

Chrissy relaxes, pops the shells from the weapon and shoves it under her arm as she closes up the barn and walks with her son back to the house. "Wanna help me hose the gazebo and lay down some sawdust and hay real quick?"

"Sure thing," he says.

"Don't dally," she says. "We've got a big gay wedding to throw tomorrow."

Barnett touches the injury above his eye. "Mom. It is tomorrow."

Chapter 19

HUNGRY animals don't care about wedding days. So when the sun starts to peek into Chrissy's big bedroom window, she's already awake.

The special day is here, she thinks, and then pulls the covers tightly to her chin, exhausted and emotional after a restless night that involved brandishing a shotgun on a trespasser. *Clay Parker. How could it be?*

Moments later, she reaches to her bedside, grabs her orange notepad, and flips to her to-do list, her to-worry-about list: "Check on Elaine, steam dress, decide on pearls or gold chain, run dishwasher again, put out fresh towels, check on Elaine again."

Elaine has been on Chrissy's mind since the vandal arrived overnight, as if the old sheep were calling to her. There was no falling back to sleep. Instead of counting sheep, counting Elaine, Chrissy has been counting odds: *Which morning will I wake to find Elaine has passed?*

And at the thought, Chrissy is up, out of bed, on her way.

She moves with purpose down the hallway. Victoria and Winston's bedroom door is closed, the couple no doubt exhausted from the night before, not to mention their busy, full-time careers of being an alcoholic and managing one, respectively.

She rushes past Ezra and Barnett's bedroom door. It's also closed, the guys almost certainly wrapped snugly together, tangled in the sheets of the childhood bedroom on the farm where they're scheduled to be married later today.

The sewing room door is closed; Paw-Paw is either asleep or lying awake, staring at the wall, a pastime that's practically an Olympic sport for people of a certain age, and especially for residents of Camille Manor Retirement Gardens.

Besides the doors closed on her, she surveys the other stretch marks left by a full house—dirty towels, dirty dishes, kitchen chairs askew, throw pillows out of place in the living room. Chrissy can hardly wait for The Baker to finish his aberration.

All of Chrissy's family and family-to-be are so supportive of the day's wedding, and yet Chrissy is the only one awake, alone in her worry not just about the crush of a wedding ceremony and party, but about the aftereffects, the trauma for the animals, the messes to clean up, both on the farm and in town, among the readership of Facebook and the *Picayune Tribune*.

Exiting that big farmhouse full of people, Chrissy feels the itch of loneliness.

Outside, the gazebo stands firm, gleaming white and drying quickly from the late-night hose-down. Sawdust and hay give the ground a fresh feel and a lovely scent, which covers the fading remnants of the more unpleasant ones.

The barn stands strong and tall, wrapped in whatever white fabric Nichole mustered up. It looks new and fresh. *Good for the party*, Chrissy thinks. *Good for them.*

The barn's highest window is dark, a sign Nichole is still asleep in the apartment up there. *No one cares as much as I do*, Chrissy thinks.

She grabs one of the barn's heavy doors and slides it slowly and carefully as always, until it's wide open, and the barn is flooded in earnest with the day's first light.

Chrissy is braced for the scene inside—the bars set up with alcohol, the potpourri of vanilla and patchouli, the chandeliers, the assortment of round paper lights of all colors, hanging from all rafters, macaws quiet, perhaps confused.

But she was not prepared to see Barnett.

"Morning!" he says. He has an Elmo Band-Aid above his eye. "Ezra insisted." He picks up a bale of hay. "Where does this go, Farmer Mom?"

"There," she says, pointing to Niles and Roz at the stables, who neigh and wiggle their lips.

"Sleep okay?" Barnett asks, but Farmer Mom is way past that—sleep seems like hours or days ago, so much lower in priority than what she's focused on right now—*Oh, Elaine*, her ward, her friend.

Elaine stirs and almost reaches for Chrissy, cries out for her with the kind of "baa" that only an aged throat can manage.

"Shh, shh," Chrissy says as Elaine stirs, trying to stand but having trouble. "It's okay, sweetie," Chrissy says. "I'm here," she says. "Please, don't go today," she whispers.

"Is it almost time?" Barnett asks. As with so many other ways of speaking the language of rural Louisiana, Barnett leaves off the rest of his question. *Is it almost time . . . to put her down?*

Elaine seems weaker, but Chrissy doesn't want to ruin the day's fun. Chrissy doesn't answer Barnett's question. She leans down and whispers to Elaine, "I love you, too."

"Do you still feed the pigs trash stew?" Barnett jokes, poking fun at the veritable feast Chrissy used to make for the pigs—a mix of sweet potato ends, cauliflower stems, browning bananas. "I can put a pot out."

"Pauley can do all that," Chrissy says.

"He's probably extra busy today," Barnett says. "I'm happy to help."

Chrissy thinks of her own wedding. Few pictures remain after floods, hurricanes, a couple of moves. And John didn't want a lot of pictures at the service. He wanted to live in the moment. She touches inside her collar, that gold chain, his old wedding band.

222 / Byron Lane

Together—mostly in silence—mother and son tend the farm, tend to the lives, including Chrissy's, that Barnett is soon to abandon. The chickens get their feed. The horses get their hay. The alpaca gets an apple first thing—he goes on a daily hunger strike without it.

By the end of their first morning's chores, mother and son find themselves again beside Elaine.

"She getting worse?" Barnett asks.

"She's tough. Mamas are tough. Mamas can handle terrible things."

Barnett shuffles past her. "You'll have to come visit us in California for future summers."

Future summers, Chrissy thinks. She immediately identifies her dysregulation, blue vibes, sadness, a reminder about what this day really means, a reminder she's truly hosting not just a wedding but a goodbye party for her son, for her hopes for him, for her hopes for her own old age and the dream of her farm living on past her through Barnett. Her happy summers with her son are over.

"You okay, Mom?"

"Yeah, yeah."

"Are you nervous?" he asks.

"More than you'll ever know."

"You still have doubts?" he asks.

"Normally I'd turn to Father Perfect to talk it out, but I hate him," Chrissy says. "I'd turn to Pauley, but he's swept up in it. I'd turn to Paw-Paw, but he's on your side, so to speak. I'd turn to you, but, you know."

Barnett looks down, nods his understanding.

"None of you are able to bring me peace with all this," Chrissy says. "I'm okay with it, more or less, but I'm not at peace with it. Not really. Not yet. You know? But I'm working on it. I really am. I understand that Ezra is special."

"I get it. And considering all that, I think what you're doing for us is pretty brave."

"Is that what it is?" Chrissy balks. "Calling it 'brave' is just another way to say it's not easy. It's better branding. But it doesn't make it right in my heart. And I'm so worried I need more time to make it right. I'm worried I need more time to process all this. And there is no more time. Sometimes I don't know if I can do it. God. I'm so sorry. Is it okay that I told you that?"

"If I don't see you at the service later today..." Barnett pauses, considers what he says next. "I won't hate you."

Chrissy laughs to herself. "I was expecting you to say something heartbreakingly devastating to me."

"No, Mom. I love you unconditionally."

They embrace and separate, and as her son walks out of the barn, out of her life, Chrissy touches her broken heart and whispers to herself, "There it is."

I love you unconditionally. Those were his exact words.

He's right, she thinks. *He loves unconditionally. And I do not.*

VICTORIA Tanner steps onto the front porch of Chrissy's home, into the early morning cool of wicked and sobering force, and takes a deep breath. "Ah, fresh air."

Her face goes instantly limp at the remark, as if all other stresses of her life evaporate and she's left with just one: *Something is terribly wrong with me.*

She glares at the Louisiana sky and hears an awful racket. Early mornings in Mader start not with the sight of sunlight but with the sound of bugs, the white noise of the day coming to life. Upon hearing the hum, Victoria sticks a finger in her ear, hoping it's something she can wiggle out.

Victoria chugs a coffee mug of La Gracè Vino. As she considers her new and increasing shakes, irritability, and sweating, she notices the dog.

The animal, a puppy, is country big. Gray like a storm cloud. Dark fur circles his caramel-colored eyes so he looks like an evil raccoon. His DNA—part terrier and part wolfhound—is perfected to quash nuisances and slaughter weaker challengers. He's a Build-a-Bear version of the perfect match for Victoria Tanner.

"Am I hallucinating?" Victoria asks, watching as the puppy moves slowly and deliberately, like a hunter, like a predator, as if he thinks he's invisible, toward her. "You do realize I can see you stalking me?"

The dog is on a mission. It is decided. He will pee on her.

The leg of Victoria Tanner, in black stockings and ballet-heel shoes, draws the little furry beast as if it's magnetic. The dog has no fear of her, though Victoria Tanner is the only person in the world who makes wearing a ballet heel look like an act of terror.

As the dog approaches, Victoria is seething at the landscape of her life—trees, humidity, insomnia. Her allergies are acting up—headache, cramps. She's shaking either from the heat or in anticipation of it. Sweating is somewhat understandable, albeit still unacceptable. And the mattresses here. *Are they stuffed with Brillo pads?* she's wondered, but hasn't—uncharacteristically—asked aloud, not even to Winston. *Something is definitely wrong with me*, she thinks. *Cancer*, she thinks. *My liver has finally turned on me*, she thinks.

The dog is closer, then closer still.

The nerve, Victoria thinks.

"Go ahead and attack," she says.

She's too irritable to be startled, a part of her even hoping for some kind of assault, any kind of bloody puncture that could get her to a hospital bed and propped up on real pillows and real painkillers.

Finally by her side, the dog makes a fatal mistake. As he lifts his leg to pee on her, he also lifts his head, and the two beings—one forged of status warfare and another of desperate escapism—make eye contact.

They share not just a look but a language, both resigned to the fact, and recognizing in the other, that neither of them belongs *there*.

Victoria Tanner's evil eye—perfected over years of scowling—penetrates deep into the dog's soul. The sheer power of her gaze, entering the dog's iris and triggering neurons and brain activity, evaporates his urge to pee. The dog puts its leg down and sits calmly beside Victoria like they've been training for this moment for both their lives.

Those caramel eyes, as if the creature has been practicing, have their own kind of magic—the opposite of an evil eye. And as Victoria's gaze penetrated him, his gaze penetrated her, in what was somehow the signaling of equals, equals among predators.

The dog looks out at the landscape of his life—trees, mystery—and looks up again at Victoria. He then looks down at the ground beside him. And back up at her.

"Oh, why not," she says. She dusts her butt, as if her sateen dress is filthier than the ground. And she sits beside the dog. He scratches himself behind his ear.

"Are you itchy, too?" she asks. She looks at the animal and he looks back at her, this time with no evil or magic or excretions exchanged.

"I don't want to murder and eat you," she says. "And that's yet another sign something is profoundly wrong with me."

CHRISSY finishes her rounds on the farm alone. She stops where she always does, in Elaine's corner. "Hang in there, sweetie," Chrissy says.

She surveys the barn again, the last time she'll see it before it's full of wedding guests and absurdities—Chrissy still doesn't understand the concept of a drag bar.

As she turns to leave, Chrissy hears something upstairs in the apartment. There's a loud mechanical sound and stomping, pacing. "Nichole," she calls out. "You okay?"

Chrissy slowly walks up the stairs until she's at the apartment door. She knocks. She hears more clamor, and Nichole shouts in distress: "Oh, shit, oh, shit!"

Chrissy grabs the doorknob—it's unlocked. She opens it slowly.

"Hatch, you goddamn monsters!" Nichole yells at a tray of firefly larvae positioned on the kitchen counter. She has a hair dryer plugged in next to the sink and is moving it wildly over the critters.

"Everything okay?" Chrissy asks.

"No!" Nichole looks up at Chrissy. Her hair is a tangled mess and her clothes are disheveled. "These stubborn firefly babies are late being born! And The Baker is having a terrible time with the crotch of the cake, and I haven't heard a whisper back from Celine Dion! Who's going to be in the dunking booth? I'm so scared I'll ruin the wedding!"

"I'm scared I'll ruin the marriage," Chrissy says.

"Hey, Nic," Pauley says, entering the apartment with an air of determination that quickly changes to a look of shock as he registers Chrissy.

"Oh, shit—I mean—shucks—I mean . . . Hey, Miss Chrissy," Pauley says. "I was just gonna tell Nichole that the valet drivers are done moving all the vehicles."

"Nic?" Chrissy asks, crossing her arms.

"Short for Nichole," Nichole says. "Thanks, Pauley."

"And what valet drivers?" Chrissy asks. "Oh God, where are you parking everyone?"

"On the street."

"That's gonna be miles away."

"Don't worry," Nichole says. "We hired the Mader High School track team to park the cars. They're great at hustling for long distances. And quickly. They have trophies."

"Do they all have driver's licenses?" Chrissy asks.

Nichole pauses, looks at Chrissy in her work garb. "I love your outfit."

Pauley pipes up. "Don't worry. Those kids are fast. They already moved all the farm's tractors and vehicles to make more room for the party."

"Wait. Did they move my Chevy?" Chrissy asks.

"They were very careful," Pauley says.

Nichole waves the hair dryer back and forth over the larvae. "It's okay, Miss Chrissy. You don't need your truck today, do you? Not planning a hasty getaway are you?"

Chrissy pauses, looks at Nichole in her sweats. "I love your outfit," she says.

VICTORIA sits on the farmhouse porch beside the pensive pup and wishes she had a cigarette they could share together. "Am I the first socialite you've ever met?" Victoria asks the dog.

Then, "Am I the saddest person you've ever met?"

Then, "Am I the sickest?"

She watches as the dog notices a fly. His eyes follow the little insect up and around and over and back again, his ears flopping in all directions like a young girl's pigtails.

"Is this the first fly you've ever seen?" Victoria asks.

But the dog's attention is already elsewhere, now watching a crow flying overhead, from one tree branch to another.

"Is this the first crow you've ever seen?" she asks.

The dog's dumbness is a sucker punch to Victoria's own sensibilities—or lack of them. She finds *herself* fascinated by the fly, by the crow. She follows the dog's gaze to a yellow flower bobbing in the breeze.

She asks, "Is that the first flower you've ever seen?"

She asks, "Is that the first flower I've ever seen? Ever *really* seen?"

As the minutes wear on, and the coffee mug of La Gracè Vino wears low, the engine in the skull of Victoria Tanner starts to roll, to warm up; old and rusted gears start to turn and almost topple from her head. The thoughts, all in a rush as if she's relieving herself, find escape in her mouth. "Nature!" she exclaims. "It's beautiful!"

A black ant trots bravely in front of her and the dog, and his big, gray, floofy paw tries to plop upon it, unsuccessfully, unsuccessfully, unsuccessfully, until finally it lands a blow, which does nothing; the ant continues on, unhurried.

Victoria marvels. "Is that the first ant we've ever seen together?"

A bee zigzags past them and the dog bounds up and goes after it. Victoria gives chase as best she can. "Come! Hey! Twat! Get back here!"

The dog bounces and bounces, a cartoon of its innocent self.

It flips and flops and twists and jumps until it's at the front of the farmhouse, in front of Paw-Paw Durang.

"Think this dog knows anything about macaws?" Victoria asks, out of breath from the exhausting jaunt of a few feet.

"Think this dog knows anything about homophobes?" Paw-Paw asks. "We got one out there by the valet."

Victoria's eyes narrow and she kicks her head back to refresh her signature steely bob. She looks at the gray, floofy beast beside her. "Ready to attack?" she asks.

Chapter 20

Countdown to Damnation:

0 days / 2 hours / 3 minutes

VICTORIA'S steps maneuver the gravel like she's Jesus walking on water, far from the performance of her first arrival to Polite Society Ranch. She passes gay pride flags on small dowels freshly planted along the walkway, a group of go-go dancers applying baby oil for the night's shift, a bank of valet attendants in rainbow sashes trying to do their job.

She spots the homophobic trespasser, a man standing by the front gate, hate in every tuck of his forehead wrinkles, raging at one of the young valet attendants. "I live in this town! I grew up in this town, right down the road there! Do you have permits for all this? All these cars out here? All this traffic? For a gay wedding? Sinners! I wanna see the permits!"

The valet attendant spots Victoria's approach and smiles. "Here she comes," he says to the angry man. "Here comes our permit right now."

The trespasser looks at Victoria and walks toward her. "Now, listen here," he starts, but Victoria holds up a finger as if to say *WAIT*.

The man stops talking. He stops moving.

Victoria advances, the dog by her side, his tail no longer wagging but stiff, unneutral, vertical for a few moments until it arches angrily over his back. His scruff stands up—and the same is happening to Victoria, the hairs on the back of her neck becoming like cactus needles; her tail would be stiff and threatening, if only she had one.

The man puffs up his chest, which only pushes forward his big belly.

Victoria and the dog, they're almost within striking distance.

"I don't believe in this," the man shouts.

Victoria Tanner is closing in on him, that finger still raised. He takes a small step back. For the first time in his life, he smells perfume that costs six hundred dollars per bottle.

"This is all the work of the devil!" he shouts.

Victoria's eyes are steely, confident, approaching.

The man steps back, again, again. "Who the hell are you?"

Victoria leans toward him. "The devil," she whispers.

BARNETT sits on his childhood bed, the one that's too small for him now, and was maybe too small for him then. The springs squeak as Ezra sits beside him, the two men freshly showered, wearing only their underwear, cleaned of the drama of the last many hours, many days, many weeks, maybe more. They're pushed together by the weight of their lives, by the crater in the mattress.

Ezra carefully peels the Elmo Band-Aid off Barnett's face. "Nothing a little concealer won't hide."

"Thanks, babe," Barnett says.

Their shoulders and thighs touching—Ezra marvels at Barnett's warmth, his blood pumping extra fast, worry rushing like a river through his veins. Barnett, in turn, marvels at Ezra's cool and calm, his steadiness in the face of pivotal life events.

Ezra puts his hand inside Barnett's, their fingers mingling so comfortably, all digits feeling at once at home, their bodies closer to peace.

"Can you believe we're doing this?" Barnett asks. He looks around his room—at the bicycle wallpaper, the old track ribbons. "Every night I slept in this room as a kid, I would fall asleep thinking about how I'd have a lonely life. How, because I was different, I'd never be able to love or get married. And now. God. Look at you. Look at us."

"How are you feeling?"

"A little sad thinking about all the gay men before us who couldn't do this. A little proud of all the heroic people who fought for us to have this day. A little nervous."

Ezra puts his arm around Barnett and squeezes. Barnett's shoulders are not the broadest Ezra has ever held. Barnett is not the most handsome, not the wealthiest, not the funniest. But none of the other men Ezra dated ever pinched his belly fat and said, "I love this part the most." No other person in Ezra's life has ever dried his tears after he cried watching a trailer for a terrible movie. No other person in Ezra's life has ever known instinctually when to bring home a pizza for dinner. Ezra Tanner never made love, not until Barnett, and each time, the act created more than something physical. Ezra Tanner, with all his crazy pagan theories about the cosmos, looks at Barnett Durang and feels a swell in his heart that makes him question whether there truly is a God, a benevolent superpower, some wisdom pulling the strings, and doing so with such perfection. Ezra laughs his too-loud laugh.

"What's so funny?"

"Want to hear some hocus-pocus?" Ezra asks.

"Absolutely."

"This bed is supporting us right now, right?"

"Barely," Barnett says with a little grin.

Ezra smiles. "What about the floor? It's supporting us?"

"Yeah."

"And under that? The dirt? It supports us?"

"I have a feeling I'm gonna need a science book soon."

"And under the dirt? The water, the magma, the minerals, they all support us? The trees, do they worry that the earth won't support them? Or that the wind is an enemy? Do the clouds worry about where they'll end up? Do birds trust their wings? A mosquito died millions of years ago—his life seems so small—until his fossil is found in tree sap, and the blood he sucked millennia ago educates and inspires generations after generations."

"You're saying I should trust you?" Barnett asks.

"I'm saying you should suck blood," Ezra jokes.

"You're my grossest lover," Barnett says.

"Nah. I'm not saying trust *me*. I'm saying trust *you*. Trust yourself. Trust nature. And remember, you're nature, too."

Barnett grabs his lover's leg, squeezing tight. "I don't always completely understand you. But I love you, my little mystery."

Ezra lets his hand fall on Barnett's bare thigh, his pinky plucking at the elastic of the underwear holding Barnett in place. "I'm just saying everything works out. And I love you, too, my little mortal."

"Shall we dress?" Barnett asks.

"I have one other question," Ezra says. "Do I wear my tux—"

"YES!" Barnett interjects quickly, knowing what's next.

"OR!" Ezra continues. "I brought my Victorian gown."

"Tux," Barnett says.

"Think about it," Ezra says, the men giggling, radiant.

THE homophobe at the front gate is soon joined by others, their dusty sedans and pickup trucks lining the ditch, the SLAM-SLAM of their vehicle doors signaling more, more, more on the way.

The growing crowd is generally well-dressed for the occasion, like they just came from Mass.

"Is everyone here?" Victoria asks. "I'd hate for anyone to miss this." She looks down at the dog. He sits, his tail frantic in the dirt, his butt wiggling with excitement.

"Shame on you!" a woman in the crowd shouts.

Another man pipes up, "It's Adam and Eve, not Adam and Steve."

"Don't make me throw up," Victoria says. "It'll ruin my lipstick."

The original trespasser, the first to confront her, looks at his cohorts. "We think homosexuality is unnatural—"

"So is Coca-Cola!" Victoria shouts. "So is your washer and dryer. So's your deodorant and ugly makeup and duvet covers and doctors and surgeries and your high cholesterol and erection medications. They're all unnatural! And who are you people, the nature police? You look like fools to me."

"Jesus is the only salvation—"

"Oh, for goodness' sake! Are your genitals clean?" Victoria asks, loudly.

"What?" the man asks with horror.

"Your penis and perineum and anus, are they clean?"

"You're a sick, sick woman!"

"Me? You brought it up! You showed up here! You seem to care so much about my son's genitals, and what my son does with his genitals, I'd like to return the favor and ask you what you do with yours. Do you have sex often? What position?"

"That is—"

"None of my business? Very nice. Very observant. And, very interesting. Because what you think is none of my business I think is certainly none of yours. And yet here you are in my face, trespassing on this beautiful farm, talking about my son, a man you've never met!"

Victoria steps forward, advancing on the man, and he steps back and back, his crowd of fellow congregants parting and swirling around him like he's thick oil and she's pure vinegar. Soon, Victoria and her dog are center stage.

Victoria turns slowly, making eye contact with as many townsfolk as she can. "You people," she says. "You're hypocrites and assholes. You're bad neighbors. You're bad Christians—Jesus was friends with prostitutes, beggars, murderers—the fun people! Is your presence here a reflection of that? No! You're the angry mob Jesus scolded! Your behavior out here is shameful, dishonorable, undemocratic, and poorly styled." Victoria allows her eyes to land on one of the more matronly dressed bigots.

"But," Victoria continues, "you're also victims. You're also confused. You've all been misled. Probably by some generic-looking old white man who gets paid a lot of money to tell you to hate someone else. What could be more evil than that? And why? Why would someone hold up an old book, originally written in a language he can't understand, and tell you what it says? And why would you believe it sight unseen? And why would you take his orders and take aggressive action on them? And *this*? *This* sin? Why *this* sin? Because it's an easy target. You're all tools for a bully. Straight married men are the biggest threat to your children—straight married men are the most likely to be pedophiles! Straight men are, by far, the most common perpetrators of assault, murder, domestic violence, child sex trafficking, and white-collar crimes that rob your pensions. Are you protesting them?"

Victoria looks around, and the dog does as well. The crowd is silent, some looking down, some embarrassed by the long-overdue scolding, as wedding attendees begin to arrive and jeer at the group. A few in the crowd still want to challenge her, but they think better of it.

"In summation," Victoria says, "gay people have been around since the beginning of time; quit acting surprised! Sodom and Gomorrah is a fictional story. Religion is a huge, profitable business and always has been. No one can turn you gay, just like no one turned you straight.

Shame on all of you for your willful ignorance, wasting everyone's precious time, and causing so much unnecessary suffering. Now, unless you have something relevant to present, get the hell off my gay future son-in-law's property! Posthaste!"

The valet kids cheer and whoop.

The dog barks and paws at the air.

The crowd becomes unnervingly quiet as a woman steps forward from the group. Her posture is stiff as Chrissy's, her graying hair swept into a tight bun. With both hands she holds a tattered Bible close to her heart. The worn book matches the worn fabric of her dress. She approaches Victoria, but then pivots to the man who started the ruckus. "Get in the truck, Earl."

The man says not another word, silenced like a smoke alarm smashed with a broom handle. His eyes lower and he takes a sip of breath, as if something inside him is drowning. He doesn't look back up. He turns. He walks away. The woman loosens her grip on the Bible. She nods once to Victoria, slowly, thoughtfully, words wholly inadequate.

Victoria nods back, like she's had this kind of conversation before, like this kind of solemn ritual is the only possible way for some women to communicate about certain men. Before Victoria can further process what happened or consider which holy spirit of persuasion swept over the tiny group at the tiny farm in the tiny town, the woman is also gone.

Victoria looks at the silent stragglers and pushes her shoulders back, trying to relieve her entire body's discomfort she's been managing the last many days. She looks around. "Now, if the rest of you will please excuse me, I think my organs are failing."

BARNETT walks up the hallway of his childhood home, glancing at the walls lined with his mother's treasured photos of him, photos of him from when he was still her boy. He looks at his young face, into his young eyes, and remembers what he was looking at in all these pictures, what was behind the camera—his mother.

Barnett's smile—all that caffeine—is really only as good as the joy he was feeling in that split second, the camera capturing the spark. If only they could zoom in, really zoom far, they'd see the spark in his eye is that of Chrissy Durang.

There he is in second grade. There he is in high school. And there she was, through all of it.

"Mom?" Barnett asks as he approaches her bedroom. The door is open, the bed is made, but his mother is not there.

Across the room, Barnett sees his reflection in his mother's mirror. He walks close and glances at his tux, then carefully studies his face. *There she is*, he thinks.

Ezra follows behind, surveying the empty room. "I'm sure she didn't get far."

He and Barnett crane to fit both their faces in the mirror, to see how they look together, on the evening of their nuptials. They're in matching tuxes, black and white, though Ezra is also wearing an ornate pin. "My touch of Victorian," he says.

Barnett fumbles with his hair, trying to get each gelled piece in place.

"How about mine?" Ezra says, brushing his fingers easily through his locks and letting each strand fall perfectly.

"So damn hot," Barnett says. He turns to face his partner.

"Shall we?" Ezra asks, offering his hand. Barnett takes it tightly.

The two men leave Chrissy's bedroom. They leave the bright-blue farmhouse and step into a wonderland of their own making—well, theirs and Nichole's.

The lights and holograms at the driveway are spectacular. They cast a glow across the entire farm, bouncing off the white draping covering the barn.

Guests are arriving in fun outfits, gleeful to have a celebration to attend. Caterers are walking around with hors d'oeuvres and champagne, and valet drivers are hustling. Vehicles pull up, limos and tractors alike, and the track stars rush to get keys and get parking.

Of all Barnett sees, it's what he doesn't that worries him. "Where's my mom?"

"I'm sure she's busy," Ezra says.

The guys make their way to the front gate and pass Victoria as she walks back to the farmhouse and festivities. "My work here is done," she says.

"Have you seen my mom?" Barnett asks.

"Nope," Victoria says. "Where are you going?"

"Welcome guests," Ezra says.

"You know, it's highly unusual for the betrothed to see each other before the service, much less welcome people," Victoria says.

"Really, Mother? A speech about tradition? At a gay wedding? With lasers and fog machines and macaws that greet people?"

"Don't get your hopes up about the macaws," Victoria says. She turns to Ezra. "And where's your bodice and skirt?"

"Ate too many beignets the other night, I'm afraid."

"That's why I get all my nutrition through red wine," Victoria says. "Grapes. The miracle food." She waves over her shoulder as she enters the blooming wedding fray, dog in tow.

Ezra reaches an arm around Barnett. "I'm sure your mom is fine," he says. "Don't worry."

Ezra and Barnett greet their guests. They embrace old friends and new. Some are clearly from the town, others not.

There's Barnett's favorite teacher, Mrs. Adams. There's his first boss from Boy Scouts camp, Miss Angie.

The people who saw Barnett as a child still do. "You look exactly the same as you did in second grade," says Mr. Monte, Barnett's childhood barber.

They almost all make the same joke. "Which one is the bride?" asks Mr. Johnston, Barnett's former school bus driver.

During the flow of incomers, Barnett looks at shoes, just as his mother taught him years ago. *Shoes don't lie*, she said. There are the fancy ones, the ones that have never made contact with gravel—the shoes of wealthy New Yorkers.

Victoria invited relatives and business associates. Ezra greets and hugs his oldest nanny and then his second-oldest nanny. He kindly ushers them, mostly, to the bar.

There are the flashy shoes—the Los Angeles contingent. These are Barnett's doctor and nurse friends, buddies from college who jab and poke their congratulations at him.

There are the boots—the locals, Chrissy's loyal friends from church. None of them mention Father Perfect.

There are the sneakers. Those are Barnett's oldest friends from Mader High School. They approach with the same speed that news and gossip travel; they tell him, loudly, "Clay's an asshole."

And then there are shoes he doesn't recognize. Nice shoes, but old, scuffed by time and wear and poverty. People who know his mother. People supporting his mother, by supporting her son, whatever his proclivities.

And then, shoes of people who drove here, within readership of the *Picayune Tribune*'s wedding announcement. Within reach of Facebook.

All the guests offer their hellos and take the path to the barn.

"Look at these twats!" the macaws shout, instead of "Welcome."

"Look at these twats!" the macaws shout, their pitch surprisingly similar to the voice of one Victoria Tanner.

Shiny high heels approach and Jessica Thoreaux introduces herself with a firm handshake. "With the *Picayune Tribune*," she says proudly. "I'd love to interview you."

"We think it's best if our vows speak for us," Ezra says.

"You don't want your side of the story published?"

"What 'sides' are you talking about?" Barnett asks.

Jessica smirks and pulls out her little tape recorder. "The grooms seem defensive," she says into the device as she walks away, dissolving into the festivities.

Officer Stolton arrives, gift in hand. "I'm off duty," he says.

"So, no gun this time?" Ezra asks, playfully. Officer Stolton doesn't answer.

"Glad to see you, Officer Stolton," Barnett says, and the two men shake hands.

"Call me Paul," he says. "I brought The Oaf."

Lionel, dressed in his best jeans—dirty but still his best—asks the same question as almost everyone else, "Where's your mom?"

Barnett steps away from the greetings, texts his mother, calls her, leaves her a voice mail: "Everyone is asking about you. Where are you? I'm getting worried."

"Babe," Ezra says sternly. "Her truck is not here."

Chapter 21

Countdown to Damnation:

0 days / 1 hour / 11 minutes

VICTORIA approaches the bar. The gray dog with caramel eyes is with her. "A glass of La Gracè Vino, please."

"I'm sorry, we don't have that," the shirtless bartender says.

"*You* don't have that," Victoria says. "*I* have plenty. The bottles are at the house. Please go fetch a couple for me. Posthaste." She waves a fifty-dollar bill around and the bartender grins, grabs the cash, and dashes away. Victoria reaches over the bar, picks up a bottle of gin, and pours herself a little sip. She quickly spits it out. "Gah!" she retches. She turns to a woman behind her in line. "I think I lost the taste for gin! Do you think I look sick?"

"Not yet," the stranger says. "But here's hoping for a good time tonight. Woo!"

"Oh, yikes," Victoria says. "You must be one of the locals."

"Hey, that yours?" the woman asks, pointing to the tail-wagging beast glued to Victoria's legs.

Victoria is reminded anew of her shadow. She touches the dog's head, the first contact between them, and the dog pushes his skull into her hand. A rare smile messes up Victoria's lipstick. "Yes," she says. "Or more accurately, I'm his."

"What's his name?"

Victoria moves her hand from the dog's head to his chin, holding his floofy face, staring into his candy eyes. "He's idiotic but flashy. I'll name him Bitcoin."

Bitcoin approaches the stranger and starts to lift his leg to pee on her.

"No!" the stranger shrieks.

"Don't you talk to him like that!" Victoria scolds. "This innocent being is frightened. He's getting adjusted. Everything is new to him. We just saw a crow for the first time!"

Bitcoin, who has perhaps never been defended in his entire life, still pees on the woman, but does so with awe.

The woman walks away in protest as the shirtless waiter returns, bottle of La Gracè Vino in hand, and pours a stiff one for Victoria. "Gee, your hand is shaking a lot there," he says. "Not getting sober on me, are ya?"

And Victoria squints, as if trying to see it, to really take it in—not the sight of her own shaking hand, but what it means, what it means when she pairs it with the sweats, the nausea, the headaches, the hell of mundane happiness. "Oh! My! God! Give me that bottle!"

The bartender hands her one of the bottles. She reads the label: "La Gracè Vino, Vin Cabernet Sauvignon, Supérieur Désalcoolisé."

"I'm filled with rage and shock," Victoria says.

The bartender's face twists with confusion. "Um, this is a wedding. You should feel good."

"I should feel drunk!"

From the gazebo comes a soft voice made booming by a microphone. "Please take your seats," Nichole says.

WINSTON Tanner sits away from the crowd, just outside the bright-blue farmhouse.

If Snow White had an eighth dwarf, named Waiting, it would be Winston's namesake. If he were the fourth wise man, he would have brought Prozac to the manger. If he were a saint, Winston's purview would be patience; Saint Winston Tanner, humble savior not of multiple souls, but of just one.

As she approaches him, Winston stands, holds his chin up.

"I'M SOBER!" Victoria cries, falling into his arms, confusion welling in her and manifesting in soft, subtle sobs.

Winston, his vocal cords in perfect working order, says, "My dear Lord, my dear wife," pulling her close to him.

Victoria pushes away to face him. "Thank God you finally said something. I was forgetting the sound of your voice."

"Do you remember the last thing I said to you?"

"No," Victoria says.

"I said I wouldn't talk to you again until you stopped drinking. I've been waiting to talk to you until you could really hear me."

"My hearing has been fine."

"But not your drinking, my Victoria."

Even Bitcoin seems to cringe, the kind that's the only natural response when someone speaks truth and it's hard to watch, hard to hear, and maybe even harder to own.

"You mean to tell me, I've been doing all this . . . everything since we got here on this farm . . . the dinners, the thing with the homophobe at the valet, the dog . . ."

Bitcoin lets out a quick whine, a plea for sympathy.

"I've been doing all this . . . unaided?" Victoria asks.

"I wondered when you'd notice." Winston smiles. "Has it been a nightmare?"

"It's been . . . Heaven," she says. Victoria puts her hands to her wet cheeks. "Are my eyes bleeding?"

"You're crying, my love. Here, here." And Winston holds his wife tightly, unreservedly, for the first time in twenty-three years.

Music begins, and the last of the wedding stragglers take their seats.

IN the living room, the boys make their final preparations, tug on their tux jackets, square away the folds of ties and shirt collars and flyaway hairs.

"What about your mom?" Ezra asks.

Barnett looks at his phone again. Nothing. "Aw, man."

"Is there something you're not telling me?"

"She was nervous. I told her it was okay if she wasn't here for the wedding."

"You told her that?"

Barnett nods, *Yeah*.

"Were you lying? Or being nice? I mean, if she's not here, is it really okay with you?"

Barnett squeezes his partner's hand. "It will be, one day."

Part 5

Cold Feet

Sweetheart, the condition of cold feet doesn't only affect boys of war. If it seems daunting that a marriage is forever, that you only get one shot to make the perfect choice, that you will be bound and judged and weighted throughout all eternity (or damnation!) to another human, I recommend simply not thinking too much about it.

> —*Mrs. Jeannie Laffite's Undisputed Guide to*
> *Respectable Southern Nuptials,*
> *volume III, page 146*
> *(copyright 1912 by Mrs. Jeannie Laffite)*

Chapter 22

Countdown to Damnation:

0 days / 0 hours / 59 minutes

ONE of the kids at the valet owes Chrissy Durang a big favor.

Little Roddy is not so little anymore. But years ago, as a kid, he had a black Lab he was supposed to put down. Roddy's father gave him a loaded pistol, said Roddy could do it wherever he wanted, just get it done, get "the thing" buried, and then, "get your ass back to work and quit cryin.'"

Where do I go? young Roddy thought. *Where do I go to do this? Or not do this?*

Black labs are loyal even unto their own demise. They hold their heads up high no matter the gray in their beard, the droop of their eyes, the heaviness of each leg—they press on and on. They love even with a gun to their head. But love is not enough on a hard farm; that's not the job description of a farm dog. A farm dog is a tool, a piece of equipment, something you don't keep past its usefulness.

Where do I go? young Roddy wondered again. His legs were wobbly and sore; his arms clung so tightly to his dear Farmer Dog, that name inscribed on a collar that was holding on by threads, a collar that was never needed in the first place because his dog was so loving, so loyal.

Sunburned and dehydrated from carrying Farmer Dog for two

miles, Roddy collapsed at the doorstep of Chrissy Durang at Polite Society Ranch, where Roddy knew dignity mattered—it said so right there on the sign out front. Roddy knew Miss Chrissy—the lady from school field trips, the lady who ran the place, the lady who once gave his class a tour—would have a spot for Farmer Dog.

Of course she did. And Chrissy had Farmer Dog for a few weeks. At first he lived in the kennel, then the barn, making easy friends with the other animals. As he got sicker, he came to live inside with Chrissy. She even let him into her bedroom, where he slept on a pile of blankets beside her bed.

During that time, Chrissy would take Roddy's meek and hushed calls to check on his dog. She'd text Roddy photos of Farmer Dog. She let Roddy come over anytime and say hello. Eventually, he came over to say goodbye. It happened in her bedroom, just under Chrissy's picture window, with Farmer Dog comfy on a pile of Chrissy's good towels, a young boy's two hands on the slowly rising and falling belly of his beloved beast. Farmer Dog twitched and tried to lick the boy's tears but couldn't muster the strength, and they fell and fell and fell to the floor just out of the dog's reach. There would be no last taste of him, this boy whom Farmer Dog watched come home from the hospital as a baby and grow up to be the young man tasked with killing him.

The dog's brown eyes were weary, clouded with the understanding that the world was closing in on him, closing him out. His old age was new fencing. Nothing tasted the same as it once had. Nothing smelled the same. The joys were fewer and further away.

And when the needle went in, Farmer Dog didn't flinch.

And as the fluid mixed with his blood, still Farmer Dog thought about how much he loved the boy, Little Roddy.

And, yes, even at the end, the irresistible urge to live still filled Farmer Dog. And fearlessly, as he lived, and optimistically, as he loved, he mustered the last strength to push himself toward the boy, unable to kiss Little Roddy one last time, but at least get close enough to breathe him, to make sure his favorite human's scent was the last to fill his lungs.

And when it was over, the boy sobbed, exhaled, and said to Farmer Dog, "I love you."

And Chrissy knelt down beside the two best friends, one living and one dead. She took the collar off Farmer Dog and handed it to the boy, to Little Roddy. And he took it into his hands, squeezed it tight, as if he could wring out a part of his bestie's soul, wash his hands in his spirit one more time. And he looked at Chrissy, his eyes pained, his breath hushed, unable to speak the words of gratitude she knew he wanted to say, but that she didn't need to hear aloud.

"He loved you, too," she told Roddy. "He loved you so much."

And Roddy left with that collar.

And he grew up.

And that's why he treasures Farmer Dog's collar.

And that's why when Miss Chrissy asked him to fetch her Chevy, he did it.

And that's why when Miss Chrissy asked for the Chevy's keys, he handed them over.

And that's why when Barnett and Ezra and Nichole asked Roddy if he'd seen Miss Chrissy, he lied. Because Miss Chrissy helped him once. And still, he's never loved any animal more. And still, this small favor doesn't adequately show his appreciation.

Where do I go? he asked himself one day, long ago, in despair. *To Chrissy Durang,* came the answer. *Of course, to Chrissy Durang, savior of misfits.*

THE Chevy is trusty no matter the day, the weather, the parking spot—even where it rests now, in a ditch near a side entrance to Polite

Society Ranch. When Chrissy turns the key, the engine roars, the tires twitch, and the steel monster makes nothing of the ground beneath it as it rips away from the wedding, the guests, the responsibility.

Where do I go? Chrissy asks herself.

The Chevy makes its trek up the highway.

Where do I go? she wonders as the sun comes down on her crisis of faith, the hour nearly upon her. *Where do I go?*

And first, she tries his house, and he's not there.

Where do I go? she asks.

And now she's off to Waffle House, and he's not there.

Where do I go? she asks.

And now she's racing Earth, daylight, darkness approaching, the wedding service soon beginning. *Where do I go?* she asks herself, as she drives farther from Polite Society Ranch.

She tries the address Miss Iva found in school records.

She tries the address she got from the man's wife.

And that's how she got the address of the man's job.

The Chevy grinds the gravel all the way up Pearl River Road, to a construction site, a soundscape of hammers clapping against nails, the occasional scream of a table saw, the fresh scent of sawdust that delights your senses only to eventually choke your throat.

It's there that Chrissy Durang finds Clay Parker.

"Working on the Lord's day?" she asks.

Clay recognizes her voice immediately. He's crouched over, hammering nails into a stud. He rises onto his knees, squeezes his handful of nails, and flips his hammer like a bartender with a bottle of vodka. He turns slowly to meet her gaze. But he says nothing.

"I asked if you were working on the Lord's day?" Chrissy repeats.

"Look who's talking," Clay says. "I didn't see you in the pew this morning."

One of Clay's coworkers at the site laughs. Chrissy can hear one of the other men saying, "Maw-Maw is out front in her Sunday best." She thinks she hears other whispers, but only makes out a few words: *farm, wedding, faggots.*

The other men laugh with immature delight.

Clay smiles with confidence. She's no match for him here, on his turf. "Are you here to threaten me with police and all that? Because—"

"No," she interrupts. "Truly. No threats. I'm less the eye-for-an-eye type and trying to be more of the love-your-neighbor type."

"Then what the hell do you want?"

Some of Clay's coworkers laugh, but not quite as many as before.

Chrissy looks down. She fluffs her dress, frilly and bright blue, perfectly matched to the structures of Polite Society Ranch, presenting as proud and strong, exactly as she requested of the salesperson. "I'm here because I think we're a lot alike."

Clay smirks. "How's that?"

"I was a vandal, too," Chrissy says. "An emotional vandal, once or twice at least." She looks from his eyes to his hands—the hammer in one, the nails in the other. "And I came here because you're someone I know won't lie to me. And I have questions I think you can help me answer."

Clay stares at her for a moment. His grip loosens and a single nail falls, landing near his foot, hitting the concrete foundation with a ting. He pays it no mind; a small hazard to deal with later. He's focused on Chrissy. He shifts his face and motions his arms, *go on, go on, what do you want?*

"Please tell me we can be people who make mistakes," Chrissy says. "Please tell me we can be people who are forgiven. Please tell me we can be people who are civil to each other. Please tell me we can be people who change, who don't cause other people to suffer. Because if I can love and forgive you, maybe Barnett can love and forgive me."

Now, the construction site is silent.

Chrissy looks not at her watch but at the sun, which is slipping away from her.

Clay feels his muscles relaxing. Relief. He doesn't have to fight. It feels free, it feels foreign. He considers that it might be nice to feel this way more often.

"Are we people who can change, be civil, be forgiven? Yeah, I *think* we are." He pauses. "But I *know* you are, Miss Chrissy."

Chrissy almost laughs at his answer; there's such ease and kindness in his compliment that it disarms her, seems to set the whole town free.

"Anything else?" he asks.

"Yeah," Chrissy says. "Which necklace?" She holds up the two options: her gold chain and a string of pearls.

Clay pauses for much longer than such a decision should take. He truly considers. "Pearls," he says. Then, loudly, "Right, guys?"

A moment floats by, then a chorus sounds, deep voices echoing louder and louder between bare studs that will one day be a home, "Yeah, yeah," Clay's fellow construction workers say. "The pearls, the pearls."

"Take care, Clay," Chrissy says.

"Take care, Miss Chrissy."

Chapter 23

Countdown to Damnation:

0 days / 0 hours / 3 minutes

Nichole's eyes are crazed. Chunks of her hair are coming unclipped. The strap on her tiny teal dress won't stay on her shoulder. She paces the living room in front of Barnett and Ezra, the men dressed, ready, and very late. "Where's your mother?"

Nichole's watch vibrates and she yells at it, "I hate you!"

Her app reads: 0 days / 0 hours / 2 minutes.

"Has she ever vanished before?" Nichole asks.

Barnett looks down at the black hardwood floor, still clean enough that it reflects the three of them standing there, as if it's made of onyx, as if it's a mirror and under them is a whole parallel world, maybe one where mothers show up for their sons; but that's not this life.

"We can't start without her!" Nichole says. "People will think something is wrong."

Barnett looks up. "Let's do it."

"Are you sure? I bet people don't mind waiting," Ezra suggests, with hope in his heart, not that Chrissy will show up for the wedding, but that she will show up for her son.

"I'm not worried about people waiting," Barnett says. "I'm worried about *me* waiting." Barnett grabs Ezra's hand. "I'm worried about *us* waiting. I can't keep waiting for people to catch up."

The two men smile. They both consider touching foreheads and kissing, but both decide to save it for the big moment, a moment that seems to be moving further and further away from them.

"This is a curse," Nichole says. "This is because you're seeing each other before the wedding!" She looks at her watch. "Goddammit! And where the hell is Celine Dion?"

OUTSIDE the farmhouse, Winston and Victoria wait anxiously for their cue to march down the aisle. Victoria fidgets with the bouquet she's being forced to carry. Bitcoin licks his crotch.

Nichole rushes up to them and stares at her mother as if in shock.

Victoria steps forward. "Oh, no. Oh, no. What's wrong?"

Nichole looks her mother up and down. "What's wrong with *you*? Something is missing."

Victoria puts her hand to her face. "It's my demon, my sin, my disease!"

"No, no. Oh, I see," Nichole says. "It's just weird to see you without a drink in your hand."

Victoria shakes her head. "See, Winston. It's a curse. I have wrists for Waterford."

Bitcoin approaches Nichole, his tail in an uncertain position. "Ew, what's that?" Nichole asks, taking a step back.

"This is Bitcoin," Victoria says. "And if he tries to pee on you, let him. It might be his only happiness."

"He's not a registered guest!" Nichole scolds.

"He's with us."

"You adopted a dog?"

Victoria opens her mouth to answer but—

"Yes," Winston says. "Yes, I believe we did."

"Dad!" Nichole shouts, bouncing on her toes. "You're talking!"

"I told your mother I'd talk to her again if she quit drinking." He looks at Victoria with longing, wishing he could sweep her up like a dog greeting its military owner at the airport, but that's not her style, and he chooses to love that about her, too.

Nichole turns to her mother. "You quit drinking?"

"It was a terrible accident," Victoria says. "But, I'm back," she says and bumps shoulders with Winston. "*We're* back, and my urine has returned to a normal color."

"Shall we, then?" Winston asks, offering his arm to Victoria. She puts hers inside his, and the two are locked together again.

"Wait, wait. No, no. You can't walk down the aisle, not yet."

"Why not?" Victoria asks. "Aren't we late?" She cranes her neck to see inside, into the farmhouse. "Are the boys okay? Are they ready?"

"Yes. They're ready. They've *been* ready. But if you go," Nichole says, "everyone will know that the mother of the other groom is missing."

"Missing?" Victoria asks.

Worry washes over Winston. "What? Should we call the police?"

"Barnett said she got cold feet," Nichole says. "So we're gonna skip the wedding party processions and just have the grooms walk."

"Absolutely not!" Victoria says. "I'm not missing out! This is my only son's wedding! Come, Winston." She pulls her husband and he moves gracefully with her toward the aisle.

"Mom! No! No! If you go, the announcer will . . . Oh, shit—"

Across the rows and rows of guests, near the gazebo, sits Wishful Willie, whose entire stock of business cards are stained in beer but nevertheless still legibly read: "New Orleans's Best DJ/Host/MC/ Certified CPR Instructor."

Wishful Willie has been sitting at the control panel all evening, behind the gazebo, regulating the music, watching the chairs fill up, watching servers circle with food and drink, waiting for his most important job—to announce the wedding party.

And then he sees his cue: Winston and Victoria walking defiantly down the aisle.

Nichole starts to run to him—but it's too far; there's no time. She waves her hands frantically, trying to signal, *No! No! Abort! Abort!*

Wishful Willie nods dismissively, ignorantly, motioning as if to say, *Don't worry! I got this!*

Barnett and Ezra step outside in time to see Nichole frantic, and to hear Wishful Willie earn his pay. He lowers the music, grabs the microphone, holds it close enough to his mouth that his voice booms, but not so close that his goatee hairs interfere. "The mother and father of the groom, Mrs. Victoria Tanner and Mr. Winston Tanner."

Heads turn to watch the couple as they emerge—Bitcoin trailing behind, gleefully, as if the ruckus is for him alone. The trio make their way down the aisle, nodding to friends, relatives, and strangers alike.

"Oh, no," Nichole whispers, watching from afar.

As Winston and Victoria take their seats, Wishful Willie strikes again, taking his next cue, the microphone to his mouth, "The mother of the groom, Mrs. Chrissy Durang."

Rows and rows of guests turn to look for her, the other mother of the other groom, the matron of Polite Society Ranch.

Barnett and Ezra cringe.

Nichole accidentally plucks out a surprising amount of her own hair.

From the crowd, a few whispers rise to a hushed din, as nearly everyone wonders—*Where is she? Where is Farmer Mom?*

Soon, the questions answer themselves. Gazes lower in disbelief; a few shake their heads in disappointment.

Jessica Thoreaux whispers, "Disaster," into her tape recorder.

It's dark. And the darkness survives despite the fairy lights overhead, despite the efforts of the blossoming moon, despite the soft glow of the farm and the house and the stables and the chicken coop. The mood is suddenly dark, too.

"Blue vibes," Ezra says softly.

"No, no. It's okay," Barnett whispers, trying to comfort his almost husband.

Ezra smiles and nods, knowing the truth: Barnett is trying to comfort himself.

Barnett's shoulders are slumped, his face long.

"She loves you," Ezra says.

Barnett looks away, into the void, toward his destiny and the increasingly disenchanted murmurs of the celebrants. He affixes a smile that presents as heartbroken but polite, exactly as he's seen on his mother's face more than a few times over the years.

Energy—the kind that skirts danger, the kind that requires you to turn off the car radio so you can make a turn—rains down upon Polite Society Ranch, a sticky disappointment, a pine sap–style humidity that'll require more than one shower. Those dark vibes hover for long enough that craning necks start to get sore, butts start to get fidgety in their seats, until the confusion yields to focus: another spirit appears, lurking on the grounds of Polite Society Ranch.

Heads cock, bodies lean forward.

Rhett stands, as if some haunting force is heading straight for him—for all of them.

Others stand as well—*Is that a ghost?*

From the darkness emerges form, white circles, floating orbs, beads—no, pearls. One pearl, then two, then a string of them, gracing the neck of a stunning Chrissy Durang as she steps into the light, into the show.

The crowd rises. She's so vibrant, every witness is forced upright just to give her momentum a proper place to flow within them.

"They're supposed to stand for you guys!" Nichole protests, but Barnett and Ezra gawk at Chrissy with boyish smiles.

"There she is," Barnett says, as they watch Chrissy step down the aisle, nodding politely at the guests as she tries to make eye contact with each, mouthing the word "Sorry" here and there, though the bright shift of life Chrissy brings renders her delay moot.

Barnett inhales sporadically, little sips of air that might count as sobs if not for the joy in his eyes, his posture firming, that smile working double time. He takes his hands out of his pockets and is about to clap—

"No, no!" Nichole says, putting her hand between Barnett's. "If you clap, they'll all clap, and this is not the time for clapping. The whole wedding could collapse!"

"Nic!" Ezra starts.

"Hey, hey," Barnett says, clearing his throat, wiping his eyes, widening his stance to deliver his message eye to eye with Nichole. "This is the happiest day of my life. And getting happier by the second." He looks out to his mother. "She would deserve it," he says.

"It's okay to have something for you," Nichole says.

Chrissy walks alone, stepping to the beat of Wishful Willie's music, carrying a modest bouquet of flowers that presents as full but affordable, exactly as she requested of the florist. The faces she sees are warm. The hearts on this farm are open.

Stiffen your spine, Chrissy thinks to herself. She smiles at Rhett; he smiles back.

The sequins on Paw-Paw's suit catch the light and make it look as if Chrissy is on a spaceship as she approaches him. He's smiling; he's crying. Chrissy wants to rush to him, to comfort him, to give him a tissue—or maybe even an Elmo Band-Aid or a fiver if needed. But he holds up his two weathered hands, palms out, and motions as if to say, *No, no*. Or, *Slow down*.

And Chrissy does both. She turns from Paw-Paw and back to the journey she must face alone, up to the front of the show, where before everyone, she's expected to give away her favorite person on earth.

Chrissy adjusts her breathing to not just slow, but also careful. The emotions are hunting her, and who knows how they'll finally make entry, perhaps through the lungs, perhaps through the sound of the vows, perhaps from the friends whose gazes she's meeting now.

Officer Stolton looks especially kind under the fairy lights. Nearby, the soft orange glow also works wonders on Lionel. Little Roddy joined the occasion, still in his valet getup. *What a great kid*, Chrissy thinks, nodding at him, nodding to the other track stars/valet drivers standing on the sidelines to watch the service.

Linda is wearing what she believes to be a dress she bought at Goodwill, though technically, it's a poncho. At this, Chrissy breaks, not into laughter, but tears. The cracks must have been bursting for Linda to be the final blow.

The emoting starts with passion, blurring Chrissy's vision as she moves down the aisle. She wipes at her tears. She tries to blink and blink away the feelings—loss? love?—as she passes Victoria, Winston, and that dog with a penchant for peeing on people.

Nichole is right about the venue, the lights, the music, Chrissy thinks.

And maybe Ezra is right about the unity and connection.

And maybe Barnett is right about following our hearts.

And, Chrissy considers, maybe she's right about the thing she always feared, that her son is a reflection of herself. She hated the reflection—so much gay muck on the mirror, she feared the reflection was a bad one. She tried to manage it, hide it, color it. When Barnett was no longer under her roof, she quit updating photos of him on the hallway wall, she quit directly answering any questions about him. But now she sees there was no severance, ever. It was only in her mind; the fears existed only in fog, her fingers that held scissors now sew sutures, trying to repair a beloved ragtag family, now larger by one serving of socialite, one squirt from a flip-top soap lid. *How beautiful*, she thinks.

She reaches her seat, her journey just beginning.

All eyes in the crowd remain on her, waiting for her to sit before they do.

But before anyone takes their seat, just as Chrissy lets go of old hopes and embraces new ones, absolute pitch darkness swallows Polite Society Ranch, as if God himself has unplugged the wedding. The carefully strung fairy lights are dead. The music goes silent. And the crowd lets out a collective, shocked, "OH!" until they, too, become soundless, quieted, listening for instruction, or danger.

Part 6

Damnation

Sweetheart, every marriage is a damnation. It is damnation of a degree of loneliness! It is damnation of a stale home! It is damnation of paths untraversed! Indeed, may anything outside of your love be damned. May it be damned straight to Hell.

—*Mrs. Jeannie Laffite's Undisputed Guide to*
   Respectable Southern Nuptials,
   volume III, page 192
   (copyright 1912 by Mrs. Jeannie Laffite)

Chapter 24

Countdown to Damnation:

0 days / 0 hours / 0 minutes

RHETT thinks he sees a spark. Paw-Paw wonders if it's a forest fire raging toward them, but there's no smoke, no thick smell of ruin. Chrissy thinks, if only for a moment, that it looks supernatural, the swirl of slowly blinking dots of bright-yellow light approaching then billowing around and over and through the crowd.

The night is soon polka-dotted with low, floating, flowing stars, hypnotizing bright freckles in the dark, which seem to come and go as if vanishing and reappearing elsewhere, defying science and sensibilities.

The lights float about, a fireworks show in slow motion, silent explosions that fizz and fumble and loop and bound.

Bitcoin barks then jumps at the miracles.

Chrissy holds out her hand and a spark lands upon it, blinking affection at her. "Fireflies," she whispers in delight.

The tiniest of wedding guests make their way around their new home, at least for the night. Their flash patterns vary—some make the shape of a hook, others loop, others shimmer as if in signal to the cosmos. They meander, they mingle.

"Damn," Lionel says, mesmerized by the display.

"They're beautiful," Rhett says. "So beautiful."

"Ew!" Linda says. She shoos them away from her and Rhett. "It's a reverse fart. That's how they do that. A reverse fart. Saw it on TV. Air goes in their butts and combines with other chemicals in there and boom, light!"

Linda and Rhett look up as the fireflies coalesce a few feet above the crowd, a storm cloud full of broken lightning. And Rhett thinks with childlike wonder, *Wow*. And Linda thinks with scientific certainty, *Farts*.

Jessica pulls her tape recorder from her purse. She fumbles, struggling to see in the dim light which button is marked "record." But slowly, a stardrop floats down to her and lands on her device, illuminating the buttons. She shakes the critter away and hits record. She says into it, softly, as if unsure she's found the right word, "Wicked."

In the awe of the moment, the fireflies lolling about like confused sparks, as each heart is warmed by the magic of Mother Earth, Wishful Willie resumes romantic and plucky music, and all eyes turn from the light show above them to the light show emerging before them— the dazzling grooms.

Barnett and Ezra stand under a blanket of jolly moving stars, as fireflies land on their shoulders and hair and bounce away again, as if even earth's bugs know this is not about them.

The two lovers look at each other and smile. "Shall we?" Barnett asks.

"Let's get married," Ezra says, tickling his fingers into Barnett's palm, the two men holding each other's hands tightly as they step, step, step to their collective fate.

They walk in sync, creating a swirl of Louisiana air that spins the fireflies into twists of enchantment. They step down the aisle, eyes focused ahead, forward, toward their future.

At the gazebo, they turn and look into each other's grinning faces.

From the crowd erupts a symphony of "aws," giddy laughs, and loving applause.

Nichole is nearly out of breath—she just ran around the audience to rip the microphone from Wishful Willie's hands and join the grooms on the gazebo as the crowd starts to quiet again. "Dearly beloved," she exhales. "We gather here today to witness the marriage of these great guys." Nichole pauses to catch her breath while applause breaks out anew, cheers from friends and family, loved ones careful to mark their support, as if to say: *Great guys, indeed.*

At all the love, Barnett and Ezra look at each other, and both blush.

"It's called 'holy matrimony,'" Nichole continues. "Those two words are part of a long-held tradition, at times both beautiful and oppressive, unifying and divisive, coveted and impossible. Tonight, our 'holy matrimony' is a union of gentle rebellion, a hard-fought civil right, and a choice, a flag planted: love is love."

Chrissy nods her agreement and looks around, taking in the other happy faces around her, and at least one happily wagging tail.

"Allow me to introduce myself. I'm Nichole, spelled n-i, like the element. And c-h-o-l-e, as in the Punjabi word for chickpeas, but pronounced traditionally 'Nicole' like Scherzinger. And I'm the officiant. I'm also Ezra's twin sister. And no, we can't read each other's thoughts." She pauses for laughter, though none comes.

"I'd like to start with a story," Nichole says. "I remember talking to Ezra after his first date with Barnett. It was exciting to see Ezra so happy. He was so intrigued by you, Barnett, and that never happens. Ezra usually thinks people are boring."

"Sad but true," Ezra says quietly.

Nichole turns to Barnett. "And, Barnett, I'm sorry but I don't remember the first time I met you in real life. And I suspect I know why—Shots! Shots!" Nichole pumps her fist in the air as if at a night-club. She pauses for laughter, though again, none comes.

"To try to remember the first time I met Barnett," she continues, "I turned to the most trusted source—Instagram. To the first time Ezra posted a photo with Barnett. The two of you were on a beach and the caption read simply, 'Happiness is.' And I relate. And I think that's why I don't remember meeting you, Barnett. You always felt like family."

Blushing Barnett reaches out his fist and Nichole happily bumps it with hers.

"What I see in you two is an easy joy," Nichole continues. "You choose each other every day, every week, year after year, since that first date. And it just keeps getting better. I marvel at your patient kindness with each other, how committed you are to caring for each other, how much fun and friendship I see, along with the steady wellspring of affection. I love you both and I'm so happy for you, and there's so much more to come."

"Hear! Hear!" someone shouts from the back, briefly confusing Nichole. She looks out suspiciously at the crowd and sees only beaming faces looking at her, seeming to will her to get on with it. She smiles.

She turns to the guys. "We will now have the exchanging of the vows, starting with you, Barnett."

He leans forward with grace, his eyes locked with Ezra's. "I never thought this kind of 'love' was for me. That I'd ever find it. Or that as a gay man, I'd ever be doing something like this. Marriage?"

A few souls in the audience laugh. Chrissy fidgets with her pearls.

"But I guess I had hope," Barnett continues. He looks out at the crowd and back to Ezra as he explains, "I like making lists—I'm like my mom that way, I guess—" He nods to Chrissy. She nods back.

"But my lists are not in my back pocket. They're in my front,"

Barnett says. "In my phone. I had a list in there of things I'd want in a partner if I ever got so lucky. I've been updating it for years. Years before I met you," he says to Ezra. "And so when it came time for me to—sorry—"

Barnett stops and reaches his hand to cover his face, to shield raw emotion he's not used to having on display.

"Green vibes?" Ezra whispers, battling his own tears and struggling to stifle a sob.

Barnett nods. He can't fully answer his lover, his best friend, his future husband, not yet. He takes a deep breath. He takes a few beats, and continues, "When it came time for me to write these vows, it wasn't hard. At all. Because everything I wanted to say was right there in my phone, right there on a list of what I was hoping to find in a relationship."

To Ezra, Barnett says, "You're the guy I wished for in my notes app. You're a magical person. Some kind of benevolent alien creature from another time or place who just showed up like I ordered you online."

"You manifested me!" Ezra shouts playfully. He wipes his eyes of the evidence of his affection.

Barnett cocks his head. "Don't get too magical on me."

Ezra nods, *Right, right, sure.*

Barnett continues. "My list includes traits like patience, kindness, thoughtfulness, humor. And passion. And just kissing you, it makes my insides melt, like sand or pressure is leaving my body. Something about you makes me feel that life is friendly, life is safe. I'm so in love, sometimes I'm scared to drive over the speed limit. I'm so in love, I'm scared to cross the street. I'm so in love, I'm scared to do anything with risk, because I'm so in love. I'm so happy, I'm scared I'll be hit by a bus and die and lose it all. You make me want to wear a bike helmet!"

The crowd laughs. Ezra squeezes his lover's hands, tears and nose running. Barnett continues. "You know that scene in one of the old *Superman* movies, where he flies with Lois Lane? He kinda lets her flail a bit up there in the air. I hated that scene as a kid. I thought Superman was being mean to Lois. I wanted him to hold her tightly. I used to think, *If I ever have a Lois Lane, I'll never let go.* But with you, I realize my dream was backward. Because when I met you, I realized you're the superman. You're the superhero. In my dreams about love, you're the magical one, the one who can fly. And in that dream, I'm not the one holding you tight. I'm the one being held, trusting you with my whole heart, flying through life, holding onto you, filled with gratitude that you chose me, that you saved me, that you let me fly with you."

Ezra squeezes Barnett's hands, both men's eyes red and strained and wet. Ezra wants to shout, "I'll never let you fall!" But he's not sure it's his time yet, not sure Barnett is finished.

Ezra studies his lover, the new redness and swelling in his face, the flaring nostrils and wet palms. The wordless presence lingers, it seems, just long enough.

"My turn?" Ezra asks.

Barnett smiles and nods, *Yes.*

"I'm screwed," Ezra says.

"Ez!" Nichole admonishes as the crowd reveals its amusement.

"I'm so screwed," he repeats. "Because I didn't write anything. I planned to wing it. But yours was just so great!"

Ezra only now realizes his mistake in planning to improvise. He made this terrible mistake hoping the cosmos would inspire him with lucid and eloquent and perfect vows on the spot. He pauses and tries to own the quiet. He tries to settle his mind, to find his feelings. The audience permits it, smiling kindly and waiting patiently. Ezra looks at Barnett. "I know I'm kind of 'out there.' Not everyone gets me. I don't even think you get me fully, huh?"

"I do not," Barnett says. "And I love that about you."

"I have to wonder," Ezra says. "How do you make a life promise if you think life is a big illusion? And how do you make a commitment if you don't believe in time? But I can say this with certainty to my core—" Ezra pauses, hoping to spit out the rest of his feelings before he's blubbering too much to do so. "The present moment is the only moment. And because of that, I will love you forever because I love you right now."

The two men touch foreheads. They feel each others' warmth and sweat, nerves that say more about excitement than fear. As is their habit, they start to lean in for a kiss.

"Not yet," Nichole whispers, and the men smile and abort the smooch. She continues. "This next part of our service isn't traditional. These guys aren't known for doing things in traditional order, anyhow. But they'd like to, now, make up for any missteps or oversights."

The guys nod to each other, then Barnett turns to Winston and Victoria. "I didn't ask earlier, not formally, but I wish I had. May I have your son's hand in marriage?" he asks.

Winston nods enthusiastically.

"Yes, yes, Jesus!" Victoria says. "Posthaste!"

Ezra turns to Chrissy. "May I . . . borrow him?" he asks.

Chrissy, tearfully, nods, *Yes*.

"Does anyone object?" Nichole asks.

Chrissy feels heat stir within her. Her list of worries is in the trash, and though the aftertaste lingers—it's also fading. There was a time when she'd have something unwise to say. But the voice that fills the cooling southern air is not hers.

"GODDAMMIT GET ON WITH IT," Paw-Paw yells.

The crowd laughs. Ezra sobs with glee.

"You okay?" Barnett whispers to him.

"I'm so happy," Ezra whispers back.

From Nichole's pocket she pulls two rings. One is carved from a chunk of a maple tree with a thin inlay of emerald. *Green vibes*, Barnett thought when he saw it, *perfect for my Ezra.*

The other ring is gold, scratched and imperfect, with an old inscription inside: *Chrissy & John.* And a new inscription just beside it, fresh, flawless, a gift from a loving mother: *Barnett & Ezra.*

Barnett recognizes his father's ring immediately and looks to his mother. She winks at him, freeing a tear from her eye and sending a smile to Barnett that says it all—*It's yours now.*

The gold ring seems alive, as if filled with the same vibrancy as all the fireflies floating about. It carries a spirit. Barnett remembers the ring from when he was a boy and his father allowed him to touch it and spin it and even wear it. Barnett would put the gold band on his tiny finger and make a fist and pump it up and jet around like he was the Green Lantern or a sorcerer, as if it held so much power.

As Barnett got older, the ring did, too; it grew steadily more worn, and more scratched, right there upon his father's finger. And Barnett grew too old to ask to touch it or spin it. Barnett grew too old to ask to wear it. After his father's death, the ring went to Chrissy, onto the thin gold chain she wears around her neck, sized just right so the ring hangs close to her heart, as if it is the first, maybe only, prized possession she would save in a house fire. All that old gold, locked in a circle, it feels like just as much of John's being as his grave out back.

Looking at the ring, Barnett prays. It's an accident that happens sometimes without his consent, like when an Our Father or a Hail Mary pops into his head while he's washing dishes or grocery shopping. *God bless you, Dad. I love you. I miss you*, Barnett prays, wishes, decrees.

"A ring can be a symbol for many things—wealth, power, infinity," Nichole says. "Today, let your rings be a symbol of companionship. Let them be a reminder that part of another life travels with you, and that a part of you travels with another. Today, let your rings be a symbol of dedication. Let them be a reminder that fates are shared. Today, let your rings be a symbol of love and a reminder that love is simple: It is making his side of the bed, squeegeeing the shower. Love is complimenting his hair, buying his favorite ice cream, picking him up at the airport, but during low traffic hours ONLY. When you look at these rings on your hands, be reminded of this moment, of your commitment, your duty of care, and the love you feel for each other."

Nichole continues, "Barnett, place the ring on Ezra's finger. Will you, Barnett, keep Ezra as your favorite person—laugh with him, have adventures with him, support him through life's tough moments, be proud of him, grow old with him, and find new reasons to love him every day?"

"I will and I do," Barnett says.

"Ezra, place the ring on Barnett's finger. Will you, Ezra, keep Barnett as your favorite person—laugh with him, have adventures with him, support him through life's tough moments, be proud of him, grow old with him, and find new reasons to love him every day?"

"I will and I do," Ezra says.

"And now, by the power vested in me by the state of Louisiana and some random website run by a guy in Austria, I now pronounce you married. Please kiss your husband!"

Barnett Durang and Ezra Tanner touch foreheads, then kiss for the first time as husbands.

The crowd cheers, a joyful racket with a blast radius of three miles.

Drones catapult into the air from the perimeter of the farm. They soar over the crowd, the grooms, the fireflies, creating hearts in the sky, a show of love true to its universal nature, one that can be seen from space.

Chapter 25

To applause and whoops and the whir of the drones, the effusive crowd's affections target the two men kissing in a gazebo. Barnett's hands tangle into Ezra's hair, pulling their faces and then mouths even closer together. Ezra's hands trace inside Barnett's tux jacket, hugging his husband in a way that's familiar, the two men maneuvering around each other as if one body, in love with all the parts.

They separate and look at each other with huge grins. They turn shoulder to shoulder and face their community. Their arms that are closest join hands to a smattering of "aws." Beaming, they extend their other arms open to the whole wide world.

Wishful Willie kicks on some music and Nichole whispers, "To the barn, guys."

Barnett and Ezra take each other's hands and step from the gazebo into what feels like a stadium full of fans. On the lower level, the crowd up front clamors to touch them, hug them, make eye contact. The kids from the valet jump onto tables, creating a mezzanine level of love. The towering trees create the feel of a balcony of attendees swaying to the music. The fireflies twisting about make it look like supporters stretch to the heavens, like all the lost souls from Polite Society Ranch are waving their flaming lighters from the nosebleed seats.

Barnett finds his mother staring up at the sky. "Your dad is watching. I know he's really proud of you."

Barnett believes it, because he believes in her. "I love you, Mom."

Chrissy sees in her son both the face of a child and an adult. It's confusing. But isn't so much of life that way.

As Ezra is smothered in the adoration of Victoria and Winston, the grooms' hands separate. Ezra turns to his husband. "See you on the dance floor?"

Barnett gives a thumbs-up as he's swept into the cheerful, joyous crowd rushing to the bars in the barn.

Inside, Nichole grabs a drink for her and Pauley and the two tour the homestead arm in arm, warmed by the sight of so many enjoying so much.

Lionel is at the wig bar, donning some of the threads of the deceased. No living soul has ever looked better in a medium, auburn, synthetic fiber, ultralightweight shag.

Paw-Paw's nurse guides him to the gift area. There's a big sign that says, "NO GIFTS," and beneath it are tons of presents. "I can take it from here," Paw-Paw tells her. "Get yourself a drink. You'll need it when you see the cake."

As she walks away, Paw-Paw rummages through the mix. Some gifts are prettily wrapped in boxes and bows, others are shabbily but thoughtfully wrapped in recycled tissue paper with the giver's name and well-wishes written in Sharpie on the outside. Paw-Paw shakes a few. *Sounds broken*, he thinks. *Sounds expensive*, he thinks. He takes a look around, smiling at the party, and then slowly, carefully stands and walks unsteadily from his wheelchair.

He digs deeper into the gifts, until finally, he finds the one. It's got a card on the front: "To Mr. B and The Bum, from Paw-Paw."

"They won't mind," Paw-Paw says to himself and carries the present away.

"Welcome, everyone," Chrissy says into a microphone. "Welcome to Polite Society Ranch."

Wishful Willie turns down the music.

Those who are dancing hold their embrace but give Chrissy their attention. Heads turn from the cocktail tables and the drag bar.

Chrissy continues, "I usually give tours to kids. I'm always telling them to calm down. Now, I see maybe that's a misstep. There's so much fun to be had here. It's wonderful to see so much excitement here. I was gonna tell you about the farm highlights, all my favorite things. But the best things are not on the tour. They're my family, my house, where I slept every night beside the love of my life and raised a son who's a delight. And now I can say I gave him away. And it was in the name of love." And with all those eyes on her, Chrissy Durang wonders briefly if she should have called it *Loving* Society Ranch, instead. "Please add to that joy. Please, let's all create some happy memories here tonight. Welcome, again. Thank you."

"Woo-hoo!" Ezra shouts from the crowd. "Cheers!"

The music, dancing, and drinking resume. Ezra makes his way to Chrissy. "Have you seen my husband?"

"He's here somewhere. No doubt looking for you," she says. As Ezra walks away, Chrissy considers her own wedding. She wonders if the start of her marriage was ever this happy, if her union was ever this hard fought.

Bitcoin, bored with pleasantries, decides on adventure. He can't shake the temptation of whatever is hiding behind a red curtain in the corner of the barn. He crouches, he crawls, a predator to a prize, toward—

"My cake!" The Baker yells in his thick French accent.

Bitcoin disappears under the curtain, but his tail gives him away, wagging so feverishly the flowing fabric parts to reveal two life-sized frosted statuesque men in embrace.

"NO! GIT!" The Baker yells. "*Connard!*"

The shouting catches Bitcoin's interest for only a moment, then he turns back to the cake, focusing on a particularly interesting, protruding part.

"I worked all day on that!" The Baker yells.

Dogs are mirrors of humans. Panic begets panic. Excitement begets excitement. And Bitcoin, in deliriously excited panic, bounds up, grabs the artfully sculped penis in his mouth, rips it from the cake, and sprints away.

"NOOOOOOOOO!" The Baker screams, his howl competing first with the music and then with laughter as the crowd catches on to what's happening.

Bitcoin makes a bold escape with his dangly trophy.

"Someone grab that dog," Wishful Willie yells into the microphone.

But Bitcoin rushes wildly out and away from the barn. He's empowered by the gawking, by people pointing and jeering. He's intoxicated by the attention paid him, the effort made to extract the marzipan member from his mouth.

He passes Nichole, getting increasingly drunk and holding up a vibrating, thrashing horse masturbator sleeve like it's a trophy, laughing with Pauley to the point of nausea.

"My erection!" Ezra yells, pointing to Bitcoin as he races past.

Bitcoin runs up the stage and past a team of musicians playing horns and brass so beautifully, he can't help but shake his tail in an attempt at dance.

Barnett is outside in the pasture with some high school classmates. They're horsing around with a lit joint and accidentally set the field on fire. Thankfully, the spread is stopped by the buffer of Nichole's urine that she has, over the last week, delicately trickled along the property line, inadvertently killing the grass with such profundity that not even flames could find life. Barnett watches Bitcoin race past with the familiar sculpture. Barnett recognizes it as part of his Ezra and seeks to find him.

Dozens of food trucks fill part of the pasture and Bitcoin sets out to have a taste from each. He spits out what's left of the marzipan. He steals scraps of carnitas, vegan nachos, half an In-N-Out burger, and a peanut-dipped vanilla ice cream cone.

As the cars dwindle and the track team has less and less to do, they find sport in, of course, racing each other. "Betcha you can't keep up, old man," Little Roddy says as Barnett walks past. Barnett sprints! He joins the kids, racing in his tux, proudly keeping up with the teenagers despite his age and dress shoes. Out of breath, he says to the kids, "I'd beat you again, but I gotta find my husband."

They hoot playfully and harass, "How can you run so fast with that heavy ball and chain?"

Paw-Paw wanders behind the barn, away from oversight, away from the crowd, not far from the graveyard home of several animals, and of his son. He unwraps the gift. It's a squirrel feeder shaped like a little picnic table. The top is a tray that holds seed. It even comes with a red umbrella that opens to protect furry heads from harmful UV rays.

Paw-Paw pulls nuts from his pockets and loads up the squirrel picnic table. He puts it down and steps a few feet away. "At least I'm good for something," he says to the creatures he's sure are hiding just out of sight.

Nichole and Pauley say their farewells under an umbrella of fireflies, the two of them exhausted from laughter, the horse semen extractor still humming beside them. "I bet there's not a single horse masturbator in all of New York City," she says.

"Maybe I'll send you one from vet school."

Nichole reaches over and turns off the device. The sound of the reception fills the void. Nichole and Pauley wiggle their bodies together, cuddling in their own special moment as the world around them prepares to spin one of them back to her lonely life in the big city and the other to his life's only dream, to help animals in need.

"I feel like I've been here before," Pauley says. "Or maybe this is happening just like in the movies, you know? Doesn't this feel familiar?"

Nichole pulls his arm tighter around her.

"Yes," she admits; the heaviness of her voice is no comfort to either of them. She knows what he's trying to say. The words are on the tip of his tongue: *Fairy tale.* And for Pauley, his hands rough but loving, his unscarred heart full and eager, the trappings apparent in this happily-ever-after moment are intoxicating and hard to abandon.

But Nichole's hands are not rough, her heart not unscarred, her world totally different from his, and she doesn't believe in fairy tales. Happily-ever-after is not for her. It's something others can maybe find. But not her. "I hope we stay in touch," she says, a damp towel over their glowing coals. It may be a cop-out, but it's undeniably a farewell.

And as the couple stills anew, neither wanting to make any move that could be construed as purposeful or manipulative, not far away, Bitcoin is reminded of his own unfinished business, his own necessary farewell.

Linda.

She's a hoarder, sure. But for Bitcoin Tanner, Linda has also been, for lack of any other, a mother.

The floofy gray dog bounds to her, its oversize paws making an easy path to her house.

The other dogs shun him, the beast formerly known as Shithead.

Linda is still wearing her poncho, still a little buzzed from champagne, re-sorting junk mail she's sorted a million times before. She stares at him, cocks *her* head for a change.

Bitcoin approaches her calmly, brushes against her leg and looks up and into her eyes.

"Don't you dare pee on me," she says.

If only he could laugh.

Bitcoin and Linda stare at each other, their minds, in their own languages, marveling at one another. They face vast differences on all levels, and yet each wants to remember the other, to memorize the smells and sounds and textures of their skin and hair and teeth.

"You come to say goodbye?" Linda asks. "I guess I don't blame ya. It's too late for me."

Bitcoin looks around, determined to remember this life, to remember the pile of eternally dirty clothes that served as his bed. He looks to the overgrown backyard, where he still knows where every single bone is buried. He looks at the microwave, still in the box, which Linda will never open, never use. He looks at her closet full of things and considers her longing for a lover, even though there's no room for anyone else. He looks at the bed, piled with unread newspapers, unspent coupons, all that promise; hope can be a death trap.

Bitcoin Tanner was never meant for all this trash.

He bounces, his butt up and his front paws down joyfully like the Great Sphinx. *Thank you*, he says, in his own way.

Linda is a little too drunk from the wedding and a lot too hardened by life to show any emotion; dulled by endless loss of things that have mattered to her and an inability to let go of things that don't. "I hope you find everything I could never give you, Shithead."

At that, Bitcoin is set free. He slides away, his first graceful move, as if where he made his first steps in puppyhood is also where he makes his last, as he steps into maturity.

If dogs mirror humans, whom do humans mirror? For Bitcoin, all humans are made in the image and likeness of nature. Every human is a different flower, a one-of-a-kind pebble, a cloud that is uniquely real for only as long as the wind holds it in place. To Bitcoin, all humans, all living things, are just animated dirt. But, wow, isn't it all fun while it lasts.

He rushes back to the party.

"Look at these twats!" the macaws shout. Bitcoin says goodbye to them, and the pig, the horses, the goats, the chickens, the farm he will soon trade for a high-rise in New York.

Bitcoin says goodbye to Elaine, curled, sweet, still. Too still, especially as people dance and frolic around her stable. He nudges her. *I hope we meet again.*

Elaine offers no response in return. Bitcoin looks up to see Chrissy watching the two of them. He's prepared for her to issue a hearty "git!" But she seems to know the only danger Elaine faces is from within.

Bitcoin's final goodbye is reserved for the reporter for the *Picayune Tribune*. He finds Jessica Thoreaux standing with a scowl, looking at an empty dunking booth, an unnaturally green pasture behind her. Bitcoin approaches stealthily, a hunter still. Her hand dangles at her side and he sees his prize. He bares his teeth. He leaps for it. He snatches her purse.

"Hey! Hey!" she screams as he makes his getaway, every tooth in his mouth exposed in an undeniable, proud smile. He hears from inside the purse the rattle of her car keys and makeup and a cigarette lighter tapping against her tape recorder with every bounce.

Near the barn, Chrissy hugs Victoria. "Thank you for everything."

"We did it," Victoria says. Her instinct is to break the embrace with Chrissy, to sever the intimacy, but Victoria makes a choice not to push Chrissy away, but to hold on even tighter.

"In my whole life, I don't think I've ever had a best friend," Victoria says quietly into Chrissy's ear, her voice so soft, it's almost as if she's unsure she's saying it at all.

And there's a pause—maybe Chrissy didn't hear it.

Victoria starts to pull away, but can't. Now, it's Chrissy who holds

Victoria tightly, whispering back, "I've been so jealous that the six-year-olds who tour the farm have besties and I don't."

At this, both women let go—of each other and of the fogs of fortunes and vices that in any other world would keep them separate. They look into each other's faces, recognizing that *mom quality*—exhaustion, love for their children so acute, it shows up in neat lines of poetry around their eyes, their mouths. Still smelling the other woman's hair and soap, still feeling the other woman's heat and heartbeat, they say nothing else. It reads on their faces—a couple of older ladies who at last understand what the kids mean by BFF.

"Hi, Moms. Have you seen Ezra?" Barnett asks.

"That way," Victoria points.

Barnett rounds the corner and sees Ezra leaning against the gazebo.

"I've been waiting all night to dance with you," Ezra says.

Barnett jumps up beside his husband and the two twirl, not to the faint music from the barn but to the song in their hearts, a dance so sincere they forget about cruel and crusty graffiti that's just a few feet away.

"By space and time standards," Ezra says, "this gazebo sure has seen some shit, huh?"

Barnett laughs. "God, don't remind me. Or actually, do remind me. Let's never forget it. We did this."

"Well, we did *some* of it. Lest we forget the workers who built this thing, my sister, your mother. It all added up to loveliness, didn't it?"

Barnett slows their dancing, lowers his voice, searches for the right words. "Are we different? I always thought getting married would give us some kind of special shine."

Ezra claims the lead, spins his husband around in the opposite direction. In the dizzying thrill of being in each other's eternal care, he says, "Aren't we lucky, babe? We had it all along."

Chapter 26

CHRISSY Durang is red from embarrassment, lost in another world, unanchored in the present moment despite the steaming cup of black coffee beside her, despite the crisp newspaper in her achy hands, the morning light on her face. She's lost in an article about the day before, an article about her farm and her family and her son and his wedding, splattered in ink under the byline of Jessica Thoreaux:

> The whole event was a sort of miracle—a word not used lightly under the controversial circumstances. It was tarnished by graffiti last week. But the attack was used against the unknown vandal as guests painted over the slur with well-wishes for love and a long life together. The messages upon the mural range from basic support like "We love you!" to more direct refutes of the original attack, like single words in bold letters, including "ICONS!" and "HEROES!"
>
> Perhaps the protesters and vandal got it wrong. Perhaps they are the scandal, the sinners, the villains.
>
> As the wedding reception was winding down, a dog stole my purse. I gave chase and eventually found it. But I ended up out of breath near the front gate. That's when a very thin

woman met my eyes. Her beauty was buoyed by otherworldly confidence, with an uncanny and shocking resemblance to singer Celine Dion. She ran past me, and in a thick French Canadian accent, she asked in a panic, "Where is the dunking booth? WHERE IS THE DUNKING BOOTH? Am I late?"

Maybe it was her, maybe not. But it made me realize something. Maybe love isn't just patient and kind, maybe it's magical, too.

"Maybe love isn't just patient and kind, maybe it's magical, too," Chrissy reads aloud, the final sentence in a long article that was once her greatest fear and is now her greatest teacher. She lays the paper down on the desk in the office. She reaches her hands to her face to cool the blushing.

She looks at the futon, briefly entertaining the faintest memory of Barnett sitting there crying in her arms—it feels like another lifetime ago—when she gave him bad advice that he thankfully didn't take.

She looks out the window.

But her beautiful farm, her life's work, can't keep her attention.

Chrissy looks back at the article in the newspaper, baffled, amused. Not even a mention of the word "gay." The photo they used from yesterday—Barnett, elated in Ezra's embrace in the gazebo—does not include her. She was so worried about how she'd look. She only now realizes how much the event was not about her. The awareness causes her to blush anew. She considers what Ezra would say about her self-centeredness, about going through the entire occasion with every color vibe except green. She has regrets, but also love. Just thinking about the concept of vibes—even the undesirable ones—she smiles with fondness for what's now her two sons, the one from birth and the one from marriage.

Chrissy gently folds the newspaper article and puts it atop a brand-new box wrapped in thick, crisp, glossy-white paper and a sturdy red-velvet ribbon tied into a perfect, big, blossoming bow. She picks up the gift and the newspaper article and seeks him. *Oh, Barnett.*

The kitchen is empty save for a mess, a smattering of hardening bagels and remnants of handfuls of cereal downed in a rushed breakfast. There's never enough time for goodbyes.

Her boy is not in the kitchen, though his spirit and history linger—the spot where he threw up brussels sprouts, the cabinet wherein he would hide with his He-Man, the sink where he ruined his church suit. Soon, all that will be left of the two most important men in her life are the scenes of their misadventures.

Chrissy carries the newspaper and the gift through the living room, past memories of John and young Barnett playing on the floor, watching *Cheers* and *Seinfeld* together. It's all fondness, as she thinks of the man she loved so much and the boy they loved together, the boy—now man, now married—who's finally flying away.

Chrissy carries the newspaper and the gift down the hallway to Barnett's room. He's not there. The room is tidy, luggage already hauled outside in preparation for the Uber. The room is back to the way it was before everyone arrived, when this trip was to be all about her and Barnett, in Chrissy's mind, at least.

The room smells like them, the two boys, Ezra and his Barnett, Barnett and his Ezra, as if their natures are in cahoots to eliminate the individuals and present to the world only a couple, two who make one, and she remembers the thrilling feeling, the feeling of excitement and love when she had that oneness with John.

She also feels mourning, as she lets go of Barnett, again, as she did when she mourned the loss of his sweet baby scent, the loss of his dependence on her as he started to walk and talk, the loss of his childhood as he became a teen, the loss marked by every great achievement—each grade advanced in school, each graduation, each job promotion—because they all meant her baby was growing further and further from her.

She eyeballs the room, considering the bicycle wallpaper, the Boy Scout badges framed on the wall. *Maybe it's time for a bigger bed in here? For when the boys come visit.*

Chrissy tenses at the sound of high heels approaching. *The shoes don't lie*, she thinks.

Victoria Tanner doesn't exit the guest room; she emerges.

"Morning," Chrissy says, but Victoria makes a show that she's on the phone, rolling her eyes and shaking her head and holding up a finger at Chrissy as if to say, "WAIT."

Chrissy stands patiently in the doorway to Barnett's bedroom, listening as her new family, her new friend, trots toward her, Bitcoin in loyal tow.

"And the whole time I was drinking the blood of Christ!" Victoria says into the phone. "Alas, I'm sober now. And I intend to be annoying about it. I'm advocating radical self-care. For all those reasons, I must decline the mother-of-the-year award at this time." She looks at Chrissy. "There's someone else who deserves it much more than me."

Behind Victoria's high heels are loafers—worn, dependable, and quiet. Winston. He steps around his wife, dragging their luggage, and hugs Chrissy. "Thank you," he says.

"You have a lovely voice," Chrissy says. She looks down at Bitcoin. "And you have a lot of luck."

His wagging tail makes for an easier goodbye.

Victoria ends her call and turns to Chrissy. "Winston and Bitcoin and I will reach out when we get to New York."

"Everyone is leaving so soon," Chrissy says.

"I have all kinds of things to do back home—find a dog trainer, find a therapist, find an Alcoholics Anonymous meeting, build a sober community of friends around me, and most importantly, find a stylist who can reset my hair."

"Come back anytime," Chrissy says. "No one is ever turned away. It's Polite Society Ranch, after all."

Victoria smiles, puts her hands on Chrissy's shoulders. "Chrissy, truer words have never been spoken." The two women hold their gaze for a moment, emoting at each other like it's a sport. Then, Victoria turns to Bitcoin and Winston. "To the limo. Posthaste."

"Have you seen Barnett?" Chrissy asks, guiding her new family outside.

Winston shakes his head.

"No," Victoria says. "We said our goodbyes to the boys already."

They walk to the carport, where their party grows by two.

"Mother?" Nichole asks, nodding awkwardly behind her, to where Pauley is standing. He waves. "Pauley and I were talking and maybe I'll stay a little longer."

"You can't possibly be serious?" Victoria says. "Stay longer... here? In this climate? And have you asked Chrissy if you can keep intruding?"

"No worries here," Chrissy says.

"Actually, Miss Chrissy," Pauley says. "I was wondering. Sorry about this. But Nichole and I were gonna maybe take a week and go to the French Quarter. She's never been. And I know my classes start soon and I only have a little time left working here and I hate to be away from you—"

"You have my blessing," Chrissy says. "Go have fun, sweetie." Then, "But not too much fun, you know?"

"Oh, shit yeah—I mean—shucks yeah, Miss Chrissy. Thank you."

"Mother, is it okay?" Nichole asks.

"Do whatever you want," Victoria says. "Just don't TOUCH the CarMax stock!"

Nichole and Pauley beam.

"And don't you dare show your breasts," Victoria says. "Unless it's for cash up front."

Once sealed in the limousine, Winston and Bitcoin struggle to get comfortable while Victoria makes short work of the minibar. A bottle of Belvedere sits in wait, in a thick, frosty glass bottle. Her eyes are wide with craving, not only for the taste of real alcohol but for the ritual, the crutch of something cool in her hand, the lovely chime of ice floating, bumping into crystal. Winston and Bitcoin watch her with reservation. She catches them staring and they both look away, partly in fear of her, and also in defeat, unsure what to do. She yanks the bottle from the ice bucket.

The limo sits in the driveway as if on a launchpad, the driver noting mileage in his diary and preparing to pull away. Just as he places it in drive, a perfectly chilled, unopened bottle of vodka goes flying out of the rear passenger window. It lands in the grass and rolls and rolls to a thud against a pine tree, like the television rolled to the curb at the end of *Poltergeist*.

"I never want to be haunted again, Winston," Victoria says. She pulls a bottle of La Gracè Vino out of her purse. She pops the cork, takes a swig, and closes it up. "I'm now a lush for overpriced grape juice."

As the limo picks up speed, Bitcoin stands on the seat and leaps up, smashing his nose against the sunroof.

"Here, buddy," Winston says, pushing the button that makes the magic happen, the sunroof peeling back, letting in fresh air and warm sunshine and fond memories.

Bitcoin's head pops from the roof of the vehicle. His ears flutter in the wind, his caramel eyes curious, pensive, sentimental.

His stature as he looks out the window gives Victoria and Winston a severe, clinical look at his underbelly. "If you pee on me—" she starts, considering her options: fur coat, disownership, abandonment. But none of those feel true. Victoria looks at Winston. "Oh, screw it. Who am I kidding?" she shrugs, saying into Bitcoin's groin, "I'll forgive you anything."

But the beast doesn't hear, doesn't understand. As the limo reaches the end of the driveway, Bitcoin becomes more frantic, desperate to take in the shrinking landscape of his life so far—the woods, the pine trees, the path to a home with Linda, the path to a new life with Victoria, the kissing boys, the trash, the hunger, the marzipan penis. Though, if his eyes are saying farewell, his tail—thrashing back and forth and slapping Winston repeatedly—signals his delight at whatever destination is next, namely, an airport, a bustling city, a thrilling future, all ahead of him.

Chrissy watches as the limo carries Victoria, Winston, and Bitcoin away. She clocks the bottle of vodka on her lawn and smiles. She pulls out her orange notepad and makes a note to collect it later. She looks back up just in time to catch Bitcoin's floofy ears flapping from the sunroof as he leaves this life behind.

Chrissy is about to shout for Barnett, but shoes catch her eyes, one pair that looks like it belongs on a stealthy ninja, and another that looks like it belongs on a big clown.

Ezra is sitting with Paw-Paw on the far side of the carport, one man in a wheelchair, the other in one of the rented chairs being prepared for pickup.

Chrissy listens quietly, politely.

"I already told Mr. B," Paw-Paw says to Ezra. "I got you a squirrel picnic table as a wedding gift. It's behind the barn. They don't like hazelnuts."

But Ezra's tone is much more serious. "Did you tell them?"

"Kid, I'm running out of evidence that I'm alive. I don't recognize myself. I'm worth more dead. My prized possessions are gone. Memory lane costs a toll that's harder and harder to pay. I'm exhausted. My friends are dead. My son is dead."

"Your grandkid isn't."

"Wanna know something terrible?"

"Always. I'm not even kidding," Ezra says.

"The grandchild thing never really did it for me. I mean, yay—a healthy kid was born and the family expands. But they're a Xerox of a Xerox of a Xerox, aren't they? They just remind me time is running out, the game is over, I'm benched, the field isn't mine anymore."

"And yet here you are," Ezra says. "Supporting your grandson."

"Barnett is different. I actually like him. I just plain like the guy." He makes eye contact with Ezra. "I just love the guy."

Ezra twists his brand-new wedding ring around and around—the emerald inlay catching his eye and producing within Ezra the vibes they're meant to represent. The twist of that ring is the easiest way for Ezra to say to Paw-Paw, without words: *Me, too.*

"Last night, your wedding was the best night of my life," Paw-Paw says.

"That's generous," Ezra laughs, "and impossible."

"You'll see someday, you bum. Experiences shine brighter on borrowed time."

"You can borrow more. You have to take your meds."

Paw-Paw has considered it, had visions of the diarrhea, the nausea, the needles, more and more tolls. "Nah. Never borrow unless you have to. I'm debt-free, you handsome devil."

Ezra considers all the tricks he uses on kids, asking about the vibes, reflecting their sentiments back to them, gently asking questions that would force self-inquiry. But, Ezra thinks, maybe he's not the teacher in this situation.

"Can I show you a secret handshake?" Paw-Paw asks.

At Ezra's enthusiastic nod, the two men clasp palms, holding tightly, the older clinging to the younger as if parting is lethal. The younger holds with curiosity—the old skin, the cool blood, the palm that indeed tells the future: age comes for all.

"Hope I come back as one of my damn squirrels," Paw-Paw says.

"We should all be so lucky."

"Love my grandson, please," Paw-Paw says, orders.

"I'm on it."

The two men tighten their grips.

And in the palm of Milford Alan Durang's hand, Ezra can feel a faint life, a slow push of warm blood to the old man's fingertips. "See you soon?"

Paw-Paw shrugs and offers a Louisiana-worthy nonresponse: "I'll be watching you."

With a polite nod, the boy is gone.

And Chrissy takes his place.

"Have you seen Barnett?" she asks, stepping forward, sitting beside Paw-Paw. He doesn't answer. Together, they watch Ezra walk away.

"Young people don't understand goodbyes," Paw-Paw says. "They can't. If they did, we'd all be paralyzed, stuck in farewells all the damn time."

"Nice shoes," Chrissy says.

Paw-Paw wiggles his feet, willing his legs to kick in a show of flamboyance, but his body refuses, and he accepts the smaller compromise. He wants to tell her they're Elmer's shoes. Then he thinks better of it, decides they're his shoes. Then he thinks better of that, for they won't be his shoes much longer. They'll go to whoever scores them when stuffy old room 102 eventually opens to a new resident, paying a new rate, again renaming the old squirrels at Camille Manor Retirement Pavements.

"My sister—goddamn her—she used to obsess over a marriage book," Paw-Paw says. "The author's name always stayed with me because it was like the pirate's name: Laffite. That book, for my sister—we were just kids back then—but for her, she was sure that book described her future. And it talked about leeches for hysteria and serving fancy meals of canned goods. And my sister was ready. She accepted all the norms and did all the holy traditions. And none of it lasted. And yet these boys—" Paw-Paw chokes up. "These boys had their own version of that book, a whole volume of hate written succinctly on the side of your damn house. But, unlike my sister, those boys, my boys, our boys—our men, damn—they said no to all that."

Paw-Paw starts to laugh, deep and cavernous laughter, the kind that forces loose from his lungs the old, bitter air of hard decades. The laughter is almost convulsive, almost appearing to be the reason for the tears pooling in his eyes. "Who's hysterical now?" he asks.

Chrissy, as if in charity, as if her own welling tears are appearing simply because Paw-Paw has too many to unleash on his own, follows his gaze not onto the farm but into the future.

"I'm so damn proud of those boys," Paw-Paw says, not wiping the tears. Maybe at his age, he doesn't feel them; maybe at his age, he doesn't fear them. "No one will ever say these boys didn't throw out the bullshit so-called traditions, that they didn't follow their hearts. Goddamn. My sister couldn't say that. I'm not sure I can say that." Paw-Paw reaches his hand out to the woman formerly known as Chrissy Boudreaux, the little girl brought to life by the love she had with his late son.

Chrissy smiles, dabs her eyes, holds his hand.

"I'm sorry Elaine is so unwell," Paw-Paw says. "I see it at the home just before, you know. I know that look on her face."

Chrissy nods. "And I know—" she pauses, tries to continue without blubbering, "and I know that look on yours."

Paw-Paw smiles. "I wish I could tell you that it's hard. To say good-bye. But it's easy. It's so easy. I'm so tired. I just have to give in. I just have to say 'Okay.' I'm just never sure. What if tomorrow they serve my favorite pudding, you know?"

Soft footsteps break the moment. Paw-Paw's nurse approaches. "Time to go?" she asks.

Paw-Paw looks at his daughter-in-law. "I believe so," he says, squeezing her hand, considering it's maybe the last time. And Chrissy savors his touch, his strong grip on her hand and her heart, and she hopes she never forgets the feeling, wishing she could save it like a voice mail to play over and over.

The nurse helps Paw-Paw into the ambulance and Chrissy can't take her eyes off him. The door slams and he's cut off, severed from her world.

Paw-Paw sits, looking out of the back window, relaxed but solemn. He doesn't flinch as the nurse slams her door closed. He doesn't change expression as the engine starts. He doesn't move an inch as the vehicle starts to drive away. He's still in his seat as the world starts to move around him.

Through that window, Paw-Paw waves goodbye.

Chrissy steps forward and waves back, faster and faster to try to distract from the lump forming in her throat.

But Paw-Paw's wave is not as energetic, and, Chrissy realizes, not for her.

Paw-Paw Durang waves not to Chrissy but to the life flowing through every tree and blade of grass, every chicken and goat. He waves goodbye to a farm he may never see again, to the fiefdom of little Chrissy Boudreaux, to the soil that nourished that dang fine kid, Mr. B. Paw-Paw waves and prays that his soul flows, somehow, someday, from the dumpster at Camille Manor Retirement Gardens, to this beautiful, perfect, and—goddammit—*polite* farm, and in that, he'll be whole again, he'll be home again, he'll be with his son, with his family, forever.

CHRISSY walks to the barn and finds Ezra outside. "Barnett in there?" she asks.

Ezra nods, *Yes*. "Miss Chrissy, before you go in there, I was wondering if I could ask you something?"

"Anything, always, anytime."

"Well, this was such a special whirlwind, I don't want to spoil it."

"I don't see how that would be possible," she says.

Ezra swallows hard. "I was thinking, maybe this could be the part where you tell me to call you 'Mom.'"

"I don't think that's this part," Chrissy says quickly.

"Not this part?"

"No."

"Got it," Ezra says.

Nearby, Roz lets out a neigh, maybe a laugh, and a huge grin appears on Chrissy's face. "But definitely later, probably," she says.

Ezra grins.

"Come here, son!" Chrissy opens her arms and hugs a giddy Ezra, the quirky young man whose name she finally committed to memory as she finally committed him to family. *Ezra*, the name Barnett threw around so often in desperate attempts to solidify him in her consciousness, the name once unheard and now etched in her mind, and heart.

"I love your vibe," she says, pulling from their hug to look him in the eyes.

Again, Roz neighs and finally Chrissy turns to her. "Hush. You have this whole farm. You can surely go entertain yourself elsewhere."

"Want to hear some hocus-pocus?" Ezra asks.

Chrissy sighs playfully. "I'll allow it only because you're leaving."

"Some people believe, since everything exists only in your mind, that talking to animals is really just talking to yourself."

Chrissy looks away and considers it for a moment. "You know what," she says, turning back to Ezra. "I'm glad that was my last hocus-pocus from you for a while." Again, she pulls him in for a hug. "Love you, Ezra."

"Love ya back," he says. He breaks their embrace and steps back. He reaches for her hands and holds them—and her gaze—tightly. When he releases her, she looks down and sees a silver square—magic chocolate—in her palm. "You and Elaine had such a nice chat last time."

"Thank you," Chrissy says.

INSIDE the barn, Chrissy finds him. *Oh, Barnett.*

His two hands are petting Elaine's chest. She's lying on her side, nearly motionless, looking unalive save for the gentle rippling of her wool as she labors for a breath, and another, and another.

Barnett doesn't want to leave Elaine and doesn't want to leave his mother. Now married, he expected it to change how he felt about her, and about how she fits into his life. But he's still worrying. He's still wondering: *Should I be doing Pauley's job? Or my mom's?*

"Do you think you'll ever want to come down here and take over?" Chrissy asks.

"It sounds so nice," Barnett says.

"But you don't know?"

"I don't know," he says. "But I'm hopeful it will all work out."

They both look at Elaine. "She's the best," he says. To Elaine, he says, "Sorry again about the Woolite thing."

"You're wasting your breath," Chrissy says. "She'll never forgive you for that."

The mother and son laugh reservedly, their joy feeling sacrilegious at the altar of Elaine, her dirty white wool gleaming atop the golden hay on which she lies, the other animals keeping their distance, as if the whole barn was built around her, as if they understand how much space Elaine commands by being Farmer Mom's favorite.

"I have something for you," Chrissy says to Barnett. She hands him the newspaper article and the small wrapped gift. "The article is about the wedding. For your scrapbook. It turned out lovely. She even called it 'wicked,' but, you know, in a good way, as you kids would say."

Barnett smiles, looks at the wrapped gift. "And this?"

"A little something from me to you."

Barnett opens the gift just as his mother knew he would—ravenously, ripping the paper and letting the ribbon and bow fall to the dirt.

Inside he finds a leather belt wrapped in a tight loop.

"What?" he says playfully, picking up the belt and letting it unroll. The leather smell brings back memories of his family, his youth, Boy Scouts.

The phrase "Just Gay Married" is smashed in neat lettering, letters that perfectly match belts of old: Farmer Mom, Farmer Dad, and a discarded one, at least for now, Farmer Son.

"Tuck it away somewhere," Chrissy says.

"Absolutely not!" Barnett stands and starts to unlatch the belt he's wearing at present. With a THWAP, THWAP, THWAP of his old boring belt lashing the loops of his pants, he tosses it on the ground and starts stringing his new belt into place. "I'll wear it every day, Mom. I love it."

Chrissy laughs. "I guess I should've gotten you matching boots."

The belt fits perfectly, of course, with dignity and style—just as Chrissy requested from the craftsman. It fits in every way, around her son's waist, and around the soft parts of each of their hearts, the parts that needed a little love, a little repair, a little cinching.

"You have your plane tickets?" Chrissy asks.

Barnett taps the right front pocket of his jeans. "In my phone."

"Of course," she says.

"Our hotel has this whole stargazing thing," Barnett says of their honeymoon to Hawaii. "So, when you look up at the stars, please think of us. Those are the same stars viewed by Galileo, Cleopatra, Jesus."

Chrissy walks Barnett out of the barn and finds Ezra with the Uber driver.

"I could take you to the airport," Chrissy says.

"Nah, the farm is the most important. I'd never ask you to leave my favorite place on earth."

The MRI would show major inflammation—the heart, the tears.

Chrissy and Barnett come together not as two halves but as two completes, two complete celestial bodies defined forever by their eclipse—a vibrant sun and a cooling moon. The two are powerhouses in their own right, but when together, they're a marvel.

"I love you, son."

"I love you, Farmer Mom."

The trunk of the Uber is full of two red suitcases and a sensible oversize black purse, lighter by a couple handfuls of psychotropic chocolates.

The car doors close, the vehicle's tires conspire with the farm's gravel, nature and science and love and life have their way, and the car drives away.

As if in slow motion, as if she were the Bionic Woman, Chrissy feels she could run after him. *Oh, Barnett.* She feels she could do it, chase the car down the highway, try to hold him and keep him. She could—but she doesn't.

And in the slow agony, her boy is gone.

And the sound that's in her heart—a throaty farewell—is voiced not from her mouth but from the barn. A cry of loss, of letting go, comes from Elaine. And Chrissy wants to shout back, to comfort her dear ward, "Hang in there!" Chrissy starts to rush to Elaine but then stops. She looks from the barn to her palm, and the silver square therein.

Chapter 27

THE screeching rips peace and quiet from every soul within a mile of Polite Society Ranch, except one. Chrissy Durang is cool and calm, even as the school bus with the loud brakes (and equally loud kids) arrives to deliver her afternoon's headache.

Polite Society Ranch, especially of late, has been a place of comings and goings, of cutting old ties and forging new ones, of marriage and dog adoptions, of parties and sobriety. Chrissy is used to being busy, so when Mader Elementary requested another tour on the day after the wedding, in the afternoon after she's said goodbye to her son and houseguests, she welcomed the distraction.

The bus lumbers to a stop, its noisy tires just as loud as on the day of Barnett's arrival; it felt like yesterday. But with this hour comes not a joyful reunion of kids and her farm, but a lingering farewell. Chrissy looks to the barn with sadness; she longs to be by Elaine's side.

Chrissy reaches into her back pocket and pulls out her orange notepad and half a pencil she once stole from Saint Michael the Archangel Catholic Church. She licks the tip of the pencil and holds it beside one of the items on her to-do list: "11 a.m., Goodbye to Barnett. She puts a checkmark beside it. 2 p.m., Tour arrives." She puts a checkmark beside it.

Chrissy steps out of her office and onto the porch, looking out over her plot of life lit by peak Louisiana sunshine. "Stiffen your spine, Lionel," she says to The Oaf. "It's gonna be a Category 4."

"Yes, ma'am," Lionel says, his white T-shirt tucked in, his pants and fingernails clean, his posture stiff and respectful, exactly as requested by his new boss, Chrissy Durang.

Chrissy misses Pauley. Though he hasn't exactly left yet, he's gone in the ways that matter, the emotional ones. Chrissy pictures him wearing his cowboy hat while showing Nichole around the French Quarter. She hopes he wears the hat to vet school. Maybe he'll come back after he graduates. Maybe he'll run this place one day instead of Barnett. Or maybe Pauley's hope to come back to Polite Society Ranch will be derailed by love, and he'll end up in some future he couldn't have imagined, maybe with Nichole, just like Chrissy so many years ago with John. Or, maybe, by the time Pauley graduates, there won't be a farm to come back to, or a Farmer Mom here to show him the old ways of dignity, of politeness.

Meantime, Lionel's training has to start at some point, and today is as good as any.

Farmer Mom tightens her belt, the old, cracking leather belt of her legacy, her life's work. Her hand finds its way into her collar, a habitual tug on the gold chain, though it's now much lighter. In a strange way it's a relief; something heavy seems lifted.

The bus doors open with such force, Lionel takes a step back. But Chrissy holds steady.

She watches the junior size-four shoes as they clomp, clomp off the bus. Shoes don't lie. Her eyes fall upon her own feet. She looks at her boots and for the first time considers what they say about her: aged, respectable, reliable, exactly as she would have requested of her maker.

Chrissy takes the kids past the macaws, who shout and jeer, "Look at these twats!!"

"What's a twat?" one of the kids asks.

"You're mishearing them," Chrissy says, dismissing Victoria's lasting contribution of vulgarity to Polite Society Ranch.

Chrissy takes the kids past the kennel, the stables, the barn, which are all still draped in white, flowy fabrics. The trees still have tables built around them. The gazebo is empty, and yet it seems full of energy—like a church that's been decommissioned. You can't suddenly make something unsacred.

"You had a big party here, huh?" a young boy asks.

"I did. My son got married."

"To a pretty girl?" the boy asks.

"To a man," Chrissy corrects. "A pretty man, if you want to know the truth."

The kids are stunned silent for a moment, then shrug and move along with their lives. *Adults sure do complicate things*, Chrissy thinks.

She shows the kids the pasture partially burned by Barnett's friends, the brand-new lake with swans who will never again get sold for wedding fodder, the chickens making peace signs in the dirt with their feet.

Chrissy doesn't take the kids to the graveyard, not today, not with the new plot carefully, freshly dug, a hole the size of a Louisiana heritage sheep.

Elaine. She's all Chrissy can think about as she goes through the motions of the tour. And as it's finally wrapping up, and the teacher begins to herd the kids toward their bus—"STOP!" a little girl yells, the volume enough to cause hearing loss in the other students who surround her. "I HATE Y'ALL!" the girl blubs, her face red, snot sneaking out. The little crowd dissipates as the girl's tears arrive.

"What's going on?" Chrissy asks.

"AHHH—"

"Hey!" Chrissy says to the crying child. "Silence the alarm for one second. You don't have to scream."

The girl does as instructed. For approximately one second, she is quiet.

"AHHH!" she resumes.

Chrissy kneels down in front of her, wincing to cope with the shrieks, wincing instead of putting her fingers in her ears.

"Want some candy?" Chrissy asks, to which the young girl mercifully, quietly, sobs. But she shakes her head, *No.* Her little fingers squeeze into each of her hands to create two rounded fists, rounding out a young body trying to figure out where to put her helplessness.

"What happened?" Chrissy asks.

"They called me loser-town."

"Loser-*TOWN*?" Chrissy asks. "Is it not enough anymore to simply call someone a loser?"

The girls face reddens anew and fresh tears begin to well in her sweet eyes.

"Sorry, sorry," Chrissy says, reaching into her front jeans pocket. She feels the crisp five-dollar bill she stuffed in there this morning. "Any chance you're a capitalist?"

The girl starts to sob again.

Chrissy's shoulders slump. The pang that hits her might be what an explorer feels when discovering a new land, the feeling of directionlessness. *What would Ezra do?*

"All right, then," Chrissy says. "What color are your body's, um, vibes right now?" Chrissy swallows hard. "Like, red and angry? Or blue and sad?"

The girl wipes her eyes, her snotty nose, blinks as if in Morse code: *I don't know.*

Chrissy tries to remember how Ezra did it. "Uh, okay," she says.

"Vibes are like radio stations. You can change the channel. If I may be so bold, you kinda look like you're having red, angry vibes in your body. Do you want to change the channel?"

The girl nods, *Yes*.

"Okay, okay," Chrissy says, in a mild panic, trying to recall what she witnessed in Ezra's process. "Wanna go to a happy place in your mind?"

The girl swallows, slows her breathing, nods, *Yes*.

"Close your eyes," Chrissy says. "Think of a happy place." She pauses. "See it?"

"Yes."

"Is it awesome?"

"Yes," the girl says, her eyes still closed, a little giggle in her voice.

"The only way you can imagine an awesome place is if you're awesome yourself. Isn't that cool? And you can't be 'loser-town' if you're awesome. So don't let some silly thing ruin your whole day." Chrissy leans in close and speaks quietly. "And between you and me, I know a thing or two about loser-town. It's a compliment! Our property values are sky high and our mayor is that chicken over there."

The girl laughs with such a spurt, a blob of snot shoots from her nostril and lands in the dirt. She quickly covers her nose with her hands and looks embarrassed.

"Not to worry, hon," Chrissy says. "I've seen worse."

The girl lowers her hands, smiles.

"Feel better?" Chrissy asks. "Green vibes or whatever?"

The girl says, "Yeah."

"Woo-hoo," Chrissy says. She puts up her hand and the girl gently high-fives it.

"Wanna meet my best friend?" Chrissy asks.

The girl nods, "Yes!"

Chrissy walks the girl into the barn, to the far side, the most sacred spot, the warmest spot in the winter and the coolest spot in the summer, the spot with the best views outside, the spot with the softest hay, the spot where Elaine lies, her three legs limp, her dark eyes searching.

Chrissy sits and the child does the same.

"This is Elaine. She's a Louisiana heritage sheep. They can only survive in Louisiana."

"Why?"

"Parasites. It's complicated. It's not important."

"Where's her other leg?"

"In a landfill, probably. But if you mean, 'What happened to it?' I can tell you that it broke when she was a lamb."

"What do sheep count as they're falling asleep?" the girl asks.

Before Chrissy can answer, before she can even begin to consider an apt response, the girl's teacher sticks her head in the barn. "Everything okay?"

Chrissy looks from the young girl to the teacher. "Yeah, just fine."

"We're loading the bus," the teacher says. "Time to say goodbye."

Now, Chrissy looks from the girl to Elaine.

Outside the barn, the school bus engine roars to life.

Inside the barn, a frail heart embraces death, with Chrissy by her side.

As the screech of the brakes (and the kids) grows more faint, Chrissy pulls out her orange notepad. A teardrop hits the page, right beside "3 p.m., Goodbye to Elaine."

Part 7

—

Gifts

Sweetheart, eschew the crystal ashtray and silver cake breaker. The best wedding gift is memory. Consider! Life is scaffolding around a vapor, until one day, in the end, suddenly, as if from nowhere, as if you weren't creating it the whole damn time, something remarkable stands. One day, they shall try to define it. One day, they shall call it an obituary. But you? Oh, you've already given it a name. You shall call it a life. You shall call it a ball!

—Mrs. Jeannie Laffite's Undisputed Guide to
Respectable Southern Nuptials,
volume III, page 208
(copyright 1912 by Mrs. Jeannie Laffite)

Chapter 28

ELAINE bounds through a field with green grass below and breezy blue sky above, a sweet sheep surrounded by the sanctuary of white picket fences, a place perfect and yet somehow familiar, almost exactly like her home, Polite Society Ranch.

She smells flowers, intensely. Nearby are white roses, a bed of them for her to nuzzle into and doze the day away. She smells apples and carrots and grapes. Nearby are baskets full of them.

"Thank you for this," a beloved voice says.

Elaine turns her head to look for her, the source of the woman's voice, the voice of Chrissy Durang. Elaine jumps and twirls playfully, but in the perfect pasture, there's no sign of her Farmer Mom.

"Sorry for these circumstances," a mysterious voice says. A man's voice, one Elaine doesn't recognize.

At this, she stops her play. She's focused now. She's curious now. She's worried now.

Elaine hasn't yet realized she's asleep in her little hay bed in the barn, dreaming. Her nose is dry. Her hooves are worn and twitching. Her wool is thin. Her breathing is labored. The flowers she smells are left over from the wedding, white roses and angel's breath rotting in the trash. The gentle breeze Elaine is dreaming about is Chrissy's hand petting her head, neck, side. Slices of Elaine's favorite treats are in Chrissy's pockets: apples, carrots, grapes.

"It's going to be okay," Chrissy whispers to Elaine. She puts the apple and carrots and grapes near Elaine, but Elaine doesn't react, or can't.

"Tell me when you want me to start," the man's voice says.

In her beautiful dreamscape, Elaine struggles to understand what's happening. She struggles to understand the voices and what they want, or what they're doing. Of late, much has been a struggle for Elaine. But she doesn't have the strength to fight. Not now. What she lacks in concern, she makes up for in trust.

On farms, trust looks like your pet forgiving you for killing them.

The man Elaine hears is The Oaf, Lionel, with all his farm experience in tow.

"I'm going to be high on magical mushrooms while you do it," Chrissy says. "Hope that's not a problem."

Lionel nods. "You'd be surprised how many tough guys had me put down one of their favorite animals, and I could smell the whiskey on their breath. No different, if you ask me."

Elaine stirs and Chrissy touches her, rubbing her finger behind and around Elaine's floppy ear. "It's okay, sweetie. You're okay."

Talking to animals is really just talking to yourself.

Chrissy considers all the things she's said to Elaine over their time together—*You're safe. You're beautiful. You're loved.* All things Chrissy maybe wishes she heard more often in her life, especially in these last years.

"You're not alone," Chrissy says to Elaine. Chrissy swallows hard, wishing away the aftertaste of Ezra's chocolate square still lightly coating her mouth. "You'll be getting all fixed up soon."

Farmers are quiet folk. Some of their rugged spouses joke that it's because farmers are full of secrets. Break the seal for one little bit of banter and it could all spill out—all sorts of truths about what's really in the soil, what's really in the animal feed, what it really takes to grow a crop, to raise a herd.

Words from a farmer's mouth are chosen carefully: "Raise" sounds way better than "harvest meat." "Herd" sounds way better than "supply chain."

The word "euthanasia" is out of place in these rural woods. It's a combination of Greek words that conspire to mean "easy death." But farmers don't talk like that, especially not in rural Louisiana. Instead of death they say, "It's time." They say, "field trip." Instead of die, they call it "retirement." They call it "going home." They call it "getting all fixed up."

Elaine twitches and her eyes open partially. She's back in the barn, awake from the pasture. She tries to stretch, to reorient her body into this world and out of her dream one. Her eyes land first on Chrissy, then on Lionel, then back on Chrissy.

"He's our friend," Chrissy says. "Don't worry, baby."

Elaine was never bred. She has no lambs. She's never known love for, or love of, offspring. She's never had a signal of her maturity, no pregnancy, nothing ever expected from her. She's had no idea of time or aging. She's lived most of her life on Polite Society Ranch, believing the entire time that she was still a young lamb, until these final months, weeks, days, hours. Time finally arrived with its cruel calling, a sudden feeling twisting in Elaine, a sudden feeling that something has run its course.

Chrissy lies in the hay beside Elaine and looks up at Lionel. "Maybe you could give us a minute?"

He nods and walks to the far side of the barn.

The space is cool and the light is dim. The fragrances left over from the wedding are mixed with the smell of the animals, giving the barn a scent similar to that of Saint Michael the Archangel Catholic Church.

Fitting, that something so simple could evoke the feeling of sanctity. *Perfect*, Chrissy thinks.

Chrissy believes crying in public is sometimes acceptable, but weeping is impolite. And because of that, Elaine is one of the only living beings to have ever seen Chrissy shed tears in earnest, the kind of tears that force themselves into being with great labor, with groans and a struggle for breath. The first time Chrissy wept was when Barnett went off to college. It was a devastating sadness. Elaine watched Chrissy cry then as she's doing now. *Maybe I'm going off to college*, Elaine thinks.

Years later, Elaine's wool again absorbed the tears of her mother. Chrissy, her eyes wet and her voice pleading, cried out, "No, no, no," over and over again. Chrissy cried out, "No, no, John. Don't leave me." Chrissy cried out, "John, John. Don't leave me alone."

John must have gone to college, too, Elaine thought.

Once, Elaine walked with Chrissy to the part of the farm called the graveyard. Elaine watched as Chrissy wept, placing a small box in a fresh hole with a gravestone marked "JD."

Soon after, it was time for Seinfeld and George and Kramer to go to college. Again, Chrissy buried three items in the backyard.

Except for Barnett—maybe because he comes back to visit—every time someone goes to college, Chrissy cries, then buries a box in the backyard. *Maybe it's a time capsule*, Elaine has wondered. *Maybe it's a human thing I'll never understand, like bathrooms*, Elaine has wondered. Today, Elaine wonders, *What will Farmer Mom bury to remember me?*

Elaine stirs and locks eyes with Chrissy. "Am I going to college?" Elaine asks, a hopeful hint of glee in the corners of a small, old smile.

High on magic mushroom chocolate from her son-in-law, though not quite high enough to dull her heartache, Chrissy's face changes from pained, as she lets out a delighted laugh at the thrill of hearing

Elaine's voice again, and in gratitude for the familiar warmth that's finally flowing through Chrissy's brain and blood, her hair mixing with Elaine's wool. *We are one.*

"Yes, sweet Elaine. You're . . . going to college," Chrissy says, struggling with the words.

"And in college I'll feel better?"

"So much better," Chrissy lies. "Good as new," Chrissy lies, again.

There are three ways to send an animal to college. The most popular is a bullet. A shotgun shell is a couple bucks, and an instruction pamphlet is free on the Internet. It includes an illustration of a sheep with a big red target printed on its forehead. In the illustration, the sheep is smiling.

"Almost time?" Lionel asks.

The second way to send an animal to college is with an air gun. It creates an opening in the head within which a device is inserted, like a small Roto-Rooter, to create the necessary destruction.

"Almost time," Chrissy says.

The third way to send an animal to college is lethal injection, which is expensive and requires an experienced hand, which could also mean a big oafish one.

"Will I see Kramer in college?" Elaine asks.

"Yes. Yes, sweetie," Chrissy says. "Everyone will be there."

Elaine had no name before she came into Chrissy's care. Elaine has never seen an episode of *Seinfeld*. She has no sense of her namesake, no sense of what the world looks like outside of Mader, barely any sense of anything outside the bounds of Polite Society Ranch.

Elaine knew nothing of playfulness until she met The Boy, who was, back then, technically an adult. She figured he was surely named "Oh Barnett" based on how often Chrissy said it. And so Elaine, in her kind ignorance, in her innocence, believed it to be so.

Elaine remembers Oh Barnett washing her with Woolite. He was so sincere. She felt like the prize of the pasture—getting The Boy's attention, feeling the cool hose on a warm day, the fresh scent of the Woolite. Elaine remembers thinking, *They must be excited because I look so awesome.*

Elaine knows little of Heaven and Hell but for the first farm where in birth she was sentenced to die, and Polite Society Ranch, where she was lucky to live.

Elaine doesn't know religion, her mind unpolluted with speculation.

"What do you hope college is like?" Chrissy asks with a hard swallow, anything to keep the sobs at bay.

Elaine considers with whatever strength remains. She wishes to roll over and think on her back, but she can't muster the movement. "I hope it's just like here." She stirs again. "I hope you come visit."

"I promise," Chrissy says.

"And I'll come back here to visit sometimes?" Elaine asks.

"All the time," Chrissy says.

Elaine's discomfort now shifts its blame from age to gravity, which seems to lie upon her mercilessly—everything is so heavy, her eyelids, her head upon the hay, her three legs limp, too heavy to adjust, relief seeming anything but possible, relief seeming pointless.

"I can see everything," Elaine says.

In the tired, glassy darkness of Elaine's eyes, Chrissy watches, with the help of psychedelic confection, a reflection of Elaine's short life. Through Elaine's blink, and then another, Chrissy watches, mesmerized, as if watching an inverted movie, as if Elaine is too weak to adjust the image, too sick to care that the life flashing before her eyes is upside down, distorted, messy, unrepairable, unable to be varnished, no time to tidy, no energy to misremember.

Chrissy watches as Elaine relives her birth—the actual moment life began for her, the moment she took in air, took a swift kick, lost a leg and a family. She remembers kooky old Chrissy Durang heading toward her. She remembers everything about the first moment with Chrissy—the smell, the warmth, the thrill.

Elaine remembers living her earliest days on a trash heap. Elaine, still so innocent, doesn't fully grasp that she was also the trash. She was going to be incinerated just like the rubbish she was picking through. She ate bags left over from pig feed. She ate moldy hay, unaware that what she didn't eat would eventually dry, would fuel the fire that would consume her body, were it not for the woman with the stiff spine coming at her, the woman with the old rugged belt that said "Farmer Mom," reaching out for her unflinchingly, her first words still ringing in Elaine's ears. "This is no way to live."

And what of the best way for Elaine to die?

Her eyes are growing darker and more vacant. Soon, gravity, as it did to Elaine's body, brings its heavy hand to her mind, and it's harder and harder for her to force forward the warm memories bringing calm to her mooring end.

She remembers John.

She remembers certain kids from tours, usually the quiet ones, the fellow misfits.

She remembers The Boy—*Oh, Barnett*—most recently dressed in a tuxedo and beaming, never happier, hand in hand with The Long-Haired Boy. And her memories have nearly reached their end, back in the present.

The gravity gets even heavier. Chrissy puts her hand on Elaine's wool. The hand upon Elaine brings her such comfort, though it adds weight, the slightest weight—how much can a hand weigh?—but it's enough to reveal the labor of breathing, the increasing labor of living.

Elaine considers her friends—the horses and the skinny pig. The alpaca with alopecia. She wishes they could join her at college. She wishes it so badly, though she is unable to express it. A generous God would surely allow such passion to count as a full-hearted goodbye.

Elaine will never see the small, rectangular hole that's been dug out back, about two feet long by one foot wide and three feet deep. She won't see the fresh, dark, unearthed dirt piled beside it, a shadow and its opposite. She'll never see the gravestone made of slate, etched with a name she'll never read: *Elaine*. Her resting place is near the one marked "JD," directly beside an empty one to be marked, one day, "CD."

Elaine doesn't hear Chrissy give the go-ahead.

She doesn't hear the THUMP-THUMP as the syringe is readied, the poison primed.

She doesn't hear Chrissy's sobs.

Elaine reaches out for her Farmer Mom. Elaine's trotter touches the dirt and her hooves make an imprint: her last.

"It's okay," Chrissy cries. "Are you ready to go run and play?"

Elaine falls back into a safer, dreamier state, seeing a field so vast and delicious, her heartbeat speeds up, her adrenaline spikes, she moans, longing for it. She sees Seinfeld and Kramer waiting for her; she sees John. She thrashes and thrashes. She looks at her body—she's young and whole! She struggles, as if in quicksand. "I'm coming! I'm coming! Wait up!" Elaine shouts.

Then, stillness. Elaine feels comfort around her, as if she's wrapped in a warm blanket, the vast field fading from her vision as she starts to let go of words and things and separation, as she becomes the field, the farm, the whole world.

Chrissy watches as Elaine's tightly closed eyes dart to and fro. Chrissy hopes Elaine is having a spectacular vision. But there are tears. Elaine is crying. Chrissy wipes Elaine's eyes and apologizes for the extremes of life, of facilitating living and its unpleasant withdrawal. "Thank you for loving me," Chrissy says.

But Elaine is not crying tears of sadness. Elaine is filled with so much, her eyes are the breaking point for release, it's her eyes that bear the brunt. She's weeping for joy, love, memories. They say the body knows when it's time, and dumps dopamine to help. They say the body knows when it's time to let go.

And all the blinks that made up little Elaine's life are given back, freely—almost with gratitude—to the land of her family, this heritage sheep living her legacy, and dying into it. For Elaine, there is nothing but Polite Society Ranch, no property lines; the earth is not round or flat but forever, just Johns and Chrissys and Oh Barnetts for miles into infinity.

What do sheep count as they're falling asleep? Blessings.

Soon, the three trotters are still, the heart stops beating, the dreams stop dazzling, the chest stops rising, the wool stops growing. Sweet Elaine exists only in memory, a whisper in the humid vapor of a faint Louisiana breeze.

At Polite Society Ranch, Elaine was already in Heaven.

Chrissy turns away from Elaine's body for a moment. Her eyes find bits of dust in the air, animated by a small gust that enters the barn and travels to Elaine and palpates her wool like the flickering of those old, silly scented candles that once burned for Barnett's soul. The dust rises again and swirls and settles into a figure, pressed as if from glass, covered in the dewy glow of hardworking skin.

"Oh, John," Chrissy says. Elaine stands beside him. She stretches, she bounces, she gives her new body a joyful test drive. John pats her head, runs his hands over her now full, beautiful wool. "Hi, friend," he says to her.

"Hi, friend," she says back to him. Elaine looks at Chrissy. "Thanks for being such a great mama. You'll never be alone. It's impossible. Life is all around you."

Chrissy laughs at all the hocus-pocus she's had to endure in the last two weeks. But she looks out at the trees waving to her in the living breeze. She looks to the blue sky barely concealing the stars slyly twinkling above—*hello Cleopatra, hello Jesus*. She looks to a tiny ant carrying a stick four times its size to its home, and to a bee buzzing around looking to get its job done.

John and Elaine walk together, out of the barn, into an almost painfully brilliant light. "You're still my sunrise, Chrissy," John says, turning to her as he walks toward the graveyard he created and now lords within.

Chrissy weeps. *Blue vibes*, she thinks, as tears dance from her eyes, down her face, like they're racing, thrilled to be alive and free, unaware of the cost of their arrival.

Chrissy considers what Ezra would say. *Go to a happy place in your mind.*

Chrissy smiles. "Ah," she says, looking around. "I'm in my happy place right now."

Chrissy stands. She wipes her eyes. She exhales.

Later, Chrissy bids Lionel a grateful farewell.

Later, Chrissy carries Elaine to her resting place. She shovels the grave closed, all that black dirt on all that white wool. She shovels a heap of sorrow. She shovels a heap of regret. She shovels a heap of loneliness. She shovels the death of her dream son. She shovels the death of her dream husband. She puts it all in a graveyard that's running out of space, as if it's all-consuming, a wildfire heading straight for her. Until there's nothing left to bury.

And Chrissy looks out at the gravestones that mark the eras of her life.

She sits and feels ethereal, as if the blades of grass beneath her are holding her up, swaying her with the breeze. She stiffens her spine, determined to present herself as confident and whole, exactly as she requested of God so many times throughout her life, and finally feeling that it's a prayer answered.

Later, Chrissy sobers from the magical chocolate.

Later, Chrissy stands and dusts herself off.

She exits the graveyard but leaves the gate open. To no one behind her or around her or even within hearing distance of her voice, she says, "Come and go as you please."

She turns to the breeze, the sky, the new gazebo, the mural of well-wishes painted with love onto the side of her house. She looks up and greets the early night and the new resident fireflies starting their late shift, showing up, dancing like stars coming down to her, landing on her, around her, so many little miracles.

And in the thick of all the undeniable life, Chrissy Durang decides to let go, to take life as it is with all its many gifts and mysteries, to stop clambering toward the future, and let the future come to her.

Epilogue

'HAWAII'   Post Card

Dear Mom,
Hi! We made
it safe & sound.
Thinking of
you. And Elaine.
I'm so sorry. She
loved her farmer
mom so much. We
wish she could have
stayed around for,
Farmer Grandma!?
What do you think?
Up for a Big Gay Adoption?
Love, Barnett,
AND EZRA! Green Vibes!
Love you!

HAWAII USA
PM
HONOLULU

HAWAII   USA
FOREVER

Mrs. Chrissy Durang
c/o Polite Society
Ranch
12443 Hwy 43
Mader, LA
70022

Acknowledgments

Thank you to my agent, Deborah Schneider. The day you said yes is still one of my happiest! And to Cathy Gleason and everyone at Gelfman Schneider and Curtis Brown.

Eternal gratitude to my editor, James Melia. I was in a parking garage having a crappy afternoon when we first spoke all those years ago. You brightened my day with that call and you've brightened my life by believing in me. A big cheers to you and everyone at Henry Holt and the Macmillan family, including Amy Einhorn, Lori Kusatzky, Jane Haxby, Molly Bloom, Marian Brown, Lulu Schmieta, Alyssa Weinberg, and Ally Demeter.

Thanks to my teammates Ashley Burns and Josie Freedman.

To Crystal Patriarch, Taylor Brightwell, Hanna Lindsley, and everyone at Booksparks, you're the best besties in all the land.

I'm a better writer and person because of Iva Turner. Thank you for the time and care you put into helping me hone these pages. Is it true? YES!

Erin Rodman, your friendship is fuel. Thanks for taking all those FaceTimes.

Stacy Saxton, don't think you can escape me by moving to Europe! Loving you!

I'm in debt to so many who have contributed along the way, including Tom Lenk, Tom DeTrinis, Jayne Entwistle, Mark Jude Sullivan, Tim McKernan, Claire Mouledoux, Rachel Sciacca, Glenn Millican, Angela Hill, Cindy Cesare, Esteban Rey, John McCoy, Michael Crowley, Heath Daniels, Nicholas Alexander Brown, Chris Neuhaus, Roswell Encina, Elissa Dauria Smith, Rob Weisbach, Kathleen Caldwell, Kyle Cummings, Rafe Judkins, Eric Brassard, Brian Larson, Michael Peters, Tobias Conan Trost, Betsy Burnham Stern, Dave Lach, Rachel Bartur, Michael Osborne, Jamie Pierce, Zac Hug, Julia Claiborne Johnson, Alisha Brophy, Michael Barnard, Matt Murphy, Matt Allard, and Austin Goodman.

Much love to Carrie Fisher, who changed my life in every way possible.

I love you, Raindrop and Shirley. And I think of you every day, sweet Tilda.

And thanks to my family, especially my sweet and supportive mother, and my husband, Steven Rowley. Although ours was a "little gay wedding," it looms large in my heart and inspired the spirit of this story. I can't believe our lovely life! Thanks for letting me eat all the peanut butter. I love you.

About the Author

Byron Lane is the author of *A Star Is Bored*, hailed by the *New York Times Book Review* as "wildly funny and irreverent." He's a playwright, screenwriter, Emmy Award–winning former journalist, and former assistant to the actress Carrie Fisher. He's originally from New Orleans and lives in Palm Springs, California, with his husband, author Steven Rowley, and their rescue dogs, Raindrop and Shirley.